LUIGI PIRANDELLO was born near A͟ a Garibaldian veteran who had grown rich in the sulphur-mining industry. After studying at the universities of Palermo, Rome, and Bonn, Pirandello lived in Rome and devoted himself to literature with an abundant production of short stories and novels in the Sicilian realist tradition. *The Late Mattia Pascal* (1904) broke this pattern and announced his dominant modernist themes of absurdity and unstable identity. In 1894 he married Antonietta Portulano who gave him three children; but, after the bankruptcy of Pirandello's father in 1903, she became increasingly unbalanced and was definitively interned in 1919, an event reflected in Pirandello's frequent representations of madness. In 1910 he began a succession of dialect comedies, followed in 1917 by *Right You Are, If You Think You Are*, his first play in standard Italian, influenced by the emerging 'theatre of the grotesque'. In 1921 the controversial *Six Characters in Search of an Author* established his international reputation as an experimental dramatist, and the breakthrough was confirmed in the following year by *Henry IV*. He joined Mussolini's Fascist party in 1924 and went on to direct the artistically successful but short-lived Arts Theatre of Rome (1925–8). The metatheatrical trilogy initiated by *Six Characters* was completed by *Each in His Own Way* (1924) and *Tonight We Improvise* (1930). A number of later plays such as *Diana and Tuda* (1927), *As You Desire Me* (1930), *Finding Oneself* (1932), and *When Someone is Somebody* (1932) derive from the dramatist's own experience and his tormented passion for the young actress Marta Abba. The *New Colony* (1928) and *Lazarus* (1929) belong to a 'myth trilogy' which should have been concluded by the unfinished *Mountain Giants*. After 1930 Pirandello spent much of his time in Germany and travelled widely. He was awarded the Nobel Prize in 1934 and died in Rome in 1936.

ANTHONY MORTIMER is Emeritus Professor of English Literature at the University of Fribourg, Switzerland, and also taught for many years at the University of Geneva. In addition to his academic work on English Renaissance poetry and Anglo-Italian literary relations, he has published verse translations of Dante (*Vita Nuova*), Cavalcanti, Petrarch, Michelangelo, Angelus Silesius, and Villon.

OXFORD WORLD'S CLASSICS

*For over 100 years Oxford World's Classics have brought
readers closer to the world's great literature. Now with over 700
titles—from the 4,000-year-old myths of Mesopotamia to the
twentieth century's greatest novels—the series makes available
lesser-known as well as celebrated writing.*

*The pocket-sized hardbacks of the early years contained
introductions by Virginia Woolf, T. S. Eliot, Graham Greene,
and other literary figures which enriched the experience of reading.
Today the series is recognized for its fine scholarship and
reliability in texts that span world literature, drama and poetry,
religion, philosophy, and politics. Each edition includes perceptive
commentary and essential background information to meet the
changing needs of readers.*

OXFORD WORLD'S CLASSICS

LUIGI PIRANDELLO

Three Plays

Six Characters in Search of an Author

Henry IV

The Mountain Giants

Translated with an Introduction and Notes by
ANTHONY MORTIMER

OXFORD
UNIVERSITY PRESS

OXFORD

UNIVERSITY PRESS

Great Clarendon Street, Oxford OX2 6DP
United Kingdom

Oxford University Press is a department of the University of Oxford.
It furthers the University's objective of excellence in research, scholarship,
and education by publishing worldwide. Oxford is a registered trade mark of
Oxford University Press in the UK and in certain other countries

Translation and editorial material © Anthony Mortimer 2014

The moral rights of the author have been asserted

First published as an Oxford World's Classics paperback 2014

Published in the United States of America by Oxford University Press
198 Madison Avenue, New York, NY 10016, United States of America

British Library Cataloguing in Publication Data
Data available

Library of Congress Control Number: 2013943740

ISBN 978-0-19-964119-2

Printed in Great Britain by
Clays Ltd, Elcograf S.p.A.

Links to third party websites are provided by Oxford in good faith and
for information only. Oxford disclaims any responsibility for the materials
contained in any third party website referenced in this work.

CONTENTS

ABBREVIATIONS

The following abbreviations are used throughout and refer to the Mondadori 'Meridiani' edition of the *Opere di Luigi Pirandello* under the general editorship of Giovanni Macchia:

MN *Maschere Nude*, ed. Alessandro d'Amico, introd. Giovanni Macchia, 4 vols. (Milan, 1986–2007).

NA *Novelle per un anno*, ed. Mario Costanzo, introd. Giovanni Macchia, 3 vols. (Milan, 1986–90).

RO *Tutti i romanzi*, ed. Giovanni Macchia and Mario Costanzo, foreword Giovanni Macchia, 2 vols. (Milan, 1973).

Texts contained in this volume are indicated as follows:

SC   *Six Characters in Search of an Author*
HIV *Henry IV*
MG   *Mountain Giants*
PSC *Preface to Six Characters*

The 'Meridiani' volume of *Saggi e interventi*, ed. Ferdinando Taviani (Milan, 2008), gives the 1908 text of *Humourism* (*L'umorismo*). Pirandello's thought, however, is clearer in the revised text of 1920 which is found in volume vi of the older Mondadori edition of Pirandello, *Saggi, poesie, scritti varii*, ed. Manlio Lo Vecchio-Musti (Milan, 1960), denoted here by the abbreviation *SP*.

All translations are my own.

INTRODUCTION

ON 10 May 1921, at the Teatro Valle in Rome, the first performance of Pirandello's *Six Characters in Search of an Author* provoked a famous theatrical brawl. The actors had to contend with shouting, whistling, and cries of 'madhouse'; counter-protests by the author's supporters led to scuffles in the street; Pirandello and his daughter Lietta were showered with insults and small coins as they sought a taxi to take them safely home. Four months later, with an audience who had been prepared both by the scandal and by publication, *Six Characters* received a better reception in Milan, and in 1923 Georges Pitoëff's imaginative Paris production set off a wave of enthusiasm that saw the play performed in almost every European capital and as far afield as New York, Buenos Aires, and Tokyo. In 1922 a similar but more immediate success greeted Ruggero Ruggeri's masterly interpretation of *Henry IV*.

Both plays are now established as seminal classics of the modern stage and there is no good reason to challenge the orthodoxy that sees them as Pirandello's most characteristic and influential achievements. But we should not, on this account, regard what came before *Six Characters* as mere apprenticeship or dismiss what came after *Henry IV* as a decline. Our vision of the two plays becomes distorted if they are detached from the broader context of Pirandello's long literary career, and the significance of that career cannot be understood solely in terms of its most notable successes.

The author who enjoyed such a sudden international breakthrough was, in fact, already in his mid-fifties and anything but a newcomer to the Italian literary scene. He had started out as a poet, but soon turned to novels and short stories, initially marked by an adherence to the school of Sicilian naturalism (*verismo*) as represented by Federico De Roberto, Luigi Capuana, and, above all, Giovanni Verga. This period culminates with *The Old and the Young* (*I vecchi e i giovani*, first part 1909, completed 1913), a long novel centred on the period between 1892 and 1894 and structured around the two poles of Rome, where the political class is mired in a grave banking scandal, and Sicily, shaken by the doomed peasant rebellion of the *fasci siciliani*. The portrayal of Sicilian society resembles that of such better-known novels as De Roberto's *The Viceroys* (1894) or Lampedusa's *The Leopard* (1958), as it traces the rapid decline of Garibaldian idealism, the compromises and collusion that link old aristocracy to raw and ruthless bourgeoisie, and the failure of the new unified Italy to provide any political solution for the stunted development, grinding poverty, and archaic social structures of the island. The author himself seems to stand behind Don Cosmo Laurentano's disenchanted withdrawal from political engagement:

One thing only is sad, my friends: to have understood the game . . . I mean the game of that playful devil that each of us has within and who amuses himself by representing to us, outside, as reality, what a moment later he will reveal as our own illusion . . . Wear yourselves out and torment yourselves, without thinking that all this will come to no conclusion. (*RO* ii. 509–10)

The Old and the Young was already something of a throwback by the time it started to appear. Five years earlier Pirandello had published *The Late Mattia Pascal* (*Il fu Mattia Pascal*, 1904) which is usually considered as announcing the new direction of his work. Here Pirandello abandons Sicily for a setting which is announced as Liguria but presented without any marked regional features. The story of the eponymous narrator emerges as a philosophical fable in a way that justifies Leonardo Sciascia's bracketing of Pirandello with Kafka and Borges.[1] Trapped in a loveless marriage, devoid of any real vocation, and leading a life that is completely beyond his control, Mattia Pascal is offered what appears to be a fresh start when a drowned corpse is officially identified and buried as his. Assuming a new identity under the invented name of Adriano Meis, he at first experiences a euphoric feeling of freedom and envisages honest and constructive relations with his fellow men. But the illusion is short-lived: freedom becomes isolation, for the lie on which the new self is based makes it impossible for him to participate in the conventions and institutions to which human relations inevitably give rise. A new marriage is out of the question in a situation where he cannot even buy a dog. Thus he will eventually suppress Adriano Meis through a faked suicide and 'die' for a second time. But a return to the old false relations is now impossible. Rather than disturb his supposed widow and her new husband, he withdraws to the decayed municipal library, significantly housed in a deconsecrated church, to write his autobiography.

[1] Leonardo Sciascia, *Pirandello e la Sicilia* (Milan, 1996), 241.

In *The Late Mattia Pascal*, as in the later novel *One, No One, One Hundred Thousand* (1926), we find many of the themes that will recur in the plays. Mattia, for all his extraordinary adventures, is a twentieth-century Everyman, plagued by the impossibility of possessing a stable identity, tormented by the 'sad privilege' of consciousness, by a 'feeling of life' that he mistakes for knowledge of it, condemned, after the failure of the 'great lanterns' of religions and ideologies, to walk by the light of his own little lamp which reveals nothing but the darkness around him (*RO* i. 484–8). This is the 'lanternosophy' expounded in the novel by the spiritualist philosopher Paleari who finds in the theatre another metaphor for the absurdity of life in a purposeless post-Copernican world. He imagines a Sophoclean drama like *Elektra* being performed in a puppet theatre when suddenly a hole appears in the painted paper sky above the stage:

Orestes would still be intent upon revenge, yet in the very moment when he is about to accomplish it with passionate intensity, his eyes would look up there, to that rent in the sky, through which all kinds of evil influences penetrate down to the stage, and his arm would fail him. Orestes, in short, would become Hamlet. Believe me, there lies all the difference between ancient and modern tragedy: a hole in a paper sky. (*RO* i. 467)

The metaphor of the world as stage is all too familiar, but where Macbeth saw human life as resembling 'a poor player', here the tragic protagonist is further reduced to a mere puppet of the kind that Pirandello must often have seen during his Sicilian childhood. The hole in the sky reveals the pitiful illusion of reality within which his action occurs. The central innovation of Pirandello's theatre will be that it calls into question not only its own power as illusion but also its communicative function as a frame that allows and contains meaning.

In the 1890s Pirandello had renounced the theatre after writing a few plays that failed to reach the stage. In 1910, however, with a difficult financial situation aggravated by the increasing insanity of his wife, he found a welcome new source of income when a fellow Sicilian, the playwright-producer Nino Martoglio, persuaded him to adapt and expand some of his short stories into dialect plays, all of which were later translated into Italian. Many of these, such as *Sicilian Limes*, *The Doctor's Duty*, and *The Jar*, were one-act affairs, but there were also more substantial works, among them *Think it Over, Giacomino* (1916) and the pastoral comedy *Liolà* (1917) which has a vitality and irreverence reminiscent of Synge's *Playboy of the Western World*. But by 1917 Pirandello was tiring of dialect theatre and his decision to write henceforth in Italian must have been reinforced by the success of two younger contemporary playwrights, Luigi Chiarelli and Rosso di San Secondo, both associated with the current known as 'the theatre of the grotesque' which takes its name from the subtitle of Chiarelli's *The Mask and the Face* (*La maschera e il volto, grottesco in tre atti*, 1916). The 'grotesque' events of this play involve a husband who, instead of killing his adulterous wife, allows her to escape with her lover while he, having confessed to drowning her, is tried, acquitted, and feted for having acted as an honourable man should do. When the deception is discovered, he is universally reviled and threatened with thirty years in prison as punishment for simulating a crime. By now, however, his wife has returned to him and, in a nicely ironic and symmetrical conclusion, the pair escape (or elope) together. Rosso di San Secondo's *Puppets, What Passion!* (1918) presents three stages of passion in characters who, like those of *Six Characters*, remain nameless. Neither Chiarelli nor Rosso di San Secondo are major innovators, but their metaphors of puppets and masks link bourgeois conventions with the lack of stable or authentic identity in a way that echoes *The Late Mattia Pascal* and anticipates Pirandello's major plays.

Right You Are, If You Think You Are (*Così è (se vi pare)*, 1917) is the first of the nine full-length plays in Italian that Pirandello wrote before *Six Characters* and is probably the most frequently performed. The plot is taken from a short story, *Signora Frola and Signor Ponza, Her Son-in-Law* (1917; *NA* iii. 772–81) and presents a mystery of the kind that would normally receive a logical solution in the last act. The survivors of an earthquake—Signor Ponza, his wife, and his mother-in-law Signora Frola—arrive in a small town. There Signora Frola, instead of living with her son-in-law, takes lodgings and has no face-to-face contact with her daughter, though she communicates by letter and by shouting up from the courtyard. Unable to restrain their curiosity, the pillars of the local community demand an explanation from Signor Ponza who tells them that the woman with whom he lives is actually his second wife, his first having died in the earthquake. His mother-in law, he asserts, is suffering from a terrible delusion and believes that her daughter is still alive; it is to preserve this illusion that he keeps his wife away from her. For Signora Frola, however, it is Signor Ponza who is deluded in believing his first wife to be dead, while she and her daughter, in his interest, accept the fiction of a second marriage. Which of these two incompatible versions is true? We receive the answer (which is not one) in the final scene when the veiled wife herself claims to be both Signora Frola's daughter *and* the second wife of Signor Ponza. To the objections that she must be one or the other, she asserts: 'No, gentlemen, I am whoever you think I am' (*MN* i. 509).

Pirandello himself described the play as 'a devilish trick',[2] but there is far more to it than the desire to frustrate conventional expectations with a demonstration of the relativity of truth. The key to what Pirandello is doing lies in the character who is absent from the short story but essential to the play: Lamberto Laudisi. For most of the play Laudisi is a *raisonneur* figure who speaks for the author and delivers a commentary on the action, deriding the quest for a straightforward solution. But it is he who finally intervenes to drive the plot to its strange unravelling. What this compassionate ironist teaches his audience, both onstage and off, is not some trite doctrine of relativism, but rather the recognition that some truths are better left veiled and that necessary illusions should be respected. Thus Signor Ponza respects what he believes is the delusion of Signora Frola and she protects what she thinks to be his. As for Signora Ponza, the objective truth of whether she is the first or the second wife is ultimately irrelevant since she completes a trinity of love by accepting both roles as 'the remedy that compassion has found' for their predicament (*MN* i. 508). Role-playing is not simply a matter of social conformism or bourgeois hypocrisy; it may also create and reveal whatever identity we have. Hence the oxymoron Pirandello chose as a title for his collected plays: *Naked Masks* (*Maschere nude*).

Philosophy and Poetics

As if it were not enough to be an inheritor of the theatre of the grotesque and a precursor of the theatre of the absurd, Pirandello has also been likened to Shaw and claimed for 'the theatre of ideas' on the grounds that many of his characters (Laudisi is a major example) spend a great

---

[2] *Il figlio prigioniero, carteggio tra Luigi e Stefano Pirandello durante la guerra 1915–1918*, ed. A. Pirandello (Milan, 2005), 191.

deal of time in what sounds like ratiocination. Moreover, some of his plays, on a first reading, do seem designed to demonstrate a philosophical point, be it the inevitability of role-playing, the multiplicity of identity, the relativity of truth, or the impossibility of real knowledge of the self or the world. Benedetto Croce, Italy's pre-eminent philosopher in the first half of the twentieth century, notoriously dismissed Pirandello's work as an awkward hybrid between art and philosophy,[3] but this is hardly surprising if we consider the contrast between Croce's own neo-idealism and the dramatist's radical pessimism, rooted in the work of Schopenhauer and his French disciple Gabriel Séailles. And even if Pirandello's ideas are no more than the common intellectual currency of his age, we still need to see how they relate to his poetics. In this context the crucial document that has served as a starting point for most later discussions of the issue is Pirandello's own lengthy essay *Humourism* (*L'umorismo*, 1908, revised 1920).

The only available English translation of *L'umorismo* is entitled *On Humor* which is unfortunate if it suggests some theory of the comic along the lines of such near-contemporary discussions as Bergson's *Laughter* (1900) and Freud's *Jokes and Their Relation to the Unconscious* (1905). There are, no doubt, points of contact with both these texts, but 'humourism', as John Barnes reminds us,[4] is no laughing matter and the immediate sources of Pirandello's thought are to be found in such less-known works as Alfred Binet's *The Alterations of Personality* (1892) and Giovanni Marchesini's *The Fictions of the Soul* (1905). The first part of *Humourism* is a fairly academic account of writers who have been described as 'humourists'; it is only in the second part of the book that Pirandello gets down to discussing what 'humourism' actually is, with a verve and an intensity that leave us in little doubt that he is defining his own poetics. At the heart of 'humourism' lies the bleak vision that had already been roughly outlined four years earlier in *The Late Mattia Pascal*. Pirandello follows Bergson is seeing life as a continuous flux, evanescent and ever-changing, which we seek in vain to halt by imposing on it the 'stable and determinate forms' constructed by the intellect. These are the concepts, ideologies, and ideals, the 'fictions' that give us a deceptive consciousness of ourselves,

---

[3] Benedetto Croce, 'Luigi Pirandello', *La Critica*, 33 (1935), 357.

[4] John C. Barnes, 'Humourism is no Laughing Matter', *Pirandello Studies*, 20 (2009), 14–20.

the illusion of some coherence in our lives. Thus life and form are at odds. At times inevitably the forms into which we try to channel our lives will be overthrown by our unruly passions and we shall be plunged back into the chaotic flux; but the alternative is a subjection to forms whose rigidity means death (*SP*, p. 151).

It is to this inevitable tension between life and form, between the absurdity of what we are and the illusion of what we think we are, that humourism directs our attention. Humourism is not a question of subject matter but of a particular kind of perception which Pirandello calls *sentimento del contrario*, 'the feeling of the opposite' or perhaps 'feeling *for* the opposite'. It begins with the awareness of some incongruity (*avvertimento del contrario*) as when we see an old lady striving and failing to appear young (*SP*, p. 127). If the experience remains at that level, it will give rise to the comic and nothing more. But the true humourist subjects it to a dispassionate reflection which 'penetrates everywhere and dismantles everything: every image of feeling, every ideal fiction, every appearance of reality, every illusion' (*SP*, p. 146). This goes beyond a derisive satisfaction at the stripping away of illusions. In the case of the old lady, for example, an understanding of the reasons why she has gone to such lengths might lead to compassion rather than laughter. Hence the *sentimento del contrario*, unlike the initial *avvertimento del contrario*, is the fruit of reflection—a distinction that, to some extent, recalls Schiller's *On Naïve and Sentimental Poetry* (1796), where 'sentimental' implies a reaction to the gap between the real and the ideal that is self-conscious and meditated as opposed to 'naive' and instinctive.

It is important to recognize that the 'feeling for the opposite' does not simply replace one response with another. The humourist, now revealed as a compassionate ironist, remains conscious of the comic aspect of experience and this generates an uncertainty or instability that is reflected, Pirandello believes, in the literary forms that humourism takes, 'disorderly, interrupted, interspersed with constant digressions', deconstructing rather than constructing, seeking contrast and contradiction where other works of art aim for synthesis and coherence (*SP*, p. 133). As a prime example of the humourist text, Pirandello cites Sterne's *Tristram Shandy*, but his own *Six Characters*, which he himself describes as 'stormy and disordered . . . constantly interrupted, sidetracked, contradicted' (*PSC*, p. 195), would fit the bill just as well. Life, for the humourist, resists the constraints of genre; it is neither a novel nor a drama. And if Sterne's narrator undermines the fiction of coherent identity by parodying and disrupting the conventions of narrative, Pirandello does the same through his recognition and subversion of the conventions of theatrical representation.

Impressive and eloquent though *Humourism* often is, it may be doubted whether Pirandello's ideas would have attracted serious attention for very long without the powerful advocacy of the philosopher-critic Adriano Tilgher in his chapter on the dramatist in *Studies in Contemporary Theatre* (1923). Tilgher does more than follow the lead of *Humourism* in seeing the tension between life and form as central to Pirandello's thought; he seizes on the paradox of a reasoning process that undermines reason to present Pirandello's art as the most powerful literary extension of a crisis in modern thought:

> Pirandello's art is not only chronologically but also ideally contemporary with the great idealist revolution that took place in Italy and Europe at the beginning of this century. It carries over into art the anti-intellectual, anti-rationalist, anti-logic current that permeates the whole of modern philosophy and is now culminating in Relativism. Pirandello's art is anti-rationalist not because it denies or ignores thought to the total benefit of feeling, passion, and affections, but rather because it installs thought at the very centre of the world as a living power struggling with the living and rebellious powers of Life.[5]

Pirandello was initially flattered by the major role thus assigned to him, but he later resented the critic's not implausible claim to have influenced some of the plays that followed *Six Characters* and *Henry IV*. More justifiably, he came to regard the Tilgher formula as reductionist and insisted that his works offer images of life which assume universal significance rather than concepts that express themselves through images. Tilgher's account of Pirandello is, no doubt, unduly dry and schematic and he has been reproached for neglecting the comic verve that so often leavens the dramatist's so-called 'cerebralism'. He has, however, the great merit of showing that Pirandello's vision tends inevitably towards the theatre which embodies and enhances the form–life duality by the very fact that it subjects a fixed text to the vagaries and hazards of performance.

---

[5] Adriano Tilgher, *Studi sul teatro contemporaneo* (Rome, 1923), 180.

Six Characters in Search of an Author

'[N]othing in this play exists as given and preconceived: everything is in the making, . . . everything is an unforeseen experiment' says Pirandello (*PSC*, p. 194). *Six Characters in Search of an Author* bears the subtitle 'a play in the making'; it is often described as 'a play within a play', and it would be equally appropriate to speak of 'a rehearsal within a rehearsal'. The audience finds the Director and the Actors apparently assembled to rehearse one of Pirandello's most successful earlier plays, *The Rules of the Game* (1918), whose Italian title, *Il giuoco delle parti* (more accurately translated as *The Game of Roles* or *Role-Playing*) reminds us that the innate theatricality of life is no new concern of the author. But whereas *The Rules of the Game* conformed to the scenic conventions of naturalist theatre—the familiar setting in a bourgeois salon and the invisible 'fourth wall' dividing audience from actors—*Six Characters* gives us a bare stage where the presence of Director and Stage Manager and the absence of props prevent any willing suspension of disbelief. Thus Pirandello subtly announces a thematic continuity combined with a revolutionary innovation in stagecraft.

The rehearsal of *The Rules of the Game* is interrupted by the arrival of the Six Characters who, having been refused by a novelist, seek to impose their drama on the Director. There is, of course, nothing very original in the conceit of fictional characters seeming to take on a life independent of an author's will, but *Six Characters*, in a typical Pirandellian move, turns the conventional scheme on its head—not an author who creates characters so alive that they escape from his control, but rather uncreated characters who need the fiat of an author in order to be given life. The idea seems to have occupied Pirandello for at least ten years. The short stories *The Tragedy of a Character* (1911, *NA* i. 816–24) and *Conversations with Characters* (1915, *NA* iii. 1138–54) already present characters who attempt to impose themselves upon the author, and a fragmentary sketch from roughly the same period gives us the Father's visit to Madame Pace's establishment, and mentions the Stepdaughter, the Mother, and the Son (*SP*, pp. 1256–8). By July 1917, in a letter to his son Stefano, we find Pirandello invoking

A strange sad thing, so sad: *Six Characters in Search of an Author: A Novel in the Making*. Perhaps you can see it: six characters caught up in a terrible drama who follow me everywhere because they want to be put into a novel; an obsession; and I don't want to hear of it and I tell them that it's useless . . . and they show me their wounds and I drive them away.[6]

The process that led from initial rejection by the novelist to a partial realization by the dramatist is discussed in the 1925 Preface, written four years after the first performance of the play. He has no interest, he explains, in the portrayal of characters unless they are 'imbued, so to say, with a distinct sense of life from which they acquire a universal significance' (*PSC*, p. 187), and he could find no such significance in the haunting image of the Six Characters. But nor can he start out from an idea and expect it to evolve into an image; to do so would be to yield to the kind of symbolism he detests 'in which the representation loses all spontaneous movement to become a mechanism, an allegory' (*PSC*, p. 187). The only solution is to begin with the image and then find an appropriate artistic form in which it will be tested to see what significance, if any, it holds. The phrasing of the letter to Stefano is revealing: Pirandello may speak of a novel, but the terms 'drama' and 'tragedy' already anticipate the theatre. It is only when their struggle for realization has been transferred from the novelist's study to the stage, when they have contended with the Director, the Actors, and all the conventions of performance, just as they contended with him, that the Six Characters will reveal their 'universal significance': 'the same pangs that I myself have suffered . . . the illusion of mutual understanding, irremediably based on the empty abstraction of words; the multiple personality of every individual according to all the possibilities of being to be found within each one of us; and finally the inherent tragic conflict between life which is ever-moving, ever-changing, and form which fixes it, immutable' (*PSC*, p. 189).

We can now see the profound sense of the play's rejection of naturalist theatre and the nineteenth-century conventions of theatrical illusion. By showing us what purports to be a rehearsal rather than a performance Pirandello stresses the creative process rather than the created work, and he does so because the drama that matters to him is not primarily the one that the Six Characters see as their own, but the drama of his own unceasing struggle for artistic expression. The Six Characters in search of an author turn out to be aspects of the

[6] *Il figlio prigioniero*, 215.

Author in search of himself, and the stage becomes a visual metaphor for the artist's mind. What Pirandello says of the surreal appearance of Madame Pace can be applied to the whole play: 'I mean that, instead of the stage, I have shown them my own mind in the act of creation under the appearance of that very stage' (*PSC*, p. 194).

The drama of the Six Characters themselves seems designed to rival Ibsen's *Ghosts* as a melodramatic naturalist taboo-breaker involving an adultery favoured by a compliant husband, illegitimate children, prostitution, a potential semi-incest, death by drowning, and suicide. But it remains, to a considerable degree, a drama frustrated or denied. One central character (the Son) refuses to take part, another (the Mother) insists on an episode (her reunion with the Son) which cannot take place. The whole story is only made available through the conflicting narratives of the Father and the Stepdaughter, as if the plot could never quite break free of its roots in an unwritten novel. Moreover, the two crucial scenes that are acted out—the episode in Madame Pace's back room and the deaths of the two younger children—are deprived of their proper emotional impact by the incessant discussion as to how they should be staged. At a superficial level, therefore, we might speak of a fictional world, that of the Six Characters, being undermined by constant interventions from the real world, that of the Director and his company. In his stage directions (considerably revised in the light of Pitoëff's production), Pirandello emphasizes the gap between the two worlds, insisting that the distinction between Characters and Actors be reinforced by all means, including lighting and grouping. All this, however, should be seen as a deliberately provocative way of foregrounding precisely the kind of hard-and-fast oppositions that *Six Characters* ultimately works to blur, disturb, and challenge. However we choose to define the polarities that govern the play—reality and illusion, truth and fiction, life and art, or, in Tilgherian terms, life and form—we shall find it impossible to align them consistently with the two groups on stage, and it is hardly surprising that directors of the play have often found it difficult to establish appropriately different acting styles for the Actors and the Characters. In his stage directions Pirandello goes so far as to suggest that the Characters should wear light masks indicative of dominant emotions such as remorse, revenge, and scorn, a device that seems dangerously close to the allegorical approach that he rejects and that would surely lead us to expect a highly stylized or artificial manner. But when Actors and Characters alternate to perform the scene, it seems that quite the opposite happens. It is the Actors whose tone and gestures appear too polished to be real while the Characters insist on taking verisimilitude so far that a crucial exchange between Madame Pace and the Stepdaughter is spoken in an inaudible whisper, to the great annoyance of the Actors. Each group has to trespass on the other's territory in order to fulfil its ambition. The real Actors have a professional interest in occupying the world of fiction; the fictional Characters need to test their truth against the real world. The Characters, we are told in the stage directions, are 'created realities, *changeless constructs of the imagination, and therefore more real and substantial than the Actors with their natural mutability*' (*SC*, p. 7). But those 'created realities' can only exist if the author, in whose imagination they have been 'born alive', consents to grant them the illusory life of art: as the Father puts it, 'What for you is an illusion that has to be created is for us, on the contrary, our only reality' (*SC*, p. 48). The paradox, of course, is that the life of art, precisely because it involves pinning characters down in a fixed immutable form, becomes a kind of death. Living human beings, however, are condemned to another sort of death or, to be more accurate, non-existence, in that their sheer mutability, their chronic lack of coherence, denies them any substantial identity.

If we [the Characters] have no reality beyond the illusion, then maybe you also shouldn't count too much on your own reality, this reality which you breathe and touch in yourself today, because—like yesterday's—inevitably, it must reveal itself as illusion tomorrow. (*SC*, p. 50)

Six Characters can be approached from many angles, most of which are complementary rather than mutually exclusive. Biographers of Pirandello have read the play as a reflection of the dramatist's own solitude and sexual anguish after his increasingly insane wife had accused him of incest with his daughter Lietta. Readers who come to it fresh from *The Late Mattia Pascal* may read it as a metaphysical drama in which the characters who seek an author are representative modern men who no longer have the Christian God to grant them substance and significance in a post-Copernican world. But what counts in the long run is that Pirandello's profound pessimism about man's capacity to distinguish between reality and illusion is the essential source of all his innovations and experiments in the theatre. In the two other plays of what we now call the metatheatrical trilogy, *Each in*

His Own Way (1924) and *Tonight We Improvise* (1930), Pirandello takes his dismantling of stage illusion and dramatic convention even further, breaking down barriers not only between actor and character, but also between the actors and the audience. Even spatial and chronological dimensions are challenged when, in *Tonight We Improvise*, we are offered the choice between a number of scenes that take place simultaneously in different parts of the theatre. In all this we should not underestimate the strong element of playfulness often verging on self-parody, but the result is to force the spectator into an unprecedented awareness and examination of the complex ways in which the theatre communicates.

Henry IV

A young man takes part in a masquerade and chooses to impersonate the eleventh-century German emperor Henry IV. The woman he loves, Matilda, participates as the emperor's historic enemy, Matilda, Countess of Tuscany. During the cavalcade 'Henry' is thrown from his horse which has been pricked by his rival Tito Belcredi. When he awakes, he really believes he is the emperor and, thanks to the generosity of his sister, is allowed to live in this illusion in a villa transformed into a medieval castle with servants as 'privy counsellors'. Twelve years later he regains his senses, but decides to maintain the pretence of madness that grants him both the freedom to construct his own little world and a standpoint from which he can challenge the shallow assumptions on which society is based. At the beginning of the play this situation has lasted about eight years, but two recent events suggest that it is under threat: Henry's sister has died and he has also lost his favourite privy counsellor. Belcredi, Matilda, her daughter Frida, Henry's nephew Di Nolli, and the psychiatrist Dr Genoni arrive at the villa with a plot, devised by the doctor, to shock Henry out of his delusion by suddenly presenting him with Frida dressed exactly as her mother had been at the cavalcade twenty years earlier. The double vision of Matilda, as she is now and as she once was, will, the doctor believes, restore Henry to real time like a stopped watch that is shaken to make it start again. In the final scene, enraged by the brutality and insensitivity of this device, Henry seizes on Frida and kills Belcredi, thus confirming the others in their belief that he is indeed insane and condemning himself to live out the rest of his life as Henry IV.

Henry IV was written in a matter of months immediately after the first performance of *Six Characters*. If, on the one hand, it develops typically Pirandellian themes and continues to explore the possibilities of metatheatre, on the other hand it seems designed to reconcile the dramatist with the audience he had just bewildered and infuriated. Instead of the amorphous 'play in the making' and the sense of experimental groping, we are offered the comfortingly recognizable genre of a 'tragedy in three acts' and the solidity of the well-made play with its exposition, complication, catastrophe, and denouement. Whereas in *Six Characters*, as the Director explains, 'We can't have one character . . . upstaging everybody else and taking over the whole scene' (*SC*, p. 44), in *Henry IV* that is precisely what happens, with a protagonist whose dominant presence, anguished self-questioning, and feigned madness recall the most celebrated tragic hero in the history of drama.

The *Hamlet* echoes may well have influenced the way in which the play has traditionally been interpreted, with 'Henry' (we never learn his real name) as a sensitive victim who attracts admiration for the way he uses his corrosive intellect not only to expose the shortcomings of society but also to pose existential questions that humanity in general would prefer to ignore. We need, however, to see that if *Hamlet* is relevant to *Henry IV*, it is primarily as an ironic counterpoint. The besetting sin of Henry's society is not so much deep-rooted corruption as sheer triviality—not murder, incest, and dynastic mayhem, but Belcredi leafing through German magazines that he cannot read, Matilda getting a fit of the giggles every time anyone looks at her with genuine sentiment, and history reduced to a fashionable masquerade. Whatever Hamlet's perplexities, he still acts on a stage where there is no hole in the ceiling and where tragic action is ultimately possible: Henry's noted seriousness traps him in a charade where he can only mime the tragedy of someone else. The result is that even his most terrible and lucid moments teeter on the edge of tantrums, the rage of the child who is losing patience with his own game. He is, moreover, less than clear-sighted about his own condition, as in the following passage where he addresses his privy counsellors after revealing that he is now sane:

do you know what it means to find yourself face to face with a madman? Face to face with someone who shakes the very foundations of everything you have built up in and around yourself—the very logic of all your constructions. Ah, what do you expect? Madmen construct without logic, lucky them! Or with a logic of their own which floats around like a feather. Changing, ever-changing! Like this today, and tomorrow who knows how? You stand firm, and they no longer stand at all. (*HIV*, p. 110)

How does this apply to his own experience? Surely, in his role as Henry IV, far from being 'changing, ever-changing', he had been the one who stood firm and therefore could not qualify as a madman. In which case, he can hardly claim the fact that he now steps out of his role as proof of his sanity. *Henry IV* links Pirandello's obsession with masks and role-playing with the question of what it means to define madness in a world that is now recognized as absurd; but this does not make Henry simply the sane madman who reveals the madness of the sane. That straightforward inversion would deny the flux that Pirandello regards as inherent in life. Like the polarities that govern *Six Characters*, madness and sanity keep changing sides until the terms become almost emptied of substance.

To understand the limits of Henry, whether as victim or critic of society, we need to look more closely at his antagonist Belcredi who is not quite the fop that he first appears to be. Pirandello's stage directions warn us that we should not underestimate the real power that lies behind the languid exterior. Nobody takes him seriously, '*or so it seems*'; he can afford to laugh at the Marchesa Matilda's sallies against him because '*What Tito Belcredi means to her only he knows*'; shrouded by the '*sleepy Arabian idleness*' is '*the supple agility that makes him a formidable swordsman*' (*HIV*, p. 71). He alone has the intelligence to see through the pseudo-scientific jargon of the Polonius-like Dr Genoni and the prescience to foresee the disastrous results of the plot; he alone shows some genuine understanding of how Henry's mind works; and in the final scene he alone comes to Frida's defence. The drama of Henry's madness is framed by Belcredi who begins it with a prick to his rival's horse and ends it by getting stabbed himself. In the intervening twenty years he has presumably possessed Matilda despite the shadowy existence of a husband somewhere along the line. Belcredi, in short, has all the fitness for life and the sexual potency that is lacking in Henry. Matilda tells us that Henry only chose the part of the emperor so that he could lie at her feet, 'like Henry IV at Canossa' (*HIV*, p. 77), a self-abasement that foreshadows some of the more embarrassing aspects of Pirandello's own relationship with the actress Marta Abba. Henry's archaic (Leonardo Sciascia would say Sicilian) attitude to women allows for sainted mothers or whores, but has no room for a lover. Thus, in his role as Henry IV, he has prostitutes brought in to satisfy his sexual needs while the only two women who have ever meant anything to him, his sister and Matilda, are transformed into mother and mother-in-law respectively. In this light, it is tempting to see his seizing of Frida and stabbing of Belcredi as a last desperate effort to abandon his womb-like retreat and re-enter the arena of sexual competition. It is also a reaction to the shock of discovering that change has become impossible because form has conquered life, the Tilgherian moment that Henry himself had described:

in all good faith, the lot of us, we've adopted some fine fixed idea of ourselves. And yet, Monsignor, while you stand fast, holding on to your sacred vestments with both hands, here, out of your sleeves something comes slipping and slithering away like a snake without you noticing. Life, Monsignor! And it comes as a surprise when you see it suddenly take shape before you, escaping like that. There's anger and spite against yourself; or remorse, remorse as well. (*HIV*, p. 89)

Many accounts of the play have pointed to the irony of a conclusion where Henry's attempt to escape from the role he has assumed ends by condemning him to it. But is he really trying to rid himself of his mask? His violent action, provoked by Belcredi's assertion 'You're not mad!', is, in fact, radically ambiguous. That brutal irruption into the real world can also be seen as deriving from a last instinctive urge to withraw into the safety of official insanity. Henry, says the stage direction, is '*appalled at the living force of his own fiction*' (*HIV*, p. 124) which has proved him unfit for life; and yet, as he gathers his counsellors around him and retreats behind his imperial mask, it is left to the reader or the actor to decide whether in his closing words—'here together, here together . . . and for ever'—the dominant emotion is one of horror, resignation, or relief.

The Mountain Giants

The Mountain Giants, the unfinished play that Pirandello was working on at the time of his death in 1936, was conceived as the last of a trilogy of myths. Myth, as Pirandello uses the term, may be taken to mean any ideal (or 'fiction') which we use to give meaning to our common experience and which, precisely because it cannot ultimately be realized in concrete terms, offers a permanent motive for change.

The first play in the trilogy, *The New Colony* (1928), examines the social myth through the attempt of a group of outcasts and idealists to create a self-sufficient Utopian community; the second, *Lazarus* (1929), takes up the religious myth in the emergence of a new nature-based and dogma-free spirituality; *The Mountain Giants* deals with the myth of art.

Pirandello had been working on the play since 1929 and this unusually long gestation can be explained by a developing crisis in his relations with Italy's Fascist regime. Disillusioned, as so many Italians were, by the failure of parliamentary democracy to fulfil the Garibaldian ideals of national unity and social justice, he had joined the party in 1924, and in public at least that adherence never wavered. There were, however, cracks beneath the surface. Mussolini failed to give full support to the dramatist's plans for a national theatre and the Fascist aesthetic found D'Annunzio's patriotic grandiloquence more to its taste than Pirandello's existential questioning. Official congratulations on the award of the Nobel Prize in 1934 were more polite than enthusiastic. The clearest sign, however, that Pirandello was now out of step with the regime came with *The Fable of the Changeling Son* (1934), the verse play that he gave as a libretto to the composer Gian Francesco Malipiero. Based on Sicilian folklore, the story is that of the beautiful Son stolen away to be brought up as a prince while a deformed changeling takes his place. At the end the Son is reunited with the Mother, returns to live a humble life with her in the sunlit South, and renounces his gloomy northern kingdom in favour of the changeling. First performed in Germany, the opera was immediately banned for fear that the deformed changeling might be associated with Hitler. In Italy also performances were cancelled after Mussolini had already excised a passage that seemed to denigrate the idea of the providential Leader: 'Believe me, change this crown of glass and paper to one of gold and precious stones, this little cape into a regal mantle, and the comic king becomes a king in earnest that you bow down before. There's nothing else needed, just as long as you believe it' (*MN* iv. 803). This is the same play that Countess Ilse and her company bring to the remote villa of the Scalognati at the start of *The Mountain Giants*.

Pirandello's experience with *The Fable of the Changeling Son* did not provoke a rejection of Fascist ideology, but it did intensify his growing concern with the role of art in society as exemplified by the theatre. In a letter to Marta Abba Pirandello described the subject of *The Mountain Giants* as 'the triumph of fantasy, the triumph of poetry, but also the tragedy of poetry in this brutal modern world'.[7] Ilse and her itinerant troupe come to the magical villa of Cotrone in the hope that he will help them arrange a public performance of *The Changeling Son*, the play written by the poet who loved her and to which she has dedicated her life. Cotrone, however, urges her to remain at the villa where the play will mysteriously create itself, freed from the constraints of the theatre and the incomprehension of a philistine society. Giorgio Strehler, whose 1967 Milan production gave *The Mountain Giants* a new lease of life, saw Cotrone and Ilse as illustrating the difference between what he called pure theatre and performance theatre.[8] Pure theatre exists only within the magic confines of the villa, a ludic and solipsistic zone of untrammelled creativity where there is no mediating factor between the imagination and its emanations. Arising from those whom the workaday world has excluded, it can exist only in isolation from that world. Thus art becomes a hermetic activity and the excluded become the exclusive. Performance theatre, on the other hand, insists on art as communication. It cannot exist without the kind of creative imagination that, for Pirandello, is the source of all art and is embodied by Cotrone; but it seeks to harness that creativity and reconnect it with the world it has abandoned. For Ilse art is an essential dimension of humanity which should be offered to all men, whether they like it or not. In her single-minded devotion to this ideal she will suffer a death reminiscent of the archetypal performer Orpheus, battered and broken by an enraged mob.

Pirandello does not ask us to choose between Cotrone and Ilse. Cotrone, the freewheeling anarchist and illusionist, is obviously the more attractive figure, especially if we think in terms of sheer spectacle. But his marvels and miracles have a superficial dazzling quality that is in tune with his regressive desire to escape adult responsibility: 'I've told you already to learn from children who first invent a game and then believe in it and live it as true . . . If we were children once, we can always be children' (*MG*, p. 179). It is not hard to see the limits of Cotrone's playpen inventiveness. If Ilse's high-minded alternative appears no less obviously flawed, this is largely because she herself is so unqualified to serve as a representative of the communicative function of the theatre. She shows no understanding of how art is shaped by the imagination and no readiness to compromise either

[7] Cited by Susan Bassnett-McGuire, *Luigi Pirandello* (London, 1983), 154.
[8] Giorgio Strehler, 'The Giants of the Mountain', *World Theatre*, 16/3 (1967), 263–9.

with her fellow actors or with her audience. Whereas Cotrone, as Strehler notes, 'sums up all the possibilities of the theatre', Ilse has no repertoire other than a single play that happens to be rooted in her own emotional experience and demands to be repeated and rejected over and over again. It is not the least of Pirandello's paradoxes that Cotrone who cuts himself off from society has the broadest of human sympathies as we see from his treatment of the various misfits who compose his group, whereas Ilse who insists on taking art out amid the world of men is an unbending fanatic who listens to nobody and sacrifices not only herself but two of her troupe.

The play as Pirandello left it breaks off as the thunderous arrival of the Mountain Giants strikes terror into the hearts of Cotrone's followers and guests. Yet in Stefano Pirandello's detailed account of his father's intentions for the unwritten conclusion it is not the Giants themselves (who never appear on stage) but their brutal workforce, coarsened by heavy manual labour, who are responsible for the riot that leads to Ilse's death. This may reflect Pirandello's reluctance to mount anything that might seem like a direct attack on a Fascist regime that still accorded him a fair measure of official respect. It is also, however, an indication that his real concern is not with any particular form of government, whether authoritarian or democratic, but with the whole of modern industrial society which has left art without a social function. The Giants, after all, behave as well as one can expect from rulers who 'are intent on vast projects to possess the powers and riches of the earth' (*MG*, p. 183): they subsidize the theatre as an entertainment for their workforce and are ready to pay compensation when things turn out badly. Despite Ilse's terrible fate, there is no suggestion that the creative activity of Cotrone's villa will be in any way disturbed, and though the Count may proclaim that poetry has died with his wife, this is pure hyperbole. Poetry will surely continue to exist, as Auden puts it, 'in the valley of its making where executives | Would never want to tamper'. The tragedy is not that art is in danger of extinction, but that marginalization and irrelevance will be the price it pays for survival.

The evolution of the theatre from nineteenth-century naturalism to the diversity of its modern modes is essentially the work of two dramatists: one is Strindberg, the other is Pirandello. In both cases the extraordinarily pervasive influence is based on a few plays which amount to a very small sample of their massive output, and in both cases much of the abundant non-dramatic work remains unfamiliar or unavailable to those who cannot read the original language. An effective summing-up of Pirandello's work would, therefore, need to take into account the difference between his achievement as it appears in its Italian context and as it appears to the world at large. Our conclusion can do no more than point to some salient aspects of the latter.

The most obvious feature of Pirandello's influence is to be found in the extensive use of metatheatrical devices by authors as diverse as Brecht, Genet, and Tom Stoppard. It is no accident that in his critical essays and especially in the Preface to *Six Characters* Pirandello uses the term 'representation' (*rappresentazione*) for a far wider variety of activities than is normal in English usage—as a synonym for description, narration, symbolic substitution, artistic realization, and theatrical performance. What this suggests is that Pirandello's metatheatre, unlike Brecht's didactic distancing effect, is deeply rooted in his conviction that we have no sure access to reality. To think of the theatre as representation is to reject the Aristotelian idea of *mimesis* on the grounds that we cannot copy what we cannot know. To the same scepticism we can also attribute Pirandello's role as a forerunner of Beckett, Ionesco, and to some degree Harold Pinter in the presentation of situations where actions are repetitive, developments illusory, and endings arbitrary since they can only leave us where we started out. Signora Ponza will continue to be both a first and second wife; the Six Characters are left still looking for an author; Henry IV remains locked in his imperial role. Action is no longer meaningful. The theatre of the absurd begins with Paleari's puppet theatre that has a hole in the sky.

One might deduce from all this that Pirandello is responsible for everything that is most bleak about the modern stage. How then do we account for the strange sense of exhilaration that his plays so often convey? Perhaps the secret lies in that very lack of conclusion, in the uncertainty of identity, in the fact that so many of his characters live in their own fictions rather than in truths. The absurdity of the world grants man the freedom to fill the void with his own inventions. The villa in *The Mountain Giants* may be labelled as unlucky (*La Scalogna*), but it contains 'a wealth beyond counting, a ferment of dreams' (*MG*, p. 153). And this, as Cotrone goes on to explain, is because 'The things around us speak and make sense only in those arbitrary forms that we chance to give them in our despair'.

NOTE ON THE TEXT

THESE translations are based on the four-volume edition of the plays, *Maschere nude* (1986–2007) edited by Alessandro D'Amico for the Complete Works of Pirandello (*Opere di Luigi Pirandello*) under the general editorship of Giovanni Macchia. *Sei personaggi in cerca d'autore* and *Enrico IV* are in volume ii and *I giganti della montagna* in volume iv.

The aim of this book is to provide an accurate, readable, and eventually actable translation of three plays by Pirandello. It is not an adaptation or what is commonly called 'an acting version'. The settings have not been updated to the twenty-first century and the idiom chosen is not so contemporary as to let us forget that Pirandello was a contemporary of Bernard Shaw. The extensive stage directions, sometimes abridged in previous translations, are here given in full because they frequently assume a narrative function, commenting on the action or providing insight into the psychology of the characters. We are reminded that for Pirandello a play is not only a performance for spectators but also a text for readers.

Act divisions are indicated only for *Henry IV*. That the intervals in *Six Characters* do not amount to act divisions is expressly stated by Pirandello himself. As for the unfinished *Mountain Giants*, the whole situation is confused by the fact that we have three numbered sections plus an account by Stefano Pirandello of a fourth 'moment' that would have constituted the third act. Under the circumstances, most editors have rightly been reluctant to label the completed sections as acts.

An asterisk in the text indicates an explanatory note at the end of the book.

For the titles 'Marchese' and 'Marchesa' in *Henry IV* I have preferred to keep the Italian terms rather than using the French-sounding 'Marquis' and 'Marquise'. For the historical figure of Matilda of Tuscany, however, I have used 'Countess' which is how she appears in most English and Italian histories of the period.

Punctuation is the one area where I have felt obliged to take some considerable liberties with the original text. The problem lies in Pirandello's repeated use of dashes, dots of suspension, and, above all, exclamation marks where there seems little to indicate a particularly agitated or emphatic utterance. One finds the same practice in Strindberg and in the German expressionists, but to reproduce it consistently in English would surely be counter-productive.

My thanks go to Simona Cain Polli, Jennifer Lorch, and Marco Sabbatini for their help and encouragement and to my editor Judith Luna for the scrupulous attention she has given to this volume. I am also grateful to Pedro Carol for keeping my files in order and to the unfailingly courteous librarians of the Bibliothèque universitaire de Genève for their assistance with inter-library loans. My greatest debt is to John C. Barnes whose meticulous and sensitive scrutiny of this translation has made it more accurate and more readable than it would otherwise have been: he has, however, always left the final decision to me and is in no way responsible for the remaining infelicities.

SELECT BIBLIOGRAPHY

In keeping with the general policy of Oxford World's Classics, this bibliography is restricted to works in English. These, fortunately, offer an abundance of perceptive comment on Pirandello and especially on the plays. Previous translations of the plays are too numerous to be listed here, but there is no complete English edition of Pirandello's theatre. The four-volume set of *Collected Plays* edited by Robert Rietti for Calder (1987–95) is the most substantial compilation to date, but omitted much of the later work for copyright reasons: it is now being re-edited and completed for Alma Classics. Pirandello's abundant production of short stories is still under-represented in translation.

Biography and Autobiography

Giudice, Gaspare, *Pirandello: A Biography*, trans. [and abridged] Alistair Hamilton (London, 1975).

Pirandello's Love Letters to Marta Abba, trans. and ed. Benito Ortolani (Princeton, 1994).

Fiction

One, No One, One Hundred Thousand, trans. William Weaver (New York, 1990).

The Late Mattia Pascal, trans. William Weaver (New York, 1964).

The Old and the Young, trans. C. K. Scott Moncrieff (London, 1928).

Shoot: The Notebooks of Serafino Gubbio, Cinematograph Operator, trans. C. K. Scott Moncrieff (New York, 1927).

Short Stories, trans. Frederick May (London, 1965).

Theoretical Writings

On Humor, trans. Antonio Illiano and Daniel P. Testa (Chapel Hill, NC, 1974).

'The New Theatre and the Old', trans. Herbert Goldstone, and 'Theatre and Literature', trans. A. M. Webb, in Haskell M. Blok and Herman Salinger (eds.), *The Creative Vision: Modern European Writers on Their Art* (London, 1960).

Criticism

Barnes, John C., '*Umorismo* is No Laughing Matter', *Pirandello Studies*, 29 (2009), 14–20.

—— 'Four Characters in Search of an Order: Some Thoughts about the Main *Dramatis Personae* of *Enrico IV*', *Pirandello Studies*, 31 (2011), 43–61.

Bassanese, Fiora A., *Understanding Luigi Pirandello* (Columbia, SC, 1997).

Bassnet-McGuire, Susan, *Luigi Pirandello* (London, 1983).

Bentley, Eric R., *The Pirandello Commentaries* (Evanston, Ill., 1991).

Bini, Daniela, 'Pirandello's Philosophy and Philosophers', in DiGaetani (ed.), *A Companion to Pirandello Studies*, 17–46.

Brustein, Robert, *The Theater of Revolt* (Boston, 1964).

Büdel, Oscar, *Pirandello* (London, 1966).

Caesar, Ann Hallamore, *Characters and Authors in Luigi Pirandello* (Oxford, 1999).

Cambon, Glauco (ed.), *Pirandello: A Collection of Critical Essays* (Englewood Cliffs, NJ, 1967).

DiGaetani, John L. (ed.), *A Companion to Pirandello Studies* (Westport, Conn., 1990).

Esslin, Martin, *Reflections: Essays on Modern Theater* (New York, 1969).

Fergusson, Francis, *The Idea of a Theater* (Princeton, 1949).

Giudice, Gaspare, 'Ambiguity in *Six Characters in Search of an Author*', in DiGaetani (ed.), *A Companion to Pirandello Studies*, 167–84.

Lorch, Jennifer, *Pirandello: Six Characters in Search of an Author; Plays in Production* (Cambridge, 2005).

MacClintock, Lander, *The Age of Pirandello* (Bloomington, Ind., 1951).

Mariani, Umberto, *Living Masks: The Achievement of Pirandello* (Toronto, 2008).

Matthaei, Renate, *Luigi Pirandello* (New York, 1973).

Mazzaro, Jerome, *Mind Plays: Essays on Luigi Pirandello's Theatre* (Bloomington, Ind., 2001).

Oliver, Roger W., *Dreams of Passion: The Theater of Luigi Pirandello* (New York, 1979).

Ragusa, Olga, *Pirandello: An Approach to His Theatre* (Edinburgh, 1980).

Starkie, Walter, *Luigi Pirandello* (rev. edn., Berkeley, 1965).

Strehler, Giorgio, 'The Giants of the Mountain', *World Theatre*, 16/3 (1967), 263–9.

Styan, J. L., *The Dark Comedy: The Development of Modern Comic Tragedy* (Cambridge, 1968).

Tilgher, Adriano, 'Life versus Form', in Cambon (ed.), *Luigi Pirandello: A Collection of Critical Essays*, 19–34.

Vittorini, Domenico, *The Drama of Luigi Pirandello* (New York, 1969).

Williams, Raymond, *Modern Tragedy* (London, 1966).

Periodicals

Modern Drama, special Pirandello issues 6/4 (1964), 20/4 (1977), 30/3 (1987).

Pirandellian Studies (University of Nebraska).

Pirandello Studies (Journal of the Society for Pirandello Studies).
PSA (Annual publication of the Pirandello Society of America).

Further Reading in Oxford World's Classics

Chekhov, Anton, *Five Plays*, trans. and ed. Ronald Hingley.
Ibsen, Henrik, *Four Major Plays*, trans. James McFarlane and Jens Arup, ed. James McFarlane.
Strindberg, August, *Miss Julie and Other Plays*, trans. and ed. Michael Robinson.
Synge, J. M., *The Playboy of the Western World and Other Plays*, ed. Ann Saddlemyer.

A CHRONOLOGY OF LUIGI PIRANDELLO

Dates in parenthesis refer to first performance for drama and to publication for all other texts.

1867 Born 28 June in villa known as Kaos near Girgenti (now Agrigento), Sicily, during cholera epidemic; P will later call himself 'a child of chaos'. His father Stefano Pirandello is a wealthy sulphur-mine contractor who served under Garibaldi in the unification campaigns of 1860–2: there is the same patriotic tradition in the family of his mother, Caterina Ricci-Gramitto.

1870–9 Elementary education at home in Agrigento. From family servant hears Sicilian folklore (the Women of the Night, the Angel Hundred-and-One) that will later appear in *The Fable of the Changeling Son* and *The Mountain Giants*. Loses his religious faith after brief period of childhood piety. First signs of literary vocation. Aged 12, writes five-act tragedy (not extant).

1880–8 Studies in Palermo where his family has moved (1880). Writes conventional late Romantic poetry. Spends three months helping father in management of sulphur mines before enrolling at University of Palermo where he gets to know future leaders of the *fasci siciliani* movement which will form background of novel *The Old and the Young* (1913). Becomes engaged to cousin Paolina.

Ibsen, *Ghosts* (1881); Strindberg, *Miss Julie* (1888).

1889 Transfers to University of Rome where he enrols in the Faculty of Letters. After writing a number of plays (now lost) that fail to reach the stage, publishes first volume of poems in late Romantic vein, *Joyful Pain*; breaks off engagement to Paolina; quarrels with Professor of Latin and transfers to University of Bonn.

Giovanni Verga, *Mastro Don Gesualdo* (1889).

1890–1 Studies at Bonn where he obtains a doctorate in Romance Philology with a thesis on the Agrigento dialect (1891). Love affair with German girl Jenny Schulz-Lander to whom he dedicates his second volume of poetry, *The Easter of Gea* (1891).

1892 Returns to Rome where he lives on allowance from father and devotes himself to literature. Meets with prominent writers, including fellow Sicilian novelist Luigi Capuana.

Italo Svevo, *A Life* (1892).

1893–4 Brutal suppression of Sicilian peasant movement (*fasci siciliani*) by government of Francesco Crispi.

Shaw, *Mrs Warren's Profession* (1893); Maeterlinck, *Pelléas and Mélisande* (1893); Federico De Roberto, *The Viceroys* (1894).

1894 First volume of short stories, *Love without Love*; translation of Goethe's *Roman Elegies*; consents to arranged marriage with Antonietta Portulano, daughter of his father's business partner.

1895–9 Birth of children: Stefano (1895), Rosalia ('Lietta', 1897), Fausto (1899). Begins teaching at college for girls, Istituto Superiore di Magistero (1898). Italian colonial expansion halted by defeat at Adwa (1896) in First Italo-Ethiopian War.

Wilde, *The Importance of Being Earnest* (1895); Jarry, *Ubu the King* (1895); Italo Svevo, *As a Man Grows Older* (1898); Ibsen, *When We Dead Awaken* (1899).

1900–3 Continues to write short stories, first published in magazines and then collected in volumes. Publishes two early novels *The Outcast* (1901) and *The Turn* (1902). Flooding of the Aragona sulphur mine (1903) in which his father had invested not only his own fortune but also the dowry of his daughter-in-law. At first paralysed by the shock, Antonietta descends into madness. P forced to supplement modest salary by taking in private pupils and working for magazines.

Freud, *The Interpretation of Dreams* (1900); Strindberg, *A Dream Play* (1901); Luigi Capuana, *The Marchese of Roccaverdina* (1901); Thomas Mann, *Buddenbrooks* (1901); Wedekind, *Pandora's Box* (1902); Gabriele D'Annunzio, *Tales of Pescara* (1902) and *The Daughter of Iorio* (1903).

1904–7 Innovative and successful third novel *The Late Mattia Pascal* (1904) leads to collaboration with publishing house Fratelli Treves and major newspaper *Corriere della Sera*.

Chekhov, *The Cherry Orchard* (1904); Yeats, *On Baile's Strand* (1904); Strindberg, *The Ghost Sonata* (1907); Synge, *The Playboy of the Western World* (1907).

1908–9 Publishes *Art and Science* and his major theoretical essay *Humourism* (*L'umorismo*, 1908) which sets off a bitter feud with Benedetto Croce. Promotion to rank of full professor at Istituto Superiore. Publishes first part of historical novel *The Old and the Young* (1909). Begins composition of novel *One, No One, One Hundred Thousand*.

Filippo Tommaso Marinetti, *The Futurist Manifesto* (1909).

1910–14 Sicilian playwright-producer Nino Martoglio persuades him to adapt short stories for the theatre (*Sicilian Limes*, 1910; *The Doctor's Duty*, 1912). Forced to halt circulation of new novel *Her Husband*

(1911) because of presumed satirical allusion to Sardinian novelist Grazia Deledda. Publishes final volume of poetry (1912) and complete version of *The Old and the Young* (1913); continues prolific production of short stories. Italian conquest of Libya (1911–12).

D'Annunzio, *The Martyrdom of Saint Sebastian*, with music by Debussy (1911); Dino Campana, *Orphic Songs* (1914).

1915–16 Increased production of Sicilian dialect plays (*Think it Over, Giacomino*; *The Cap and Bells*; *Liolà*; *The Jar*). Novel *Shoot* (1916, later renamed *The Notebooks of Serafino Gubbio*) testifies to P's interest in the cinema. Italy enters war against Austria (1915); Stefano Pirandello volunteers, is taken prisoner (1916), and begins sustained correspondence with father.

Giorgio De Chirico founds movement of 'Metaphysical Painting' (1915); Giuseppe Ungaretti, *The Buried Port* (1916); Luigi Chiarelli, *The Mask and the Face* (1916).

1917–20 With *Right You Are, If You Think You Are* (1917) begins a new series of plays in standard Italian and with bourgeois settings (*The Pleasure of Honesty*; *The Grafting*; *It Can't Be Serious*; *The Rules of the Game*; *Man, Beast and Virtue*; *As Before, Better than Before*; *All for the Best*; *Signora Morli, One and Two*). P's work now staged by the most prominent actors and directors: Angelo Musco (for the dialect plays), Ruggero Ruggeri, Virgilio Talli. First collection of plays published as *Naked Masks* (*Maschere nude*, 1918). Stefano returns from captivity; Antonietta, increasingly disturbed, accuses her husband of incestuous relations with Lietta, and is moved to mental home (1919) where she remains until her death forty years later. War ends (1918) with Italian victory over Austria and territorial gain of South Tyrol. D'Annunzio leads group of ultra-nationalist veterans (*irredentisti*) to seize port of Fiume (1919), later ceded to Italy.

Rosso di San Secondo, *Puppets, What Passion!* (1918); Giuseppe Ungaretti, *The Joy of Shipwrecks* (1919); Shaw, *Heartbreak House* (1919); Joyce, *Ulysses* (1920).

1921–2 Catastrophic Rome premiere of *Six Characters in Search of an Author* (10 May 1921) is followed by success in Milan later the same year. Pitoëff's 1923 Paris production assures P's international fame and *Six Characters* is translated and performed throughout Europe. Similar success greets *Henry IV* (February 1922). *To Clothe the Naked* staged in same year. First four volumes of collected short stories published under the title *Stories for a Year* (*Novelle per un anno*, 1922). Fascist March on Rome; Mussolini appointed prime minister (1922).

T. S. Eliot, *The Waste Land* (1922).

1923–4 New plays, *The Man with the Flower in His Mouth* (1923), *The Life I Gave You* (1923), and *Each in His Own Way* (1924) which develops the metatheatrical discourse initiated by *Six Characters*. Special Pirandello season in New York (1923–4) presents *Six Characters*, *Henry IV*, and *As Before, Better Than Before*. Adriano Tilgher's discussion of the plays' philosophical implications (1923). 'Pirandellism' becomes a byword. Government in danger of collapse after murder of Socialist deputy Matteotti (1924). P joins the Fascist party. Mussolini weathers the storm and builds totalitarian state.

Italo Svevo, *Zeno's Conscience* (1923); Shaw, *Saint Joan* (1923); Thomas Mann, *The Magic Mountain* (1924).

1925–7 New edition of *Six Characters* (1925), revised in the light of Pitoëff's production. Founds Arts Theatre of Rome with official state sponsorship. Writes and directs new plays, including *Our Lord of the Ship* (1925) and *Diana and Tuda* (1927). Increasingly involved with practical side of theatre as director and manager. Completion and publication of last novel, *One, No One, One Hundred Thousand* (1926). Passionate and probably unconsummated love for company's leading young actress, Marta Abba.

Gide, *The Counterfeiters* (1925); Eugenio Montale, *Cuttlefish Bones* (1925); Proust, *In Search of Lost Time* (1927); Woolf, *To the Lighthouse* (1927); Grazia Deledda awarded Nobel Prize (1926).

1928–9 New work includes the first two plays of the myth trilogy, *The New Colony* (1928) and *Lazarus* (1929). Despite successful tours abroad (England, France, Germany, Brazil, Argentina), the Arts Theatre is dissolved in 1928. P blames lack of adequate government support and will continue to resent Mussolini's reluctance to fund a national theatre company. Member of Royal Academy of Italy (1929). Lateran Treaty (1929) settles relations between the Italian state and the Vatican.

Claudel, *The Satin Slipper* (1929); Alberto Moravia, *The Time of Indifference* (1929).

1930–3 Last play in metatheatre trilogy, *Tonight We Improvise* (1930) with satirical allusion to German director Max Reinhardt ('Dr Hinkfuss'). *As You Desire Me* (1930) and *Finding Oneself* (1932), like the earlier *Diana and Tuda*, written with Marta Abba in mind. *When Someone is Somebody* (1933) reflects P's own experience as a celebrated ageing artist. Travels widely (Paris, Lisbon, Prague, Los Angeles, Montevideo), but now resides in Germany where some of his plays receive their first performance.

Brecht, *The Rise and Fall of the City of Mahagonny* (1930); O'Neill, *Mourning Becomes Electra* (1930).

1934–5 Awarded Nobel Prize for Literature (1934). *The Fable of the Changeling Son* (1934), opera by Malipiero with libretto by P, performed in Germany and Italy and quickly banned by both regimes. Publishes first and second parts of *The Mountain Giants* (1934), conceived as conclusion to myth trilogy. Still seeking state funding for a national theatre, makes fulsome speech in Mussolini's presence supporting Italian invasion of Ethiopia (1935).

1936 Marta Abba leaves for the United States. P dies 10 December in Rome and is cremated. His will forbids funeral ceremonies of any kind. Italian military help to Nationalists in Spanish Civil War.

1937 First performance of unfinished *Mountain Giants*, Florence, 5 June.

SIX CHARACTERS IN SEARCH OF AN AUTHOR

A Play in the Making

CHARACTERS

The Characters of the Play in the Making

The Father
The Mother
The Stepdaughter
The Son
The Young Boy (non-speaking)
The Little Girl (non-speaking)
Madame Pace

The Theatre Company

The Director
The Leading Lady
The Leading Man
The Second Actress
A Young Actor
A Young Actress
Other Actors and Actresses
The Stage Manager
The Prompter
The Property Man
The Technician
The Director's Secretary
The Usher
Stagehands and Staff

The action takes place in daytime on the stage of a theatre. The play has no act or scene divisions, but the performance is interrupted twice: first when, with the curtain still up, the DIRECTOR *and the* FATHER *withdraw to compose the scenario and the* ACTORS *clear the stage; second, when the* TECHNICIAN *lowers the curtain by mistake.*

On entering the theatre, the audience finds the curtain raised and the stage as it is during the day, with neither wings nor scenery, empty and almost in darkness, so that right from the start the impression is that of an improvised performance.

Stairways, left and right, connect the stage with the auditorium. On the stage the cover has been removed from the PROMPTER's *box and lies next to the hatch. On the other side, downstage, for the* DIRECTOR, *a small table and an armchair with its back turned to the audience. Also downstage two more tables, one larger and one smaller, with several chairs, ready for use if needed in rehearsal, other chairs scattered right and left for the* ACTORS; *upstage, to one side, a half-hidden piano.*

When the houselights go down, the TECHNICIAN, *in dark blue overalls and with tool bag at his belt, enters through the stage door: from a corner at the back, he takes a few planks, comes forward, and kneels down to nail them together. The noise of hammering brings the* STAGE MANAGER *running from the dressing rooms.*

STAGE MANAGER. Hey! What are you doing?

TECHNICIAN. What am I doing? I'm knocking in these nails.

STAGE MANAGER. What? Now? [*Looks at his watch*] It's already half past ten. Any moment now the Director will be here for the rehearsal.

TECHNICIAN. But I need some time to do my job as well.

STAGE MANAGER. You'll have it; but not now.

TECHNICIAN. So when?

STAGE MANAGER. When it's not rehearsal time. Come on. Take all that stuff away, and let me get the stage ready for the second act of *The Rules of the Game.**

Mumbling and grumbling, the TECHNICIAN *picks up the planks and goes off. In the meantime the* ACTORS OF THE COMPANY, *men and women, start coming in through the stage door, first singly, then in pairs, in no special order, until there are nine or ten, about as many as are needed for the rehearsal of Pirandello's play* The Rules of the Game, *which is scheduled for that day. They enter, greet the* STAGE MANAGER, *and say their good mornings to each other. Some of them set off towards the dressing rooms; others, including the* PROMPTER *with his script rolled up under his arm, remain on the stage, waiting for the* DIRECTOR *to come and begin the rehearsal. They sit or stand around in groups, and chat; one starts smoking, another complains about his part, a third reads aloud to his group from some theatre magazine. Both* ACTRESSES *and* ACTORS *should wear bright cheerful clothes, and the way this first scene is improvised should be very lively as well as natural. At a given moment one of the cast sits at the piano and plays a dance tune; the younger* ACTORS *and* ACTRESSES *start dancing.*

STAGE MANAGER [*clapping his hands to call them to order*]. Come on now, pack it in! Here's the Director.

The music and the dancing stop abruptly. The ACTORS *turn to look out into the auditorium as the* DIRECTOR *enters through a door at the back. With bowler hat on head, walking stick under arm, and fat cigar in mouth, he walks up the aisle between the seats, is greeted by the cast, and mounts one of the stairways up to the stage. The* SECRETARY *hands him the mail: a few newspapers and a script in a wrapper.*

DIRECTOR. Any letters?

SECRETARY. None. That's all the mail there is.

DIRECTOR [*handing back the script*]. Put it in my office. [*Then, looking around and turning to the* STAGE MANAGER] Can't see a thing here. Give us a bit more light, please.*

STAGE MANAGER. Right away.

He goes to pass on the order and soon the whole right side of the stage, where the ACTORS *are, is flooded with white light. By now the* PROMPTER *has taken his place in the box, switched on his lamp, and opened out his script.*

DIRECTOR [*clapping his hands*]. Right then, come on, let's get started. [*To the* STAGE MANAGER] Is anyone missing?

STAGE MANAGER. The leading lady.

DIRECTOR. As usual. [*Looks at his watch*] We're already ten minutes late. Do me a favour: make a note of it. That'll teach her to be on time for rehearsals.

Before he has even finished this reprimand, the voice of the LEADING LADY *is heard from the back of the theatre.*

LEADING LADY. No, no. Please don't! Here I am, here I am!

Dressed in white from head to foot, with a dashing broad hat on her head and a charming lapdog in her arms, she runs down the central aisle and hurries up the steps onto the stage.

DIRECTOR. You never miss an opportunity to keep us waiting.

LEADING LADY. So sorry. I tried so hard to find a taxi and get here on time. But I can see you haven't started yet. And I'm not on stage straightaway. [*Calls the* STAGE MANAGER *by name and hands him the dog*] Please lock him in my dressing room.

DIRECTOR [*grumbling*]. And now the dog as well. As if there weren't enough dogs here already! [*Clapping his hands again and turning to the* PROMPTER] Right then, let's go: Act Two of *The Rules of the Game*. [*Sits in the armchair*] Your attention, ladies and gentleman! Who's on stage?

The ACTORS *and* ACTRESSES *clear the front of the stage and go to sit at the side—all except for the three who are supposed to be on stage and the* LEADING LADY *who, paying no attention to the* DIRECTOR, *has gone to sit at one of the two small tables.*

DIRECTOR [*to the* LEADING LADY]. So you're on stage, are you?

LEADING LADY. Me? No, sir.

DIRECTOR [*annoyed*]. Then get out of the way, for God's sake!

The LEADING LADY *gets up and goes to sit with the other* ACTORS *who have already withdrawn to one side.*

DIRECTOR [*to the* PROMPTER]. Let's get started, let's get started.

PROMPTER [*reading from the script*]. 'In the house of Leone Gala. A strange room, both dining-room and study.'

DIRECTOR [*turning to the* STAGE MANAGER]. We'll use the red set.

STAGE MANAGER [*noting it down on a piece of paper*]. The red one. Right.

PROMPTER [*still reading from the script*]. 'Table ready laid and desk with books and papers. Bookshelves and china cabinets displaying precious ware. Exit rear leads to Leone's bedroom. Side exit left for the kitchen. Main exit on the right.'

DIRECTOR [*standing up and pointing*]. So now pay attention. Main exit over there. Kitchen exit over here. [*Turning to the* ACTOR *who plays Socrates*] You enter and exit here. [*To the* STAGE MANAGER]

We'll have the doorway at the rear and put up curtains. [*Sits down again*]

STAGE MANAGER [*noting it down*]. Right.

PROMPTER [*reading as before*]. 'Scene One. Leone Gala, Guido Venanzi, Filippo known as Socrates.' [*To the* DIRECTOR] Do I have to read the stage directions as well?

DIRECTOR. Yes, yes. I've told you a hundred times.

PROMPTER [*reading*]. 'As the curtain rises Leone Gala, wearing a chef's hat and apron, is busy beating an egg in a bowl with a wooden spoon. Filippo, also dressed like a cook, is beating another egg. Guido Venanzi sits and listens.'

LEADING MAN [*to the* DIRECTOR]. But look, do I really have to wear a chef's hat?

DIRECTOR [*annoyed by the question*]. You certainly do. Since that's what's written there. [*Pointing to the script*]

LEADING MAN. Sorry, but it's ridiculous!

DIRECTOR [*jumping up in a fury*]. Ridiculous! Ridiculous! What can I do about it if we don't get any more good plays from France, so that we're reduced to putting on stuff by Pirandello that you have to be super-clever to understand, plays that seem cut out to please nobody—not the actors, not the critics, not the public? [*The* ACTORS *laugh; he rises, goes right up to the* LEADING MAN *and shouts*] The chef's hat, yessir! And beat those eggs! You think that beating eggs is all you'll have to do? No such luck. You need to represent the shell of the egg you're beating! [*The* ACTORS *laugh again and exchange ironic remarks*] Silence! And listen to me when I explain things. [*Turning to the* LEADING MAN *again*] Yes, sir, the shell: that's to say the empty form of reason, without the content of instinct which is blind. You are reason and your wife is instinct in a play of fixed roles where you, by playing your part, are deliberately the puppet of yourself.* You understand?

LEADING MAN [*opening his arms*]. Not me.

DIRECTOR [*going back to his chair*]. Neither do I. Let's get on with it. Anyway, you'll love the way it ends up. [*In a friendlier tone*] Do me a favour, turn round a bit, almost facing the audience. Because otherwise, what with the obscurity of the dialogue and the fact that you can't be heard, the whole thing falls apart. [*Clapping his hands again*] Attention, please, attention! Let's get started.

PROMPTER. Sorry, boss, but do you mind if I put the cover back on the prompt box? There's a bit of a draught.

DIRECTOR. Sure, sure, just do it!

In the meantime the USHER, *wearing his braided cap, has entered the auditorium; making his way down the aisle, he has come up to the stage to announce to the* DIRECTOR *the arrival of the* SIX CHARACTERS *who have also entered and are following some way behind, looking around, somewhat lost and bewildered.*

In the staging of this play all available means should be employed to ensure the crucial effect which is the avoidance of any confusion between the SIX CHARACTERS *and the* ACTORS OF THE COMPANY. *The placing of the two groups, indicated by the stage directions, when the* CHARACTERS *climb onto the stage, will obviously come in useful here, as will a different colouring obtained by appropriate lighting. But the most effective and fitting means suggested here is the use of special masks for the* CHARACTERS—*masks of some material that does not lose its form with sweat but that is still light enough for the actors to wear, designed and cut out so as not to cover the eyes, nostrils, and mouth. This brings out the underlying meaning of the play. The* CHARACTERS *should not appear as* phantoms, *but as* created realities, *changeless constructs of the imagination, and therefore more real and substantial than the* ACTORS *with their natural mutability. The masks help create the impression of figures fashioned by art, each fixed immutably in the expression of its own fundamental feeling*—Remorse *for the* FATHER, Revenge *for the* STEPDAUGHTER, Scorn *for the* SON, *and* Sorrow *for the* MOTHER *with static wax tears welling from her dark eyes and running down her cheeks, as in the painted and sculpted images of the* Mater dolorosa *in churches. And her clothing should be of some special material and style, sober, with stiff folds and statuesque volume; in short, not looking like a material you could buy in any old shop to be cut out and sewn by any old dressmaker.*

The FATHER *is about fifty, thinning at the temples, but not bald, with reddish hair and thick moustaches curling round a young-looking mouth, often open in an uncertain vacuous smile. His pallor is particularly noticeable on his broad forehead; blue oval eyes, bright and intelligent; he wears light-coloured trousers and a dark jacket; sometimes mellifluous, sometimes abruptly harsh and grating.*

The MOTHER *seems frightened and crushed by some unbearable burden of shame and humiliation. With her widow's veil of thick crêpe, she dresses in humble black; and when she lifts the veil, her face seems not so much marked by suffering as made of wax; her eyes remain downcast.*

The STEPDAUGHTER, *eighteen years of age, is defiant, almost impudent. Very beautiful, she too wears mourning, but with conspicuous elegance. She shows her contempt for the timid, suffering, lost air of the* YOUNG BOY, *her brother, a miserable fourteen-year-old, also dressed in black; she is, however, full of tenderness towards her sister, a* LITTLE GIRL *of about four, wearing white, with a black silk sash round her waist.*

The SON *is twenty-two, tall and stiff in his contained scorn for his* FATHER *and his sullen indifference towards his* MOTHER; *he wears a mauve overcoat and a long green scarf round his neck.*

USHER [*cap in hand*]. Excuse me, sir.

DIRECTOR [*brusque, surly*]. What is it now?

USHER [*timidly*]. There are some people here asking to see you.

The DIRECTOR *and the* ACTORS *turn round in surprise and look down from the stage into the auditorium.*

DIRECTOR [*furious again*]. But I'm in the middle of a rehearsal! And you know perfectly well that nobody's allowed in during a rehearsal! [*Calling out to the back of the auditorium*] Who are you people? What do you want?

FATHER [*coming forward to one of the two sets of steps, followed by the others*]. We've come here in search of an author.

DIRECTOR [*half-puzzled, half-angry*]. An author? What author?

FATHER. Any author, sir.

DIRECTOR. But there's no author round here because we're not rehearsing any new play.

STEPDAUGHTER [*brightly as she hurries up the steps*]. So much the better, so much the better, sir! So we could be your new play.

SOME OF THE ACTORS [*amid the laughter and comments of the others*]. Oh, hear that, hear that!

FATHER [*following the* STEPDAUGHTER *onto the stage*]. Could be. But if there's no author . . . [*To the* DIRECTOR] Unless you'd like to be . . .

The MOTHER *climbs the first few steps, holding the* LITTLE GIRL *by the hand and followed by the* YOUNG BOY. *They wait there, while the* SON *remains sullenly behind.*

DIRECTOR. Are you people joking?

FATHER. How can you say such a thing! Quite the contrary—we bring you a very distressing drama.

STEPDAUGHTER. And one that could make your fortune!

DIRECTOR. Do me a favour and clear off. We've got no time to waste with a bunch of loonies!

FATHER [*honey-voiced and hurt*]. Oh sir, you must know that life is full of endless absurdities, so barefaced that they don't even need to seem real, because they *are* real.

DIRECTOR. What the devil are you trying to say?

FATHER. I'm saying that what really does seem crazy, yes, sir, is to insist on doing the opposite; that is, to create lifelike situations so that you can make them seem real. But let me remind you that if this is madness, it's still the only purpose of your profession.

The ACTORS *protest, indignant.*

DIRECTOR [*rising and facing up to him*]. Oh yes? So you think that ours is a profession for madmen?

FATHER. Well, passing off as real what isn't real at all; for no good reason, sir: just as a game . . . Isn't it your job to give life on the stage to imaginary characters?

DIRECTOR [*without hesitation, voicing the growing indignation of the Actors*]. I beg you to believe, my dear sir, that the profession of acting is a highly noble one. Even if, as things stand nowadays, the new playwrights give us silly comedies and puppets instead of real men, you should know that we can still boast of having given life—here, on these boards—to immortal works!

The ACTORS *show their satisfaction and approval by applauding their* DIRECTOR.

FATHER [*interrupting and seizing on the topic*]. That's it! Quite right! Life to living beings, more alive than those who breathe and wear clothes! Not as real, perhaps; but more true! We're in perfect agreement!

The ACTORS *look at each other in amazement.*

DIRECTOR. Hold on! A moment ago you were saying . . .

FATHER. No, sorry, I was saying it for you, sir, because you shouted that you had no time to waste with lunatics, whereas nobody should know better than you that nature employs the human imagination as an instrument to pursue its work of creation at a higher level.

DIRECTOR. Fine, fine. But what are you trying to prove with all this?

FATHER. Nothing, sir. Just to show you that one can be born into life in so many ways, so many forms: tree or stone, water or butterfly . . . or woman. And one can also be born as a character.

DIRECTOR [*with mock ironic surprise*]. And so you, and these people around you, were all born as characters?

FATHER. Exactly, sir. And alive, as you see.

The DIRECTOR *and the* ACTORS *burst into laughter as if at a joke.*

FATHER [*hurt*]. I'm sorry to hear you laugh like that; let me repeat that we bring with us a most painful drama, as you might guess from this woman with the black veil.

So saying, he gives his hand to the MOTHER *to help her up the last steps, and then, with a solemn and tragic air, leads her to the other side of the stage which is immediately illuminated by an unreal light. The* LITTLE GIRL *and the* YOUNG BOY *follow their* MOTHER; *then comes the* SON *who goes to stand apart upstage; finally the* STEPDAUGHTER *who also stands apart, but downstage, leaning against the proscenium arch. The* ACTORS, *at first surprised but then impressed by this development, burst into applause as if at a performance given specially for them.*

DIRECTOR [*first shocked, then indignant*]. Pipe down! Let's have some silence! [*Turns to the* CHARACTERS] And you lot can clear off! Get out of here! [*To the* STAGE MANAGER] For God's sake, get them out of here!

STAGE MANAGER [*comes forward, but then stops as if held back by a strange fear*]. Out! Out!

FATHER [*to the* DIRECTOR]. But no, you see, we . . .

DIRECTOR [*shouting*]. Now look! Some of us here have got work to do.

LEADING MAN. And we're not to be made fools of . . .

FATHER [*coming forward, determined*]. I'm really surprised by your lack of faith. As if you weren't used to seeing characters spring to life and face each other on this stage—the characters created by an author. Maybe it's because we're not in any script down there. [*Points to the* PROMPTER's *box*]

STEPDAUGHTER [*coming up to the* DIRECTOR, *smiling, seductive*]. Believe me, sir, we are six *very* interesting characters! Even if we're lost.

FATHER [*moving her aside*]. Yes, lost, that's the word for it! [*To the* DIRECTOR *without a break*] Lost, you see, in that the author who created us alive either wouldn't or in practice couldn't bring us into the world of art. And that truly was a crime, sir, because someone who has the luck to be born as a living character can laugh even at death. He never dies. The man will die, the writer, the instrument of creation; but the creature never dies! And to live for ever he doesn't even need to have any extraordinary gifts or to do marvellous deeds. What about Sancho Panza? What about Don Abbondio?* And yet they live for ever because— living seeds—they had the luck to find a fertile soil, an imagination able to feed them, form them, and grant them life for all eternity!

DIRECTOR. That's all very fine! But what do you want with us?

FATHER. We want to live, sir!

DIRECTOR [*ironic*]. For all eternity?

FATHER. No, sir: just for a moment. In you.

AN ACTOR. Hear that!

LEADING LADY. They want to live in us!

YOUNG ACTOR [*pointing to the* STEPDAUGHTER]. I wouldn't say no, so long as I get that one!

FATHER. Now see here, see here. This show must go on. [*To the* DIRECTOR] But if you agree, and if your actors agree, we can soon fix it up among ourselves.

DIRECTOR [*annoyed*]. What's there to fix up? We don't do fix-ups round here. We perform tragedies and comedies.

FATHER. That's right. And that's what we've come here for, here to you!

DIRECTOR. And where's the script?

FATHER. It's in us, sir. [*The* ACTORS *laugh*] The play's in us and we are the play. And we're burning to act it, driven by the passion within!

STEPDAUGHTER [*scornfully, with the wicked charm of outrageous impudence*]. My passion, sir; if only you knew! My passion . . . for him! [*Points to the* FATHER *and seems about to embrace him, but then bursts into a shrill laugh*]

FATHER [*with sudden anger*]. You just behave yourself for a moment. And don't laugh like that.

STEPDAUGHTER. No? Then, if you allow me, gentlemen—although it's only two months since I became an orphan—just see how I can sing and dance.

With a malicious air she launches into 'Beware of Chu Chin Chow'* by Dave Stamper, in the French version arranged by Francis Salabert as a foxtrot or slow one-step, dancing as she sings the first verse.

> Les chinois sont un peuple malin,
> De Shangaï à Pékin,
> Ils ont mis des écriteaux partout!
> Prenez garde à Tchou-Tchin-Tchou!

As she dances, the ACTORS, *especially the young ones, move towards her as if drawn by some strange attraction, raising their hands slightly as if to grasp her. But she evades them; and when the* ACTORS *burst into applause and the* DIRECTOR *protests, she becomes withdrawn and distant.*

THE ACTORS AND ACTRESSES [*laughing and applauding*]. Bravo! Splendid! Good for you!

DIRECTOR [*angry*]. Silence! Do you think you're in a cabaret! [*Rather worried, taking the* FATHER *aside*] Just tell me, is she mad?

FATHER. Not in the least! It's worse than that!

STEPDAUGHTER [*immediately running up to the* DIRECTOR]. Worse! Worse! Oh sir, much worse! Listen, please: do let us put on this play straightaway, because you'll see that at a certain moment, I . . . when this little darling here [*taking the hand of the* LITTLE GIRL *who is with the* MOTHER *and leading her up to the* DIRECTOR]—see how pretty she is [*hugging and kissing her*] dear, dear child! [*Puts her down and adds with almost involuntary emotion*] Well, when God suddenly takes this little darling from her poor mother there: and when this little idiot [*pushing forward the* YOUNG BOY, *grasping him by the sleeve*] does the silliest thing you can think of, like the cretin that he is [*shoving him back towards the* MOTHER]—then you'll see how I take flight, yes, sir, take flight! Flight! And I just can't wait, believe me, can't wait. Because after the very intimate thing that happened between me and him [*pointing to the* FATHER *with a horrible wink*] I can't stand being in this company, can't stand seeing how Mother suffers for that weird type over there [*pointing to the* SON]—look at him! look at him! Cold as ice, couldn't care less—because he's the legitimate son, he is! And he despises me, and him [*indicating the* YOUNG BOY] and that poor little creature. Because we're all bastards—do you see? bastards. [*Goes up to the* MOTHER *and embraces her*] And this poor mother, the mother to all of us—he won't even recognize her as *his* mother. He looks down on her, as if she were only the mother of us three bastards—the coward!

She says all this in a very rapid and agitated manner. After raising her voice on 'bastards', she speaks the final 'coward' softly, as if spitting it out.

MOTHER [*deeply distressed, to the* DIRECTOR]. I implore you, in the name of these two helpless little ones . . . [*feeling faint, on the verge of collapsing*]—Oh my God . . .

FATHER [*rushing to support her, joined by most of the* ACTORS *in amazement and dismay*]. A chair, for pity's sake! A chair for this poor widow!

ACTORS [*running to help*].—Is it real, then? Is she really fainting?

DIRECTOR. Get a chair, quick!

One of the ACTORS *provides a chair; the others gather anxiously round. The* MOTHER, *seated, tries to prevent the* FATHER *from raising the veil that hides her face.*

FATHER. Look at her, sir. Look at her . . .

MOTHER. No. Stop it, for heaven's sake!

FATHER. Let them see you! [*He lifts the veil*]

MOTHER [*rising and hiding her face in her hands for despair*]. Oh sir, I implore you, don't let this man go through with his plan—it's horrible for me!

DIRECTOR [*bewildered, stunned*]. Now I'm lost. I don't understand where we are or what it's all about! [*To the* FATHER] Is this your wife?

FATHER [*promptly*]. Yes, sir, my wife.

DIRECTOR. So how can she be a widow, if you're still alive?

The ACTORS *find relief for their astonishment in a loud burst of laughter.*

FATHER [*wounded, bitterly resentful*]. Don't laugh! Don't laugh like that, for God's sake! Because, sir, that's just where her drama lies. She had another man. Another man who should be here!

MOTHER [*with a scream*]. No! No!

STEPDAUGHTER. Luckily for him, he's dead: two months ago. I told you that. We're still wearing mourning, as you can see.

FATHER. He's not here; but, you see, it's not so much because he's dead. He's not here because—just look at her and you'll understand! Her drama couldn't be about the love of two men, because she's quite incapable of feeling anything for either of them—except perhaps a touch of gratitude (for the other one, not me!)—She's not a woman: she's a mother! And her drama—how powerful it is!—is all there, in fact, in these four children by the two different men that she had.

MOTHER. I had them? You dare to say that I had them, as if I'd wanted them myself? It was him, sir. He forced that other man on me. He made me go away with him, he made me do it.

STEPDAUGHTER [*suddenly indignant*]. Not true.

MOTHER [*stunned*]. What do you mean, not true?

STEPDAUGHTER. Not true. It's not true.

MOTHER. And what can you know about it?

STEPDAUGHTER. It's not true! [*To the* DIRECTOR] Don't you believe her. You know why she says it? For him, over there. [*Indicating the* SON] That's why she says it. Because she's wasting away and tor-turing herself, and all for the indifference of that son there. She wants him to think that if she abandoned him when he was two, it was because *he* [*referring to the* FATHER] forced her into it.

MOTHER [*vehemently*]. He did, he forced me: God be my witness! [*To the* DIRECTOR] Go and ask him if it isn't true. [*Pointing to her husband*] Let him tell you himself! . . . She can't know anything about it. [*Indicating her daughter*]

STEPDAUGHTER. I know that as long as my father was alive you lived with him calm and content. Deny it, if you can.

MOTHER. I don't deny it, no . . .

STEPDAUGHTER. Always full of loving care for you. [*To the* YOUNG BOY, *angrily*] Isn't it true? Tell him. Why don't you speak up, you idiot?

MOTHER. Leave the poor boy alone! Why do you want to make me look ungrateful? I don't want to insult your father's memory. I told this gentleman that it wasn't my fault, and it wasn't for my own pleasure that I left his house and abandoned my son.

FATHER. It's true, sir. It was my doing.

Pause

LEADING MAN [*to his fellow actors*]. How's that for a show!

LEADING LADY. One that they're putting on for us.

YOUNG ACTOR. For once in a while.

DIRECTOR [*beginning to get seriously interested*]. Give them a hearing. Let's give them a hearing.

So saying, he goes down the steps into the auditorium and stands facing the stage as if to survey the scene from a spectator's viewpoint.

SON [*without moving from his place; cold, quiet, ironic*]. Yes indeed. Now just wait for his chunk of philosophy! He'll tell you all about the Daemon of Experiment.

FATHER. You're a cynical fool, and I've told you so a hundred times. [*To the* DIRECTOR *down in the auditorium*] He mocks me because of this phrase that I use in my own defence.

SON [*with scorn*]. Phrases!

FATHER. Phrases! Phrases! As if, when we're faced by some inexplicable fact, some devouring evil, we didn't all find comfort in a word that means nothing and that simply serves to calm us down.

STEPDAUGHTER. And calm your remorse as well. That above all.

FATHER. Remorse? It's not true. Words alone have never calmed my remorse.

STEPDAUGHTER. No, it took a bit of money too; yes, yes, a bit of money! Like the hundred lire he wanted to pay me, gentlemen.

The ACTORS *recoil in horror.*

SON [*to his half-sister, with contempt*]. That's despicable.

STEPDAUGHTER. Despicable? It was there in a blue envelope on the mahogany table in Madame Pace's back room behind the shop. You know, sir. One of those *madames* who use the pretext of selling *Robes et Manteaux** to attract us poor girls from good families into their *ateliers*.

SON. And she's bought herself the right to bully the whole family with that hundred lire he was going to pay her—and which, luckily— mark my words—he had no call to pay.

STEPDAUGHTER. But we were right on the verge, you know. [*With a burst of laughter*]

MOTHER [*protesting*]. Shame on you, daughter! Shame!

STEPDAUGHTER [*sharply*]. Shame? It's my revenge! I'm burning, burning, sir, to live that scene! The room . . . over here the window with the cloaks; over there the sofa bed; the mirror, a screen; and in front of the window the little mahogany table with the pale blue envelope containing the hundred lire. I can see it. I could take it. Oh, but you gentlemen should turn your backs: I'm almost naked! I'm not blushing now, though; now it's his turn to blush! [*Pointing to the* FATHER] But I can assure you he was very pale, very pale in that moment! [*To the* DIRECTOR] Believe me, sir.

DIRECTOR. I don't understand a thing any more.

FATHER. I bet you don't. After being set on like that. Call everyone to order, and let me have my say; and pay no attention to her vicious slanders about me, until you've heard all the explanations.

STEPDAUGHTER. No stories here. No telling stories.

FATHER. I'm not telling stories. I want to explain to him.

STEPDAUGHTER. Yes, in your own way! Very nice!

At this point the DIRECTOR *climbs back onto the stage to restore order.*

FATHER. But this is where all the trouble starts! With words! We all have a world of things inside us; everyone has his own world of things! And how can we understand each other if in my words I put the meaning and the value of the things inside me; while my listener inevitably receives them with all the meaning and value that they have for him, in his own inner world? We think we understand each other: we never understand each other! Look here: my pity, all my pity for this woman [*referring to the* MOTHER] has been taken by her as the most ferocious cruelty.

MOTHER. But if you drove me out?

FATHER. There. Do you hear that? Drove her out. She thinks I drove her out.

MOTHER. You know how to talk; I can't . . . But, believe me, sir: after he married me . . . who knows why, a poor simple woman . . .

FATHER. But that's just it, I married you for your simplicity; it's what I loved in you, I thought . . . [*He breaks off at her signs of protest. Seeing how impossible it is to make himself understood, he throws wide his arms in a gesture of despair and turns to the* DIRECTOR] No, you see? She says no. It's frightening, sir, frightening, [*striking his forehead*] her deafness, her mental deafness! A good heart, yes, for her children! But deaf, brain-deaf, desperately deaf!

STEPDAUGHTER. Yes, but now get him to tell you how lucky we've been to profit from his intelligence.

FATHER. If only we could foresee all the evil that can come from the good we think we're doing.

The LEADING LADY *has had enough of seeing the* LEADING MAN *flirting with the* STEPDAUGHTER; *she now comes forward to the* DIRECTOR.

LEADING LADY. Excuse me. Are we going to carry on with the rehearsal?

DIRECTOR. Of course, of course! Just let me hear this out!

YOUNG ACTOR. It's such an unusual case!

YOUNG ACTRESS. And so interesting!

LEADING LADY. For those who are interested! [*With a dark look at the* LEADING MAN]

DIRECTOR [*to the* FATHER]. But you'll need to explain things clearly. [*Sits down*]

FATHER. Well now, you see, sir, there was a poor fellow who worked for me, my assistant, my secretary, loyal to the core. And he got along absolutely perfectly with her [*indicating the* MOTHER]; without the faintest shadow of any wrongdoing, mind you! Good and simple, like her. Both of them incapable of any evil in deed or thought.

STEPDAUGHTER. Instead, he thought it up for them—and did it!

FATHER. Not true! What I did I meant for their good—and my own too, I admit. I had reached the point where I couldn't say a word to one or the other without seeing them exchange a glance of mutual understanding, without seeing one looking straight in the other's eyes for advice on how to take my words so as not to make me angry. This, of course, as you must understand, was enough to keep me in a state of permanent anger, unbearable exasperation.

DIRECTOR. So why didn't you sack him then, this secretary chap?

FATHER. Good question. In fact, I did sack him, sir. But then I saw this poor woman mooning around the house like a lost soul, like some stray animal you'd take in out of pity.

MOTHER. Well, no wonder.

FATHER [*suddenly turning, as if to forestall her*]. It's about our son, isn't it?

MOTHER. He'd torn my son from my breast!

FATHER. But not out of cruelty. To make him grow up strong and healthy, in contact with the earth.

STEPDAUGHTER [*pointing to the* SON, *ironic*]. And how it shows!

FATHER [*immediately*]. Am I to blame if he grew up like this? I gave him to a wet-nurse in the country, sir, a peasant girl, because his mother didn't seem strong enough, for all her humble birth. It was the same impulse that had made me marry her. A silly prejudice, perhaps; but that's the way it is. I've always had these damned yearnings towards a kind of solid moral health. [*Another loud burst of laughter from the* STEPDAUGHTER] Make her stop that! It's unbearable!

DIRECTOR. Stop that! Let me hear him out, for God's sake!

Once again, she responds to the reproaches of the DIRECTOR *by becoming withdrawn and distant, her laughter suddenly cut off. The* DIRECTOR *goes down from the stage again so that he can get an overall view of the scene.*

FATHER. I couldn't bear to see this woman next to me any longer. [*Pointing to the* MOTHER] But not so much, believe me, because of what I went through—the suffocation, the real suffocation—as for the pity—the terrible pity that I felt for her.

MOTHER. And he sent me away!

FATHER. Well provided for in every way, to that man, yes, sir—to set her free from me.

MOTHER. And to free himself.

FATHER. Yes, to free myself as well—I admit it. And a great evil came of it. But I acted with a good intention—and more for her than for myself, I swear. [*He folds his arms; then suddenly turning to the* MOTHER] Did I ever stop looking after you, tell me, did I ever let you out of my sight? Not until he took you away, from one day to the next, without me knowing it, to another town. Because he was so stupid as to misunderstand my pure interest, pure, sir, without the slightest ulterior motive. I watched the new family that was growing up around her with incredible tenderness. *She* can vouch for that. [*Points to the* STEPDAUGHTER]

STEPDAUGHTER. And how! When I was still a little girl, little, you know, just so high—with plaits down to my shoulders and drawers longer than my skirt—I used to see him at the school gate when I came out. He came to see how I was growing up . . .

FATHER. That's vicious! Scandalous!

STEPDAUGHTER. No, why?

FATHER. Scandalous, scandalous! [*Turning abruptly to the* DIREC-TOR *in agitated explanation*] When she went away, sir [*referring to the* MOTHER], the house suddenly seemed empty. She had been a constant burden; but she filled the house for me. Left alone in those rooms I felt like some mindless fly. That boy there [*indicating the* SON] brought up away from home—I don't know—when he came back, he no longer seemed to be mine. With no mother to be a link between us, he grew up by himself, quite alone, having no intellectual or emotional connection with me. And then (it may be strange, sir, but that's how it is) I became at first fascinated and then gradually attracted by that family of hers which I had brought into being. The thought of them began to fill the void that I felt around me. I needed, I really needed to believe she was at peace, busy with the simple cares of life, lucky in being away from me, far from the complex torments of my soul. And to prove it I would go to see this child as she came out of school.

STEPDAUGHTER. That's true. He used to follow me in the street, smiling, and when I got home he'd wave his hand to me—like this. I looked at him with wide eyes, suspicious. I didn't know who he was. I told Mother, and she must have understood immediately. [*The* MOTHER *nods agreement*] At first, for several days, she stopped sending me to school. When I did go back, there he was at the school gate—looking silly—holding a large paper package. He came up to me, patted me, and took from the package a lovely big Florentine straw hat with a border of rosebuds—just for me!

DIRECTOR. But this is all anecdote, narrative.

SON [*scornfully*]. Of course. Literature, literature.

FATHER. Literature, you say! This is life, sir. Passion.

DIRECTOR. Maybe. But it's not for the stage.

FATHER. Agreed, sir. Because all this only leads up to the action. And I don't say it should be staged. In fact, as you can see, [*pointing to the* STEPDAUGHTER] she's no longer a little girl with plaits on her shoulders . . .

STEPDAUGHTER. And drawers showing beneath her skirt!

FATHER. Now comes the drama, sir. New, complex . . .

STEPDAUGHTER [*sombre, proud, coming forward*]. As soon as my father was dead . . .

FATHER [*quickly, leaving her no time to speak*]. The misery of it, sir! They came back here without letting me know, thanks to her stupidity. [*Indicating the* MOTHER] She hardly knows how to write; but she could have got her daughter to do it, or that boy there, to tell me they were in need.

MOTHER. You tell me, sir, how I could have known that he felt all this.

FATHER. That's just what's wrong with you. You've never been able to imagine any of my feelings.

MOTHER. After so many years apart, and everything that had happened . . .

FATHER. And was it my fault if that fine fellow carried you off like that? [*Turning to the* DIRECTOR] From one day to the next, I say . . . because he'd found some job or other elsewhere. I wasn't able to trace them; and so, naturally, my interest faded as the years passed. The drama breaks out, violent and unforeseen, on their return; at just the wrong time for me, driven by the needs of the flesh, still unabated . . . Ah, what misery, what real misery, for a lonely man who had never wanted degrading relationships; not yet old enough to do without a woman, and no longer young enough to go out and look for one, simply and without shame. Misery, did I say? More like horror, horror, because no woman can give her love to him any more—And when a man realizes this, he should learn to go without . . . Easy to say! Every man, sir, wears his dress of dignity—outside, before other people. But within he knows only too well the unspeakable things going on in the secret depths of his being. We give in, give in to temptation; even if only to pick ourselves up immediately after, in a great hurry to reconstruct our dignity, solid and unbroken, like the slab on a grave, hiding and burying from our eyes every trace and even the very memory of our shame. And it's the same for everybody. Though not everybody has the courage to talk about such things.

STEPDAUGHTER. But when it comes to doing them, everyone's got the guts for that!

FATHER. Yes, everyone. But in secret. That's why it takes more courage to talk about them. Because it's enough for a man to speak out and hey presto! He's branded as a cynic. But it's not true, sir: he's just like all the others; better, in fact; better because he's not afraid of using the light of his intelligence to reveal the blushing shame that lies in the bestiality of mankind that always closes its eyes so as not to see. Take woman, for example. What about her? She looks at you, provocative, inviting. You seize her, and no sooner do you hold her close than she closes her eyes. It's the sign of her commitment, the sign that tells a man: 'I'm blind, now blind yourself!'

STEPDAUGHTER. And when she stops closing them? When she no longer needs to hide her blushing shame from herself by closing her eyes; and when instead, dry-eyed and impassive, she sees the shame of the man who has blinded himself, even without love? Ah, how repulsive, how disgusting, all those intellectual complexities, all that philosophy that first reveals the beast and then wants to save and excuse it . . . I can't listen to him, sir. Because when a man feels obliged to 'simplify' life like that—so bestially—shrugging off all the trammels of being 'human', every chaste longing, every pure feeling, idealism, duty, modesty, shame . . . then nothing is more contemptible, more sickening than certain kinds of remorse: crocodile tears!

DIRECTOR. Let's come to the facts, ladies and gentlemen, the facts. This is just talk.

FATHER. Indeed, sir. But a fact is like a sack: when it's empty it won't stand up. To make it stand you have to fill it with the motive and sentiments that determined it. When that man died and they came back here penniless, I couldn't know that she [*pointing to the* MOTHER] had been looking around for work as a dressmaker to support her children, and that she had ended up taking a job precisely with that . . . that Madame Pace!

STEPDAUGHTER. And a very fine dressmaker she is, if you want to know. She may seem to be serving the most respectable ladies, but she has fixed everything so that those respectable ladies serve her instead . . . without spoiling things for the other ladies who are, well . . . so–so.

MOTHER. Believe me, sir, when I say that it never even crossed my mind, the idea that that witch had given me a job because she'd set her sights on my daughter . . .

STEPDAUGHTER. Poor Mother! You know, sir, what that woman would do whenever I brought her the work that my mother had done? She'd show me how my mother had ruined the things she'd been given to sew. And then she'd start deducting, deducting. So that, you see, I ended up paying, while my poor mother thought she was sacrificing herself for me and for those two by staying up at night to sew for Madame Pace.

Exclamations and signs of disgust from the ACTORS.

DIRECTOR [*quickly*]. And that's where, one day, you met . . .

STEPDAUGHTER [*pointing to the* FATHER]. Him, him, yes sir! An old client! You'll see how it works on the stage. Superb!

FATHER. Then, when she came in, her mother . . .

STEPDAUGHTER [*quick and vicious*]. Almost in time!

FATHER [*shouting*]. No, in time, in time! Because luckily I recognized her in time. And I took them all back home with me, sir. Now picture this new situation, sir. Hers and mine. Her the way you see her; and me unable to look her in the face.

STEPDAUGHTER. Very funny! But could I be expected—'after that'—to be still the modest, virtuous, well-bred young lady, to suit his damned aspirations towards 'a solid moral health'?

FATHER. Here's where the whole drama is for me, sir: in the conviction I have that each one of us, you see, believes that he is 'one'; but it's not true: he's 'many', sir, 'many', according to all the possibilities of being that exist within us—'one' with this man here, and 'one' with that man there. All very different. And with the illusion all along that we are 'one for everybody', and always the same 'one' in every single thing we do.* It's not true, not true. We realize this when, by some wretched bad luck, something that we do leaves us suddenly hooked up and hanging: I mean that we realize we are not wholly represented by that action and so it would be a horrible injustice to judge us by that action alone, to keep us hooked up and hanging, in the pillory for a whole lifetime, as if a whole life were summed up in that action. Now do you see the malice of this girl? She caught me in a place where she shouldn't have known me, doing something that should not have concerned her. And she wants to give me a reality that I could never have expected to take on for her, in one fleeting, shameful moment of my life! This, sir, is what I feel most deeply. You'll see that it gives the drama a very special significance. But then there's the situation of the others. His . . . [*Indicates the* SON]

SON [*with a scornful shrug of the shoulders*]. Leave me out of it; I don't come into this.

FATHER. You don't come into it?

SON. I don't come into it, and I don't want to come into it, because you know very well that I'm not cut out to be seen here with you lot.

STEPDAUGHTER. Common we are! Not refined like him! But you can see, sir, that whenever I look at him and fix him with my scorn, he lowers his eyes—because he knows the harm he's done me.

SON [*hardly looking at her*]. Me?

STEPDAUGHTER. You. You. If I've gone on the streets, I've got you to thank. You! [ACTORS *recoil in horror*] Did you or did you not deny us, by the way you behaved—I won't say the intimacy of your home—but the simple charity that relieves guests in trouble? No, we were intruders, come to invade the realm of your 'legitimacy'. Sir, I would like you to observe a few little scenes just between him and me. He says that I bullied everyone into submission. But you see, it was precisely his behaviour that made me use the argument that he calls 'despicable'; the argument that brought me into his house as its mistress, along with my mother—who is his mother too.

SON [*slowly coming forward*]. How they enjoy it, sir, how easy it is to gang up on me! But just imagine a son, living quietly at home, until, one fine day, what does he see coming his way but a young lady, head held high like this and bold as brass, who asks to see his father because she has something or other to tell him. And then she comes back, with the same haughty air, bringing that little one there, and treats his father—who knows why?—in a very ambiguous and brusque manner, asking for money in a way that suggests he must, absolutely must pay up, because he's under an obligation . . .

FATHER. But I really do have that obligation; it's for your mother.

SON. What do I know about that? When did I ever see her, sir? When did I ever hear her mentioned? And then one day she turns up with *her* [*pointing to the* STEPDAUGHTER], with that boy, and that child. And they tell me 'Oh, didn't you know? She's your mother too.' Then, from the way she carries on [*indicating the* STEPDAUGHTER *again*], I manage to grasp why, from one day to the next, they suddenly came into my home . . . Sir, what I feel and what I experience is something I can't say, something I don't want to say. The most I could do is confess it in secret, but I wouldn't—not even to myself. So, as you see, there's no way it can give rise to any action on my part. Believe me, sir, I'm a character who has not been 'realized' in dramatic terms; and I'm ill at ease, truly ill at ease in their company. They can leave me out of it!

FATHER. Now wait a minute. It's just because you're like that . . .

SON [*violent, exasperated*]. How do you know what I'm like? When did you ever care about me?

FATHER. Granted, granted! But isn't this an awkward situation too? Your setting yourself apart, so cruel to me, so cruel to your mother who comes home and sees you for more or less the first time, grown-up like that, and doesn't recognize you, but knows you're her son . . . [*Turning to the* DIRECTOR *and pointing to the* MOTHER] There, look, she's crying!

STEPDAUGHTER [*angrily, stamping her foot*]. Like an idiot!

FATHER [*to the* DIRECTOR, *quickly indicating the* STEPDAUGHTER *as well*]. And she can't stand him, that's clear. [*Referring to the* SON *again*] He says he doesn't come into it. But he's practically the hinge of the whole action. Look at that little boy there, always close up by his mother, lost and humiliated . . . He's like that because of *him*. Maybe his situation is the hardest of all: he feels most like a stranger, and he's bitterly mortified, poor lad, to be taken in like this, out of charity. [*Confidentially*] Just like his father, humble, silent . . .

DIRECTOR. But that won't work out. You've no idea how much trouble children are on the stage.

FATHER. Oh, but he won't trouble you for long. Nor will that little girl: she'll be the first to go.

DIRECTOR. Right. Excellent! I must say that I find all this interesting, exceptionally interesting. I feel, I just feel that this material could be worked up into a splendid drama.

STEPDAUGHTER [*trying to get in on the act*]. With a character like me!

FATHER [*pushing her off, eager to hear the* DIRECTOR'*s intentions*]. You shut up!

DIRECTOR [*continuing, ignoring the interruption*]. Something new, yes . . .

FATHER. Very new, sir.

DIRECTOR. But it takes some nerve—I mean—to come and shove it in my face like this . . .

FATHER. Well, you know, sir: born for the stage as we are . . .

DIRECTOR. Are you amateur actors?

FATHER. No. I say born for the stage because . . .

DIRECTOR. Come off it, you must have done some acting!

FATHER. No, sir, not really. Only the way everyone acts the part he's given himself, or that he's been given by others in this life. And then, with me, as soon as it gets intense—as it does with everyone—it's the passion itself that always becomes a bit theatrical.

DIRECTOR. Let's drop it, let's drop it. You'll understand, dear sir, that without an author . . . I could put you in contact with someone . . .

FATHER. No. Look here: you do it.

DIRECTOR. Me? What are you talking about?

FATHER. Yes, you, you! Why not?

DIRECTOR. Because I've never been an author.

FATHER. So why not be one now? There's nothing to it. So many people do it. And your job will be easier because you've got us lot, living, standing here before you.

DIRECTOR. But that's not enough.

FATHER. Why isn't it enough? When you see us living out our drama . . .

DIRECTOR. Fair enough. But you still need someone to write it.

FATHER. No. Someone to write it down, if anything. Transcribe it as it happens, scene by scene, in front of you. It should be enough to jot down something, a rough sketch—and then try it out.

DIRECTOR [*tempted, climbing back onto the stage*]. Well . . . I might just about . . . just for fun . . . we really could try it out.

FATHER. Yes indeed, sir! Wait and see what scenes you'll get out of it. I can show you some of them right now.

DIRECTOR. I'm tempted . . . I'm tempted. Let's give it a try . . . Come with me to my office. [*Turning to the* ACTORS] You can take a break, but don't go far. Be here again in fifteen, twenty minutes. [*To the* FATHER] Now let's see, we could try . . . Maybe something extraordinary will come out of this.

FATHER. No doubt about it. Don't you think it would be better if they came along? [*Indicating the other* CHARACTERS]

DIRECTOR. Yes, come along, all of you. [*He starts to go off, then turns to the* ACTORS] And remember, eh, punctual. In fifteen minutes' time.

The DIRECTOR *and the* SIX CHARACTERS *cross the stage and go out. The* ACTORS *stand looking at each other, as if stunned.*

LEADING MAN. Is he serious? What's he thinking of?

YOUNG ACTOR. This is downright madness.

THIRD ACTOR. He wants us to improvise a play—on the spot!

YOUNG ACTOR. Right. Like the Commedia dell'Arte.*

LEADING LADY. Well, if he thinks I'm going to stoop to that kind of game . . .

YOUNG ACTRESS. He can count me out as well.

FOURTH ACTOR. I'd like to know who these people are. [*Referring to the* CHARACTERS]

THIRD ACTOR. Who do you think? Lunatics or crooks.

YOUNG ACTOR. And yet he listens to them?

YOUNG ACTRESS. Vanity, vanity. He wants to pass for an author . . .

LEADING MAN. Who ever heard of such a thing! If the theatre must sink to this . . .

FIFTH ACTOR. I find it fun.

THIRD ACTOR. Well, I don't know. After all, let's see how it turns out.

Talking thus among themselves, the ACTORS *leave the stage, some leaving by the door at the back and some returning to their dressing rooms. The curtain remains up. There is an interval of about twenty minutes.*

The theatre bell announces that the play is about to restart.

The ACTORS, *the* STAGE MANAGER, *the* TECHNICIAN, *the* PROMPTER, *and the* PROPERTY MAN *come back onto the stage from the dressing rooms, the entrance, and even the auditorium. At the same time the* DIRECTOR *comes from his office with the* SIX CHARACTERS. *Once the lights of the auditorium are out, the stage is lit as before.*

DIRECTOR. Come on, ladies and gentlemen. Are we all here? Now listen, listen. Let's get started. Technician!

TECHNICIAN. Here I am.

DIRECTOR. Get the drawing-room set ready. Two wings and a

backdrop with a door, that should be enough. And be quick about it, please.

The TECHNICIAN *hurries off to get it done. While the* DIRECTOR *discusses the forthcoming performance with the* STAGE MANAGER, *the* PROPERTY MAN, *the* PROMPTER, *and the* ACTORS, *he mounts the set required: striped pink and gold, two wings and a backdrop with a door.*

DIRECTOR [*to the* PROPERTY MAN]. Go and see if we've got a settee in the storeroom.

PROPERTY MAN. Yes, sir. We've got the green one.

STEPDAUGHTER. No, no. Not green. It was yellow, flowered, made of plush—very big, and so comfortable.

PROPERTY MAN. Well, we don't have one like that.

DIRECTOR. It doesn't matter. Use the one we've got.

STEPDAUGHTER. You say it doesn't matter? Madame Pace's famous sofa!

DIRECTOR. It's just for the rehearsal. Please stop interfering. [*To the* STAGE MANAGER] See if there's something like a shop window, rather long and low.

STEPDAUGHTER. The table, the little mahogany table for the blue envelope.

STAGE MANAGER [*to the* DIRECTOR]. There's the little gilded one.

DIRECTOR. Right. Fetch that.

FATHER. A mirror.

STEPDAUGHTER. And the screen. Don't forget a screen. Otherwise, how will I manage?

STAGE MANAGER. Yes, madam, we have plenty of screens, don't worry.

DIRECTOR [*to the* STEPDAUGHTER]. And some hatstands, right?

STEPDAUGHTER. Lots of them.

DIRECTOR [*to the* STAGE MANAGER]. Go and see how many there are and have them brought here.

STAGE MANAGER. Leave it to me.

The STAGE MANAGER *in his turn hurries off to get things done.* STAGEHANDS *bring on the furniture required and he arranges them as he thinks best while the* DIRECTOR *carries on talking with the* PROMPTER *and then with the* ACTORS *and the* SIX CHARACTERS.

DIRECTOR [*to the* PROMPTER]. Now you take your place. Look, here's the outline, scene by scene, act by act. [*Showing him some sheets of paper*] But now we need you for something very special.

PROMPTER. Shorthand?

DIRECTOR [*surprised and delighted*]. Excellent! You know shorthand?

PROMPTER. I may not be much good as a prompter, but shorthand . . .

DIRECTOR. All the better! [*Turning to a* STAGEHAND] Go and get some paper from my office—plenty of it—as much as you can find.

The STAGEHAND *hurries off and returns with a thick wad of paper which he hands to the* PROMPTER.

DIRECTOR [*still speaking to the* PROMPTER]. Follow the scenes as they are performed, and try to get down the dialogue—at least, the most important bits. [*Then, turning to the* ACTORS] Clear the stage! Here, all on this side [*pointing to his left*], and pay careful attention.

LEADING LADY. If you don't mind, we . . .

DIRECTOR [*forestalling her objection*]. Don't worry. There'll be no improvising.

LEADING MAN. So what are we supposed to do?

DIRECTOR. Nothing. For the moment just watch and listen. Later on, each of you will get a written part. But for now, as best we can, we'll have a rehearsal. They'll do it. [*Indicating the* SIX CHARACTERS]

FATHER [*totally lost amid the confusion on stage*]. Us? What do you mean, a rehearsal?

DIRECTOR. A rehearsal—a rehearsal for them. [*Pointing to the* ACTORS]

FATHER. But if we are the characters . . .

DIRECTOR. Sure, you're the 'characters'; but here, my dear sir, characters don't act. Here it's the actors who act. And the characters stay there in the script [*pointing to the* PROMPTER]—when there is a script!

FATHER. That's just it. Since there is no script and you ladies and gentlemen are lucky enough to have the characters here alive before you . . .

DIRECTOR. Oh that's splendid! So you want to do everything by yourselves—you do the acting, you present yourselves before the public?

FATHER. Well, yes. The way we are.

DIRECTOR. Believe me, you'd put on a wonderful show!

LEADING MAN. And how about us lot? What would we be hanging around for?

DIRECTOR. You don't really think you can act, do you? You make people laugh . . . [*The* ACTORS *do, in fact, laugh*] See, they're laughing. [*Remembering*] And that reminds me. The casting. Easy enough: the play casts itself. [*To the* SECOND ACTRESS] You, madam, are the Mother. [*To the* FATHER] We'll need to find her a name.

FATHER. Amalia, sir.

DIRECTOR. But that's your wife's name. We certainly don't want to use her real name.

FATHER. Why not? If that's what she's called . . . But maybe you're right, if it's to be this lady . . . [*gesturing vaguely towards the* SECOND ACTRESS]. This is the woman [*indicating the* MOTHER] that I see as Amalia. But do as you please . . . [*increasingly confused*] I don't know what to say . . . somehow, my own words are beginning to sound different, sound false.

DIRECTOR. Don't you worry about it, don't worry. Leave us to find the right tone. And as for the name, if you want Amalia, Amalia let it be; or else we'll find her another. For now we'll refer to the characters like this: [*to the* YOUNG ACTOR] you the Son; [*to the* LEADING LADY] you, of course, the Stepdaughter.

STEPDAUGHTER [*excessively amused*]. What, what? That woman there—as me? [*Bursts into laughter*]

DIRECTOR [*annoyed*]. What's there to laugh about?

LEADING LADY [*indignant*]. Nobody has ever dared to laugh at me. I expect to be respected: if not, I'm out of here.

STEPDAUGHTER. Look, sorry, I wasn't laughing at you.

DIRECTOR [*to the* STEPDAUGHTER]. You should feel honoured to be played by . . .

LEADING LADY [*prompt and bitter*]. 'That woman there'.

STEPDAUGHTER. But I wasn't thinking about you, believe me! I was thinking of myself, because I just don't see myself in you. That's all. I don't know, you're nothing like me.

FATHER. Precisely so. You see, sir! Our way of expression . . .

DIRECTOR. What about your way of expression? Do you think it's something you've got within you, this expression? Not a bit of it!

FATHER. What! We don't have our own expression?

DIRECTOR. Not in the least! Here your expression becomes material, given body and figure, voice and gesture, by the actors—and they, I'd have you know, have given expression to matter of a far higher order, while yours is so insignificant that if it gets by on the stage, all the merit, believe me, will belong to my actors.

FATHER. I wouldn't dare to contradict you. But, believe me, it's horribly distressing for us who are the way you see us, with these bodies, these looks . . .

DIRECTOR [*cutting him off, losing patience*]. But we take care of that with make-up, make-up, my good man, at least for the faces.

FATHER. Yes, but the voice, the gestures . . .

DIRECTOR. Oh, now look! You as yourself have no business here. Here it's the actor who represents you. Let that be the end of it!

FATHER. I understand, sir. But now perhaps I also begin to see why our author, who saw us alive as we are here and now, decided not to put us on the stage. I don't want to offend your actors—far from it! But the idea of seeing myself represented by . . . whoever . . .

LEADING MAN [*rising haughtily and coming up to him, followed by laughing young* ACTRESSES]. By me, if you have no objection.

FATHER [*honey-voiced and humble*]. I'm honoured, sir [*with a bow*]. Look, I think that however hard this gentleman tries to identify with me, for all his art and all his goodwill . . . [*He loses the thread*]

LEADING MAN. Finish it off, finish it off. [*Laughter from the* ACTRESSES]

FATHER. Well, I say, his performance, even going heavy with the make-up to look like me . . . I mean, with his height . . . [*all the* ACTORS *laugh*] he'll be hard put to represent me as I really am. It will be more like—forget the way I look—more like his *interpretation* of what I am, how he feels me—if he feels me—and not the way I feel myself deep down. And I reckon this is something that should be kept in mind by whoever's called on to judge us.

DIRECTOR. So now you're worried about the critics? And I still stood there listening! Let the critics say what they like. We'd do better to think about putting on this play—if we can! [*Stepping aside and looking around*] Come on, come on. Is the set ready yet? [*To the* ACTORS *and* CHARACTERS] Clear out of the way, out of the way. Let me see. [*He comes down from the stage*] Let's stop wasting time. [*To the* STEPDAUGHTER] Do you think the set's all right like that?

STEPDAUGHTER. Dunno. Can't say I recognize it, to be honest.

DIRECTOR. Come off it! You can't expect us to reconstruct the back room of the shop, exactly as you know it at Madame Pace's. [*To the* FATHER] You said a room with flowered wallpaper?

FATHER. Yes, sir. White.

DIRECTOR. Well it's not white, it's striped; but it doesn't matter. I think we've got the furniture more or less right. That little table, bring it forward a bit. [STAGEHANDS *oblige. To the* PROPERTY MAN] You go and find an envelope, pale blue if possible, and give it to this gentleman. [*Indicating the* FATHER]

PROPERTY MAN. An envelope for letters?

DIRECTOR AND FATHER. Yes, letters, letters.

PROPERTY MAN. Right away. [*He goes off*]

DIRECTOR. Come on now. The first scene is with the Young Lady. [*The* LEADING LADY *comes forward*] No, you wait! I said the Young Lady [*indicating the* STEPDAUGHTER]. You stay there and watch . . .

STEPDAUGHTER [*adding immediately*]. How I bring it to life!

LEADING LADY [*stung*]. But I shall bring it to life as well, don't worry, once I get started.

DIRECTOR [*his head in his hands*]. Ladies and gentlemen, let's stop nattering! Now, the first scene is the Young Lady with Madame Pace. Oh [*looking around as if lost, he gets back on to the stage*], where's this Madame Pace?

FATHER. Not with us, sir.

DIRECTOR. So how do we manage?

FATHER. But she's alive like us. She's alive too.

DIRECTOR. Yes, but where is she?

FATHER. Hold on. Let me say something. [*Turning to the* ACTRESSES] If you ladies would do me the favour of lending me your hats for a moment.

ACTRESSES [*surprised and amused, in chorus*]. What?—Our hats?—What do you mean?—Why?—How's that then?

DIRECTOR. What do you want with the ladies' hats? [*The* ACTORS *start laughing*]

FATHER. Oh, nothing. Just to put them on these pegs for a moment. And some of you should be so kind as to take off your coats as well.

ACTORS [*as above*]. Coats as well—What next?—He must be crazy.

ACTRESSES [*as above*]. But why?—Only our coats?

FATHER. To hang them up for a moment . . . Do me this favour. Would you mind?

ACTRESSES [*taking off their hats, and some their coats as well; still laughing, they go and hang them on the racks*]. Why not?—Here you are—You know, it's seriously funny—Should they be on display?

FATHER. Yes, that's right, on display, like that.

DIRECTOR. But can you tell us what it's all in aid of?

FATHER. Well, sir, maybe if we dress the set a little better, who knows, she might be attracted by the objects of her trade and come and join us . . . [*Pointing to the door at the back of the stage*] Look there! Look there!

The door at the back of the stage opens and, taking a few steps forward, in comes MADAME PACE, *a monstrously fat harridan, with a showy carrot-coloured woollen wig and a flaming red rose on one side, Spanish-style; heavily made-up, dressed with awkward elegance in gaudy red silk; in one hand is a feather fan, the other is raised to hold a cigarette between two fingers. At the sight of this vision, the* ACTORS *and the* DIRECTOR *dash from the stage with a shout of fear and jump down the steps as if to escape up the aisle. The* STEPDAUGHTER, *however, hurries to greet* MADAME PACE *respectfully as her employer.*

STEPDAUGHTER [*running up to her*]. Here she is! Here she is!

FATHER [*radiant*]. It's her. Didn't I tell you? Here she is.

DIRECTOR [*overcoming his initial amazement, indignant*]. What kind of trickery is this?

    The ACTORS *join in, speaking at more or less the same time.*

LEADING MAN. What's going on, anyway?

YOUNG ACTOR. Where did they get that one from?

YOUNG ACTRESS. They were keeping her in reserve.

LEADING LADY. It's all a conjuring trick.

FATHER [*quelling the protests*]. Just a moment! Why, in the name of some crude truth, some mere fact, do you want to spoil this miracle of a reality that is brought to birth, evoked, attracted, shaped by the stage itself*—and has more right to live here than you do, because it is far more true than you are. Which of you actresses will play the part of Madame Pace? Well, that's Madame Pace there! You'll admit that the actress who plays her will be less true than that woman there, who is Madame Pace in person. Look, my daughter has recognized her and gone straight up to her. Just wait a bit and watch, watch this scene.

Hesitantly, the DIRECTOR *and the* ACTORS *climb back onto the stage. But already, during the protests of the* ACTORS *and the* FATHER*'s reply, the scene between the* STEPDAUGHTER *and* MADAME PACE *has begun, in undertones, quietly, in short naturally, as would not normally be possible on a stage. The* ACTORS, *alerted by the* FATHER, *turn to watch and see* MADAME PACE *with her hand already under the* STEPDAUGHTER*'s chin to make her lift her head; hearing* MADAME PACE *talking in a way that is totally unintelligible, they listen carefully for a moment before showing their disappointment.*

DIRECTOR. Well?

LEADING MAN. What's she saying?

LEADING LADY. You can't hear a thing.

YOUNG ACTOR. Louder! Louder!

STEPDAUGHTER [*leaving* MADAME PACE, *whose face wears a priceless smile, and coming down to the group of* ACTORS]. Louder, eh. Louder? These are hardly things one can say out loud. I could say things aloud about *him* [*indicating the* FATHER] to put him to shame and get my revenge. But with Madame, it's different, gentlemen: it could mean prison.

DIRECTOR Oh, fine! Is that the way it is? But here, my dear, you have to make yourself heard. We can't hear you, and we're on the stage. Just imagine when there's an audience in the theatre. This scene has to be properly staged. And anyway, you can speak out loud to each other because we won't be here to listen the way we are now. Pretend you're alone in the room, at the back of the shop, where no one can hear you. [*The* STEPDAUGHTER, *gracefully and with a malicious smile, wags her finger to say No*] Why not?

STEPDAUGHTER [*in a muted mysterious tone*]. There's someone who'll hear us if she [*indicating* MADAME PACE] speaks out loud.

DIRECTOR [*very worried*]. You don't mean someone else is going to pop up?

The ACTORS *get ready to quit the stage again.*

FATHER. No, no, sir. She's referring to me. I have to be there, waiting behind that door; and Madame knows it. In fact, if you allow me. I'd better go and be ready. [*Starts to go off*]

DIRECTOR [*stopping him*]. No, wait. The stage has its rules. Before you get ready . . .

STEPDAUGHTER [*interrupting him*]. Yes, right now, right now. I tell you I'm dying to live it, to live this scene. If he wants to start now, I'm more than ready.

DIRECTOR [*shouting*]. But first we need to get clear this scene between you and that woman! [*Pointing to* MADAME PACE] Can't you understand?

STEPDAUGHTER. Oh, for God's sake, sir; she's only been telling me what you already know—that Mother's work is badly done yet again, that the dress is ruined, and that I shall need to be patient if I want her to keep helping us in our wretched state.

MADAME PACE [*coming forward with a self-important air*]. That's right, señor, porqué I no like take profit . . . make advantage . . .

DIRECTOR [*sounding scared*]. What? Does she really talk like that?

Loud laughter from all the ACTORS.

STEPDAUGHTER [*laughing too*]. Yes, sir. She does speak like that, mixing up the languages in such a funny way.

MADAME PACE. Ah, not me seems bona maniera laugh with me while I tries hablar italiano, señor.

DIRECTOR. No, no. Quite the contrary. Speak like that, speak just like that, Madame. It'll go down perfectly. Nothing better for a bit of comic relief in a rather sordid situation. Go on speaking like that. It's fine.

STEPDAUGHTER. Fine, indeed! To hear certain proposals made in that kind of language. It goes down perfectly because it sounds almost like a joke, sir. It's a real laugh to hear that there's a 'viejo señor' who wants to 'amusarse con migo'.* Isn't that true, Madame?

MADAME PACE. So he old, vièjo, my pretty. Is better for you. You no like him, but he come with prudencia.

MOTHER [*rising up to the amazement and dismay of all the* ACTORS *who have been paying her no attention: now, when they hear her shout, they laugh and try to hold her back because she has already torn off* MADAME PACE's *wig and thrown it on the floor*]. Witch, you witch! Murderess! My daughter!

STEPDAUGHTER [*rushing to restrain her* MOTHER]. No, no, Mother, please!

FATHER [*hurrying towards her at the same time*]. Calm down, calm down. Come and sit down!

MOTHER. Then get her out of my sight.

STEPDAUGHTER [*to the* DIRECTOR *who has hurried to join them*]. There's no way, no way Mother can be here.

FATHER [*also to the* DIRECTOR]. They can't be together. And that's why, you see, that woman wasn't with us when we came. If they're together, you understand, we give away the whole story.

DIRECTOR. Doesn't matter. Doesn't matter. For now this is just a first sketch. Everything helps me pick up all the various elements, however muddled they are. [*Turning to the* MOTHER *and taking her back to her chair*] Come along, my dear lady. Calm and easy now. Sit yourself down again.

> *The* STEPDAUGHTER, *returning to the middle of the stage, addresses* MADAME PACE.

STEPDAUGHTER. So let's get on with it, Madame.

MADAME PACE [*offended*]. Ah no, muchas gracias! Here I do nada with your madre presente.

STEPDAUGHTER. Oh, come on. Show him in, this 'viejo señor, porqué se amusi con migo'. [*Turning towards everyone majestically*] After all, we have this scene to play out. Let's get on with it. [*To* MADAME PACE] You can go.

MADAME PACE. I go, I go, seguramente I go. [*She exits in a fury, picking up her wig and glaring defiantly at the* ACTORS *who applaud and giggle*]

STEPDAUGHTER [*to* FATHER]. And you make your entrance. No need to turn away. Come here. Pretend you've just come in. Now then. Here I am with my head bowed, all modesty! Come on, speak up. In a fresh voice, as if you've just come in from outside: 'Good afternoon, miss . . .'

DIRECTOR [*already off the stage*]. See that! Who's the director here, you or me? [*To the* FATHER *who looks on, puzzled and tense*] Do what she says. Go to the back, but don't go out. Then come forward again.

The FATHER *obeys, bewildered. He looks very pale; nevertheless, already possessed by the reality of his created life, he smiles as he approaches from the back of the stage, as if still unaware of the drama that is about to overwhelm him. The* ACTORS *are immediately intent on the unfolding scene.*

DIRECTOR [*in a hurried whisper to the* PROMPTER *in his box*]. And you, follow carefully, follow and write it down.

THE SCENE

FATHER [*coming forward, with a fresh voice*]. Good afternoon, miss.

STEPDAUGHTER [*head bowed, controlling her disgust*]. Good afternoon.

FATHER [*peering under the brim of the hat that almost hides her face, he sees that she is very young: caught between satisfaction and the fear of being compromised in a risky affair, he exclaims, almost to himself*]. Ah . . . But, I say, it's not the first time, is it? That you come here.

STEPDAUGHTER [*as above*]. No, sir.

FATHER. So you have been here before? [*And since the* STEPDAUGHTER *nods*] More than once? [*Pauses for a reply, then goes back to peering under her hat; he smiles, then says*] Come now, no need to be like this . . . Allow me to remove that hat.

STEPDAUGHTER [*quickly, unable to control her disgust*]. No, sir. I'll do it myself. [*She does so in a nervous hurry*]

From the side of the stage opposite to the ACTORS, *the* MOTHER *is following the scene, together with the* SON *and the two smaller children who are more her own and who always stand next to her. Anxious and tense, she accompanies the words and actions of the* FATHER *and* STEPDAUGHTER *with exclamations varying from sorrow and scorn to anxiety and horror, sometimes hiding her face and sometimes moaning.*

MOTHER. God, Oh my God!

FATHER [*hearing her moan, he remains motionless for a long moment, then continues in the same tone as before*]. There. Give it to me. I'll put it down. [*Takes the hat from her hands*] Now on a lovely little head like yours I should like to see a more worthy hat. So wouldn't you like to help me choose one from Madame's collection?—No?

YOUNG ACTRESS [*interrupting him*]. Hey, watch out. Those are our hats.

DIRECTOR [*really angry*]. Shut up, will you! Don't try to be funny. We're in rehearsal. [*Turning to the* STEPDAUGHTER] Where you left off, please.

STEPDAUGHTER [*continuing*]. No, thank you, sir.

FATHER. Oh, come on. Don't say no. Do accept it. I'll be upset if you don't . . . Look, there are some very pretty ones. And think how happy we'll make Madame. She displays them here on purpose.

STEPDAUGHTER. No, sir, you see: I could never wear it.

FATHER. Perhaps you're saying that because of what they might think at home when they see you come back with a new hat. But come on! Don't you know what to do? What to say at home?

STEPDAUGHTER [*agitated, unable to stand it*]. But that's not it, sir. I couldn't wear it because I'm . . . as you see me: you might have already noticed. [*She shows her black dress*]

FATHER. So you're in mourning! Forgive me. Now I see. I do beg your pardon. Believe me, I'm truly mortified.

STEPDAUGHTER [*summoning up strength and courage to overcome her contempt and revulsion*]. Enough, sir, enough. I should be thanking *you*; and you shouldn't feel mortified or distressed. Please think no more about what I said. I too, you can imagine . . . [*with a forced smile she adds*] I really shouldn't remember that I'm dressed like this. ·

DIRECTOR [*interrupting, turning to the* PROMPTER *in his box and climbing back onto the stage*]. Wait, wait! Don't write that down. Cut out that last line. [*Turning to the* FATHER *and the* STEPDAUGHTER] Splendid! Splendid! [*Then only to the* FATHER] Then you carry on the way we decided. [*To the* ACTORS] Delightful, this little scene with the hat, don't you think?

STEPDAUGHTER. Oh, but the best is what comes next. Why don't we go straight on with it?

DIRECTOR. Have patience for a moment. [*Turning to the* ACTORS] Of course, it needs to be handled with a light touch . . .

LEADING MAN. Easy, smooth . . .

LEADING LADY. Why not? There's nothing to it. [*To the* LEADING MAN] We could have a go straightaway, couldn't we?

LEADING MAN. No problem for me. Right, I'll go round to make my entrance. [*He goes out so that he can re-enter through the door at the back of the set*]

DIRECTOR [*to the* LEADING LADY]. Now then, let's say the scene between you and Madame Pace is over. I'll write it up later. Now you should place yourself . . . No, where are you going?

LEADING LADY. Wait, I'm going to put my hat back on . . . [*She goes to take her hat from the hatstand*]

DIRECTOR. Ah yes, good . . . Right then, you place yourself here with your head bowed.

STEPDAUGHTER [*amused*]. But if she's not even dressed in black!

LEADING LADY. I shall be, and it will suit me much better than it does you.

DIRECTOR [*to the* STEPDAUGHTER]. Please keep quiet, can't you. Just watch. You might learn something. [*Clapping his hands*] Let's go, let's go! Entrance!

He comes down from the stage so that he can get an overall impression of the scene. The door at the back of the set opens and the LEADING MAN *comes forward, with the smooth roguish air of an ageing seducer. Right from the start the* ACTORS' *performance of the scene should seem quite different from what we have already witnessed, but it should not be remotely like a parody: more like a polished version of the original. Unable to recognize themselves in the* LEADING LADY *and the* LEADING MAN *and hearing their own words spoken by others, the* FATHER *and* STEPDAUGHTER *respond in a variety of ways, using gestures, smiles, and open protest to convey their reactions of surprise, wonder, suffering, etc., as will be seen in due course. The voice of the* PROMPTER *in his box is clearly heard.*

LEADING MAN. 'Good afternoon, miss . . .'

FATHER [*promptly, unable to control himself*]. No, no!

Seeing the way the LEADING MAN *makes his entrance, the* STEPDAUGH-TER *bursts out laughing.*

DIRECTOR [*furious*]. Pipe down, you lot. And you stop laughing once and for all. We can't carry on like this.

STEPDAUGHTER [*coming from the front of the stage*]. I'm sorry, sir, but it's only natural. That young lady [*indicating the* LEADING LADY] is just there, stock still; but if she's supposed to be me, then let me tell you that if I'd heard someone say 'good afternoon' in that tone and in that way, I'd have burst out laughing—just the way I did.

FATHER [*taking a few steps forward*]. Yes, indeed . . . the manner, the tone . . .

DIRECTOR. Manner and tone be damned! Stand aside and let me see the rehearsal.

LEADING MAN [*making his way downstage*]. If I have to play an old man who comes to a house of ill fame . . .

DIRECTOR. Yes, yes. Don't listen to them, for heaven's sake. Get on with it, take it from there, it's going splendidly. [*Waiting for the* LEADING MAN *to start*] Well . . .

LEADING MAN. 'Good afternoon, miss . . .'

LEADING LADY. 'Good afternoon . . .'

LEADING MAN [*imitating the* FATHER's *gesture of peering under the hat, but distinguishing clearly between the two emotions, expressing first the satisfaction and then the fear*]. 'Ah . . . but I say, it's not your first visit . . .'

FATHER [*unable to resist correcting him*]. Not 'your first visit'—'the first time, is it?' 'Is it?'

DIRECTOR. He says 'is it?' Question mark.

LEADING MAN [*nodding to the* PROMPTER]. I heard 'visit'.

DIRECTOR. It's all the same! 'Is it?' or 'visit'. Now get on with it. Only maybe a bit less emphasis . . . Here, I'll show you. Watch me . . . [*comes back onto the stage and then takes up the part, starting from the entrance*] 'Good afternoon, miss . . .'

LEADING LADY. 'Good afternoon.'

DIRECTOR. 'Ah . . . but I say' [*turns to the* LEADING MAN *to point out the way in which he peered under the hat*] Surprise . . . fear and satisfaction . . . [*continuing, now addressing the* LEADING LADY] 'It's not the first time, is it? That you come here . . .' [*Turning again to the* LEADING MAN *with a meaningful look*] Is that clear? [*To the* LEADING LADY] And then you come in with 'No, sir'. [*To the* LEADING MAN *again*] Now how can I put it? *Souplesse!* [*He comes down from the stage*]

LEADING LADY. 'No, sir . . .'

LEADING MAN. 'So you have been here before? More than once?'

DIRECTOR. No, wait! First let her nod agreement [*indicating the* LEADING LADY]. 'So you have been here before?'

The LEADING LADY *raises her head a little with eyes half-closed to suggest disgust; then, when the* DIRECTOR *says 'Now', she nods her head twice.*

STEPDAUGHTER [*unable to resist*]. Oh my God! [*And she puts a hand to her mouth, stifling her laughter*]

DIRECTOR [*turning round*]. What is it?

STEPDAUGHTER. Nothing, nothing.

DIRECTOR [*to the* LEADING MAN]. Now you, now you. Take it from there.

LEADING MAN. 'More than once? Come now, no need to be like this . . . Allow me to remove that hat.'

The LEADING MAN *says the last line with such a voice, accompanied by such a gesture, that the* STEPDAUGHTER, *even with her hands at her mouth, cannot keep from laughing, however hard she tries. The laugh escapes between her fingers, loud and irresistible.*

LEADING LADY [*indignant, going back to her seat*]. I'm not going to play the fool for that woman!

LEADING MAN. Me neither! Let's have done with it.

DIRECTOR [*shouting at the* STEPDAUGHTER]. Pack it in! Pack it in!

STEPDAUGHTER. I will, I'm sorry . . . so sorry . . .

DIRECTOR. Atrocious manners! A little guttersnipe, that's what you are! Arrogant too!

FATHER [*trying to intervene*]. Quite right, sir, quite right. But you must forgive her . . .

DIRECTOR [*coming back onto the stage*]. How can you expect me to forgive her? It's disgraceful!

FATHER. Yes, sir, it is. But believe me, all this gives us such a strange feeling . . .

DIRECTOR. Strange? Strange in what way? Why strange?

FATHER. I admire your actors, sir, I really admire them: that gentleman there [*pointing to the* LEADING MAN], that lady [*indicating the* LEADING LADY], but the fact is . . . well, they're just not us . . .

DIRECTOR. You bet they're not you! How can they be? They're the actors.

FATHER. That's just it, actors. And they both do our parts very well. But, you see, to us it looks like something different, something that tries to be the same, and yet it isn't.

DIRECTOR. What do you mean, 'it isn't'? What is it then?

FATHER. Something that . . . becomes theirs. It's no longer ours.

DIRECTOR. But there's no other way. I've told you that already.

FATHER. Yes, I understand, I understand . . .

DIRECTOR. So that's enough! [*Turning to the* ACTORS] This means that later on we'll rehearse on our own, the proper way. For me it's always been a curse, having to rehearse with the authors present. They're never satisfied. [*Turning to the* FATHER *and* STEPDAUGHTER] Right then, we'll go back to doing it with you; and let's see if you can stop laughing.

STEPDAUGHTER. I won't laugh. I won't laugh! Now comes the best part for me; you can count on it.

DIRECTOR. So then, when you say 'Think no more about what I said . . . I too, you can imagine . . .' [*turning to the* FATHER] you come straight in with 'I see, ah, I see' and then you ask her . . .

STEPDAUGHTER [*interrupting*].—Ask what? What does he ask?

DIRECTOR. The reason why you're in mourning.

STEPDAUGHTER. Not at all, sir. Look, when I told him that I really shouldn't remember the way I'm dressed, do you know what he answered? 'Very well, then. Let's take it off, let's take this little dress off straightaway.'

DIRECTOR. Splendid! Wonderful! That'll bring the house down.

STEPDAUGHTER. But it's the truth.

DIRECTOR. You and your truth, do me a favour! This is the theatre. Truth, yes, up to a certain point.

STEPDAUGHTER. So what do you want to do then?

DIRECTOR. You'll see, you'll see. Now leave it to me.

STEPDAUGHTER. No, sir. Out of my revulsion, out of all the factors, one more vile and cruel than the next, that have made me the way I am, do you want to cobble up some soppy sentimental romance? With him asking why I'm in mourning and me answering in tears that my papa died two months ago? No, no, my dear sir. He must say what he did say: 'Let's take this little dress off straightaway.' And with all that grief in my heart, after barely two months, I went there, do you see? There, behind that screen, and with these fingers, trembling with shame and disgust, I undid my corset, my skirt . . .

DIRECTOR [*with his hands in his hair*]. For God's sake! What are you saying?

STEPDAUGHTER [*shouting, frantic*]. The truth! The truth, sir!

DIRECTOR. Yes, I'm sure it's the truth. I don't deny it . . . and I understand, I really do, all the horror you feel. But then you must understand that all this is quite impossible on the stage.*

STEPDAUGHTER. Impossible? Then thanks very much, you can count me out of it.

DIRECTOR. No, look . . .

STEPDAUGHTER. Count me out! Count me out! What's possible on the stage is something you've cooked up back there, the two of you, thanks a lot. I know perfectly well what's going on. He wants to get straight to the scene of his [*with ironic emphasis*] 'spiritual torments'; but I want to act out *my* drama. Mine!

DIRECTOR [*irritated, with an angry shrug of his shoulders*]. Oh, give it a break! Yours! There's not just your drama, you know. There are the others too. There's his [*indicating the* FATHER], there's your mother's. We can't have one character pushing forward like this, upstaging everybody else and taking over the whole scene. They must all be contained in a harmonious framework and act out what can be acted. I know very well that everyone has a whole interior life that he or she would like bring out into the open. But that's where the difficulty lies: how to bring out only what matters in relation to the other characters; and, at the same time, with the little that is shown, suggest all the life that remains within. It would all be too easy if every character could be given a monologue or . . . why not? . . . a lecture where he could serve up to the audience whatever's cooking in his head. [*In a good-natured conciliatory tone*] You must control yourself, young lady. And believe me, it's in your own interest; because, I warn you, you can give a very bad impression with all this destructive fury, this extreme revulsion— especially, if I may say so, when you yourself have admitted that you went with other men at Madame Pace's, and more than once.

STEPDAUGHTER [*bowing her head and speaking in a deep voice, after a meditative pause*]. That's true. But remember that for me all those others were him too.

DIRECTOR. How do you mean, the others were him?

STEPDAUGHTER. When someone falls into evil ways, sir, isn't the one who caused the first fall responsible for all the evils that follow? Well, for me that's him, and has been since before I was born. Look at him and see if it isn't true.

DIRECTOR. Very well. And don't you think the remorse that weighs on him should count for something? Give him the chance to act it out.

STEPDAUGHTER. How can he do that? Tell me how he can act out all his 'noble remorse', all his 'moral torments' if you choose to spare him the horror of being one fine day in the arms of a woman, after suggesting she take off her dress, her mourning dress—and then discovering that this woman, this fallen woman, is the same little girl he used to go and watch as she came out of school?

She says these last words in a voice that trembles with emotion. The MOTHER, *hearing her speak like this, is overwhelmed by an unbearable anguish, expressed first by stifled sobs and then by a flood of tears. Everyone is deeply moved. A long pause.*

STEPDAUGHTER [*grave and resolute, as soon as the* MOTHER *seems to be calming down*]. Here and now there's only us; the audience hasn't heard of us yet. Tomorrow you can make of us whatever spectacle you like, arranged as you think fit. But do you really want to see this drama? See it explode the way it actually did?

DIRECTOR. I ask for nothing better, so that I can already take whatever I can use.

STEPDAUGHTER. Then have my mother go out.

MOTHER [*rising up from her weeping with a cry*]. No, no. Don't allow it, sir. Don't allow it!

DIRECTOR. But it's only for us to see, madam.

MOTHER. I can't. I can't!

DIRECTOR. But if it's all happened already? I don't understand.

MOTHER. No, it's happening now, it happens all the time. My agony's not feigned, sir. I'm alive and present, always, in every moment of my torment which is itself renewed, alive and ever-present.* But those two little ones there, have you heard them speak? They can no longer speak, sir. They still cling on to me to keep my torment alive and present; but as themselves they are not there, they no longer exist! And this girl, sir [*indicating the* STEPDAUGHTER], she's gone away, run away from me, and now she's lost, lost . . . If I see her here now, it's only for that—always, always to renew, alive and present, the torment that I have suffered on her account as well.

FATHER [*solemnly*]. The eternal moment, as I told you, sir. She [*indicating the* STEPDAUGHTER] is here to catch me, fix me, hold me hooked and hanging, pilloried for ever, in that one fleeting shameful moment of my life. She can't give it up, and you, sir, can't really spare me.

DIRECTOR. Exactly. I don't say we shouldn't play the scene: in fact, it will be the nucleus of the whole first act right up to the moment when she discovers you. [*Indicates the* MOTHER]

FATHER. That's it. Yes. Because that's my condemnation. All our passion must reach a climax in her final cry! [*He too points to the* MOTHER]

STEPDAUGHTER. It's still ringing in my ears. It has driven me insane, that cry. You can have me played any way you like, sir: it doesn't matter. Even clothed, provided at least the arms are bare— only the arms because, look, as I stood like this [*she goes up to the* FATHER *and leans her head on his chest*], with my head like this and my arms round his neck, I could see a vein throbbing in my arm here; and then, as if it were only that vein that made me shudder, I closed my eyes, just like this, and hid my head on his chest. [*Turning towards the* MOTHER] Scream, Mama, scream! [*She buries her head in the* FATHER's *chest, and with her shoulders hunched as if not to hear the cry, adds in a voice of stifled suffering*] Scream, the way you screamed then!

MOTHER [*rushing in to separate them*]. No! Daughter, my daughter! [*And when she has torn her daughter from his arms*] Brute, you brute! Don't you see that she's my daughter?

DIRECTOR [*backing up to the footlights as he hears the cry, amid the bewildered* ACTORS]. Splendid, yes, splendid. And then, curtain, curtain!

FATHER [*hurrying to him in excitement*]. That's it, yes. Because it really was like that, sir.

DIRECTOR [*with admiration, convinced*]. Yes, right here. Absolutely! Curtain, curtain!

At the repeated shouts of the DIRECTOR, *the* TECHNICIAN *lowers the curtain, leaving the* DIRECTOR *and the* FATHER *standing outside in front of the footlights.*

DIRECTOR [*looking up with arms raised*]. What an idiot! I say 'curtain' meaning that this is where the act should end, and he really goes and lowers the curtain! [*Lifting the hem of the curtain in order to go back on stage, to the* FATHER] Splendid! Marvellous! A real knockout. There's our ending for Act One. A knockout! Take my word for it!

DIRECTOR *and* FATHER *go off behind the curtain.*

The curtain rises again to reveal that the TECHNICIANS *and* STAGE-HANDS *have dismantled the improvised set and replaced it with a small garden fountain.*

On one side of the stage, sitting in a row, are the ACTORS; *on the other the* CHARACTERS. *The* DIRECTOR *stands in the middle of the stage, raising a closed fist to his mouth, thinking hard.*

DIRECTOR [*straightening up after a brief pause*]. Right now, let's get to Act Two. Leave it to me, leave it all to me as we agreed at the outset, and everything will be fine.

STEPDAUGHTER. It's when we come into his house [*indicating the* FATHER], in spite of that fellow over there [*referring to the* SON].

DIRECTOR [*impatient*]. Yes, yes. But leave it to me, I say.

STEPDAUGHTER. As long as it's clear how spiteful he was.

MOTHER [*from her side, shaking her head*]. For all the good it did . . .

STEPDAUGHTER [*rounding on her*]. It doesn't matter. The more suffering for us, the more remorse for him!

DIRECTOR [*impatiently*]. All right, I know; I've got the message. And I'll keep it in mind, especially at the beginning. Don't worry.

MOTHER [*imploring*]. But please, sir, for the sake of my conscience, make it absolutely clear that I did everything I could . . .

STEPDAUGHTER [*interrupting indignantly and taking up the speech*]. To calm me down, to advise me not to offend him. [*To the* DIRECTOR] So satisfy her, give her what she wants, because it's true. In the meantime I'm thoroughly enjoying it because, as you can see, the more she implores, the more she tries to touch his heart, the more distant, the more *absent* he becomes. What a treat!

DIRECTOR. Now could we finally get started on this second act?

STEPDAUGHTER. I won't say another word. But I warn you; it won't be possible to do it all in the garden the way you want.

DIRECTOR. Why won't it be possible?

STEPDAUGHTER. Because he [*indicating the* SON] stays out of the way all the time, closed up in his room. And then everything to do with that poor lost boy there has to happen inside the house. I told you.

DIRECTOR. Yes, I see. But on the other hand, you must understand that we can't put up signs or change the set three or four times in one act.

LEADING MAN. They used to once . . .

DIRECTOR. Yes, maybe when the audience was like that little girl over there.

LEADING LADY. And the illusion much easier to create.

FATHER [*jumping up*]. The illusion? For God's sake, don't say the illusion! Don't use that word which is especially hurtful for us.

DIRECTOR [*stunned*]. Why on earth?

FATHER. Oh yes, cruel, cruel! You should understand that!

DIRECTOR. What should we say then? The illusion that we create, here, for our spectators . . .

LEADING MAN. Through our performance . . .

DIRECTOR. The illusion of a reality.

FATHER. I understand, sir. But maybe it's you who doesn't understand us. Forgive me. Because, you see, for you and for your actors here, it's only—as is right and proper—a matter of playing your game.

FIRST LADY [*interrupting, indignant*]. What game? We're not a bunch of children. Here we take our acting very seriously.

FATHER. I don't deny it. What I mean, in fact, is the game of your art, your playing which—as the gentleman says—should give a perfect illusion of reality.

DIRECTOR. That's it. Exactly.

FATHER. Now, if you consider that we, as ourselves [*indicates himself and gestures vaguely towards the other five* CHARACTERS], have no reality other than this illusion.

DIRECTOR [*dumbfounded, looking at his* ACTORS *who are no less dazed and bewildered*]. Which means what?

FATHER [*after pausing to look at them, with a pale smile*]. Yes, indeed, sir. What other reality do we have? What for you is an illusion that has to be created is for us, on the contrary, our only reality. [*Brief pause. He takes a few steps towards the* DIRECTOR *and adds*] But not just for us, come to that. Just think about it. [*Looking him in the eye*] Can you tell me who you are? [*He stands pointing at him*]

DIRECTOR [*troubled, with a half-smile*]. What? Who am I? I'm me.

FATHER. And if I said that's not true because you are me?

DIRECTOR. I'd answer that you were mad.

The ACTORS *laugh.*

FATHER. You're right to laugh: because here we're all playing a game; [*to the* DIRECTOR] and so you can object that it's only in play that the gentleman there [*indicating the* LEADING MAN] who is *him* must be *me* who, on the other hand, am this *me* myself. Do you see how I've caught you in a trap?

The ACTORS *laugh again.*

DIRECTOR [*annoyed*]. But we've heard all this already. So we're back where we started?

FATHER. No, no. In fact, I didn't mean that. On the contrary, I was inviting you to come out of this game [*with a warning look at the* LEADING LADY]—of art! Art!—which you play here with your actors; and I ask you once again quite seriously: who are you?

DIRECTOR [*turning to the* ACTORS, *astonished and also irritated*]. Well, what a bloody nerve! Someone who claims to be a character comes and asks me who I am!

FATHER [*dignified, but not overbearing*]. A character, sir, may always ask a man who he is. Because a character really has a life of his own, marked by his own traits, which means that he is always 'someone'. But a man—I'm not talking about you, but about man in general— a man may well be 'nobody'.

DIRECTOR. Maybe. But you're asking me, me the Director, the boss! Have you got that?

FATHER [*almost under his breath, modestly soft-spoken*]. It's a matter of knowing, sir, whether you, as you are now, really see yourself . . . in the same way, for example, as you see in retrospect what you once were, with all the illusions you then had; with all those things within and around you, as they then seemed—and indeed truly were for you. Well, sir, when you think back on those illusions which you now no longer have, on everything that no longer 'seems' what once for you it 'was'—don't you feel, not the boards of this stage, but the earth, the earth itself, give way beneath your feet? For you must conclude that in the same way all 'this' that you feel now, all your reality of today, as it is, is destined to seem illusion tomorrow.

DIRECTOR [*not understanding much and stunned by the specious argument*]. So what? What are you trying to prove?

FATHER. Oh, nothing, sir. Only to make you see that if we [*indicating himself and the other* CHARACTERS] have no reality beyond the illusion, then maybe you also shouldn't count too much on your own reality, this reality which you breathe and touch in yourself today, because—like yesterday's—inevitably, it must reveal itself as illusion tomorrow.

DIRECTOR [*deciding to take it as a joke*]. Oh, that's wonderful! And now tell me that you, and this play you've come here to put on for me, are more real and true than I am.

FATHER [*deeply serious*]. There's no doubt about it, sir.

DIRECTOR. Really?

FATHER. I thought you'd understood that right from the start.

DIRECTOR. More real than me?

FATHER. If your reality can change from one day to the next . . .

DIRECTOR. Of course it can change, and how! It changes all the time. Like everyone else's.

FATHER [*shouting*]. But not ours, sir! There's the difference, you see. It doesn't change, it can't change, it can never be different because it's fixed—like this; it's 'this'—for ever—a terrible thing, sir!—an immutable reality that should make you shudder to come near us.

DIRECTOR [*jumping up, struck by a sudden idea*]. But what I'd like to know is who has ever seen a character step out of his part and start lecturing about it the way you're doing, expounding it and explaining it? Can you tell me that? I've never seen such a thing.

FATHER. You've never seen it, sir, because authors usually hide the labour of their creation. When characters are alive, truly alive before their author, all he does is follow them in the actions, words, and gestures that they, indeed, set before him. And he must wish them to be as they themselves wish to be; otherwise he runs into trouble! When a character is born he immediately obtains such an independence, even from his author, that everyone can imagine him in a host of situations that the author never thought of—and he sometimes acquires a significance that the author never dreamed of giving him.

DIRECTOR. As if I didn't know that!

FATHER. Then why are you so surprised by us? Imagine what it's

like for a character to have the misfortune I've already told you
about—to have been born alive from the imagination of an author
who then decided to deny him life; and tell me if that character,
abandoned like that, living and without a life, isn't right to start
doing what we're doing here, before you, after already doing it for so
long, so long, believe me, before our author—urging him, persuading
him, appearing before him, each of us in turn: me, her [*indicating
the* STEPDAUGHTER], that poor Mother there . . .

STEPDAUGHTER [*coming forward as if in a trance*]. It's true. Me too,
sir, me too! Tempting him so often in the gloom of his study, at
twilight, as he lay listless in an armchair, unable to decide whether
or not to switch on the light, letting the darkness invade the room,
a darkness swarming with us who came to tempt him . . . [*As if she
could see herself still there in that study and felt disturbed by the presence of all the* ACTORS] If only you'd all clear off and leave us alone!
Mother there with that son of hers—me with my little sister—that
boy there always by himself—and then me with *him* [*hardly gesturing towards the* FATHER]—and then me alone, all alone . . . in the
shadows. [*Starting up, as if she wanted to grasp that vision of herself,
alive and shining in the shadows*] Ah, my life! What scenes, what
scenes we used to offer him! And I tempted him most of all.

FATHER. You certainly did. But perhaps it was your fault; precisely
because you insisted too much, because you kept going too far!

STEPDAUGHTER. Not in the least! Since that's the way he willed me
to be. [*Coming close to the* DIRECTOR, *confidentially*] I think, sir, it
was discouragement rather, or contempt for the kind of theatre
that the public nowadays usually wants and gets.

DIRECTOR. Let's get on with it, for God's sake, and let's go straight
to the action. Ladies and gentlemen, please.

STEPDAUGHTER. Well, I reckon you've got more than enough
action, with us coming into his house [*indicating the* FATHER]. And
you said you couldn't put up signs or change the set every five
minutes.

DIRECTOR. So I did. That's just the point. We need to combine the
episodes, unite them in one single simultaneous concise action,
and not do things the way you want, with first your little brother
who comes back from school and wanders through the rooms like

a shade, hiding behind doors and brooding on some plan that would make him—how did you put it? ...

STEPDAUGHTER. Sapless, sir, totally sapless.

DIRECTOR. That's a new one on me! But all right, and then: 'Only his eyes seem to grow larger', wasn't that it?

STEPDAUGHTER. Yes, sir. There he is. [*Pointing to where he stands next to the* MOTHER]

DIRECTOR. Well done! And then, at the same time, you want this little girl to be playing in the garden, all unawares. One in the house and the other in the garden, is that possible?

STEPDAUGHTER. Ah, happy in the sunshine, sir! It's my only reward—her happiness, her delight, in that garden; saved from the misery and the squalor of that horrible room where we slept, all four of us—and me with her—me, just think of it! With the horror of my contaminated body next to hers as she hugged me tight, so tight, in her innocent and loving little arms. As soon as she saw me in the garden she used to run and take me by the hand. She didn't even notice the bigger flowers; she went looking for all the 'teeny-weeny ones' to show me, with such joy, such delight!

This said, distraught at the memory, she breaks into a loud despairing lament as she drops her head into her arms outstretched on the table. The emotion is general. The DIRECTOR *comes up to her, paternal and comforting.*

DIRECTOR. We'll have the garden, we'll have the garden, don't you worry. You'll like it, I promise. We'll set all the scenes round the garden. [*Calling a* STAGEHAND *by name*] Hey, lower me down a few tree pieces! Two cypresses in front of this fountain.

Two cypresses descend onto the stage. The TECHNICIAN *hurries in to nail them down.*

DIRECTOR [*to the* STEPDAUGHTER]. Something simple for now. Just to give an idea. [*Calling the* STAGEHAND *again*] Now give me a bit of sky.

STAGEHAND [*from up above*]. What?

DIRECTOR. A bit of sky. A backdrop, coming down here behind the fountain. [*A white cloth is lowered onto the stage*] But not white! I said sky! Oh well, never mind. Leave it. I'll fix it. [*Calling out*] Hey there, lighting. All lights out and then give me a bit of atmosphere ...

moonlight . . . dark blue, use the blues in the batten, and a blue spot on the backdrop . . . Like that. That's it!

His orders produce a mysterious moonlit scene which leads the ACTORS *to speak and move as they would at evening in a garden under the moon.*

DIRECTOR [*to the* STEPDAUGHTER]. There, look! And now the young boy, instead of hiding behind doors in the house, can wander here in the garden and hide behind the trees. But you can see it will be hard to find a little girl who can pull off that flower scene with you. [*Turns to the* YOUNG BOY] Come here, come up here, we'll start with you. Let's see how it works out. [*And since the* BOY *does not move*] Come on, come on. [*Pulling him forward and trying in vain to make him lift his head*] He's a real problem, this lad . . . What's up with him? Oh, for God's sake, he'll have to say something . . . [*He goes up to him, lays a hand on his shoulder and leads him behind the stage trees*] Come on, come here a bit. Let's see. Hide yourself here a moment . . . like this . . . try to stick your head out a bit, to spy on them . . . [*He steps back to look at the effect; the* ACTORS *watch, impressed and rather worried, as the* YOUNG BOY *performs the action*] Splendid . . . splendid . . . [*Addressing the* STEPDAUGHTER] And what if the little girl catches him spying like that? Couldn't we have her run up and wrench a few words out of him?

STEPDAUGHTER [*getting to her feet*]. There's no hope of him speaking as long as that fellow's around [*indicating the* SON]. You'd need to send him away first.

SON [*advancing decisively towards the steps down from the stage*]. Right now! My pleasure! I couldn't ask for anything better.

DIRECTOR [*holding him back*]. No. Where are you off to? Wait!

The MOTHER *jumps up in alarm, worried that the* SON *is really about to leave, and instinctively she raises her arms as if to hold him back, though she does not move from her place.*

SON [*already at the footlights, to the* DIRECTOR *who is holding him back*]. I've got absolutely nothing to do with all this! Let me go, will you! Just let me go!

DIRECTOR. What do you mean, you've got nothing to do with it?

STEPDAUGHTER [*calm and ironic*]. No need to hold him back. He won't leave.

FATHER. He has to act out the terrible scene in the garden with his mother.

SON [*prompt, resolute, proud*]. I shall act out nothing. I said so from the start. [*To the* DIRECTOR] Let me go!

STEPDAUGHTER [*hurrying to the* DIRECTOR]. Do you mind, sir? [*Making him let go of the* SON] Let him go! [*Then, turning to him as soon the* DIRECTOR *has released his grip*] Well then, go!

The SON *remains where he is, straining towards the steps but unable to descend, as if held back by some mysterious power; then to the amazement and concern of the* ACTORS, *he moves slowly along the footlights towards the other stairway leading down from the stage. But there too he remains transfixed, unable to go down. The* STEPDAUGHTER, *who has been watching him with a defiant look, bursts out laughing.*

STEPDAUGHTER. He can't, you see, he can't. He has to stay here, he must, bound fast to the chain. When what has to happen happens, I will fly away—precisely because I hate him so much, precisely because I can't stand the sight of him. Well, then, if, for all that, I'm still here, putting up with his face and his presence, it's unthinkable that he could clear off. No, he has to stay, really stay here with that fine father of his and that mother there who has no other children left but him . . . [*Turning to the* MOTHER] It's your turn, Mother! Come along . . . [*Drawing the* DIRECTOR*'s attention to her*] See, she got up, she got up to hold him back . . . [*To the* MOTHER, *attracting her as if by magic*] Come on, come on . . . [*Then, to the* DIRECTOR] Imagine if she has the heart to show her feelings to your actors. But her craving to be near him is so great that—there, you see? She's ready to live her scene!

In fact, the MOTHER *has gone up to the* SON *and, at the* STEPDAUGHTER*'s last words, opens her arms to show her consent.*

SON [*quickly*]. Oh no, not me! If I can't get away, then I shall stay here; but I repeat: I'm not acting anything.

FATHER [*worked up, to the* DIRECTOR]. You can make him, sir.

SON. Nobody can make me do anything.

FATHER. I'll make you.

STEPDAUGHTER. Wait! Wait! First the child at the fountain. [*She runs to pick up the* LITTLE GIRL, *crouches before her, holds the little face between her hands*] Poor little darling, how lost you look with those lovely big eyes: who knows where you think you are! We're on a stage, my love. What's a stage? Well now: it's a place where you play at being serious. It's where they put on plays. And now we're going to put on a play. I mean really, you know, seriously. You too . . . [*She embraces her, clasping the child to her breast, and rocking her a little*] Oh my darling, my little darling, what a nasty play for you, what a terrible part you've been given! The garden, the bowl of the fountain . . . It's a pretend fountain, of course. But that's just the problem, my love: everything here is pretend. But maybe, after all, you prefer a pretend fountain to a real one—a fountain to play games in, right? But no, it'll be a game for the others. Not for you, I'm afraid, because you're real and you play in a real fountain. A nice, big, green bowl, with bamboos reflected in the pool and giving shade; and there are ducklings, lots and lots of them, swimming around and breaking the shade. You want to catch one, one of those ducklings . . . [*With a terrifying scream*] No, Rosetta, no! Mama's not watching you because of that wretched son there! My mind's somewhere else, struggling with my own demons . . . And that creature . . . [*Leaving the* LITTLE GIRL *and turning with her usual scorn towards the* YOUNG BOY] What are you doing, hanging around here like a beggar? It's your fault too that this child was drowned— your fault for being the way you are, as if I hadn't paid for everyone when I got you all into this house! [*Seizing his arm and forcing him to take his hand out of his pocket*] What have you got there? What are you hiding? Out with it, out with it! [*She forces his hand out of his pocket and, to general horror, discovers that he is holding a revolver. She gives him a brief satisfied glance, then says grimly*] So. Where and how did you get hold of it? [*And since the* YOUNG BOY, *wide-eyed and distraught, does not answer*] You idiot! If I were you, instead of killing myself, I'd have killed one of those two; or both of them, father and son.

She shoves him back behind the cypresses where he had been spying; then she takes the LITTLE GIRL *and lowers her into the fountain, laying her down so that she is hidden from view; finally, she sinks down with her face in her arms that rest on the rim of the fountain.*

DIRECTOR. Splendid! [*Turning to the* SON] And at the same time . . .

SON [*with scorn*]. What do you mean, at the same time? It's simply not true. There was no scene between me and her. [*Indicating the* MOTHER] Let her tell you herself how it was.

In the meantime the SECOND ACTRESS *and the* YOUNG ACTOR *have moved away from the group of* ACTORS *so that they can observe closely the* MOTHER *and the* SON *whose parts they will play later.*

MOTHER. Yes, it's true, sir. I had gone into his room.

SON. Into my room. You heard that? Not into the garden.

DIRECTOR. But that's not important. We have to reorder the episodes, I've told you that already.

SON [*noticing the* YOUNG ACTOR *observing him*]. What do you want?

YOUNG ACTOR. Nothing. I'm simply observing you.

SON [*turning to the other side and seeing the* SECOND ACTRESS]. Ah—and so you're here too? To take on her part? [*Indicating the* MOTHER]

DIRECTOR. Exactly! Exactly! And I think you should be grateful for their attention.

SON. Oh yes. Thank you very much! But haven't you understood yet that you can't possibly do this play? We're not inside of you, and your actors only stand and look at us from the outside. Do you think we can keep on living in front of a mirror, and one that is not content with freezing us in our own expression, but sends that image back to us as an unrecognizable caricature of ourselves?

FATHER. That's true. That's true. You've got to believe it.

DIRECTOR [*to the* YOUNG ACTOR *and the* SECOND ACTRESS]. All right, you get out of the way.

SON. It's no use. I won't have anything to do with it.

DIRECTOR. Keep quiet now, and let me hear your mother. [*To the* MOTHER] Well then, you went in?

MOTHER. Yes, sir, into his room, because I couldn't stand it any longer. To empty my heart of all the anguish that weighs me down. But as soon as he saw me come in—

SON. No scene! I simply left, I left so as not to make a scene. I've never made scenes. Never, you understand?

MOTHER. It's true. That's the way it is.

DIRECTOR. But now we really must have this scene between you and him. We can't do without it.

MOTHER. For my part, sir, I'm here. If only you'd just give me some way of speaking to him for a moment, to tell him all that's in my heart.

FATHER [*fiercely as he goes up to the* Son]. You'll do it! For your mother's sake, your mother's sake!

SON [*more stubborn than ever*]. I'll do nothing of the sort.

FATHER [*seizing him by the jacket and shaking him*]. For God's sake, do as you're told. Do as you're told. Can't you hear what she's telling you? Do you call yourself a son?

SON [*grappling with him*]. No! No! And let that be the end of it.

General consternation. The frightened MOTHER *tries to intervene and separate them.*

MOTHER. For heaven's sake! For heaven's sake!

FATHER [*not letting go*]. You must do as you're told. You must.

SON [*struggling with him and finally throwing him to the floor near the stairway, to the horror of the onlookers*]. What's this madness that's taken hold of you? Can't she stop shaming herself and us in public? I'll have no part in it, no part in it! And in that way I enact the will of the author who didn't want to put us on the stage.

DIRECTOR. But still you all came here.

SON [*indicating the* FATHER]. Him, not me.

DIRECTOR. So you're not here?

SON. He's the one who wanted to come, dragging us all along and then going off with you to fix up this play about what really happened—and, as if that weren't enough, about what never happened at all.

DIRECTOR. So tell me, at least tell me what did happen. You left your room without saying anything?

SON [*after a moment's hesitation*]. Nothing. Precisely because I didn't want to make a scene.

DIRECTOR [*urging him on*]. Right. And then? What did you do?

SON [*taking a few steps across the stage as everyone looks at him with*

agonizing attention]. Nothing . . . As I was crossing the garden . . .
[*He breaks off, dark and brooding*]

DIRECTOR [*still urging him to say more, impressed by his reluctance*]. Well then, as you were crossing the garden?

SON [*exasperated, hiding his face with his arm*]. But why do you want me to say it, sir? It's horrible!

The MOTHER *is all trembling as she looks towards the fountain with stifled groans.*

DIRECTOR [*in a low voice, as he notices that look, turning to the* SON *with growing apprehension*]. The little girl?

SON [*looking straight ahead into the auditorium*]. There, in the bowl of the fountain . . .

FATHER [*still on the ground, with a pitying gesture toward the* MOTHER]. And she was following him, sir.

DIRECTOR [*to the* SON, *anxiously*]. And then you?

SON [*slowly, still looking straight ahead*]. I ran, I rushed to fish her out . . . But suddenly I stopped, because behind those trees I saw something that froze my blood: the boy, the boy who was standing there, stock still, with mad eyes, looking at his sister drowned in the fountain.

The STEPDAUGHTER, *still bent over the rim of the fountain hiding the* LITTLE GIRL, *responds with desperate sobs, like an echo from the deep. Pause.*

SON. I started towards him; and then . . .

A pistol shot is heard from behind the trees where the YOUNG BOY *is hiding.*

MOTHER [*with a terrible scream, running in that direction together with the* SON *and with all the* ACTORS *in the general uproar*]. My son! My son! [*And then, amid the cries and confusion*] Help! Help!

DIRECTOR [*amid the shouting, trying to make his way through, while the* YOUNG BOY *is lifted by the head and feet and carried off behind the white backdrop*]. Is he wounded? Is he really wounded?

Except for the DIRECTOR *and the* FATHER, *who is still on the ground near the stairway, everybody has disappeared behind the sky backdrop where they remain talking in anxious whispers. Then, from both sides of the backdrop, the* ACTORS *come back onto the stage.*

LEADING LADY [*entering from the right, distressed*]. Dead! Poor boy, he's dead! Dead. What an awful thing!

LEADING MAN [*entering from the left, laughing*]. Dead, my foot! It's only pretending, pretending! Don't you believe it!

OTHER ACTORS ON THE RIGHT. Pretending? No, it's real, it's real! He's dead.

OTHER ACTORS ON THE LEFT. No. It's just make-believe, make believe!

FATHER [*standing up and shouting*]. How can you say make-believe? It's reality, ladies and gentlemen, reality! [*He too goes off in despair behind the backdrop*]

DIRECTOR [*at the end of his tether*]. Make-believe! Reality! The Devil take the lot of you! Lights! Lights! Lights!

All of a sudden the stage and the whole auditorium is flooded with light. The DIRECTOR *takes a deep breath as if released from a nightmare, and they all look at each other, dazed and uncertain.*

DIRECTOR. Well, I've never seen anything like this. They've made me waste a whole day.* [*He looks at his watch*] Off you go, off you go! What do you think you can do now? It's too late to pick up the rehearsal. See you tonight. [*As soon as the* ACTORS *have left, he calls out*] Hey, you at the lights, switch everything off. [*Before he even finishes speaking, the whole theatre is plunged into total darkness*] Oh for God's sake! Leave me enough to see where I'm going.

Immediately, as if through some faulty connection, a green spotlight comes on behind the backdrop, projecting large and clear the silhouettes of the CHARACTERS, *except for the* YOUNG BOY *and the* LITTLE GIRL. *When the* DIRECTOR *sees them he scutters from the stage in terror. At the same time the spotlight goes out, and the stage is once more bathed in the blue of night.*

Slowly, from the right side of the backdrop, the SON *comes forward, followed by the* MOTHER *with arms outstretched towards him; then from the left comes the* FATHER. *They stop at centre stage, motionless like figures in a dream. Finally, from the left, comes the* STEPDAUGHTER *who runs towards one of the stairways. With her foot on the top step, she stops for a moment, looks at the other three and breaks into a shrill laugh before hurrying down the steps and running up the aisle between the seats.*

She stops once again and laughs once more as she looks back at the other three up there on the stage. At last, she vanishes from the auditorium and her laugh can still be heard echoing from the foyer. There is a brief pause before the curtain falls.

HENRY IV

A Tragedy in Three Acts

LIST OF CHARACTERS

'Henry IV'
Marchesa Matilda Spina
Frida, her daughter
The young Marchese Carlo di Nolli
Baron Tito Belcredi
Doctor Dionisio Genoni
The Four Supposed Privy Counsellors:
   1) Landolph (Lolo)
   2) Harold (Franco)
   3) Ordulph (Momo)
   4) Berthold (Fino)
Giovanni, an old retainer
Two valets in costume

An isolated villa in the Umbrian countryside. The present day.

ACT ONE

A spacious room in the villa, carefully furnished to resemble the throne room of Henry IV in the imperial palace at Goslar. But, amid all the antiques, two life-size modern portraits in oils stand out on the back wall, placed just above floor level on a projecting ledge of carved wood that runs the whole length of the wall and is broad enough to sit on like a bench. They are placed on either side of a throne that interrupts the ledge with its imperial seat and low canopy. The two portraits show a gentleman and a lady, both young and dressed in carnival costumes, the former as 'Henry IV' and the latter as 'Countess Matilda of Tuscany'. Exits to right and left.

    As the curtain rises, the TWO VALETS, *who have been lounging on the ledge, jump to their feet as if surprised and go to stand with their halberds like statues on either side of the throne. Almost immediately from the second right exit come* HAROLD, LANDOLPH, ORDULPH, *and* BERTHOLD—*young men paid by the* MARCHESE CARLO DI NOLLI *to act the part of 'Privy Counsellors'—vassals drawn from the minor aristocracy at the court of Henry IV, and thus dressed as eleventh-century German knights. For* BERTHOLD *(real name, Fino), it is his first day in this job. His three companions enjoy teasing him as they brief him on his duties. The whole scene should be played in a bright and lively manner.*

LANDOLPH [*to* BERTHOLD, *as if continuing an explanation*]. And this is the throne room.

HAROLD. At Goslar.

ORDULPH. Or, if you like, in the Harzburg.

HAROLD. Or at Worms.*

LANDOLPH. Like us, it switches here or there, depending on the event we're playing.

ORDULPH. Saxony.

HAROLD. Lombardy.

LANDOLPH. On the Rhine.

ONE OF THE VALETS [*impassive, hardly moving his lips*]. Psst! Psst!

HAROLD [*turning round*]. What is it?

FIRST VALET [*still like a statue, under his breath*]. Is he coming in or not? [*Referring to* HENRY IV]

ORDULPH. No, no. He's asleep. Relax.

SECOND VALET [*as both valets stand easy and breathe a sigh of relief; going to stretch out on the ledge*]. You could have told us, damn it!

FIRST VALET [*going up to* HAROLD]. You wouldn't have a match?

LANDOLPH. Hey! Not a pipe. Not in here.

FIRST VALET [*while* HAROLD *strikes a match for him*]. No, it's just a cigarette. [*Lights up, then goes to sprawl on the ledge and smoke*]

BERTHOLD [*a half-amazed and half-puzzled observer, looking around the room and then inspecting his own clothes and those of his companions*]. But, hold on . . . this room . . . these costumes . . . Which Henry IV? . . . I'm not sure I get it:—It is the French one, isn't it? [LANDOLPH, HAROLD, *and* ORDULPH *burst out laughing*]

LANDOLPH [*still laughing and pointing at* BERTHOLD *as if urging his companions to keep up their mockery*]. The French one, he says.

ORDULPH. He thought it was the French one.*

HAROLD. Henry IV of Germany, old boy. The Salian dynasty.

ORDULPH. The great and tragic emperor!

LANDOLPH. The one who came to Canossa. Day after day we act out the terrible war between Church and State. Oh yes.

ORDULPH. The Empire against the Papacy. Oh yes.

HAROLD. Anti-popes against popes.

LANDOLPH. Kings against anti-kings.

ORDULPH. And war against the Saxons.

HAROLD. And all the rebel princes.

LANDOLPH. Against the Emperor's own sons.

BERTHOLD [*covering his head with his hands to ward off this flood of information*]. Now I see! Now I see! That's why I didn't get it, when I saw myself dressed up like this and coming into this room. I was right: just not sixteenth-century costume.

HAROLD. Nowhere near sixteenth-century!

ORDULPH. Here we're somewhere in the eleventh century.

LANDOLPH. Work it out for yourself. If on 25 January 1071, we're at Canossa . . .*

BERTHOLD [*more lost than ever*]. God, what a mess-up!

ORDULPH. Well, of course! If he thought he was at the French court.

BERTHOLD. After all that history I read up . . .

LANDOLPH. We're four centuries earlier, dear chap! To us you're still a child.

BERTHOLD [*angrily*]. But for Christ's sake, they could have told me it was the German one and not Henry IV of France! The books I've skimmed through in the fortnight they gave me to get ready; you've no idea!

HAROLD. Hold on, didn't you know that poor Tito was Adalbert of Bremen?

BERTHOLD. What Adalbert? I didn't know a damn thing!

LANDOLPH. No, don't you see? When Tito died the young Marchese di Nolli . . .

BERTHOLD. He was the one, the young Marchese! Why couldn't he have told me?

HAROLD. Maybe he thought you already knew!

LANDOLPH. He didn't want to take on anyone as a replacement. He thought the three of us who were left would be enough. But *him*, he started shouting 'Adalbert's been driven out'—because for him, you see, it wasn't that poor old Tito was dead. No. As Bishop Adalbert, he'd been driven away from the court by the rival bishops of Cologne and Mainz.

BERTHOLD [*burying his head in his hands*]. But I don't know the first thing about all this stuff.

ORDULPH. Then you've got a real problem, old chap.

HAROLD. And the trouble is that *we* don't know who you are either.

BERTHOLD. Not even you? Who am I supposed to act? Don't you know?

ORDULPH. Hm. Berthold.

BERTHOLD. What Berthold? Why Berthold?

LANDOLPH. 'They've driven out Adalbert? Then I want Berthold! I want Berthold!' That's what he started shouting.

HAROLD. We three just looked at each other: who on earth is this Berthold?

ORDULPH. And here you are, dear boy—Berthold!

LANDOLPH. And you'll be absolutely splendid!

BERTHOLD [*protesting and about to leave*]. Ah, but I just won't do it! Thanks very much. I'm off! I'm off out of here! I'm off!

HAROLD [*amid laughter, helping* ORDULPH *to hold him back*]. No. Calm down, calm down!

ORDULPH. You're not, by any chance, the Berthold of the folk tale?*

LANDOLPH. If it's any comfort, we don't know who we are either, come to that. He's Harold, he's Ordulph, I'm Landolph . . . That's what he calls us. We're used to it. But who are we? Period names! And you must have a period name as well: Berthold. Only poor old Tito had a really good role, one you can read about in history: Bishop of Bremen. He really did look like a bishop. Splendid he was, poor old Tito!

HAROLD. No wonder, with all those books where he could read up the part!

LANDOLPH. He even gave orders to His Majesty: he took over, guided him like a tutor, like a counsellor. We're 'privy counsellors' too, of course, but just to make up the numbers; because history tells us that Henry IV was hated by the great lords for surrounding himself at court with young nobles of lower rank.

ORDULPH. Meaning us.

LANDOLPH. Just so. Minor royal vassals; devoted, a bit dissolute, cheerful . . .

BERTHOLD. I'm supposed to be cheerful as well?

HAROLD. And how! Just like us!

ORDULPH. And it's not all that easy, you know.

LANDOLPH. It's really a pity! Because, as you see, all the trappings are there; our wardrobe would make a fine show in one of those historical dramas that are such a success in the theatre nowadays. As for subject matter, oh, the story of Henry IV would be matter enough for several tragedies, not just one. Instead of which, all four of us, and those two poor devils over there [*pointing to the* VALETS] when they're standing stiff before the throne, we're . . . well, we're there with nobody to set us up and give us a scene to act. We've got . . . how can I put it? . . . we've got the form without the content!—We're worse off than the real privy counsellors of Henry IV; granted, nobody had given them parts to act either; but at least they didn't know they were supposed to be acting. They played their parts because they played their parts: in short, it wasn't a part, it was their life. They looked after their own interests at the expense of others, sold investitures and who knows what. Not like us lot. We're all here, dressed up like this, in this splendid court . . . to do what? Nothing. Like six puppets hanging on the wall, waiting for someone to take them down and move them this way or that, and give them a few words to say.

HAROLD. Ah no, my friend. Pardon me! You have to give the right answer, know the right answer! Big trouble if he speaks to you and you're not ready to answer the way he wants.

LANDOLPH. Well, yes, that's right. That's dead right.

BERTHOLD. That doesn't help me much! How can I give him the right answers when I get all ready for Henry IV of France and then, lo and behold, up pops Henry IV of Germany? [LANDOLPH, ORDULPH, *and* HAROLD *start laughing again*]

HAROLD. Well, you'd better start putting that right straightaway.

ORDULPH. Don't worry. We'll help you out.

HAROLD. We've got so many books in there! Give them a good lookover. That'll do for a start.

ORDULPH. You must have some general idea . . .

HAROLD. Look there! [*Turning him round and showing him the portrait of the Countess Matilda on the back wall*] For example, who's that?

BERTHOLD [*looking*]. That one? Well, I'm sorry, but to start with, it's hopelessly out of place: two modern paintings in the middle of all these genuine antiques.

HAROLD. You're right. And, in fact, they weren't there at the beginning. There are two niches behind those paintings. The original idea was to have two statues, carved in period style. But since the niches stayed empty, they covered them with those two paintings.

LANDOLPH [*interrupting and continuing*]. Which certainly would be out of place if they were real paintings.

BERTHOLD. So what are they? Aren't they paintings?

LANDOLPH. Yes, if you go and touch them, they're paintings. But for *him* [*pointing mysteriously to the right, referring to* HENRY IV]— who never touches them . . .

BERTHOLD. No? So what are they for him?

LANDOLPH. Oh, it's just my impression, mind you. But I think that deep down it's right. They're images. Images like . . . well, like something reflected in a mirror, see what I mean? That one over there [*pointing to the portrait of* HENRY IV] represents him, alive the way he is, standing in this throne room, which is also, as it should be, in period style. So what's so surprising? If they put a mirror in front of you, wouldn't you see yourself, alive, here and now, dressed up like this in ancient costume? Well then, it's as if there were two mirrors, giving living images here in the midst of a world that—don't worry, you'll see, you'll see, when you've been with us for a while, how all that comes to life as well.

BERTHOLD. Now look, I'm not going to let this place drive me crazy!

HAROLD. What do you mean, crazy? You'll enjoy it.

BERTHOLD. Let me just say . . . well, how did you all get to be so knowledgeable?

LANDOLPH. My dear chap, you don't go back through eight hundred years of history without gathering a bit of experience along the way.

HAROLD. Come on, come on. You'll see, it won't take long for us to give you the hang of it.

ORDULPH. And in that school you'll become pretty knowledgeable yourself.

BERTHOLD. Yes. But for God's sake, help me out right now. At least, give me the outlines.

HAROLD. Leave it to us! A bit from one, a bit from another . . .

LANDOLPH. We'll tie your strings and fix you up like the best and handiest of puppets. Come along! [*He takes him by the arm to lead him off*]

BERTHOLD [*stopping and looking at the portrait on the wall*]. Wait! You haven't told me who *she* is. The Emperor's wife?

HAROLD. No, the Emperor's wife is Bertha of Susa, sister of Amadeus II of Savoy.

ORDULPH. And the Emperor who'd like to be young with us can't stand her and is thinking of casting her off.

LANDOLPH. That woman there is his fiercest enemy: Matilda, Countess of Tuscany.

BERTHOLD. I've got it, the one who played host to the Pope . . .

LANDOLPH. At Canossa. Exactly.

ORDULPH. Pope Gregory VII.

HAROLD. Our bête noire! Come on, let's go!

As they all move towards the right exit through which they came, the old tailcoated servant GIOVANNI *enters left.*

GIOVANNI [*hastily, anxious*]. Hey! Psst! Franco! Lolo!

HAROLD [*stopping and turning*]. What's up?

BERTHOLD [*surprised to see someone in a tailcoat entering the throne room*]. What's this? What's he doing in here?

LANDOLPH. A twentieth-century man! Get out! [*Joined in the joke by the other two, he runs menacingly at* GIOVANNI *as if to drive him out*]

ORDULPH. A messenger from Gregory VII. Off with him.

HAROLD. Off with him! Off with him!

GIOVANNI [*annoyed, fending them off*]. Pack it in, will you!

ORDULPH. No! You can't set foot in here!

HAROLD. Out! Out!

LANDOLPH [*to* BERTHOLD]. Witchcraft, you know! A devil conjured up by the wizard of Rome! Draw your sword! [*He makes as if to draw his own sword*]

GIOVANNI [*shouting*]. I said, pack it in! Don't play the fool with me! The Marchese has arrived with a number of guests.

LANDOLPH [*rubbing his hands*]. Ah, splendid! Are there any ladies?

ORDULPH [*in the same vein*]. Old? Young?

GIOVANNI. There are two gentlemen.

HAROLD. But the ladies, who are the ladies?

GIOVANNI. The Marchesa with her daughter.

LANDOLPH [*surprised*]. What? How on earth?

ORDULPH. You said the Marchesa?

GIOVANNI. The Marchesa! The Marchesa!

HAROLD. And the gentlemen?

GIOVANNI. I don't know.

HAROLD [*to* BERTHOLD]. They're coming to give us our content, you see.

ORDULPH. All of them messengers from Gregory VII! What fun we'll have!

GIOVANNI. Now look! Are you going to let me speak?

HAROLD. Go on! Go on!

GIOVANNI. It seems that one of these two gentlemen is a doctor.

LANDOLPH. Oh, we know. One of the usual doctors.

HAROLD. Bravo, Berthold! You bring us luck.

LANDOLPH. You'll see how we get to work on this doctor fellow!

BERTHOLD. I reckon I'm going to find myself dumped straight into a right mess!

GIOVANNI. Now listen to me! They want to come into this room.

LANDOLPH [*surprised, in dismay*]. What! Her? The Marchesa, in here?

HAROLD. Now that's 'content' for you!

LANDOLPH. The birth of a real tragedy!

BERTHOLD [*curious*]. But why? Why?

ORDULPH [*pointing to the portrait*]. Because it's *her* over there. Don't you see?

LANDOLPH. The daughter is engaged to the Marchese.

HAROLD. But what have they come for? Can you tell us that?

ORDULPH. If he sees her, there'll be trouble!

LANDOLPH. Maybe he won't recognize her by now.

GIOVANNI. If he wakes up, you'll have to keep him out of here.

ORDULPH. Oh yes? And how? You must be joking.

HAROLD. You know the way he is!

GIOVANNI. Good God, by force if that's what it takes! Those are my orders! Go on, go on!

HAROLD. Yes, yes. He may already be awake!

ORDULPH. Come on, come on!

LANDOLPH [*going out with the others, to* GIOVANNI]. But you'll explain it later.

GIOVANNI [*shouting after them*]. Lock that door and hide the key. And the other door as well!

He points to the other exit on the right. LANDOLPH, HAROLD, ORDULPH, *and* BERTHOLD *leave by second right exit.*

GIOVANNI [*to the* TWO VALETS]. You as well. Out! Out there! [*Pointing to first right exit*] Lock the door and hide the key!

The TWO VALETS *leave by the first right exit.* GIOVANNI *goes to the left exit and opens the door to admit the* MARCHESE DI NOLLI.

DI NOLLI. Have you passed on my orders?

GIOVANNI. Yes, my lord. There's nothing to worry about.

DI NOLLI *goes out for a moment to bring the others in. Enter* BARON TITO BELCREDI *and* DR DIONISIO GENONI, *followed by* LADY MATILDA SPINA *and the young marchesa* FRIDA. GIOVANNI *bows and leaves.* LADY MATILDA SPINA *is about forty-five, still beautiful and with a good figure, though she repairs the inevitable ravages of age rather too obviously with a heavy but skilful make-up that gives her the proud air of a Walkyrie. This make-up provides a sharp and disturbing contrast with the lovely sorrowful mouth. Widowed many years ago, she now has* TITO BELCREDI *as her friend—a man whom neither she nor anyone else has ever taken seriously, or so it seems. What* TITO BELCREDI *really means to her only he knows, and thus he can afford to laugh if his lady friend needs to pretend not to know—always laugh in response to the laughter that the* MARCHESA's *sallies provoke at his expense. Slim, prematurely grey, slightly younger than the* MARCHESA, *he has a curious birdlike head. He would be very lively if the supple agility that makes him a formidable swordsman were not, as it were, enveloped in a sleepy Arabian idleness, evident in his strange nasal drawl.* FRIDA, *the daughter of the*

MARCHESA, *is nineteen years of age. Languishing in the shadow cast by her overbearing and striking mother, she is also offended, in that shadow, by the loose gossip that the* MARCHESA *provokes—now more damaging to her daughter than to herself. Fortunately, she is already engaged to the* MARCHESE DI NOLLI, *a stiff young man, very indulgent towards others, but fixed and reserved in his attitude to that small worth that he believes he possesses in the world—though deep down, perhaps, what that worth consists in even he does not know. He is, in any case, dismayed by the many responsibilities that, he thinks, weigh upon him. So that others can go on chattering, yes, others can go and amuse themselves, lucky them! He can't; and it's not that he wouldn't like to, but that he simply can't. He is dressed in strict mourning for the recent death of his mother.* DR DIONISIO GENONI *has the fine shameless ruddy face of a satyr, with protruding eyes and a beard that is short and pointed, shining and silvery: elegant manners; almost bald. They all seem anxious, almost afraid, looking round the room with curiosity (except for* DI NOLLI*); at first they speak in low voices.*

BELCREDI. Ah, magnificent! Magnificent!

DOCTOR. Most interesting. The madness comes out even in the details. Magnificent, yes, yes, magnificent.

LADY MATILDA [*finding the portrait she has been looking for and going up to it*]. Ah, there it is! [*Inspecting it from the proper distance, with mixed feelings*] Yes, yes. Oh, look . . . My God . . . [*calls her daughter*] Frida, Frida . . . look.

FRIDA. Ah, your portrait?

LADY MATILDA. No. Look! It's not me: it's you!

DI NOLLI. It is, isn't it? I told you so.

LADY MATILDA. I would never have believed it! [*Shuddering as if a shiver had run down her spine*] God, what a feeling! [*Then, looking at her daughter*] What do you say, Frida? [*Drawing Frida close, with an arm round her waist*] Come now, don't you see yourself in me there?

FRIDA. Well, frankly, I . . .

LADY MATILDA. Don't you see it? How can't you see it? [*Turning to Belcredi*] Tito, you take a look. You tell her!

BELCREDI [*without looking*]. Oh no, I'm not looking. On principle. No.

LADY MATILDA. You fool! He thinks he's paying me a compliment! [*Turning to* DR GENONI] You say something, doctor!

DR GENONI *starts to move towards the portrait.*

BELCREDI [*his back turned, with feigned secrecy*]. Psst! No, doctor! For heaven's sake, don't get involved!

DOCTOR [*puzzled and smiling*]. And why shouldn't I get involved?

LADY MATILDA. Don't listen to him. Come here! He's unbearable!

FRIDA. He makes a profession of being stupid, didn't you know?

BELCREDI [*seeing the doctor go over*]. Mind your feet, mind your feet, doctor! Your feet!

DOCTOR. My feet? Why?

BELCREDI. Because you have hobnailed boots.

DOCTOR. Me?

BELCREDI. Yessir. And you're about to step on four tiny little feet of glass.

DOCTOR [*with a loud laugh*]. Not at all! I reckon that—after all— there's nothing surprising about a daughter looking like her mother.

BELCREDI. Scrunch! Ouch! That's done it!

LADY MATILDA [*ostentatiously angry, going up to* BELCREDI]. Why 'Scrunch, Ouch'? What's that? What are you on about?

DOCTOR [*innocently*]. Aren't I right?

BELCREDI [*answering the* MARCHESA]. He said there was nothing surprising about it; but you were very surprised indeed. How come, if now you think it's so natural?

LADY MATILDA [*even angrier*]. Idiot! You idiot! Just because it *is* so natural. Because that's not my daughter there. [*She points to the painting*] That's my portrait! And finding my daughter there instead of me, that was what took me by surprise. And my astonishment was quite genuine, believe me; and I forbid you to cast any doubt on it.

After this violent outburst there is a moment of awkward silence all round.

FRIDA [*quietly annoyed*]. Oh God, always the same . . . arguing over every little thing.

BELCREDI [*also quietly, his tail between his legs, apologetically*]. I didn't cast doubt on anything. I simply noticed, right from the start, that you didn't share your mother's surprise. Or if anything surprised you it was the the fact that the portrait looked so much like yourself.

LADY MATILDA. That's just it. She can't recognize herself in me as I was at her age, whereas I can very easily recognize myself in her as she is now.

DOCTOR. Absolutely! Because a portrait is always fixed in a given moment—for the young marchesa it's far off and with no memories; but for the Marchesa herself, everything that it recalls, movements, gestures, glances, smiles, so many things that aren't there . . .

LADY MATILDA. Just so! Precisely!

DOCTOR [*continuing*]. You, of course, can see them all again, living now, in your daughter.

LADY MATILDA. But *he* always has to spoil the slightest indulgence in any spontaneous emotion, just for the pleasure of annoying me.

DOCTOR [*dazzled by the light he has thrown on the topic, starts up again, addressing* BELCREDI *in a professorial tone*]. Resemblance, my dear baron, is often the result of imponderables. And that, in fact, is why . . .

BELCREDI [*interrupting the lecture*]. Why someone could even find a resemblance between me and you, dear professor!

DI NOLLI. Now drop it, please; please drop it! [*He gestures towards the two right exits to warn that there's somebody who might be listening*] We played about too much on the way . . .

FRIDA. Not surprising. When he's around. [*Indicating* BELCREDI]

LADY MATILDA [*quickly*]. Which is just why I didn't want him to come.

BELCREDI. But you made everyone laugh so much at my expense. Now there's ingratitude!

DI NOLLI. That's enough, Tito, please. We have the doctor with us, and we've come for a very serious purpose; you know how much it matters to me.

DOCTOR. That's it, yes. First of all, let's see if we can clarify a few points. This portrait of you, Marchesa, if you don't mind; how did it get here? Did you give it to him as a present, back then?

LADY MATILDA. No, no. What possible reason could I have had to do that? Back then I was like Frida is now, and not even engaged. I let him have it three or four years after the accident on the insistence of *his* mother. [*Indicating* DI NOLLI]

DOCTOR. Who was *his* sister. [*Pointing to the right exits and referring to* HENRY IV]

DI NOLLI. Yes, doctor: we're paying a debt—coming here—a debt owed to my mother who passed away a month ago. Instead of being here, she [*indicating* FRIDA] and I should be off travelling . . .

DOCTOR. With your minds on very different matters. I understand.

DI NOLLI. Anyway, she died with the firm conviction that her beloved brother was about to recover.

DOCTOR. And could you tell me what signs induced her to think so?

DI NOLLI. Obviously some strange things that he said to her, shortly before she died.

DOCTOR. Something he said? Well, well . . . By Jove, it would be very useful, so useful if we could know what it was!

DI NOLLI. Ah, that I don't know. I know that Mother came back from that last visit very upset; Because it seems that he was unusually tender with her, as if he foresaw that she was about to die. On her deathbed she made me promise that I would never neglect him, that I would have him seen and examined.

DOCTOR. Very well. Let's see, first of all let's see . . . So often the slightest causes . . . So that portrait . . .

LADY MATILDA. For heaven's sake, doctor, I don't think we should give it such huge importance. It struck me like that because I hadn't seen it for so many years.

DOCTOR. Please, please, give me a minute . . .

DI NOLLI. Of course. It's been there about fifteen years . . .

LADY MATILDA. More. More than eighteen, by now.

DOCTOR. Please, if you don't mind! You still don't know what I want to ask. I attach considerable significance to these two portraits—both painted, I imagine, before that famous and catastrophic cavalcade; am I right?

LADY MATILDA. Of course.

DOCTOR. Therefore, when he was perfectly in his right mind—this is what I meant to say—Did he give you the idea of having it done?

LADY MATILDA. No, doctor. Many of us who took part in the pageant had them done. As a memento.

BELCREDI. I had mine done too, I was Charles of Anjou.*

LADY MATILDA. As soon as the costumes were ready.

BELCREDI. Because, you see, the original idea was to hang them all together, as a record of the occasion, in the drawing room of the villa where we had the pageant—like an art gallery. But then everyone wanted to keep his own.

LADY MATILDA. And I gave up mine, as I said just now—without much regret—because his mother . . . [*Again indicating* DI NOLLI]

DOCTOR. You don't know whether he asked for it himself?

LADY MATILDA. Ah, that I don't know. Maybe. Or else his loving sister thought it might help.

DOCTOR. Another thing, another thing. Was the cavalcade his idea?

BELCREDI [*quickly*]. No, no. It was mine, mine.

DOCTOR. Go on . . .

LADY MATILDA. Don't listen to him. It was poor Belassi's.

BELCREDI. Belassi, my foot!

LADY MATILDA [*to the* DOCTOR]. Count Belassi who died two or three months after, poor fellow.

BELCREDI. But if Belassi wasn't even there when . . .

DI NOLLI [*annoyed at the threat of another argument*]. Forgive me, doctor, but do we really need to establish whose idea it was?

DOCTOR. Well, yes, it would help me.

BELCREDI. But it was my idea! Oh, this is a good one! It's not as if I'd be proud of it, considering the result. Look, doctor—I remember it very well—it was one evening early in November at the Club. I was looking through an illustrated magazine, a German one—just looking at the pictures, of course, because I don't know any German. And in one picture there was the Emperor, visiting some university town where he'd been a student.

DOCTOR. Bonn, Bonn.*

BELCREDI. Bonn, that's it. On horseback, dressed up in one of those strange traditional costumes of the ancient German student guilds; followed by a procession of other noble students, also mounted and in costume. I got the idea from that picture. Because you need to know that at the Club we were thinking of putting on some big pageant for the next Carnival. I proposed this historical cavalcade: historical in a manner of speaking; more like the Tower of Babel. Each of us was to choose a character from this or that century: king or emperor or prince, with his lady beside him, queen or empress, on horseback. The horses caparisoned, of course, according to the fashion of the period. And my proposal was accepted.

LADY MATILDA. My invitation came from Belassi.

BELCREDI. Breach of copyright, that's what it was, if he told you it was his idea. I tell you he wasn't even there that evening at the Club when I made the proposal. And come to that, neither was *he*! [*Referring to* HENRY IV]

DOCTOR. And so he chose the character of Henry IV?

LADY MATILDA. Because of my choice. Given my name, and not thinking all that much about it, I said I wanted to be the Countess Matilda of Tuscany.

DOCTOR. Sorry . . . I don't quite see the connection.

LADY MATILDA. Well, you know, neither did I at the beginning, when I heard him answer that in that case he'd be at my feet like Henry IV at Canossa. Yes, I knew something about Canossa, but, to be quite frank, I couldn't remember the whole story. And when I brushed it up in preparation for my role, it felt strange to be cast as a faithful and zealous friend of Pope Gregory VII in his bitter struggle against the German empire. Then I understood why, since I had chosen to impersonate his most implacable enemy, he wanted to be by my side in the cavalcade as Henry IV.

DOCTOR. Ah, because perhaps . . .

BELCREDI. For heaven's sake, doctor! Because he was courting her relentlessly, and she [*indicating the* MARCHESA] naturally . . .

LADY MATILDA [*stung, fiery*]. Naturally, exactly! Naturally! And more 'naturally' than ever in those days!

BELCREDI [*with a demonstrative gesture*]. There you are: she couldn't stand him.

LADY MATILDA. It's not true. I didn't dislike him. Quite the contrary. But with me, as soon as someone wants to be taken seriously . . .

BELCREDI [*completing the sentence*]. She takes it as the clearest proof of his stupidity.

LADY MATILDA. No, dear, not in this case. He was nowhere near as stupid as you.

BELCREDI. I've never tried to be taken seriously.

LADY MATILDA. And don't I know it! But with him it was no laughing matter. [*Changing tone and turning to the* DOCTOR] One of the many misfortunes of us women, dear doctor, is to find ourselves every now and then looking into two eyes that hold an intense unspoken promise of everlasting love. [*She breaks into shrill laughter*] There's nothing funnier! If only men could see themselves with that 'everlasting' in their eyes . . . It has always made me laugh like this! And especially then. But I must make a confession: I can make it now after twenty years and more.—When I laughed at him like that, it was also out of fear. Because perhaps a promise in those eyes could be believed. But it would have been very dangerous.

DOCTOR [*with intense interest, concentrating*]. Yes, yes, I see—that's what I would really like to know about. Very dangerous?

LADY MATILDA [*lightly*]. Simply because he wasn't like the others. And since I'm also . . . well, yes, after all . . . a bit like that . . . to be quite frank, more than a bit . . . [*looking for an understatement*] impatient, yes, impatient of everything that's formal and stuffy! But then I was too young, you understand? And a woman. I had to rein myself in. It would have taken the kind of courage that I felt I didn't have. So I laughed at him as well. With remorse. In fact, I was disgusted with myself when I saw that my laughter was no different from that of all the other fools who made fun of him.

BELCREDI. More or less as they make fun of me.

LADY MATILDA. You make people laugh with that humble look you always put on, my dear, while he was quite the opposite. There's a big difference! And then with you, people laugh in your face.

BELCREDI. Better than behind my back, I say.

DOCTOR. Let's get back to the subject, can we! So he already showed a bit of nervous excitement, if I've understood it right?

BELCREDI. Yes, doctor, but in such a strange way!

DOCTOR. How do you mean?

BELCREDI. Well, I'd say . . . deliberately . . .

LADY MATILDA. Deliberately—that's nonsense! That's the way he was, doctor: a bit strange, certainly, but only because he was full of life, so original.

BELCREDI. I'm not saying he faked his excitement. In fact, quite the contrary, he often really did get excited. But I could swear, doctor, that he was watching himself getting excited. And I think this must have been the case even in his most spontaneous actions. I'd go further: I'm sure he suffered from it. Sometimes he had really comic fits of anger against himself.

LADY MATILDA. That's true.

BELCREDI [*to* LADY MATILDA]. And why? [*To the* DOCTOR] I reckon it was because that sudden clarity of vision excluded him, all at once, from every intimacy with his own feelings. To him those feelings then seemed—not fake because they were real enough—but like something which, right there, he had to assess as . . . how can I put it? . . . as an act of intelligence, to make up for that warmth of heartfelt sincerity that he felt was lacking. And so he'd talk away, exaggerate, let himself go—anything that would make him too dazed to see himself any longer. He seemed erratic, fatuous, and . . . let's be honest . . . sometimes downright ridiculous.

DOCTOR. And . . . would you say unsociable?

BELCREDI. Anything but! He was into everything. Famous for organizing pageants, balls, shows for charity; just for fun, of course. But he was very good at acting, you know.

DI NOLLI. And in his madness he has become a magnificent and terrifying actor.

BELCREDI. Right from the start. Just imagine, when the accident happened, after he fell off his horse . . .

DOCTOR. Striking the back of his head, right?

LADY MATILDA. Oh, it was horrible! He was next to me. I saw him under the hoofs of his horse as it reared up.

BELCREDI. But at first we didn't think he'd done himself much harm. Yes, the cavalcade came to a stop and there was a spot of confusion: people wanted to see what had happened. But he had already been picked up and carried to the villa.

LADY MATILDA. There was nothing, you know. Not a scratch. Not a drop of blood.

BELCREDI. We thought he'd just fainted . . .

LADY MATILDA. And when, about two hours later . . .

BELCREDI. Exactly, when he reappeared in the room—what I mean to say is . . .

LADY MATILDA. Oh, the look on his face! I realized immediately.

BELCREDI. No, you can't say that. None of us realized, doctor, believe me.

LADY MATILDA. Of course you didn't. Because you were all behaving like madmen.

BELCREDI. Everyone was having fun acting his own part. It was a real Babel.

LADY MATILDA. You can imagine how alarmed we were when we realized that, unlike us, he had taken on his role in deadly earnest.

DOCTOR. Ah, because he too then . . .

BELCREDI. Yes. He came and joined in. We thought he'd recovered and that he'd started acting again, like the rest of us . . . better than the rest of us, because, as I told you, he was a splendid actor. In short, we thought he was joking.

LADY MATILDA. They started ragging him.

BELCREDI. And then—he was armed, like a king—then he drew his sword and assaulted two or three of us. Everyone was terrified.

LADY MATILDA. I shall never forget that scene, with all our faces masked, distorted, amazed, facing his terrible mask which was no longer a mask at all, but sheer madness!

BELCREDI. There he was, Henry IV! Henry IV in person, and in a fit of fury!

LADY MATILDA. I say he must have been affected by his obsession with that pageant, doctor, an obsession that he'd been nursing for over a month. It kept coming into whatever he did.

BELCREDI. And all his research in preparation! Down to the smallest details . . . the most minute . . .

DOCTOR. Ah, that's quite straightforward. What had been a transitory obsession became a fixation with the fall and the blow to the back of his head that caused the brain damage. It became fixed, self-generating. It can make a man a halfwit, or it can make him mad.

BELCREDI [*to* FRIDA *and* DI NOLLI]. You see how strangely things turn out, my dears. [*To* DI NOLLI] You were four or five; [*to* FRIDA] your mother thinks you've taken her place in that portrait there, though at the time she had no idea she'd bring you into the world: I've already gone grey. But *him*, there he is [*indicating the portrait*]—bang! a knock on the head—and from then on he hasn't budged: Henry IV.

DOCTOR [*emerging from a meditative pause, opens his hands before his face as if to concentrate the attention of the others and prepares to deliver his scientific explanation*]. Well then, well then, ladies and gentlemen; it is precisely this . . .

But suddenly the first door on the right, the one nearer to the footlights, opens to admit an alarmed-looking BERTHOLD.

BERTHOLD [*bursting in like someone who can stand it no longer*]. May I? I beg your pardon . . . [*He stops short, seeing the sudden confusion that his entrance has created*].

FRIDA [*with a scream of fear, shrinking back*]. Oh God! Here he is!

LADY MATILDA [*shrinking back in dismay, with one arm raised so as not to see him*]. Is it him? Is it him?

DI NOLLI [*promptly*]. No, no. Calm down.

DOCTOR [*stunned*]. Who is it then?

BELCREDI. Some survivor of our pageant.

DI NOLLI. He's one of the four young men we keep here to humour his madness.

BERTHOLD. I beg your pardon, my lord . . .

DI NOLLI. My pardon, be damned! I ordered that the doors should be locked and that nobody be allowed in here.

BERTHOLD. Yessir, but I can't take it any more. I'm asking permission to leave.

DI NOLLI. Ah, you're the one who was to start service this morning?

BERTHOLD. Yessir, and I'm saying that I can't stand it.

LADY MATILDA [*very anxious, to* DI NOLLI]. So he's not as calm as you said?

BERTHOLD [*quickly*]. No, no, my lady. It's not him. It's the three others who work with me. You say 'humour him', my lord? Well, if that's 'humouring'! They're not humouring anyone. They're the real madmen! I come in here for the first time, and instead of helping me, my lord . . .

LANDOLPH *and* HAROLD *enter through the same downstage right door as* BERTHOLD; *though anxious and in haste, they hesitate at the door before coming forward.*

LANDOLPH. Excuse me.

HAROLD. Excuse us, my lord.

DI NOLLI. Come in. What is it now? What are you doing?

FRIDA. Oh God, I'm going to run away, get away from here: I'm scared. [*She makes towards the door on the left*]

DI NOLLI [*holding her back*]. No, Frida.

LANDOLPH. My lord, this idiot . . . [*Pointing to* BERTHOLD]

BERTHOLD [*protesting*]. Ah no, thanks very much, my friends. I won't take it, not like that. I won't take it!

LANDOLPH. What do you mean, you won't take it?

HAROLD. He's ruined everything, my lord, by rushing off here.

LANDOLPH. He's driven him absolutely furious. We can't hold him back there. He's given orders for his arrest and he wants to 'deliver judgement' from the throne right now!—What can we do?

DI NOLLI. Close the door. Go and close that door. [LANDOLPH *goes to close the door*]

HAROLD. Ordulph won't be able to hold him back all on his own.

LANDOLPH. My lord, perhaps if we could announce your visit straightaway, it might at least distract him. If you ladies and gentlemen have already thought of what roles to assume . . .

DI NOLLI. Yes, yes, we've thought of everything. [*To the* DOCTOR] Doctor, if you think you could examine him right now . . .

FRIDA. Not me, not me, Carlo! I'm leaving. And you too, Mother, for heaven's sake, come away, come away with me.

DOCTOR. I say . . . he's not still armed, is he?

DI NOLLI. Armed, doctor? Of course not. [*To* FRIDA] Forgive me, Frida, but this fear of yours is really childish. It was you who wanted to come.

FRIDA. Oh no, it wasn't. It was Mother.

LADY MATILDA [*firmly*]. And I'm ready for it. So now what must we do?

BELCREDI. Now look, do we really have to dress up in some costume?

LANDOLPH. Indispensable. Indispensable, sir. Unfortunately, he sees us this way [*showing his costume*], and there'd be real trouble if he saw you gentlemen like that, in modern clothes.

HAROLD. He'd think it was some diabolical disguise.

DI NOLLI. Just as they seem disguised to you, so we would appear disguised to him, dressed in our normal clothes.

LANDOLPH. And maybe it wouldn't matter, my lord, if he didn't think it was all the doing of his mortal enemy.

BELCREDI. Pope Gregory VII?

LANDOLPH. Exactly. He says he was 'a pagan'.

BELCREDI. The Pope? Not bad!

LANDOLPH. Yessir. And that he conjures up the dead. He accuses him of all the diabolical arts. He's terribly frightened of him.

DOCTOR. Persecution mania.

HAROLD. He'd be furious.

DI NOLLI [*to* BELCREDI]. But you don't have to be there. We shall all go into the other room. It's enough for the doctor to see him.

DOCTOR. You mean . . . by myself?

DI NOLLI. But they'll be here. [*Indicating the three young men*]

DOCTOR. No, no . . . I mean, if the Marchesa . . .

LADY MATILDA. Oh yes, I want to be here as well. I want to be here. I want to see him again.

FRIDA. But why, Mother? I beg you. Come with us.

LADY MATILDA [*imperiously*]. Leave me alone! This is what I've come for. [*To* LANDOLPH] I shall be Adelaide, the mother.*

LANDOLPH. Right. Very good. The mother of Empress Bertha, splendid! It should be enough for your ladyship to wear a ducal coronet and a cloak that covers you completely. [*To* HAROLD] Off you go, Harold.

HAROLD. Wait. What about the gentleman? [*Indicating the* DOCTOR]

DOCTOR. Ah, yes . . . I think we said the bishop, Bishop Hugh of Cluny.

HAROLD. Would you be meaning the Abbot, sir? Very well, Hugh of Cluny.*

LANDOLPH. He's already been here so often.

DOCTOR [*puzzled*]. Been here already?

LANDOLPH. Don't worry. I mean that since it's such an easy disguise . . .

HAROLD. We've used it on other occasions.

DOCTOR. But . . .

LANDOLPH. There's no risk of him remembering. He looks more at the costume than at the person.

LADY MATILDA. That's good for me as well, then.

DI NOLLI. We'll leave them, Frida. Come on, Tito, come with us.

BELCREDI. Oh no. If she's staying [*indicating the* MARCHESA], I stay too.

LADY MATILDA. But I really don't need you.

BELCREDI. I'm not saying you need me. I'd like to see him again too. Isn't that allowed?

LANDOLPH. Well, after all, it might be better if there were three of you.

HAROLD. And so the gentleman?

BELCREDI. Just see if you can find some simple disguise for me as well.

LANDOLPH [*to* HAROLD]. Hold on, I've got it: a Cluniac.

BELCREDI. A Cluniac? Meaning what?

LANDOLPH. The habit of a Benedictine monk of the Abbey of Cluny. You'll be one of the Abbot's retinue. [*To* HAROLD] Off you go. Go! [*To* BERTHOLD] And you too, out! And stay out of sight for the rest of the day. [*But as soon as he sees them leaving*] Wait! [*To* BERTHOLD] You bring here the clothes that he gives you. [*To* HAROLD] And you go immediately to announce the arrival of 'the Duchess Adelaide' and 'Monsignor Hugh of Cluny'. Understood?

HAROLD *and* BERTHOLD *exit by the first door on the right.*

DI NOLLI. Then we'll withdraw. [*He exits with* FRIDA *by the door on the left*]

DOCTOR. Since I'm here as Hugh of Cluny, I should think he'll be glad to see me.

LANDOLPH. Very glad. Rest assured. Monsignor has always been received here with great respect. And you too, my lady, may rest assured. He always remembers that when he'd been waiting in the snow for two days, almost frozen to death, it was only thanks to the intercession of you two that he was finally admitted to the castle of Canossa and to the presence of Gregory VII who had refused to receive him.

BELCREDI. And what about me?

LANDOLPH. You stand respectfully to one side.

LADY MATILDA [*irritated, very nervous*]. You'd do well to clear off.

BELCREDI [*in a low voice, annoyed*]. You're very worked up.

LADY MATILDA [*haughtily*]. I'm the way I am. Leave me in peace!

BERTHOLD *returns with the costumes.*

LANDOLPH [*seeing him*]. Ah, here are the clothes. This cloak for my lady.

LADY MATILDA. Wait while I take off my hat. [*She does so and hands it to* BERTHOLD]

LANDOLPH. Take it into the other room. [*Then to the* MARCHESA *as he prepares to set the coronet on her head*] Allow me.

LADY MATILDA. For heaven's sake, don't we have a mirror here?

LANDOLPH. There are mirrors through there. [*Indicating door on the left*] If my lady would prefer to do it herself.

LADY MATILDA. Yes, yes, that would be better. Give it here. I'll do it right away.

She takes back her hat and goes out with BERTHOLD *who carries the cloak and the coronet. In the meantime the* DOCTOR *and* BELCREDI *are left to don their Benedictine habits as best they can.*

BELCREDI. Honestly, this dressing up as a Benedictine is something I would never have expected. But I say, this is a madness that costs a mint of money.

DOCTOR. Well, so do a lot of other madnesses, frankly . . .

BELCREDI. When you've got a fortune to back them up.

LANDOLPH. Yes, sir. We have an entire wardrobe back there, all period costumes, perfectly copied from models of the time. This is my special responsibility: I buy from very reliable theatrical suppliers. We spend a lot.

LADY MATILDA *returns decked in her cloak and coronet.*

BELCREDI [*at once, lost in admiration*]. Magnificent! Truly regal!

LADY MATILDA [*seeing* BELCREDI *and bursting into laughter*]. Good God! No. Get yourself out of here. You're impossible. You look like an ostrich dressed up as a monk.

BELCREDI. Well, look at the doctor.

DOCTOR. We shall just have to put up with it.

LADY MATILDA. No, no. The doctor's not so bad. But you! You really look ridiculous.

DOCTOR [*to* LANDOLPH]. So do you have many of these receptions here?

LANDOLPH. It all depends. Often he summons this or that character. And then we have to find someone who's ready to do it. Women too . . .

LADY MATILDA [*hurt, but trying to hide it*]. Ah, women too?

LANDOLPH. In the early days, yes . . . A lot.

BELCREDI [*laughing*]. Oh, that's nice! In costume? [*Indicating the* MARCHESA] Like that?

LANDOLPH. Well, you know, the sort of women who . . .

BELCREDI. Who do that sort of thing. I quite understand. [*Maliciously to the* MARCHESA] Watch out! This is getting risky for you.

The second right door opens and HAROLD *enters: after a discreet sign that all conversation in the room should cease, he solemnly proclaims:*

HAROLD. His Majesty the Emperor!

The TWO VALETS *enter and go to stand at the foot of the throne. Then* HENRY *enters between* ORDULPH *and* HAROLD *who remain a respectful distance behind. He is nearing fifty, very pale, and already grey at the back of his head; at temples and forehead, however, he seems blond, for his hair is dyed in a very obvious and almost childish way. No less obvious is the doll-like make-up imposed on the tragic pallor of his cheeks. Over his regal robes he wears penitential sackcloth, as at Canossa. His eyes are fixed in an agonizing stare that is frightening to see: this conflicts with a bearing which is intended to show humble penitence and which is all the more ostentatious because he feels that the humiliation is undeserved.* ORDULPH *holds the crown in both hands,* HAROLD *the sceptre with the eagle and the orb with the cross.*

HENRY IV [*bowing first to* LADY MATILDA, *then to the* DOCTOR]. My lady . . . Monsignor . . . [*He looks at* BELCREDI *and is about to bow, but then turns to* LANDOLPH *who has drawn near and asks in a suspicious whisper*] Is that Peter Damian?*

LANDOLPH. No, Your Majesty, he's a monk from Cluny who's here with the Abbot.

HENRY IV [*once again he examines* BELCREDI *with growing distrust; noticing how* BELCREDI *turns to* LADY MATILDA *and the* DOCTOR *with an irresolute and embarrassed look as if seeking advice, he straightens up and shouts*]. It *is* Peter Damian! No use looking at the Duchess, Father [*Suddenly turning to* LADY MATILDA *as if to ward off some danger*] I swear, I swear, my lady, that my feelings towards your daughter have changed. I confess that if he [*indicating* BELCREDI] had not come to forbid it in the name of Pope Alexander, I would have repudiated her. Yes, there was someone who was ready to support repudiation—the Bishop of Mainz,* in exchange for a hundred-and-twenty manors. [*He casts a bewildered sidelong glance at* LANDOLPH, *then says quickly*] But this is no time to speak ill of bishops. [*Humbly to* BELCREDI *again*] I'm grateful now, Peter Damian, believe me, very grateful that you prevented me. My whole life has been made of humiliations—my mother, Adalbert, Tribur,* Goslar—and now this sackcloth that you see me wearing. [*He suddenly changes tone and speaks like someone going over his part in a knowing aside*] No matter! Clear ideas, perspicacity, resolute bearing, patience in adversity! [*Then, turning to them all with contrite gravity*] I know how to correct the error of my ways: and before you too, Peter Damian, I humble myself. [*He bows deeply and remains bent before him, as if weighed down by some sudden obscure suspicion which now makes him add, almost against his will, in a menacing tone*] Unless it was you who started the obscene rumour that my sainted mother Agnes has an illicit relationship with Bishop Henry of Augsburg!

BELCREDI [*since* HENRY IV *remains bent over and pointing a threatening finger*, BELCREDI *puts his hand on his heart in denial*]. No, not me, no . . .

HENRY IV [*straightening up*]. No, is it true? An infamous slander! [*Fixes him for a moment, then says*] I don't believe you're capable of it. [*He approaches the* DOCTOR *and pulls his sleeve with a sly wink*] It's 'them'. Always the same crew, Monsignor.

HAROLD [*low and sighing, as if to prompt the* DOCTOR]. Ah yes, those rapacious bishops.

DOCTOR [*keeping up the act, turning to* HAROLD]. Them, ah, yes, of course . . . them . . .

HENRY IV. Nothing was enough for them!—Just a poor lad, Monsignor, playing all day long, the way a boy does, even if he's king without knowing it. Six years old* I was when they stole me from my mother and used me, all unsuspecting, against her and against the very powers of the Dynasty, profaning everything, robbing, robbing; one more greedy than the other: Anno worse than Stephen, Stephen worse than Anno!

LANDOLPH [*softly persuasive, bringing him back to the present*]. Your Majesty . . .

HENRY IV [*turning round*]. Ah yes, indeed! At a time like this I mustn't speak ill of bishops.—But this infamous slander about my mother, Monsignor, goes beyond all bounds! [*More tenderly, as he looks towards the* MARCHESA] And I can't even mourn her, my lady. I appeal to you; for surely you have a mother's heart. She came here from her convent to see me about a month ago. Now they tell me she's dead.* [*A long pregnant pause: then, with a wry smile*] I can't mourn her because if you're here and I'm like this [*showing his sackcloth*], it means that I'm twenty-six years old.

HAROLD [*in a low comforting whisper*]. And that, therefore, she's alive, Your Majesty.

ORDULPH [*as above*]. Still in her convent.

HENRY IV [*turning to look at them*]. Of course, and so I can put off my grief until some other time. [*Showing the* MARCHESA *his dyed hair with a touch of coquetry*] Look, still fair . . . [*Then softly confidential*] I did it for you. I wouldn't need it myself. But some external sign comes in useful. Age limits, if you see what I mean, Monsignor? [*Returning to the* MARCHESA *and examining her hair*] Ah, but I see . . . you too, Duchess . . . [*With a wink and an expressive gesture*] Now that's Italian . . . [*as if to say 'false', but without a shadow of contempt, more like malicious admiration*] God forbid that I should seem disgusted or surprised! What hopeless longings! Nobody wants to recognize the dark and fatal power that puts limits to our will. But there they are, since we're born and we die.—To be born, Monsignor: did you want to be born? I didn't. And between one event and the other, both independent of our will, so many things happen that we all wish didn't happen; and we only resign ourselves to them with great reluctance.

DOCTOR [*just to say something while he studies him attentively*]. All too true!

HENRY IV. Just so. When we can't resign ourselves, out come the hopeless longings. A woman who wants to be a man, an old man who wants to be young. None of us is lying or pretending—That's just the way it is: in all good faith, the lot of us, we've adopted some fine fixed idea of ourselves. And yet, Monsignor, while you stand fast, holding on to your sacred vestments with both hands, here, out of your sleeves something comes slipping and slithering away like a snake without you noticing. Life, Monsignor! And it comes as a surprise when you see it suddenly take shape before you, escaping like that. There's anger and spite against yourself; or remorse, remorse as well. Ah, if only you knew how much remorse I have found in my way—with a face that was mine, and yet so horrible that I could not bear to look on it . . . [*Going back to the* MARCHESA] Has it never happened to you, my lady? You really remember being always the same, do you? Oh God, but one day— how could you? how could you do such a thing? [*He looks at her so intensely that she turns pale*]—yes, 'that thing'—we understand each other (Oh, rest assured, I won't tell anyone). And that you, Peter Damian, could be a friend of someone like . . .

LANDOLPH [*as above*]. Your Majesty . . .

HENRY IV [*promptly*]. No, no, I won't name him! I know how much it upsets him. [*Turning to* BELCREDI, *as if in passing*] What did you think, eh? What did you think of him? . . . And yet, in spite of everything, we all still stick to our idea of ourselves, just as some-one who's growing old dyes his hair. What does it matter that you know this tint isn't the real colour of my hair? You, my lady, surely don't dye your hair to deceive others, or yourself; but only to deceive a little—a very little—your image in the mirror. I do it for a laugh, you do it in earnest. But I assure you, however much in earnest you are, you too are still wearing a mask, my lady; and I don't mean the venerable coronet that adorns your brow and before which I bow, or your ducal mantle either. I only mean that memory you now seek to fix by artificial means, the memory of the blond hair that once pleased you so much—or the dark hair if you were dark—the fading image of your youth. For you, however, Peter Damian, the memory of what you have been and what you have done now seems like a recognition of past realities that remain within you—isn't that so?—like a dream. For me too—like a dream—and so many of them, as I look back, inexplicable. Well, nothing surprising in that, Peter Damian; that's what our life today will become tomorrow. [*All of a sudden he flies into a rage and grasps his sackcloth*] This sackcloth here! [*With a fierce joy he starts to tear it off, while* HAROLD, LANDOLPH, *and* ORDULPH, *alarmed, hurry to restrain him*] Ah, by God! [*Backing away, he takes off the sackcloth and shouts*] Tomorrow, at Brixen,* twenty-seven German and Lombard bishops will sign with me the destitution of Pope Gregory VII—no Pontiff, but a false monk!

ORDULPH [*with the other two, begging him to be quiet*]. Your Majesty, Your Majesty, in God's name!

HAROLD [*signalling that he should put the sackcloth back on*]. Be careful what you say.

LANDOLPH. Monsignor is here, and the Duchess too, to intercede on your behalf. [*He makes discreet and urgent signs to the* DOCTOR *that he should say something without delay*]

DOCTOR [*confused*]. Er, well . . . yes . . . We're here to intercede . . .

HENRY IV [*repenting immediately, almost frightened, letting the three of them put the sackcloth back on his shoulders, and clutching it to himself with nervous hands*]. Forgive me, yes, yes, forgive me, Monsignor; forgive me, my lady . . . I feel it, I swear that I feel it, all the weight of the anathema. [*He bends forward with his head in his hands, as if expecting something to come and crush him; he remains so for a while and then, with altered voice but not changing his posture, says to* HAROLD *and* ORDULPH *in a confidential whisper*] I don't know why it is, but today I can't manage to be humble before that fellow there. [*With a stealthy gesture towards* BELCREDI]

LANDOLPH [*softly*]. But that's because Your Majesty insists on believing that he's Peter Damian, and he's not.

HENRY IV [*with a fearful sidelong glance*]. Not Peter Damian?

HAROLD. No, Your Majesty, just a poor monk.

HENRY IV [*sadly, sighing with exasperation*]. Well, none of us can judge what we're doing when we act on instinct . . . Perhaps you, my lady, can understand me better than the rest because you're a woman. [This is a solemn and decisive moment. Now, you see, in this very moment as I speak to you, I could accept the help of the Lombard bishops and have the Pope in my power, besieging him here in this castle; and then I could hurry to Rome and elect an anti-pope; offer an alliance to Robert Guiscard.* Gregory VII would be lost! I resist the temptation, and, believe me, I'm wise to do so. I feel the spirit of the age and the majesty of a man who knows how to be what he must be: a Pope! Perhaps you feel like laughing at me now, seeing me like this? But you'd be fools, because you would not have understood the political wisdom that leads me to wear this sackcloth. I tell you that tomorrow the roles could be reversed. And then what would you do? Would you, by any chance, laugh at the Pope in prison garb? No. We would be even.—Me today, masked as a penitent; him tomorrow, masked as a prisoner. But woe betide the man who knows not how to wear his mask, whether as King or Pope.—This time, perhaps he is a shade too cruel: yes, that he is.]* Think, my lady, about your daughter Bertha, towards whom, I repeat, my heart has changed [*turning suddenly to* BELCREDI *and shouting in his face as if he had been contradicted*], changed, yes, changed—because of the love and devotion she has shown me in this terrible moment! [*He stops, shaken by the angry outburst, and makes an effort to control himself with an exasperated groan; then he turns again to the* MARCHESA, *humbly sorrowful and sweet*] She has come here with me, my lady; she is down there in the courtyard; she chose to follow me like a beggarwoman; and now she is cold, freezing cold, from two nights out in the open, out in the snow. You are her mother. In the bowels of mercy you should be moved to go with him [*indicating the* DOCTOR] to implore the pardon of the Pope—and that he grant us audience!

LADY MATILDA [*trembling, in a whisper*]. Of course, of course, immediately . . .

DOCTOR. We'll do it, yes, we'll do it.

HENRY IV. And another thing. One more thing. [*He calls them around him and whispers secretively*] Granting an audience won't be enough. You know that he can do anything—anything, I say. He even conjures up the dead. [*Beating his breast*] Here I am! You see me!—And there's no magic art that he doesn't know. Well, Monsignor and my lady, my real punishment is this—or *that*—look at it [*pointing, as if in fear, to his portrait on the wall*], the fact that I can never free myself from that magic work.—Now I am penitent and I shall remain so; I swear that I shall remain penitent until he receives me. But then, once he has lifted my excommunication, you two must beg him—for only he can do it—to set me free from *that* [*again indicating the portrait*] so that I can live it all out, the whole of this poor life of mine, from which I am cut off . . . One can't be twenty-six for ever, my lady. And I ask you this for your daughter's sake as well, so that I can love her as she deserves, well disposed as I now am, moved as I am by her compassion. There. That's all. I am in your hands. [*Bowing*] My lady, Monsignor.

He is about to bow his way out through the door by which he entered when he suddenly notices that BELCREDI, *who has drawn near to hear him, has turned his head to look upstage. Thinking that* BELCREDI *wants to steal the imperial crown which has been placed on the throne,* HENRY *runs back, seizes it, and hides it under his sackcloth amid general surprise and dismay. Then, with his eyes and mouth set in a cunning smile, he resumes his incessant bowing and disappears. The* MARCHESA *is so overcome that she collapses fainting onto a chair.*

Curtain.

ACT TWO

Another room in the villa, adjoining the throne room. Severe antique furniture. On the right, raised about a foot above the floor, there is a kind of platform with a wooden railing around it on little pillars. Steps lead up to it at the front. On this platform there is a table with five period chairs, one at the head and two on either side. The main entrance is at the back of the stage. To the left two windows look out onto the garden; to the right a door leads to the throne room. Late afternoon of the same day.

LADY MATILDA, *the* DOCTOR, *and* TITO BELCREDI *are already in conversation.* LADY MATILDA *is gloomily aloof, clearly annoyed by what the others are saying; but she cannot help listening because in her present restless state everything interests her in spite of herself, preventing her from grasping and developing an irresistible idea which has flashed temptingly across her mind. Her attention is attracted by the words of the others because in that moment she feels instinctively that she needs to be restrained.*

BELCREDI. It may be as you say, dear doctor, but that's my impression.

DOCTOR. I'm not saying you're wrong; but believe me when I say that it's only an impression.

BELCREDI. Come on: he even said so, and clearly. (*Turning to the* MARCHESA) Isn't that so, Marchesa?

LADY MATILDA [*distractedly, turning round*]. Said what? [*Then, disagreeing*] Oh yes . . . But not for the reason you think.

DOCTOR. He meant the clothes we put on: your cloak [*referring to* LADY MATILDA], our Benedictine habits. And all this is childish.

LADY MATILDA [*abruptly, turning again, indignant*]. Childish? What do you mean, doctor?

DOCTOR. On the one hand, yes, childish. Just let me finish, Marchesa. But on the other hand far more complex than you can imagine.

LADY MATILDA. On the contrary, for me it's perfectly clear.

DOCTOR [*with the indulgent smile that a specialist bestows on the uninformed*]. Ah yes. You need to understand the special psychology of the mad. You can be sure, for example, that a madman is perfectly capable of recognizing a disguise when he sees it; and he accepts it as such. And yet, my good friends, he can still believe in it, like a child for whom it's both play and reality. That's why I called it childish. But then it's complicated in this sense, see: that he is and must be completely aware of being an image in and to himself— that image of himself in there! [*Pointing to the left and referring to the portrait in the throne room*]

BELCREDI. That's what he said.

DOCTOR. Right, fine!—An image that has been faced by other images—our own, if you follow me. Now in his delirium, but sharp-witted and clear-headed, he immediately noticed a difference between his image and our images—that in us, in our images, there was something fictive. And he became suspicious. All madmen are armed with a constant and vigilant distrust. But that's all there was to it. Naturally, he couldn't see that our game, in response to his, was being played out of pity for him. And his game seemed to us all the more tragic in that he wanted to reveal it precisely as a game—as a kind of challenge, coming from his distrust, if you take my meaning. Yes, his too, presenting himself with the dye on his temples and a spot of rouge on his cheeks, and telling us he'd done it deliberately for a laugh.

LADY MATILDA [*breaking out again*]. No, that's not it, doctor, that's simply not it!

DOCTOR. And why isn't that it?

LADY MATILDA [*firm and vibrant*]. Because I'm absolutely sure that he recognized me.

DOCTOR. Impossible, quite impossible.

BELCREDI [*at the same time*]. Come off it!

LADY MATILDA [*even more decisive, trembling with emotion*]. He recognized me, I tell you. When he came up close to speak to me and looked me in the eyes, straight in the eyes—he recognized me.

BELCREDI. But he was talking about your daughter . . .

LADY MATILDA. Not true. About me. He was talking about me.

BELCREDI. Yes, perhaps, when he mentioned . . .

LADY MATILDA [*at once, unashamed*]. My dyed hair! Didn't you notice that he immediately added 'or the dark hair if you were dark'? He remembered perfectly well that I was dark-haired at the time.

BELCREDI. Don't you believe it!

LADY MATILDA [*ignoring him and turning to the* DOCTOR]. In fact, doctor, my hair is dark—just like my daughter's. And that's why he started to talk about her.

BELCREDI. But he doesn't know your daughter. Never even seen her.

LADY MATILDA. Exactly. You don't understand a thing. When he talked about my daughter he meant me; me as I was back then.

BELCREDI. This madness is catching! It must be catching!

LADY MATILDA [*in a low scornful voice*]. You and your 'catching'! Idiot!

BELCREDI. Hold on. Have you ever been his wife? In his madness, it's your daughter who's his wife, Bertha of Susa.

LADY MATILDA. Exactly! Because I appeared before him—not dark, as he remembers me, but like this, fair, presenting myself as 'Adelaide', the mother. My daughter doesn't exist for him—he's never laid eyes on her, you said so yourself. So how can he know whether she's dark or fair?

BELCREDI. But he said dark-haired in a general kind of way, for God's sake, meaning that a man might want to fix the memory of his youth in the colour of a woman's hair, whether it's dark or fair. And you're letting your imagination run riot as usual. Doctor, she says I shouldn't have come here, but she's the one who shouldn't have come.

LADY MATILDA [*cast down for a moment by* BELCREDI's *remarks and lost in thought, she now recovers; but her tone is desperate with doubt*]. No . . . no . . . he was talking about me . . . speaking to me all the time, with me, about me . . .

BELCREDI. Lord have mercy! He didn't give me a moment to catch my breath and you say he was talking about you all the time? Unless you think he was talking about you even when he was speaking with Peter Damian.

LADY MATILDA [*with a defiant air, as if unrestrained by decorum*]. And who's to say that he wasn't? Can you tell me why, right from the start, from the very first moment, he took such a dislike to you, and only you?

The tone of the question invites the more or less explicit reply: 'Because he understood that you're my lover.' BELCREDI *grasps this so well that for the moment he just stands there as if lost, with a vacuous smile.*

DOCTOR. But, if I may, it could also be because the only visitors announced were the Duchess Adelaide and the Abbot of Cluny. When he was faced by a third visitor, who had not been announced, then the mistrust . . .

BELCREDI. That's it, exactly, the mistrust made him see me as his enemy Peter Damian—But since she keeps insisting that he recognized her . . .

LADY MATILDA. There's no doubt about it. He eyes told me as much, doctor: you know, when someone looks at you in a way that . . . that leaves no room for doubt. Maybe it was just a moment, what can I say?

DOCTOR. A lucid moment can't be excluded.

LADY MATILDA. Maybe that's it. And then I felt that everything he said was so full of regret for my youth and his, for this horrible thing that happened to him and locked him up there, in the mask he has never been able to escape, and which he longs, longs so much to escape!

BELCREDI. Of course! So that he can start making love to your daughter. Or to you, as you seem to think—moved to it by your compassion.

LADY MATILDA. Which is very great, I can assure you.

BELCREDI. That's obvious, Marchesa. So obvious that a miracle-worker would think it was probably a miracle.

DOCTOR. Do you mind if I speak now? I don't perform miracles, because I'm a doctor, not a miracle-worker. I listened very carefully to everything he said, and I repeat that in him that element of ana-logical elasticity which is typical of all systematized delirium is clearly already . . . how can I put it? . . . considerably slackened. In short, the various aspects of his delirium are no longer mutually supportive. Now, I think, he's reached a stage where he finds it very difficult to achieve a balance in this superimposed personality of his, because sudden recollections jerk him out—and this is very encour-aging—not from a state of incipient apathy, but rather from morbid relaxation into a state of reflexive melancholy, which indicates . . . yes, truly considerable cerebral activity. Very encouraging, I repeat. Now then, if by this violent trick we've agreed on . . .

LADY MATILDA [*turning to the window, in a querulous tone*]. Why hasn't the car come back yet? Three and a half hours . . .

DOCTOR [*taken aback*]. What's that?

LADY MATILDA. That car, doctor. It's more than three and a half hours!

DOCTOR [*fishing out his watch*]. Eh, more than four by this.

LADY MATILDA. It could have been here half an hour ago, at least. But as usual . . .

BELCREDI. Perhaps they can't find the gown.

LADY MATILDA. But I told them exactly where it is. [*Highly impatient*] And what about Frida? Where's Frida?

BELCREDI [*leaning slightly out of the window*]. Maybe she's in the garden with Carlo.

DOCTOR. He'll be persuading her to overcome her fear.

BELCREDI. But it's not fear, doctor, don't you believe it! She's just fed up with all this.

LADY MATILDA. Do me a favour and don't even try to convince her. I know how she is.

DOCTOR. We'll have to be patient and wait. In any case, it will all be over in a moment and it has to be at night. If we succeed in shaking him up, I was saying, if, with this sudden wrench, we can suddenly break the already loosened threads that still bind him to his fiction, giving him what he himself requests (he said 'One can't be twenty-six for ever, my lady'), I mean freedom from this sentence, from what he himself considers a sentence—In short, if we succeed in suddenly giving him a sense of the distance in time . . .

BELCREDI [*cutting in*]. He'll be cured! [*Then, with ironic stress on every syllable*] We'll pull him out of it!

DOCTOR. We can hope to restart him, like a watch that has stopped at a certain hour. Yes, almost as if, with our watches in our hands, we were waiting for that hour to come round again—and then, give it a shake—and let's hope that it starts marking the time again after being stopped for so long.

> At this point the MARCHESE CARLO DI NOLLI *comes in through the main entrance.*

LADY MATILDA. Ah, Carlo . . . And Frida? Where's Frida gone?

DI NOLLI. She's coming, she'll be here in a moment.

DOCTOR. Has the car arrived?

DI NOLLI. Yes.

LADY MATILDA. Ah yes, and with the gown?

DI NOLLI. It's been here quite some time.

DOCTOR. Excellent!

LADY MATILDA [*trembling*]. Where is it? Where is it?

DI NOLLI [*shrugging his shoulders with a sad smile, as if lending himself reluctantly to a joke in bad taste*]. Well . . . Now you'll see. [*Indicating the main entrance*] Here she is . . .

　　Berthold appears on the threshold and solemnly announces:

BERTHOLD. Her Highness the Countess Matilda of Canossa.

FRIDA *enters immediately, stately and beautiful, dressed in her mother's original gown as 'Countess Matilda of Tuscany', so that she seems to be the living image of the figure represented in the throne-room portrait.*

FRIDA [*with haughty disdain to* BERTHOLD *who bows as she passes by*]. Of Tuscany, of Tuscany, please. Canossa is one of my castles.

BELCREDI [*admiring*]. Look at her! Just look at her! She seems another woman.

LADY MATILDA. She seems *me*.—Heavens above, do you see that?—Stop there, Frida—You see? She's my portrait come to life.

DOCTOR. Yes, yes . . . Perfect. Perfect. The portrait.

BELCREDI. Yes, indeed. There's no question. She's really it. Just look at her. What class!

FRIDA. Don't make me laugh or I shall burst. I say, Mother, what a tiny waist you had! I had to hold my breath to get into it.

LADY MATILDA [*nervously adjusting the gown*]. Hold on . . . Stand still . . . These creases . . . Is it really so tight on you?

FRIDA. I can hardly breathe! Let's get it over quickly, for heaven's sake.

DOCTOR. But we have to wait until tonight . . .

FRIDA. Oh no, I can't hold out that long, not until tonight.

LADY MATILDA. So why did you have to put it on so early?

FRIDA. As soon as I saw it. Sheer temptation. Irresistible.

LADY MATILDA. You could at least have called me. Let me help you . . . Good Lord, it's still all creased.

FRIDA. So I've seen, Mother. But old creases . . . It won't be easy to get them out.

DOCTOR. It doesn't matter, Marchesa. The illusion's perfect. [*Then drawing closer to* LADY MATILDA *and motioning her to stand slightly in front of her daughter but without hiding her*] If you don't mind. You stand like this—here—at a certain distance—a bit further forward . . .

BELCREDI. To suggest the distance in time.

LADY MATILDA [*hardly turning to him*]. Twenty years later! A disaster, don't you think?

BELCREDI. Let's not exaggerate.

DOCTOR [*embarrassed and trying to put things right*]. No, no! I was saying that . . . I meant for the gown . . . just to see . . .

BELCREDI [*laughing*]. But for the gown, doctor, it's not twenty years; it's more like eight hundred. An abyss! Do you really want to shove him into jumping over it? [*Indicating first* FRIDA *and then the* MARCHESA] From there to here? You'll be collecting bits and pieces of him in a basket! Think about it, my friends; I really mean it: for us it's a matter of twenty years, two costumes and a pageant. But for him, as you say, doctor, time has stopped; if he's living back there with her [*indicating* FRIDA] eight hundred years ago; then I say that the dizziness of that jump will be so great that when he falls into our midst . . . [*The* DOCTOR *wags his finger in disagreement*] You don't think so?

DOCTOR. No, because life, my dear baron, starts all over again. Our life, here, will immediately become real for him too; and it will take hold of him right away, wrenching him out of the illusion and showing him that those eight hundred years of yours are only twenty. Look, it will be like one of those old tricks; for example the leap into the void in the Masonic rites, where you think it's heaven knows what and in the end you've only gone down one step.

BELCREDI. Now there's a discovery! But look at Frida and the Marchesa, doctor. Who is further ahead? We old folks, doctor. Yes, the young may think they're ahead, but it's not true: we're further ahead insofar as time is more ours than theirs.

DOCTOR. If only the past didn't take us further away.

BELCREDI. Not in the least! Further away from what? [*He gestures towards* FRIDA *and* DI NOLLI] If they still have to do what we've already done, doctor: grow old, repeating more or less the same silly old antics . . . This is the illusion: that we leave this life by a door that lies ahead of us. It's not true. If you start dying as soon as you're born, the one who started first is the furthest ahead. And the youngest of all is Old Father Adam. Look there [*showing* FRIDA], eight hundred years younger than the rest of us, Countess Matilda of Tuscany. [*He bows deeply to her*]

DI NOLLI. Please, Tito, let's not make a joke of it.

BELCREDI. If you think I'm joking . . .

DI NOLLI. Of course you are, God knows . . . ever since you came.

BELCREDI. What! I even dressed up as a Benedictine.

DI NOLLI. Exactly. To do something serious.

BELCREDI. Well, what I say is, if it's been serious for the others . . . for Frida now, for example . . . [*Then, turning to the* DOCTOR] I swear to you, doctor, that I still don't understand what you're trying to do.

DOCTOR [*annoyed*]. You'll see. Leave it to me . . . Of course, when you see the Marchesa still dressed like this . . .

BELCREDI. You mean that she too will have to . . .

DOCTOR. Absolutely, with another gown from in there, for the times when he believes he's with the Countess Matilda of Canossa.

FRIDA [*who is talking quietly with* DI NOLLI, *noticing the* DOCTOR'*s mistake*]. Tuscany! Of Tuscany!

DOCTOR [*as above*]. It's all the same.

BELCREDI. Ah, I understand. He'll find himself in front of two . . . ?

DOCTOR. Two of them, precisely. And then . . .

FRIDA [*calling him aside*]. Come here, doctor, listen!

DOCTOR. Here I am. [*He goes up to the young couple and pretends to explain something*]

BELCREDI [*quietly, to* LADY MATILDA]. For God's sake. So you are going to . . .

LADY MATILDA [*turning to him with a firm look*]. What?

BELCREDI. Does it really interest you so much? So much that you'll lend yourself to this. It's an extraordinary thing for a woman.

LADY MATILDA. For an ordinary woman.

BELCREDI. No, my dear, for any woman in this case. It's an act of self-denial.

LADY MATILDA. I owe it to him.

BELCREDI. Don't lie to me. You know it won't harm your reputation.

LADY MATILDA. So where does the self-denial come in?

BELCREDI. There's not quite enough in it to shame you in the eyes of others, but there's enough to offend me.

LADY MATILDA. Who cares about you at a time like this!

DI NOLLI [*coming forward*]. Here. So then, yes, yes, we'll do it that way . . . [*Turning to* BERTHOLD] Oh, you, go and call one of those three in there.

BERTHOLD. Right away. [*He leaves by the main door*]

LADY MATILDA. But first we have to pretend to take our leave.

DI NOLLI. Exactly. I'm calling him so that he can arrange for your leavetaking. [*To* BELCREDI] You needn't bother with it. Stay here.

BELCREDI [*nodding his head ironically*]. Right. I won't bother with it, I won't bother.

DI NOLLI. Partly so as not to make him suspicious again, you understand?

BELCREDI. Of course! *Quantité négligeable!**

DOCTOR. We must make him certain, absolutely certain that we've left.

LANDOLPH *enters through the right door, followed by* BERTHOLD.

LANDOLPH. May I?

DI NOLLI. Come in, come in. Right now . . . You're Lolo, aren't you?

LANDOLPH. Lolo or Landolph, as you wish.

DI NOLLI. Good. Look. The doctor and the Marchesa will now take their leave.

LANDOLPH. Very good. It should suffice to say that they have persuaded the Pope to grant him an audience. He's there in his rooms, groaning with repentance for everything he said and losing all hope of being pardoned. If you would come this way . . . and if you don't mind putting the costumes back on.

DOCTOR. Yes, yes, let's go.

LANDOLPH. Just a moment. May I suggest something? You should add that the Countess Matilda of Tuscany joined you in imploring the Pope to grant him an audience.

LADY MATILDA. There! You see that he recognized me.

LANDOLPH. No. Forgive me. It's that he's so afraid of the hostility of this Countess who received the Pope in her castle. It's strange. In history, as far as I know—but you ladies and gentlemen must know better than I—it's not said, is it, that Henry IV was secretly in love with the Countess of Tuscany?

LADY MATILDA [*hastily*]. No, not in the least. Quite the contrary.

LANDOLPH. That's what I thought. But he says he loved her—he keeps saying so. And now he's afraid that her scorn for this secret love will work against him with the Pope.

BELCREDI. You must convince him that this hostility no longer exists.

LANDOLPH. Right. Excellent!

LADY MATILDA [*to* LANDOLPH]. Excellent, indeed! [*Then, to* BELCREDI] Because in fact, in case you don't know, history says precisely that the Pope gave in to the pleading of the Countess Matilda and the Abbot of Cluny. And I can tell you, my dear Belcredi, that back then, when we had the cavalcade, I intended to use the occasion to show that my mind was no longer so firmly set against him, as he imagined.

BELCREDI. Well, that's wonderful, dear Marchesa. Just keep on following history.

LANDOLPH. Well, in that case, obviously, the Marchesa could save herself the bother of a double disguise and present herself with Monsignor [*indicating the* DOCTOR] as the Countess of Tuscany.

DOCTOR [*at once, with force*]. Oh no. Not that, for heaven's sake! It would ruin everything. The effect of the confrontation must be immediate, sudden. No, no. Let's go, Marchesa, let's go. You will appear once again as the Duchess Adelaide, mother of the Empress. And we shall take our leave. And one thing is absolutely necessary: that he should know we have left. Come on, let's not waste any more time, we still have so much to get ready.

The DOCTOR, LADY MATILDA, *and* LANDOLPH *go out by the right door.*

FRIDA. I'm beginning to get scared again.

DI NOLLI. All over again, Frida?

FRIDA. It would be better if I'd seen him first.

DI NOLLI. Believe me, there's nothing to worry about.

FRIDA. But isn't he raving mad?

DI NOLLI. Not at all. He's perfectly calm.

BELCREDI [*with ironic sentimental affectation*]. Melancholic. Didn't you hear that he loves you?

FRIDA. Thanks a lot. That's the problem!

BELCREDI. He won't want to harm you.

DI NOLLI. It will all be over in a moment.

FRIDA. All right. But there in the dark, with him . . .

DI NOLLI. Only for a moment, and I'll be next to you, and the others will be waiting behind those doors, ready to rush in. As soon as he sees your mother before him, your part will be over.

BELCREDI. What I'm afraid of is something else: that the whole thing will be a flop.

DI NOLLI. Don't start. I think it could be a very effective cure.

FRIDA. So do I, so do I . . . I can already feel it . . . I'm trembling all over.

BELCREDI. But madmen, my dear friends—though unfortunately they don't know it—madmen have a kind of happiness that we don't realize.

DI NOLLI [*interrupting him, annoyed*]. So now it's happiness! Do me a favour!

BELCREDI [*vehemently*]. They don't reason.

DI NOLLI. Sorry, but what's reasoning got to do with it?

BELCREDI. What! Don't you think that, if we're right, there's a lot of reasoning he'll have to do when he sees her [*indicating* FRIDA] and her mother? But we're the ones who've set this whole thing up!

DI NOLLI. No, not in the least. There's no reasoning involved.

We present him with a double image of his own fiction, as the doctor said.

BELCREDI [*with a sudden reaction*]. Listen: I've never understood why they take degrees in medicine.

DI NOLLI [*puzzled*]. Who?

BELCREDI. Psychiatrists.

DI NOLLI. So what on earth do you want them to take degrees in?

FRIDA. If they're going to be psychiatrists.

BELCREDI. In law, of course, my dear. Because it's all talk! And the best talker is the best psychiatrist. 'Analogical elasticity', 'a sense of the distance in time'! And then the first thing they say is that they don't work miracles—just when a miracle is what's needed. But they know that the more they say they're not miracle-workers the more people take them seriously. They don't work miracles, and yet by some miracle they always fall on their feet.

BERTHOLD [*who has gone to peep through the keyhole of the door to the right*]. Here they are! Here they are! They're coming this way.

DI NOLLI. Are they?

BERTHOLD. It looks as if he's going to come with them . . . Yes, yes, here he is!

DI NOLLI. Then we should get out of the way. Right now. [*Turning to* BERTHOLD] You stay here.

BERTHOLD. Must I stay?

Without answering him, DI NOLLI, FRIDA, *and* BELCREDI *escape through the main door, leaving* BERTHOLD *uncertain and bewildered. The right door opens and* LANDOLPH *enters first, bowing immediately as he is followed by* LADY MATILDA, *wearing the same gown and ducal coronet as in Act One, and the* DOCTOR *in the habit of the Abbot of Cluny. Between them, in his regal robes, is* HENRY IV. *Last come* ORDULPH *and* HAROLD.

HENRY IV [*continuing a speech presumably begun in the throne room*]. And I ask you, how can I be cunning if you think I'm being stubborn?

DOCTOR. No, not stubborn, surely not.

HENRY IV [*with a satisfied smile*]. So you think I really am cunning?

DOCTOR. No. Neither stubborn nor cunning.

HENRY IV [*stopping and protesting; like someone pointing out, benevolently yet also ironically, that something does not make sense*]. Monsignor! If stubbornness is a vice that cannot coexist with cunning, I had hoped that in denying me one, you would grant me at least a little of the other. I can assure you that I am in great need of some cunning. But if you want to keep it all for yourself . . .

DOCTOR. What? Me? Do I strike you as cunning?

HENRY IV. No, Monsignor. What a question! Far from it. [*Breaking off in order to speak to* LADY MATILDA] If you don't mind, just a word in private to my lady the Duchess. [*He leads her aside and asks her in an anxious and highly secretive way*] Is your daughter truly dear to you?

LADY MATILDA [*perplexed*]. Yes, of course.

HENRY IV. And you want me to give her all my love, all my devotion, to make up for the grave wrongs I've done her? Though you mustn't believe in the debauchery that my friends accuse me of.

LADY MATILDA. No, I don't believe it. I've never believed it.

HENRY IV. So you do want it?

LADY MATILDA [*still perplexed*]. Want what?

HENRY IV. Want me to start loving your daughter again. [*He looks at her and quickly adds in a mysterious warning tone*] Don't make friends with her, don't make friends with the Countess of Tuscany.

LADY MATILDA. But I tell you again that she begged and beseeched to obtain that pardon for you, no less than we did.

HENRY IV [*in a rapid, trembling whisper*]. Don't tell me. Don't tell me that. By heavens, my lady, can't you see how it affects me?

LADY MATILDA [*looks at him, then in a low intimate tone*]. Do you still love her?

HENRY IV [*dismayed*]. Still? You say 'still'? So perhaps you know? Nobody knows. Nobody must know.

LADY MATILDA. But maybe she does, yes, maybe she knows, since she pleaded for you with such fervour.

HENRY IV [*looks at her for a moment and then says*]. And do you love your daughter? [*A brief pause before he addresses the* DOCTOR *in a jocular tone*] Ah, Monsignor, this wife of mine—it was late, too late, before I knew I had a wife. And even now, yes, I know I have her; there's no doubt that I have her—but I could swear to you that I hardly ever think of her. It may be a sin, but I simply don't feel her in my heart. What's strange, however, is that even her mother doesn't feel her in her heart. Confess, my lady, that you care very little about her. [*Turning to the* DOCTOR, *exasperated*] She keeps speaking to me about the other one [*increasingly agitated*] with an insistence that I simply can't explain.

LANDOLPH [*humbly*]. Perhaps, Majesty, to correct a negative opinion that you may have formed in regard to the Countess of Tuscany. [*Fearful because he has allowed himself this comment, he quickly adds*] Of course, I mean now, at this time . . .

HENRY IV. Because you too maintain that she has taken my part?

LANDOLPH. Yes, at this specific time, yes, Your Majesty.

LADY MATILDA. There, that's exactly why . . .

HENRY IV. I understand. It means you don't believe that I love her. I understand. I understand. Nobody has ever believed it, or even suspected it. So much the better! Enough. Enough. [*He breaks off and turns to the* DOCTOR *with an entirely different manner and expression*] Monsignor, do you realize? The conditions the Pope has attached to the lifting of my excommunication have absolutely nothing to do with the reason why he excommunicated me in the first place. Tell Pope Gregory that we shall meet again at Brixen. And you, my lady, if by any chance you meet your daughter down in the courtyard of this castle, the castle of your friend the Countess—what can I say? Have her come up, we shall see if I manage to hold her close by my side as wife and Empress. Many women have come here, assuring me, claiming to be her—and I, knowing she's mine—yes, sometimes I even tried—(Nothing shameful in that: it's with my wife, after all!)—Now I don't know why it is, but all of them started to laugh as soon as they told me they were Bertha and from Susa. [*Confidentially*] You know what I mean—in bed; me without this robe, and her too, yes, for God's sake, naked, just a man and a woman, it's natural! You don't think anymore about who you are. The cast-off robe hangs there like a ghost! [*Still confidentially to the* DOCTOR, *but in a changed tone*] And I think, Monsignor, that in general ghosts are basically nothing more than small disturbances of the spirit, images that we fail to confine to the realm of dreams: they show themselves also when we're awake, in daytime, and they frighten us. I'm always so afraid at night when I see them before my eyes—so many disordered images, dismounted from their horses and laughing. Sometimes I'm even afraid of my own blood pulsing in my veins like the dull thud of steps in distant rooms during the silence of the night . . . Enough! I've kept you standing here too long. Ever your servant, my lady; my respects, Monsignor.

He accompanies them to the threshold of the main door where he takes leave of them as they bow in return. LADY MATILDA *and the* DOCTOR *go out. He closes the door behind them and then turns, suddenly changed.*

HENRY IV. Clowns! Clowns! Clowns! A whole keyboard of colours. As soon as I played her, white, red, yellow, green . . . And that other one there, Peter Damian. Ah, I got him all right. Perfect. He was too scared to show himself again.

He says this in a sudden frenzy of joy, pacing to and fro, his glance darting here and there, until it suddenly falls on BERTHOLD, *who is more terrified than stunned by the sudden change.* HENRY IV *stops in front of him and points him out to his three companions who also seem lost and astounded.*

HENRY IV. Now look at this idiot here who's standing and staring at me with his mouth open. [*He shakes him by the shoulders*] Don't you understand? Don't you see how I dress them up, how I set them up, how I make them come before me like a bunch of frightened clowns. And they're only scared of one thing: that I'll tear off their silly masks and show that they're all in disguise. As if it weren't me who had forced them to wear masks in the first place, to satisfy my taste for playing the madman!

LANDOLPH, HAROLD, ORDULPH [*confused, in shock, looking at each other*]. What! What's he saying? Does it mean that . . . ?

HENRY IV [*at these exclamations, turns suddenly with an imperious shout*]. Enough! Let's have done with it! I'm fed up! [*Then suddenly, as if, on second thoughts, he cannot let go or believe what he has seen*] By God, what insolence to come here, to me, now—along with her fancyman. And behaving as if they were doing it out of pity, so as not to madden a poor devil already out of the world, out

of time, out of life! Because otherwise just imagine whether the
poor devil would put up with that kind of persecution. They go on,
yes, every day, every moment, expecting others to be the way they
want them. But this isn't persecution! No, no. It's the way they
think, the way they feel and see: everyone has his own. And you
have *your* own, don't you, eh? Of course you do. And now what
can yours be? That of the herd—wretched, fleeting, uncertain.
And they take advantage of it, they make you accept and submit to
theirs, so that you feel and see as they do. Or at least that's what
they tell themselves. Because, after all, what do they manage to
impose? Words! Words that everyone hears and repeats in his own
way. And yet that's how what they call common ideas take shape.
And Lord help the man who one fine day finds himself stamped
with one of those words that everybody repeats! For example:
'madman'. For example, let's say, 'imbecile'. Well, you tell me
how a man can sit there quietly, knowing that there's someone
who's busy persuading others that you're the way he sees you,
fixing his judgement of you in their minds? 'Madman', 'madman'!
Now I'm not saying that I do it as a joke. Before, before I hit my
head falling from the horse . . . [*He stops short, seeing how nervous
the four of them are, more shocked and confused than ever*] You look
each other in the eyes? [*With gross mimicry of their amazement*] Ah,
yes, What a revelation! Am I or am I not? Ah, come on, yes, I'm
mad! [*With a formidable air*] Well then, down on your knees, by
God! Down on your knees! [*One by one, he forces them to kneel*] I
command you all to kneel before me—like that. And touch the
ground three times with your forehead. Down, all of you! That's
how everyone should be before the mad! [*At the sight of the four of
them on their knees, his ferocious gaiety suddenly evaporates, much to
his annoyance*] All right, up you get, you sheep! So you obeyed me?
You could have put me in a straitjacket . . . To crush someone with
the weight of a word. Nothing to it! What is it? Swatting a fly! All
life is crushed like that under the weight of words. The weight of
the dead.—Look at me here: can you seriously believe that Henry
IV is still alive? And yet here I am, speaking and giving orders to
you, the living. This is the way I want you! Do you think this is a
joke as well, that the dead go on acting out life? Yes, here it's a joke:
but go out from here, into the living world. Day is breaking. Time
lies before you. Dawn. This day ahead of us, you say, we shall be

the ones who make it. Oh yes? You will? Goodbye to all traditions! Goodbye to all the old customs and costumes! Start talking and you'll repeat all the words that have always been said. You think you're alive, but you'll be chewing over the life of the dead! [*He stops in front of* BERTHOLD, *by now completely dumbfounded*] You don't understand a thing, do you? What's your name?

BERTHOLD. Me? Er . . . Berthold.

HENRY IV. Don't give me Berthold, you fool. Here, just between us, what's your name?

BERTHOLD. My re . . . my real name is Fino.

HENRY IV [*turning to silence the other three with a slight warning gesture*]. Fino?

BERTHOLD. Fino Pagliuca, yessir.

HENRY IV [*turning back to the others*]. Yes, I've heard the names you give each other, so many times. [*To* LANDOLPH] Are you Lolo?

LANDOLPH. Yes, sir. [*Then, with a joyful start*] Oh my God, but then?

HENRY IV [*rapid, brusque*]. Then what?

LANDOLPH [*turning pale*]. No . . . I mean . . .

HENRY IV. That I'm no longer mad? Of course I'm not. Can't you see? We're playing a joke on those who think I am. [*To* HAROLD] I know you're called Franco. [*To* ORDULPH] And you, wait . . .

ORDULPH. Momo.

HENRY IV. That's it. Momo. Splendid, isn't it?

LANDOLPH. But then, oh God . . .

HENRY IV. Then nothing. Let's sit here and have one good, long, enormous laugh. [*He laughs*] Haha, haha, haha!

LANDOLPH, HAROLD, ORDULPH [*looking at each other, uncertain, torn between joy and consternation*]. Is he cured? Can it be true? What's going on?

HENRY IV. Quiet! Quiet! [*To* BERTHOLD] You're not laughing. Are you still offended? Don't be. I didn't mean you, you know. It suits everyone, you see. It suits everyone to convince others that certain people are mad, so there's a good excuse for keeping them locked up. Do you know why? Because it's unbearable to hear them speak. What do I say about those people who have just left? That one is a whore, that the other is a filthy libertine, and that the third is an impostor. It's not true. No one can believe it! Yet they all stand there listening to me, scared stiff. Now I'd like to know why, if it isn't true. After all, you can't believe what madmen say. And yet they stand there listening like this, wide-eyed with fear. Why? You tell me why. Look, I'm quite calm.

BERTHOLD. Because . . . maybe they think that . . .

HENRY IV. No, my dear chap, no. Look me straight in the eye—I'm not saying it's true, don't worry—Nothing is true—But look me straight in the eye.

BERTHOLD. Yes, all right. And so?

HENRY IV. There! You see it, don't you? Yes, now you have it too, that fear in your eyes. Because now I strike you as mad. That proves it! That proves it! [*He laughs*]

LANDOLPH [*exasperated, summoning up his courage and speaking for the others*]. What proves it?

HENRY IV. This dismay of yours because now you think I'm mad again. And yet, for God's sake, you know! You believe me. Until now you thought I was mad. Is it true or not? [*He looks at them for a moment and sees that they are terrified*] But can you see it? Do you feel how this dismay of yours can turn into terror, as if something were making the earth give way beneath your feet and taking away the air you breathe? Inevitably, gentlemen. Because do you know what it means to find yourself face to face with a madman? Face to face with someone who shakes the very foundations of everything you have built up in and around yourself—the very logic of all your constructions. Ah, what do you expect? Madmen construct without logic, lucky them! Or with a logic of their own which floats around like a feather. Changing, ever-changing! Like this today, and tomorrow who knows how? You stand firm, and they no longer stand at all. Changing, ever-changing! You say: 'This can't be so'—and for them anything can be. But you say it's not true. And why? Because it doesn't seem true to you, or you, or you [*indicating three of them*] or to a hundred thousand others. Ah, my dear friends! We'd do well to see what seems true to these hundred thousand others who are not called mad, and what kind of show they make of their agreements, their flowers of logic. I know that when I was a child the moon in the well seemed real. So many things seemed real and true. I believed everything that others told me, and I was happy. Because terrible things await you unless you hold fast to what seems true to you today, to what will seem true tomorrow, even if it's the opposite of what seemed true yesterday. And how terrible if, like me, you should sink into this horrible thought which truly drives one mad: that if you stand beside someone and look into his eyes—as one day I looked into a certain pair of eyes— then you'll know what it's like to be a beggar standing before a door through which he can never enter: the one who enters will never be you, with your own inner world as you see it and touch it; instead it will be someone you do not know, just as that other person, in his own impenetrable world, sees and touches you . . .

A long pause. The shadows deepen in the room, increasing that sense of uncertainty and anxiety which envelops the four masqueraders and distances them ever further from the great Masquerader who remains absorbed in the contemplation of a terrible sadness that is not his alone but that of all mankind. At last he pulls himself together, seems to look for the four whom he no longer feels around him, and says:

HENRY IV. It's gone dark in here.

ORDULPH [*coming forward at once*]. Shall I go and get the lamp?

HENRY IV [*ironic*]. The lamp, yes . . . you think that I don't know that as soon as I turn my back and go off to bed holding my oil lamp, you go and switch on the electric light for yourselves, here and in the throne room too? I pretend not to see it.

ORDULPH. Ah, so you'd rather . . .

HENRY IV. No, it would dazzle me. I want my lamp.

ORDULPH. Right. It will already be waiting for you, here behind the door.

He goes to the main door, opens it, goes out for a brief moment and returns with an antique lamp, the kind that is held by a ring at the top.

HENRY IV [*taking the lamp and pointing to the table on the platform*]. Here, a bit of light. Now sit down there around the table. But not like that. In nice relaxed poses. [*To* HAROLD] Here, you like this [*arranges his pose; then to* BERTHOLD] And you like this, so [*posing him*]. And me here. [*He sits down himself and turns his head towards one of the windows*] We should get the moon to send down a fine decorative beam. It's useful to us, the moon, it really is. I certainly feel the need of it and I often lose myself in gazing at it from my window. Looking at that moon, who would believe that she must know how eight hundred years have passed and how I can't be Henry IV sitting at the window and looking at the moon like any common man? But look, look, what a magnificent nocturnal scene: the Emperor among his faithful counsellors . . . Aren't you enjoying it?

LANDOLPH [*to* HAROLD, *in a low voice so as not to break the enchantment*]. Well, you understand? Knowing it wasn't true . . .

HENRY IV. What wasn't true?

LANDOLPH [*hesitating, seeking an excuse*]. No . . . it's that with him [*indicating* BERTHOLD] being new to the job, I was saying this very morning what a pity . . . dressed like this, and with so many fine costumes in the wardrobe, and with a throne room like that. [*Gesturing towards the throne room*]

HENRY IV. And then? It's a pity, you say?

LANDOLPH. Yes . . . that we didn't know . . .

HENRY IV. That all this play-acting was just a joke?

LANDOLPH. Because we believed that . . .

HAROLD [*helping him out*]. Yes, that it was serious.

HENRY IV. So what is it then? Do you think it's not serious?

LANDOLPH. Well, if you say . . .

HENRY IV. I say you're a bunch of fools. You should have been able to play out this whole deception for yourselves: not to perform it for me or before the visitors who come here from time to time, but like this, for the way you are naturally every day, without spectators [*to* BERTHOLD, *taking him by the arms*], for yourself, you understand; because this was a fiction where you could eat, sleep, and even scratch your shoulder if it itched; [*turning to the others*] feeling yourselves alive, truly alive in eleventh-century history, here at the court of your Emperor Henry IV. And to think from here, from this remote age, so colourful and sepulchral—to think that in the meantime, eight whole centuries further on, men of the twentieth century are struggling and striving, with a restless burning desire to know how their affairs will turn out, to see what they will add up to, all those events that keep them in such agonizing suspense. While you are already a part of history. With me! However sad my fortunes and terrible my troubles, bitter my struggles and grievous their outcomes, now they're all history and they won't change, they can't change, you understand? Fixed for ever so that you can feel at ease with them, admiring how every effect follows obediently from its cause with perfect logic and how every event unfolds clear and coherent in every detail. Ah the pleasure, the pleasure of history, how great it is!

LANDOLPH. Wonderful, wonderful!

HENRY IV. Yes, wonderful; but that's enough! Now that you know, I couldn't go on with it. [*He takes the lamp to go off to bed*] And nor could you, for that matter, if you still haven't grasped the reason behind it. Now I'm sick of it. [*Almost to himself, with repressed rage*] But by God, I'll make her sorry she came here! Dressed up as my mother-in-law . . . and him as an abbot. And they bring along a doctor to examine me. Who knows, they may even hope to cure me. Clowns! I'm looking forward to giving one of them a slap in the face: *him!* A fine swordsman, isn't he? So he'll run me through, will he? We'll see about that. [*Someone knocks at the main door*] Who is it?

GIOVANNI [*off*]. Deo gratias.

HAROLD [*delighted, anticipating a joke*]. Ah, it's Giovanni coming to play the poor monk as he does every evening.

ORDULPH [*rubbing his hands*]. Yes, yes, let's have him do it, let him do it.

HENRY IV [*immediately severe*]. Idiot! Don't you see? Why? To play a joke at the expense of a poor old man who's doing this for my sake?

LANDOLPH [*to Ordulph*]. It must seem true! Don't you see?

HENRY IV. Exactly. It must seem true. Because that's the only way truth stops being a joke. [*He goes to open the door for* GIOVANNI *who enters dressed as a humble friar with a roll of parchment under his arm*] Come in, Father, come in. [*Assuming a voice of tragic gravity and dark resentment*] All the documents relative to my life and reign that spoke in my favour were deliberately destroyed by my enemies: the only surviving record is this account of my life written by a humble monk* who is devoted to me. And you want to laugh at him? [*He turns affectionately to* GIOVANNI *and invites him to sit at the table*] Sit here, Father. With the lamp beside you. [*He puts down the lamp he has been holding*] Write, write.

GIOVANNI [*unrolls the parchment and prepares to take dictation*]. I'm ready, Your Majesty.

HENRY IV [*dictating*]. The peace proclaimed at Mainz gave sustenance to the poor and the righteous, just as it confounded the wicked and the mighty. [*As the curtain slowly descends*] It brought abundance to the former, hunger and poverty to the latter . . .*

Curtain

ACT THREE

The throne room, dark. In the darkness the back wall can hardly be seen.
The canvases with the two portraits have been removed and in their place,
in the frames that enclose the niches, holding the same poses as the
portraits, stand FRIDA, *as we saw her in Act Two, dressed as the 'Countess*
of Tuscany', and CARLO DI NOLLI *in the costume of 'Henry IV'.*

As the curtain rises, the stage seems empty for a moment. The left door
opens and HENRY IV *enters, holding the lamp by its ring and turning to*
speak to the four young men offstage who are presumably in the adjoining
room with GIOVANNI, *as at the end of Act Two.*

HENRY IV. No, stay where you are. I'll manage by myself. Goodnight.

Closing the door, sad and tired, he starts to cross the room towards the
second right door which leads to his apartments.

FRIDA [*as soon as she sees that he has passed the throne, she whispers from*
the niche like someone fainting with fear]. Henry . . .

HENRY IV [*stopping at the voice as if treacherously stabbed in the back,*
he casts a terrified look at the back wall and instinctively half-raises his
arms to ward off a blow]. Who's calling me?

It is less a question than an exclamation which breaks out with a shudder-
ing of fear and does not expect a reply in the terrible silence and darkness
of the room which for him are suddenly heavy with the suspicion that he
might indeed be mad.

FRIDA [*at that terrified exclamation, no less terrified herself by what she*
has agreed to do, repeats a little louder]. Henry . . .

FRIDA *cranes her neck out a little, looking towards the other niche, though*
still trying to play the part assigned to her. HENRY IV *drops the lamp with*
a great cry, holds his head in his hands, and makes ready to flee. She
jumps down from the niche onto the ledge screaming madly:

FRIDA. Henry . . . Henry . . . I'm frightened . . . I'm frightened.

DI NOLLI *also jumps down from his niche onto the ledge and then onto the*
floor and runs to FRIDA *who is still screaming and seems about to faint: at the*
same time from the left door, all the others burst in: the DOCTOR, LADY
MATILDA, *also dressed as the 'Countess of Tuscany',* TITO BELCREDI,

LANDOLPH, HAROLD, ORDULPH, BERTHOLD, GIOVANNI. *One of them quickly switches on the light—a strange light coming from bulbs hidden in the ceiling so that only the space high above the stage is really illuminated. While* HENRY IV *looks on, stunned by this sudden invasion after the terrifying moment that has left his whole body shaking, the others pay him no attention and hurry to support and comfort* FRIDA *who is still trembling, sobbing, and raving in the arms of her fiancé. General confusion as they all speak at the same time.*

DI NOLLI. No, no, Frida . . . Here I am . . . I'm with you.

DOCTOR [*arriving with the others*]. That's enough! That's enough! There's nothing more we need to do.

LADY MATILDA. He's cured, Frida. Look, he's cured. Don't you see?

DI NOLLI [*astonished*]. Cured?

BELCREDI. It was just for a laugh. Don't worry.

FRIDA. No! I'm afraid. I'm afraid!

LADY MATILDA. What of? Look at him. None of it was true, it wasn't true.

DI NOLLI. It wasn't true? What do you mean? That he's cured?

DOCTOR. So it seems. If you ask me . . .

BELCREDI. Of course he's cured. They told us. [*Indicating the four young men*]

LADY MATILDA. Yes, and for quite some time. He admitted as much when he told them.

DI NOLLI [*now more indignant than surprised*]. How on earth? When just now he was still . . .

BELCREDI. That's it. He was playing a part so he could have a laugh at your expense, and at ours too, since we all honestly believed . . .

DI NOLLI. Is that possible? Even at his sister's expense, right up to her death?

HENRY IV, *peering now at one and now at the other, has remained hunched up under the hail of accusations and derision for what all consider as a cruel joke that has now been revealed. His flashing eyes show that he is meditating a revenge which the scorn raging within prevents him from seeing clearly. At this point, wounded as he is, he breaks out with the intention of assuming as true the fiction that they have insidiously set up for him, shouting at his nephew:*

HENRY IV. Go on with it, go on!

DI NOLLI [*stunned by Henry's shouting*]. Go on with what?

HENRY IV. It's not only 'your' sister who's dead?

DI NOLLI. 'My sister'! I mean your sister whom you forced to come here, right to the end, as your mother Agnes.

HENRY IV. And wasn't she your mother?

DI NOLLI. My mother? Of course she was my mother.

HENRY IV. But when she died I was old and far away, whereas you've just jumped down, spanking fresh, from up there. [*Pointing to the niche*] And how do you know that I didn't weep for her, long, long and in secret, even dressed like this?

LADY MATILDA [*anxious, looking at the others*]. What's he saying?

DOCTOR [*highly impressed, observing him*]. Go easy, easy, for heaven's sake!

HENRY IV. What am I saying? I'm asking you all if Agnes wasn't the mother of Henry IV. [*He turns to* FRIDA, *as if she really were the Countess of Tuscany*] You, Countess, you should know, I'd say.

FRIDA [*still frightened, clinging more tightly to* DI NOLLI]. No, not me. Not me.

DOCTOR. It's the delirium coming back . . . Go easy, go easy, my friends.

BELCREDI [*scornful*]. Delirium? Come off it, doctor! He's simply gone back to play–acting.

HENRY IV [*quickly*]. Me? It's you who've emptied those two niches there. He's the one standing before me dressed as Henry IV.

BELCREDI. That's enough. It's time we dropped this joke.

HENRY IV. Who used that word 'joke'?

DOCTOR [*raising his voice, to* BELCREDI]. Don't provoke him, for God's sake!

BELCREDI [*paying him no attention, louder*]. They did! [*Indicating the four young men*] They told me. Them, them!

HENRY IV [*turning to look at them*]. You? Did you say it was a joke?

LANDOLPH [*timid, embarrassed*]. No, not really . . . more like that you were cured.

BELCREDI. And so that's it. It's all over. [*To* LADY MATILDA] Don't you think it's becoming unbearably infantile, the way he looks [*indicating* DI NOLLI], and you too, Marchesa, dressed up like this.

LADY MATILDA. Oh shut up! Who cares about the costumes if he's really cured!

HENRY IV. Cured? Yes, I'm cured. [*To* BELCREDI] But not to have it all over and done with just like that, the way you think. [*Aggressively*] Do you know that in twenty years nobody has ever dared to appear before me dressed like you and this gentleman? [*Indicating the* DOCTOR]

BELCREDI. Of course, I know that. In fact, this morning I too appeared before you dressed . . .

HENRY IV. As a monk!

BELCREDI. And you took me for Peter Damian. And I didn't laugh, because I believed . . .

HENRY IV. That I was mad. Do you feel like laughing now, seeing her in that state, now that I'm cured? Yet, after all, you might have thought that to my eyes the way she looks now . . . [*He breaks off with a burst of scorn*] Ah! [*Addressing the* DOCTOR] Are you a doctor?

DOCTOR. Yes I am.

HENRY IV. And was it you who decided to dress her up as the Countess of Tuscany, her as well? Do you realize, doctor, that for a moment you risked darkening my brain all over again? For God's sake—making portraits speak, making them jump down from their frames . . . [*He looks at* FRIDA *and* DI NOLLI, *then at the* MARCHESA, *and finally at his own costume*] Eh, a very pretty stratagem . . . Two couples . . . Nice, doctor, very nice: for a madman . . . [*Gestures slightly towards* BELCREDI] To him it's like carnival out of season, eh? [*Turning to look at him*] So off with it then, off with my carnival costume as well. So I can come along with you, right?

BELCREDI. With me? With us!

HENRY IV. Where? To the club? In white tie and tails? Or back to the Marchesa's house, the two of us together?

BELCREDI. Wherever you like. After all, would you rather remain here, all alone, perpetuating what was a disastrous carnival-day game? It's incredible, really incredible, how you managed to go on with it, once you'd recovered from its disastrous effects.

HENRY IV. Yes, but you see, when I fell from my horse and hit my head, I really did go mad. I don't know for how long.

DOCTOR. Ah, indeed, indeed. And was it a long time?

HENRY IV [*very quickly, to the* DOCTOR]. Yes, doctor, a long time: about twelve years. [*Addressing* BELCREDI *again*] And I saw nothing of all that happened after that carnival day, happened for you, not for me—how things changed, how friends betrayed me, how someone took my place, for example . . . well, let's say in the heart of the woman I love: and who had died and who had disappeared . . . all that, you know, it wasn't just a joke for me, as you seem to think!

BELCREDI. Hold on, I'm not saying that. I mean afterwards.

HENRY IV. Ah yes? Afterwards? One day . . . [*He stops and turns to the* DOCTOR] A most interesting case, doctor. Study me, study me carefully. [*Trembling as he speaks*] I don't know how, but one day, the damage here [*touching his forehead*] simply repaired itself. I open my eyes little by little, not knowing at first whether I'm awake or asleep; but yes, I'm awake; I touch this and that: I start to see things clearly again. Ah then, as he says [*nodding to* BELCREDI]— away with it, off with this pageant costume, this nightmare! Open the windows, let's breathe the air of life. Let's run outside, off and away! [*Suddenly checking his ardour*] Where? To do what? To be pointed at by everybody, on the sly, as Henry IV, no longer like this, but arm-in-arm with you, among my dear friends in this life?

BELCREDI. Not at all. What do you mean? Why on earth?

LADY MATILDA. Who could behave like that? It's unthinkable. After all, it was an accident.

HENRY IV. But they all said I was mad, even before. [*To* BELCREDI] And you know it. You were the angriest of all when someone tried to defend me.

BELCREDI. Oh come on! It was just for a joke.

HENRY IV. And here, look at my hair. [*Showing him the hair on the nape of his neck*]

BELCREDI. But my hair's grey as well.

HENRY IV. Yes, with this difference: that I went grey here, as Henry IV, you see? And I hadn't the faintest idea. I realized it all of a sudden, in one day, the day I opened my eyes, and it was a shock because I immediately understood that it wasn't just my hair that had gone grey like that, but everything, everything collapsed, everything over and done with; and I saw that I'd be arriving at a banquet, hungry as a wolf, only to find the whole feast already cleared away.

BELCREDI. And what about the others?

HENRY IV [*quickly*]. I know, they couldn't wait around for me to be cured, not even those who were behind me in the pageant and pricked my caparisoned horse until it bled.

DI NOLLI [*shocked*]. What? What?

HENRY IV. Oh yes, a nasty trick to make the horse rear up and throw me off.

LADY MATILDA [*horrified*]. This is the first I've heard of it.

HENRY IV. Maybe that was meant for a joke as well.

LADY MATILDA. But who was it? Who was riding behind the two of us?

HENRY IV. It doesn't matter who. All those who carried on feasting and who by then would have left me their scraps, Marchesa—their leftovers of pity, fat or lean, or some fishbone of remorse stuck to the dirty plate. Thank you very much! [*Suddenly turning to the* DOCTOR] And so, doctor, see if this case isn't something really new in the annals of madness. I preferred to stay mad, finding everything here ready and prepared for this new form of pleasure— to live out my madness with a perfectly lucid mind, and thus to avenge myself for the brutality of a stone that had bruised my head. This solitude—squalid and empty as it seemed when I opened my eyes—I chose at once to clothe it again, but better, with all the colours and the splendour of that far-off carnival day, when you [*looking at* LADY MATILDA *and indicating* FRIDA], yes, you there, Marchesa, had your triumph. And so—now, by God, for my own amusement—I could force all those who came before me here to carry on with that famous old pageant which—for you and not for me—had been the game of a single day. To make it become for ever—not a game, no, but a reality, the reality of a true madness: here, all of you disguised, with a throne room, and these four counsellors of mine—privy counsellors and, of course, traitors. [*Turning to them abruptly*] I'd like to know what you gained by telling them I was cured. If I'm cured, you're no longer needed, so you can be fired. Confiding in someone, yes, that's real madness. Well, now, it's my turn to denounce you. You know something? These men thought they could join with me and have their own share in this joke at your expense.

He bursts out laughing. Laughter, somewhat uncertain, also from the others, except for LADY MATILDA.

BELCREDI [*to* DI NOLLI]. Hear that! Not bad.

DI NOLLI [*to the four young men*]. You?

HENRY IV. Forgive them. This [*shaking his clothes*], this for me is a caricature, an obvious and deliberate caricature of that other constant incessant masquerade in which we play involuntary clowns [*pointing to* BELCREDI] when, without knowing it, we disguise ourselves as what we think we are. Forgive them because they still don't see the costume, their costume, as their real self. [*Turning again to* BELCREDI] It's easy to get used to it, you know. Nothing's simpler than strutting round like a tragic character [*he mimes the action*] in a room like this. Listen to this, doctor. I remember a priest—an Irishman for sure—a handsome chap—who was sleeping in the sunshine one November day, resting his arm on the back of a park bench, basking in the golden pleasure of that mild warmth, which to him must have felt like summer. You can be sure that in that moment he didn't know where he was or that he was a priest. He was dreaming. And who knows what he was dreaming! A little urchin passed by who had just plucked a flower, stem and all. As he went past, he tickled the priest with it, here on the neck. I saw him open his smiling eyes and his mouth too was all smiling in the blessed smile of his dream—oblivious. But then, I tell you, he immediately pulled himself together, stiffening into his priestly garb; and back into his eyes came the very same seriousness that you have seen in mine. Because Irish priests defend the seriousness of their Catholic faith as zealously as I defend the sacred rights of hereditary monarchy. Ladies and gentlemen, I'm cured because I am perfectly aware that I'm playing the madman, and I do it in all tranquillity. The problem is yours, because you live out your madness in such a turmoil, neither knowing nor seeing it as madness.

BELCREDI. There you are, the conclusion is that we're the madmen now!

HENRY IV [*with a violent reaction that he seeks to control*]. But if you weren't mad, both you and her [*pointing to the* MARCHESA], would you have come here to see me?

BELCREDI. Well, actually, I came here thinking you were the madman.

HENRY IV [*raising his voice and pointing to the* MARCHESA *again*]. And her?

BELCREDI. Ah, her, I couldn't say . . . I see that she's spellbound by what you say . . . fascinated by this 'conscious' madness of yours! [*Turning to her*] Dressed up the way you are, you could stay here and live it out yourself, Marchesa.

LADY MATILDA. Now you're being insolent!

HENRY IV [*at once, trying to calm her down*]. Take no notice of him, take no notice. He keeps trying to provoke me. And yet the doctor warned him to avoid all provocation. [*Turning to* BELCREDI] But why should I still be worked up about what happened between us, the part you played in my bad luck with her [*indicating the* MARCHESA, *then turning to her and pointing to* BELCREDI], the part he plays for you now! My life is *this*. It's not like yours. Your life, the life that you've grown old in, is one that I haven't lived! [*To* LADY MATILDA] Is this what you wanted to tell me, is this what you wanted to prove, with your sacrifice, dressed up like this on the doctor's advice? Oh, well done! as I told you, doctor: 'What we were then, eh? and how we are now?' But I'm not a madman in your sense, doctor. I know very well that he [*indicating* DI NOLLI] can't be me, because I'm the one who is Henry IV—and have been, here, for the last twenty years, you see. Fixed in the eternity of this disguise. She has lived those twenty years [*indicating the* MARCHESA], she has enjoyed them, to end up . . . look at her . . . as someone I no longer recognize: because I know her like this [*indicating* FRIDA *and going up to her*]. For me this is how she is, always and for ever . . . You all seem like children that I can scare to bits. [*To* FRIDA] And you, my child, were really frightened by the game they persuaded you to play, not understanding that for me it couldn't be the game they thought, but this tremendous miracle—the dream that has come to life in you more than ever! Up there you were an image: they have made you into a living being—you are mine, mine! Mine by right!

He puts his arms around her, laughing like a madman, while everyone cries out in horror; but as they run to tear FRIDA *from his arms, he assumes a fearsome air and calls to his four young men:*

HENRY IV. Hold them back! Hold them back! I command you to hold them back.

The four young men, dazed, but as if under a spell, automatically try to restrain DI NOLLI, *the* DOCTOR, *and* BELCREDI.

BELCREDI [*breaking free and hurling himself against Henry IV*]. Let her go! Let her go! You're not mad!

HENRY IV [*in a flash, drawing the sword that hangs from the belt of* LANDOLPH, *who is standing next to him*]. So I'm not mad? Take that!

He wounds him in the stomach. With a cry of horror, everyone runs to help BELCREDI, *shouting amid the confusion,*

DI NOLLI. Has he wounded you?

BERTHOLD. He's wounded! Yes, he's wounded!

DOCTOR. I warned you.

FRIDA. Oh God!

DI NOLLI. Frida, come here!

LADY MATILDA. He's mad! He's mad!

DI NOLLI. Keep hold of him!

BELCREDI [*as they carry him off through the left door, protesting violently*]. No, you're not mad! He's not mad! He's not mad!

They go out through the left door, shouting and they keep on shouting offstage until, high above the other voices, comes the shrill scream of LADY MATILDA, *followed by silence.*

HENRY IV *has remained on the stage with* LANDOLPH, HAROLD, *and*
ORDULPH. *His eyes are wide and appalled at the living force of his own
fiction that, in one short moment, has driven him to commit a crime.*

HENRY IV. Now, yes . . . there's no other way . . . [*calling them around
   him, as if seeking protection*] here together, here together . . . and for
   ever!

Curtain

THE MOUNTAIN GIANTS

A Myth

CHARACTERS

The Theatre Company of the Countess

Ilse, also called the Countess
The Count, her husband
Diamante, the second female lead
Cromo, the character actor
Spizzi, the young actor
Battaglia, the female impersonator
Sacerdote
Lumachi, who draws the cart

Residents of the Villa 'La Scalogna' (the Scalognati)*

Cotrone, known as the Magician
Quaquèo, the dwarf
Duccio Doccia
La Sgricia
Milordino
Mara-Mara, with the umbrella, also known as the
    Scotswoman
Magdalen

Puppets
Apparitions
The Angel Hundred-and-One and his Cohort

Indeterminate time and place, on the border between fable and reality.

I

A villa known as 'La Scalogna' where Cotrone lives with his Scalognati.

Almost midstage, on a small elevation, stands a tall cypress; old age has reduced its trunk to a mere pole and its top to something like a cornice-brush.

The villa is plastered with a faded reddish colour. To the right all that can be seen is the main entrance and the four steps leading up to it, set between two small curved balconies protruding on either side, with little pillared balustrades and columns to support the cupolas. The door is old and still retains traces of its original green paint. To right and left, on the same level as the door, two French windows open onto the balconies.

The villa, once rather grand, is now decayed and neglected. It stands alone in the valley and before it there is a small lawn, with a bench to the left. The path to this spot descends steeply as far as the cypress and then continues to the left, crossing a little bridge over an invisible stream. This bridge with its two parapets must be practicable and clearly visible on the left of the stage. Beyond it can be seen the wooded slopes of the mountain.

When the curtain rises it is almost evening. From inside the villa, accompanied by strange instruments, comes the leaping rhythm of a song which sometimes bursts into sudden shrills and sometimes plunges into dangerous glissades, drawn into a kind of vortex from which all of a sudden it breaks away, taking flight like a shying horse. This song should give the impression of a danger being overcome: we wait anxiously for it to end so that everything can go quietly back to its proper place, as when we emerge from certain inexplicable moments of madness.

Through the two French windows giving onto the balconies one can see that the interior of the villa is illuminated by strangely coloured lamps which confer a ghostly mysterious aspect on LA SGRICIA *who is sitting calm and immobile in the right balcony and on* DOCCIA *and* QUAQUÈO *in the left, the former with his elbows on the balustrade and his head in his hands, the latter sitting on the balustrade with his back to the wall.* LA SGRICIA *is a little old woman with a lace bonnet untidily knotted under her chin, a purple shawl over her shoulders, a pleated black-and-white check dress, and net mittens. She always sounds irritated when she speaks and she keeps blinking her cunning restless eyes. Every now and then she wrinkles her nose and wipes it swiftly with her finger.* DUCCIO DOCCIA, *small, of uncertain age, and completely bald, has two grave protruding eyes and a thick pendulous lower lip in a long, pale, skull-like face: his hands are long and soft, and he walks with bent legs as if always looking for somewhere to sit down.*

QUAQUÈO *is a fat dwarf dressed as a child, with red hair, a large brick-red face, and a wide smile that seems foolish on his lips, but malicious in his eyes. As soon as the song coming from the villa is over,* MILORDINO *emerges from behind the cypress. He is a young man of about thirty, with an unhealthy air and a sickly stubble on his cheeks, wearing a top hat and a tailcoat green with age which he insists on keeping so as not to lose his genteel aspect. In a panic, he announces:*

MILORDINO. Oh, oh! People coming! People coming here! Quick, let's have thunder and lightning, and the green tongue of fire on the roof!

LA SGRICIA [*getting up, opening the window, and calling into the villa*]. Help! Help! People coming here! [*Then, leaning out from the balcony*] What people, Milordino, what kind of people?

QUAQUÈO. In the evening? If it were daytime, I'd believe it. They must have got lost. Now they'll turn back; you'll see.

MILORDINO. No, no. They're really coming this way. They're already here below. A lot of them, more than ten.

QUAQUÈO. So many. Enough to make them bold.

He jumps down from the balustrade onto the steps leading up to the door and from there he goes down to the cypress to look out with MILORDINO.

LA SGRICIA [*screaming into the villa*]. The lightning! The lightning!

DOCCIA. Hold on! Lightning's expensive.

MILORDINO. They've got a cart as well; they're drawing it themselves, one pulling between the shafts and two pushing from behind.

DOCCIA. Must be people going up the mountain.

QUAQUÈO. Eh, no. It looks as if they're really heading for us. And, oh, they have a woman on the cart. Look, look! The cart's full of hay and the woman's lying on top.

MILORDINO. At least get Mara to go down onto the bridge, with her umbrella.

MARA-MARA *comes running from the door of the villa, shouting:*

MARA-MARA. Here I am! Here I am! The Scots lass will scare them off!

MARA-MARA *is a little woman who could be presented as swollen and stuffed like a bale, with a tiny tartan plaid skirt over the stuffed part, bare legs, and woollen stockings folded back on her calves; she wears a stiff-brimmed green oilcloth hat with a cock's feather on the side, holds a small parasol-type umbrella, and has a haversack and flask slung over her shoulder.*

MARA-MARA. Hey, give me some light from the roof. I don't want to break my neck.

She runs to the bridge and climbs on the parapet where, lit up and given a spectral air by a green spotlight from the villa roof, she walks up and down pretending to be a ghost. Broad flashes of light come from behind the villa, like summer lightning, accompanied by the thunder of clanking chains.

LA SGRICIA [*to the two who are watching*]. Are they stopping? Are they turning back?

QUAQUÈO. Call Cotrone!

DOCCIA. Call Cotrone!

LA SGRICIA. He's got an attack of gout.

Both LA SGRICIA *and* DUCCIO DOCCIA *have come down from the balconies and are now standing anxiously on the lawn in front of the villa. Through the door comes* COTRONE, *a bulky bearded man with a handsome open face, large eyes that shine with smiling serenity, and a fresh mouth which also shines thanks to the healthy teeth amid the warm blond of his unkempt moustaches and beard. His feet are rather delicate and he is carelessly dressed in a loose black jacket and floppy light-coloured trousers, an old Turkish fez, and a pale blue open-neck shirt.*

COTRONE. What's going on? Aren't you ashamed of yourselves? You're trying to scare someone off and you're scared yourselves?

MILORDINO. There are hordes of them coming up. More than ten.

QUAQUÈO. No. Eight. I counted. There are eight of them, including the woman.

COTRONE. A woman too? Cheer up then! Maybe she's a dethroned queen. Is she naked?

QUAQUÈO [*startled*]. Naked? No, she didn't look naked to me.

COTRONE. Naked, you fool! Lying on the hay in a cart, a naked woman, breasts free to the air and red hair spread out like blood in a tragedy. Her exiled ministers pull her along—in shirtsleeves so as not to sweat so much. Come on, wake up, use your imagination! Don't start going all rational on me. You know we're in no danger, and reason's made for cowards. And, by Jove, the night is coming on, the night, our kingdom!

MILORDINO. Fair enough! But if they don't believe in anything . . .

COTRONE. And do you need people to believe in you before you can believe in yourself?

LA SGRICIA. Are they still coming up?

MILORDINO. The lightning can't stop them. Nor can Mara.

DOCCIA. Well, if it's not working, it's a waste. Switch it off.

COTRONE. Yes, switch it off up there! Cut out the lightning! Mara, you come here. If they're not frightened, it means they're our kind and we'll get along with no trouble. The villa's big enough. [*Struck by an idea*] Oh, hold on a moment! [*To* QUAQUÈO] Did you say there were eight of them?

QUAQUÈO. Eight, yes, that's what I thought . . .

DOCCIA. And you're supposed to have counted them! Tell me another.

QUAQUÈO. Eight, yes, eight.

COTRONE. So not all that many.

QUAQUÈO. Eight, and a cart; you think that's not many.

COTRONE. Perhaps because some of them have disbanded.

LA SGRICIA. You mean they're bandits?

COTRONE. Bandits, my foot! You pipe down. Nothing's impossible for the mad. Maybe it's them.

DOCCIA. Them! Who?

QUAQUÈO. Here they are.

The flashing lightning and the spotlight that illuminated MARA *on the bridge have been turned off and the stage is left bathed in a tenuous twilight which slowly gives way to moonlight. From the path behind the cypress come the* COUNT, DIAMANTE, CROMO, *and* BATTAGLIA *the female impersonator.*

The COUNT *is a pale blond young man, lost-looking and very tired. His present poverty can be gathered from his dress: a threadbare morning coat of a greenish hue and slightly tattered, a white waistcoat, and an ancient straw hat. And yet his features and manners still betray the disenchanted gloom of great nobility.*

DIAMANTE *is nearing forty. Above a shapely generous bust she holds her head high and firm, with a certain swagger; her face is violently painted, armed with tragic eyebrows over two deep grave eyes separated by an imperious haughty nose. At the corners of her mouth she has two inverted commas of jet-black hair and there are a few more metallic curls on her chin. She always seems about to give vent to her protective compassion for the unfortunate young* COUNT *and her indignation towards* ILSE, *his wife, whose victim she believes him to be.*

CROMO *is strangely bald at the forehead and temples so that his carroty hair makes two triangles whose points meet at the top of his head; pale, freckled, and with light green eyes, he speaks with a cavernous voice and with the tone and gestures of someone who takes offence on the slightest occasion.* BATTAGLIA, *though a man, has the horsey face of a depraved old spinster and all the simpering manners of a sick monkey. He acts both male and female parts (the latter in a wig) and also acts as prompter. Though his face bears the marks of vice, his eyes are suppliant and mild.*

CROMO. Ah, thank you, my friends. A great help. We were at the end of our tether.

DOCCIA [*puzzled*]. Thank you? For what?

CROMO. Well, of course, for the signals you sent out to show that we'd finally reached our destination.

COTRONE. That's it, then. It's really them.

BATTAGLIA [*indicating* MARA]. This lady was wonderful. There's courage for you.

CROMO. And how! On the parapet of the bridge. Magnificent. With her umbrella!

DIAMANTE. And the lightning was really lovely. That green flame on the roof!

QUAQUÈO. Hear that. They took it for a show. But we were trying to do ghosts . . .

MILORDINO. They actually enjoyed it.

DIAMANTE. Ghosts? What ghosts?

QUAQUÈO. Yes, ghosts, apparitions to scare people off.

COTRONE. Now that's enough. [*To* CROMO] The Theatre Company of the Countess?* Just what I was saying . . .

CROMO. Here we are.

DOCCIA. The Company?

BATTAGLIA. The remnants of it.

DIAMANTE. Absolute nonsense! Say the pillars of it, thank heaven, the pillars. And here, first and foremost, the Count. [*She takes him by the hand and puts an arm round his shoulder as if he were a little boy*] Now come on, step forward.

COTRONE [*offering his hand*]. Welcome, my lord Count.

CROMO [*declaiming*]. A count without a county and nothing left to count.

DIAMANTE [*indignantly*]. When will you stop letting yourselves down by humiliating . . .

COUNT [*annoyed*]. No, dear, I'm not humiliated.

CROMO. All right, let's call him Count; but, take it from me, with the state we're in, it might be as well to play it down.

BATTAGLIA. When I said 'the remants of it' I was speaking for myself . . .

CROMO [*putting him in his place*]. Yes, we all know how modest you are.

BATTAGLIA. Not really. More like distracted, because I'm tired and hungry.

COTRONE. But you can have a rest here and . . . yes, I reckon we can rustle up a bite of something.

LA SGRICIA [*quick, cold, decisive*]. The fire's out in the kitchen.

MARA-MARA. We could always light it again, but at least you could tell us . . .

DOCCIA. Who these people are.

COTRONE. Yes, right away. [*To the* COUNT] And the Countess, may I ask?

COUNT. She's here, but so very tired . . .

BATTAGLIA. She can't even stand any more.

QUAQUÈO. Is that her on the cart? A Countess? [*Clapping his hands and raising a foot*] Now we get it. You've set up a surprise performance for us.

COTRONE. No, my friends, let me explain . . .

QUAQUÈO. Of course. And that's why they took what we did as a performance.

COTRONE. Because they belong to our family, more or less. You'll see. [*To the* COUNT] Does the Countess need some help?

DIAMANTE. She could make the effort to walk up here by herself.

COUNT [*suddenly angry, shouting in her face*]. No. No, she can't!

CROMO. Lumachi is bracing himself . . .

BATTAGLIA. Calling on his last reserves . . .

CROMO. For this last haul.

COTRONE [*solicitous*]. But I can lend a hand as well.

COUNT. No, there are two others there with Lumachi. But there is something I'd like you to tell us; [*looking around, seeming lost*] I can see that we're in a valley, at the foot of a mountain . . .

CROMO. So where are the hotels?

BATTAGLIA. And the restaurants?

DIAMANTE. And the theatre where we're supposed to act.

COTRONE. Give me a moment and I'll explain—to you and to my own people as well. We've all got it wrong, my friends, but we shouldn't let such a little thing bother us.

From offstage come the voices of the YOUNG ACTOR, SACERDOTE, *and* LUMACHI *who are pushing the haycart with the* COUNTESS *lying on top.*

OFFSTAGE VOICES. Go on!! Heave! Heave! We've made it! Gently, gently now; not too hard!

    Everyone turns to look as the cart appears.

CROMO. Behold the Countess!

COUNT. Watch out for the cypress! The cypress! [*He and* COTRONE *run to help*]

When the cart reaches the lawn, LUMACHI *lowers the two props attached to the shafts so that the cart remains upright without any other support. Then he comes out from between the shafts and steps aside. All the others look anxiously at the* COUNTESS *who is lying with her warm copper-coloured hair spread out dishevelled on the green hay; she wears a sad and sober dress of violet voile, low-necked and rather worn, with long ample sleeves that easily fall back to bare her arms.*

MILORDINO. My God, how pale she is!

MARA-MARA. She seems dead.

SPIZZI. Silence!

ILSE [*after a moment's pause, sitting up on the cart and speaking with deep emotion*].

> If you would stay to hear this tale,
> Not heard before,
> Look on these rags and mark them well,
> Wretched and poor.
> Mark even more these eyes that flow
> With tears I shed for a cruel fate,
> A cruel fate . . .*

At this point, as if reacting to a cue, the COUNT, CROMO, *and the whole* COMPANY OF THE COUNTESS *burst into a many-voiced chorus of incredulous laughter. Just as suddenly they stop and* ILSE *continues:*

ILSE.

> This is the way they laugh at me,
> The clever folk, who see me weep
> And are not moved . . .

COTRONE [*recovering from his astonishment*]. But you're acting!

MILORDINO. How splendid!

MARA-MARA. They're acting!

SACERDOTE. Quiet. Now she's got started, we should go along with her.

ILSE [*continuing*].

> Instead, it grates upon their nerves:
> 'You stupid fool!, you fool!', they cry
> And shout it in my face because

They can't believe it's true
That my dear son, my lovely child . . .
And yet you must believe me now;
For here I bring you witnesses;
Poor mothers all of them, like me—
Neighbours, who know each other well
And know that this is true.
[*She gestures to call them*]

COUNT [*bending over her, gently*]. No, my dear, no more now . . .

ILSE [*with impatient gestures*]. The Women . . . the Women . . .*

COUNT. The women? Don't you see? Right now there are no women.

ILSE [*as if awakening*]. No women? Why not? Where have you brought me?

COUNT. We've just arrived. Now we'll find out . . .

MILORDINO. How well she performed!

LA SGRICIA. Pity she stopped, I was enjoying it.

DOCCIA. Especially hearing them laugh together like that.

QUAQUÈO [*to Cotrone*]. You see I was right; it's true, isn't it?

COTRONE. Of course it's true. They're acting. What else do you expect? After all, they're theatre people.

COUNT. For heaven's sake, don't say that in front of my wife.

ILSE [*climbing down from the cart, with a few wisps of hay still in her hair*]. Why shouldn't he say it? Let him say it! I like to hear it.

COTRONE. Forgive me, I meant no offence.

ILSE [*as if delirious*]. Theatre people, yes, theatre people! Not him! [*indicating her husband*] but me, yes, by blood, by birth. And now he's been dragged down to my level.

COUNT [*trying to interrupt her*]. No, for God's sake, what are you saying?

ILSE. Yes, dragged down with me, from his marble palaces to wooden sheds! And even in the public square, out in the square! Where are we now? Lumachi, where are you? Lumachi? Go and sound the trumpet. Let's see if we can get a bit of a crowd. [*Looking around, delirious and terrified*] O God! Where are we now? Where are we? [*She takes refuge in the arms of* SPIZZI *who has drawn near*]

COTRONE. Have no fear, Countess, you're among friends.

CROMO. She's feverish. Delirious.

QUAQUÈO. Is she really a countess?

COUNT. Is my wife a countess!

COTRONE. Shut up, Quaquèo!

MARA-MARA. Well if you don't tell us anything . . .

DOCCIA. To us they seem crazy.

COUNT [*to* COTRONE]. We were directed to you.

COTRONE. Yes, dear Count; please forgive them: I forgot to inform them in advance. I used that expression for their benefit, but I do understand that . . .

SPIZZI *interrupts him.* SPIZZI *is hardly more than twenty, pale, with sad sick eyes and blond hair that may once have been dyed but is now discoloured; a rosebud mouth rather spoiled by the large overhanging nose; pathetically elegant in his faded sporting outfit; knee-breeches and thick woollen stockings.*

SPIZZI. You understand nothing. You can't possibly know anything about the heroic suffering of this woman.

ILSE [*suddenly resentful, breaking away from him*]. Spizzi, I forbid you to speak. [*Then, still quivering with anger, attacking* CROMO] If only I hadn't been born an actress, you see. Here's what disgusts me: that it has to be you, of all people, you lot, who are the first to believe it and to convince others . . . 'You want a good contract?— Sell yourself!', 'Clothes, jewels?—Sell yourself!' Even for a wretched write-up in some rag of a newspaper!

CROMO [*stunned*]. What do you mean? Why are you turning on me?

ILSE. Because you said it?

CROMO. Me? I said it? When? Said what?

COUNT [*imploring his wife*]. Don't lower yourself by speaking of such things. Not you. It's horrible.

ILSE. No, dear, it's good to speak of them, now that we've come to the end of the road, mere shadows of what we used to be . . . [*To* COTRONE *for a moment, then to all the others*] You know, we all sleep together . . . in the stables . . .

COUNT. Not true.

ILSE. Not true? Only yesterday . . .

COUNT. But it wasn't a stable, my dear. You slept on a bench in the railway station.

CROMO. Third-class waiting-room.

ILSE [*continuing, to* COTRONE]. As people stretch and toss and turn, the words just come out, the words that hurt . . . [*To* CROMO] Because you can't see in the dark, you think nobody can hear either, but I heard you.

CROMO. What did you hear?

ILSE. Something as I lay there, wrapped in those webs . . . maybe they were spiders' webs . . .

COUNT. No, Ilse, where could that be?

ILSE. Or shreds of the darkness flapping cold in my fevered face . . . yes, yes, breathing on me. [*To* CROMO] As soon as I heard you . . . hehee, hehee . . . I laughed like that, but then suddenly I shuddered and clenched my teeth, holding myself in so as not to howl like a beaten dog. [*Suddenly turning on* CROMO *again*] Didn't you even hear that laugh?

CROMO. Me? No.

ILSE. Oh yes, you heard it all right. But you didn't think it could be me. There in the dark you thought it was someone else, someone who agreed with you.

CROMO. I don't remember a thing.

ILSE. I remember everything.

SPIZZI. So come on, what did he say?

ILSE. That instead of this heroic suffering, as you call it, and instead of making the rest of you suffer along with me, it would have been so much better, he said . . .

CROMO [*understanding at last and protesting*]. Oh, that! Now I get it. But we've all said the same thing, not just me. And those who haven't said it have thought it. Him too, I bet! [*Indicating the* COUNT]

COUNT. Me? What did I think?

ILSE. That on this noble brow, my darling [*taking his head in her hands*], 'with a quick deal' [*turning to* CROMO], that's exactly what you said, isn't it?

CROMO. Yes, with a quick deal, a quick deal. And we wouldn't all be starving the way we are now.

ILSE. —That on this brow I should have planted a magnificent pair of horns. [*She is about to reach out to his forehead with the standard cuckold gesture when she is seized by an overwhelming impulse of anger and disgust*] Ah!

She quickly changes the ugly gesture into a loud slap on CROMO's *cheek, then staggers and falls to the ground in a violent spasm of laughter and tears.* CROMO *nurses his cheek in amazement. Taken aback by the sudden violent action, everyone starts to talk at the same time, some commenting and some running to help. They split up into four groups. In the first, trying to help the* COUNTESS, *are the* COUNT, DIAMANTE, *and* COTRONE; *in the second,* QUAQUÈO, DOCCIA, MARA-MARA, *and* MILORDINO; *in the third,* SACERDOTE, LUMACHI, BATTAGLIA, *and* LA SGRICIA; *in the fourth,* SPIZZI *and* CROMO. *Each group should complete its four lines of dialogue at the same time.*

COUNT. Oh God, she's going mad. Ilse, Ilse, for the Lord's sake. We can't carry on like this.

DIAMANTE. Calm down, Ilse, calm down. At least for your husband's sake.

COTRONE. Countess . . . Countess. Let's take her inside. That's the best thing to do.

ILSE. No, leave me alone, leave me alone. I want everyone to hear.

QUAQUÈO. What a wretched play! And she says it isn't.

DOCCIA. She's terrific. She doesn't mince her words.

MARA-MARA. She gave that bully what for!

MILORDINO. Who on earth let these people loose?

BATTAGLIA. Dig, dig, and you make your own grave.

LUMACHI. Why does she have to make such a fuss over nothing?

SACERDOTE. But it's true that we all said it.

LA SGRICIA [*crossing herself*]. It's like being stuck with a bunch of heathens.

SPIZZI [*facing up to* CROMO]. You coward! How dare you?

CROMO [*pushing him back*]. Out of the way. It's time we put an end to all this.

SPIZZI. 'A quick deal', to keep the show on the road . . . You'd have sold your own wife!

CROMO. What show on the road, you idiot! I was talking about the fellow who killed himself.

ILSE [*breaking away from those who are trying to restrain her and coming forward*]. Did you all say it?

SPIZZI. No, that's not true.

DIAMANTE. I said nothing.

BATTAGLIA. Neither did I.

ILSE [*to her husband*]. Is it true that you thought so as well?

COUNT. Of course not, Ilse. That's absolute nonsense. And in front of strangers . . .

COTRONE. If that's what's troubling you, Count . . .

ILSE. That's just what does trouble us. Arriving here like this . . .

COTRONE. Don't worry about us. We're on holiday here and we're open-hearted, dear Countess.

ILSE. Countess? I'm an actress, and I've had to remind him [*indicating* CROMO] that it's an honourable title—remind him, who's an actor like all the others.

CROMO. And I don't boast of it, no, and neither should you, not in front of me, at least. Because I've always been an actor, a respected actor, and I've followed you as far as this. But you—remember, there was a time when you chose not to be an actress any longer.

COUNT. Not true. It was me who forced her to give up the stage.

CROMO. And you did very well, old chap! If it had stayed that way— you a count and me a poor wretch—I wouldn't be using such familiar terms right now. [*To the* COUNTESS] You had married a count—[*to the others, as an aside*] he was rich—[*to the* COUNTESS *again*] you weren't an actress any longer, anxious to remain chaste, chaste as you had so proudly kept yourself up to then—I know, I understood that's what you meant to say . . .

ILSE. Yes, that's it, yes.

CROMO. But you made a bit too much of your chastity, dear. For heaven's sake, you were a countess now. And surely, as a countess, you could have given him a pair of horns. Countesses are more generous; they do these things. Then that poor devil wouldn't have killed himself, and you yourself, and that sad chap over there, and all the rest of us—we wouldn't be in the mess we're in now.

ILSE *holds herself straight, rigid, almost stony; then with a sudden tremor that seems to surge up from her very entrails, she breaks into the same convulsive laughter that she spoke of before.*

ILSE. Hehee, hehee, hehee . . . [*Lifting her hands and using her index fingers to make the sign of horns on her forehead, gasping out in a raucous voice*] On butterflies they're called antennae.

COUNT [*barely controlling his anger, going up to* CROMO]. Clear off! Just go! You can't stay with us.

CROMO. Go? Me? And where do you reckon I can go now? What will you pay me with?

ILSE [*promptly, to her husband*]. That's right. What will you pay him with? Did you hear him? [*Turning to* COTRONE] That's the whole problem, sir: we don't make enough to pay the wages.

SPIZZI. Ah no, Ilse, you can't say that about us.

ILSE. I was talking about *him*. What's it got to do with you?

CROMO. It's not true. You can't say it about me either. Pay? If it were pay, I'd have left long ago, like the others. I'm still here because I admire you. I speak out because you make me so angry, still so . . .

ILSE [*with a despairing cry*]. What more do you want me to do?

CROMO. Nothing now, I know that. I'm talking about before. Before that fellow killed himself and became, for you and for all of us, the cancer that's eaten into our very bones. Look at us: mangy dogs, starving strays, kicked around from pillar to post . . . and you there, with high head and drooping wings, like a dangling bird, one of those they sell in bunches, strung up through holes in their beaks.

QUAQUÈO. But who killed himself?

The question falls amid the violent emotions of CROMO's *companions who have been upset by his words. Nobody answers.*

LA SGRICIA. One of them?

ILSE [*noticing her, with a sudden impulse of sympathy*]. No, dear granny, not one of them. Someone who was on a higher plane than ordinary people. A poet.

COTRONE. Ah no, madam, forgive me. Not a poet!

SPIZZI. The Countess is speaking of the author of *The Fable of the Changeling Son* which we have been performing for the past two years.

COTRONE. I guessed as much.

SPIZZI. And you dare to say he wasn't a poet.

COTRONE. If he was, that wasn't why he killed himself.

CROMO. He killed himself because he was in love with her! [*Pointing to the* COUNTESS]

COTRONE. Ah, that's it. Because the Countess, I suppose, being faithful to her husband, chose not to return his love. Poetry's got nothing to do with it. A poet writes poetry: he doesn't kill himself.

ILSE [*gesturing towards* CROMO]. He says I should have responded to that love, didn't you hear? Now that I was a countess! As if the title gave me the right . . .

COUNT. And not the heart.

CROMO. You keep quiet. She loved him too!

ILSE. Me?

CROMO. Yes, you; yes, you did. And I think a lot better of you for it. Otherwise I wouldn't be able to understand anything. [*Points to the* COUNT] And now he's paying for the sacrifice you made when you didn't give in. Which goes to show that you should never disobey when the heart commands.

COUNT. Have you finished telling our business to all and sundry?

CROMO. Since we're already talking about it. I wasn't the one who started.

COUNT. Yes, you started it.

QUAQUÈO. So much so that you even got a slap for it. [*General laughter at this sally of* QUAQUÈO]

ILSE. Yes, poor dear, a slap in the face [*she goes up to* CROMO *and strokes his cheek*] which now I'll cancel like this. You're not the enemy, even if you do show me up in public.

CROMO. No, not me.

ILSE. Yes you do, and you stab me in front of all these onlookers.

CROMO. Stab you? Me?

ILSE. That's how I feel it . . . [*Turning to* COTRONE] But it's natural, once we show ourselves in public. [*To the* COUNT] Poor man, you'd like to keep your dignity. Don't worry, it will be over soon enough, I can feel we're near the end.

COUNT. No, Ilse. You just need to rest a while.

ILSE. What do you still want to hide? And where? If your soul hasn't sinned, you can show it like a child, naked or in rags. The sleep in my eyes, that too has been torn away in rags . . . [*Looking around and gazing into the distance*] We're in the country here, oh heaven, and it's evening . . . And these people in front of us . . . [*To her husband*] I loved him, you see. And I made him die. Now that he's dead I can say that, my dear, say it of someone who got nothing from me. [*She goes up to* COTRONE] Sir, this feels almost like a dream, or another life, after death . . . This sea that we crossed . . . In those days I was called Ilse Paulsen.

COTRONE. I know, Countess.

ILSE. I had left a good name on the stage . . .

COUNT [*glaring at* CROMO]. Unsullied!

CROMO [*sharply*]. Whoever said it wasn't! She was always some kind of wild enthusiast. Just imagine, before she married him she wanted to become a nun.

SPIZZI. You can say that and still argue that once she became a countess . . .

CROMO. I've already explained why I said that.

ILSE. For me it was a sacred debt! [*To* COTRONE *again*] There was a young man, his friend [*gestures towards her husband*], a poet: one day he came to read me a play he was writing—for me, he said— but with no hope of seeing me perform it because I was no longer an actress. But I thought it was so beautiful that, yes, [*looking across at* CROMO] I became wildly enthusiastic right away. [*To* COTRONE *again*] But a woman doesn't take long to notice these things—I mean when a man thinks about her in a certain way. And I understood perfectly well that through the fascination of that play he wanted to lure me back to my old life; not for the sake of the play itself, but to have me for his own. Yet I felt that if I rejected him outright, he would leave it unfinished. And so for the sake of that play's beauty, not only did I not reject him, but I fed his illusion right up to the end. When the play was finally completed, I drew back from the fire—but I was already aflame. How can't you understand, since you see me reduced to this. He's right [*referring to* CROMO], I was never to break free of him. The life I denied to him I now had to give to his work. And even he understood it [*indicating her husband*] and agreed that I should return to the stage in order to pay this sacred debt. Return for this one play.

CROMO. Consecration and martydom! Because he [*meaning the* COUNT] was never jealous, even afterwards.

COUNT. I had no reason to be.

CROMO. But don't you feel that for her he isn't dead? She wants him to live. And there she is, ragged as a beggar, dying of it and condemning the rest of us to death, all so that he can live on.

DIAMANTE. Now who's jealous!

CROMO. Well done, you guessed it.

DIAMANTE. See, you're all in love with her.

CROMO. No, it makes me angry—and sorry for her.

ILSE [*at the same time, to* SPIZZI]. He wants to drag me down, and he lifts me even higher.

SPIZZI. He wants to seem nasty, even though he's not.

BATTAGLIA [*also at the same time*]. What a spiritual earthquake! I'm shaken to bits.

LUMACHI [*folding his arms*]. I ask you, is this situation really possible?

ILSE [*to* CROMO]. Of course I'm dying of it. I've accepted that, like an inheritance. Though I must say that at the start I little thought that, with his work, he would bring me all this suffering, the suffering that he knew and that I have found there.

COTRONE. And this play—the work of a poet, but performed before the ignorant crowd—has been your ruin? How I understand! How I understand!

BATTAGLIA. Right from the first performance.

COTRONE. Nobody was interested?

SACERDOTE. They all hated it.

CROMO. Booing that shook the walls.

COTRONE. Really? Really?

ILSE. You're glad, are you?

COTRONE. No, Countess, it's just that I understand it so well. The work of a poet . . .

DIAMANTE. Nothing did any good. Not even the most amazing stage-sets ever seen! The dogs!

BATTAGLIA [*sighing as usual*]. And the lighting! What lighting!

CROMO. All the wonders of a spectacular production. Forty-two of us, what with actors and extras . . .

COTRONE. And now you're down to so few?

CROMO [*showing his clothes*]. And like this. That's the work of a poet.

COUNT [*bitter, scornful*]. You too!

CROMO [*showing the* COUNT]. A whole estate eaten up.

COUNT. I don't regret it. It was my choice.

ILSE. How lovely! And worthy of you!

COUNT. That's not it. I'm not some wild enthusiast. I really believed in the play.

COTRONE. Ah, but you know, Countess, when I said 'the work of a poet', I wasn't damning the play: on the contrary, I was damning the people who turned against it.

COUNT. For me to belittle the play is to belittle her [*referring to his wife*] and to belittle the price I put on what she has done. I've paid for it with my whole estate, and I don't care and I regret nothing. As long as she can hold her head up high, and as long as the state I've been reduced to is at least ennobled by the grandeur and beauty of the work itself. If not, then the contempt of those people . . . you know what I mean . . . and the laughter . . . [*he is stifled with emotion*]

COTRONE. But my dear Count, I hate those people myself. That's why I live here. The proof? See this. [*He shows the fez that he has been holding ever since the visitors' arrival and shoves it on his head*] I used to be a Christian; now I'm a Turk.

LA SGRICIA. Oh, oh. Let's not touch religion. Not religion!

COTRONE. Calm down, dear, nothing to do with Mohammed. I say

I'm a Turk because there's no poetry left in Christianity. But good God, was there really so much hostility?

COUNT. No, not really. We did find friends here and there . . .

SPIZZI. Full of enthusiasm . . .

DIAMANTE [*glumly*]. But not many.

CROMO. And the theatre managers cancelled our contracts and kept us out of the big cities with the excuse that we no longer had the numbers, or the scenery and the costumes.

COUNT. And it's not true. We still have everything we need to put on the play.

BATTAGLIA. The costumes are over there in those bags.

LUMACHI. Under the hay. . .

SPIZZI. And in any case, they're not absolutely necessary.

CROMO. And the scenery?

COUNT. We've always managed so far.

BATTAGLIA. Some of the roles can be doubled. I play both a man and a woman.

CROMO. Offstage as well.

BATTAGLIA [*with a feminine wave of the hand*]. Now that's mean!

SACERDOTE. In short, we can handle anything.

DIAMANTE. And we leave nothing out. What we can no longer perform, we read.

SPIZZI. And the play's so wonderful that nobody cares if we're a few actors short or if some of the props are missing.

COUNT [*to* COTRONE]. There's nothing missing, nothing! Don't listen to him. Always this damned old relish for running ourselves down!

COTRONE. I admire your spirit; but believe me, you don't need to convince me that it's a fine play and an excellent spectacle. You were directed to me by a friend who lives rather far away. Perhaps he couldn't contact you, or maybe he was too late, but he didn't pass on my advice, which was to stop you from venturing as far as this.

COUNT. Oh yes? Why?

SPIZZI. So there's nothing doing here?

CROMO. I told you so.

LUMACHI. I guessed as much. Up in those mountains!

COTRONE. Now just be patient. Don't lose heart. We'll fix up something.

DIAMANTE. But where, if there's nothing here?

COTRONE. Not in town, that's for sure. And if you've left your things there, you'd better go and pick them up.

COUNT. Isn't there a theatre in the town?

COTRONE. Yes, infested with mice and always closed. And even if it were open, nobody would go there.

QUAQUÈO. They're thinking of pulling it down . . .

COTRONE. To make a little stadium . . .

QUAQUÈO. For racing and wrestling.

MARA-MARA. No, no. I heard they want to turn it into a cinema.*

COTRONE. Don't even think of it!

COUNT. So where then? There are no houses round here.

DIAMANTE. Where have we ended up?

SPIZZI. They did refer us to you.

COTRONE. And here I am. Entirely at your service, along with my friends. Don't you worry: we'll see, we'll think it over, we'll come up with something. In the meantime, if you would care to come in . . . You must be tired. We should be able to put you up for the night somehow. It's a large house.

BATTAGLIA. A bite of supper?

COTRONE. Yes, but you'd do well to follow our example.

BATTAGLIA. Which is?

DOCCIA. Do without everything and have no need of anything.

QUAQUÈO. Don't scare them.

BATTAGLIA. What if you need everything?

COTRONE. Come on in!

BATTAGLIA. How can you go without everything?

COTRONE. My lady Countess . . . [*Now slumped on the bench*, ILSE *shakes her head*] You won't come in?

QUAQUÈO [*to* DOCCIA]. You see, she doesn't want to go inside.

COUNT. She will. Later. [*To* COTRONE] Look after the others, by all means.

DIAMANTE. You think we should accept?

CROMO. At least get a roof over your heads. You don't want to stay out here in the damp of the night.

BATTAGLIA. And we do need something to eat.

COTRONE. Of course, of course. We'll find something. You see to it, Mara-Mara.

MARA-MARA. Yes, yes. Come on in, come on.

LUMACHI. Well we certainly can't go all the way back to town. I do have the cart, thanks very much! The problem is that I have to pull it myself!

SACERDOTE [*to* BATTAGLIA *as he makes his way into the house*]. The less you eat the better you sleep.

BATTAGLIA. At first, yes. But then, old boy, it starts gnawing away and wrecks both your sleep and your stomach.

COTRONE [*to* LUMACHI]. The cart can stay here outside. [*To* DOCCIA] Doccia, you think about finding everybody a place.

SPIZZI. Especially the Countess!

CROMO. Let's hope there'll be room for everyone.

MILORDINO. Everyone, everyone. There are rooms to spare.

LA SGRICIA [*to* COTRONE]. Not mine, though. I'm not giving up mine for anybody.

COTRONE. Not yours. Don't worry. We all know. It's the old chapel, with the organ.

QUAQUÈO [*pushing them on with glee*]. In we go! In we go! What fun! I'll be a naughty boy. I'll dance on the keyboard like a cat.

They all go into the villa, except for ILSE, *the* COUNT, *and* COTRONE.

A brief pause

II

The last gleams of twilight fade and the lights dim on the stage. Moonlight slowly floods the scene. COTRONE *waits until all the others have gone inside and then, after a brief pause, resumes the conversation in a calmer tone.*

COTRONE. For the Countess there's the old master-bedroom just as it was. It's the only one that still has a key, and I've got it.

ILSE [*still sitting in silence, brooding: then in a distant voice*].

> Five bold tomcats in a ring,
> Prowling and miaowling round,
> Eager all to spring and mate with
> Pretty puss who's panting for it.
> But when one dares to make a move
> All the others jump upon him,
> Scuffling, scratching, fighting, biting,
> Chasing and escaping . . .

COTRONE [*aside to the Count*]. Is she going over her lines?

COUNT [*answering in a whisper*]. No, it's not her part. [*Angrily picking up the refrain*]

> 'Yes, yes, yes!'

ILSE.

> And do these cats delight to play
> Such tricks upon a baby's head?
> Behold, behold!

COUNT. 'And what should I behold?'

ILSE. Here, this plait of woven hair. [*She immediately changes her tone to that of a mother protecting her baby's head by clasping it to her breast*] No, no, my golden child. [*Then, in the same tone as before*]

> Do you see it? Woe betide
> Us all if ever comb should touch
> Or scissors cut that plait, for then
> The child would surely die.

COTRONE. The Countess has an enchanting voice . . . I think she might feel better if she came into the house for a while.

COUNT. Come, Ilse, come on, dear. At least you'll get a bit of rest.

COTRONE. We may lack the essentials but we have such an abundance of the superfluous. Just you wait and see. Even outside. The wall of this facade. It's enough for me to give a shout . . . [*Cups his hands round his mouth and shouts*] Holà! [*Immediately, at the sound of his voice, the facade of the villa is flooded with a fantastic dawn light*] And the walls send forth light!

ILSE [*entranced like a child*]. Oh, how lovely!

COUNT. How did you manage that?

COTRONE. They call me Cotrone the Magician. I make a modest living from these spells. I create them. And now just watch. [*He cups his hands around his mouth again and calls*] Blackout! [*The faint moonlight returns as the light on the facade goes out*] It seems that the night makes this kind of darkness for the fireflies who break it as they fly here and there—who knows where—with their faint flashes of green. Well, look: there . . . there . . . there . . .

As he speaks he points in three different directions and for a moment, as far away as the foot of the mountain, three green apparitions glimmer like fading phantoms.

ILSE. Good Lord, what was that?

COUNT. What are they?

COTRONE. Fireflies. Mine. The Magician's fireflies. Here, Countess, it's like being on the borders of life. At a word, those borders dissolve, and the invisible enters in: phantoms loom in the mist. It's natural. Things happen that usually happen only in dreams. I make them happen while we are awake as well. That is all. Dreams, music, prayers, love . . . all that is infinite in man—you will find it within or around this villa.

> *At this point, looking very annoyed,* LA SGRICIA
> *reappears on the threshold.*

LA SGRICIA. Cotrone, you'll find that we get no more visits from the Angel Hundred-and-One;* I'm warning you.

COTRONE. Of course he'll come, Sgricia, don't worry! Come over here.

LA SGRICIA [*approaching*]. After the kind of talk I've been hearing from those devils back there!

COTRONE. Don't you know that you should never be afraid of words? [*Presenting her*] Here's the one who prays for us all. La Sgricia of the Angel Hundred-and-One. She came to live here with us because the Church wouldn't recognize the miracle that the Angel Hundred-and-One worked specially for her.

ILSE. Hundred-and-One?

COTRONE. Yes, because he's in charge of a hundred souls in Purgatory, and he leads them out every night on holy missions.

ILSE. Oh yes? And what was the miracle?

COTRONE [*to* LA SGRICIA]. Go on, Sgricia. Tell the story, tell it to the Countess.

LA SGRICIA [*frowning*]. You won't believe it.

ILSE. Of course I'll believe it.

COTRONE. Nobody could be more inclined to believe it than the Countess. It was when she had to go to a nearby village where her sister lived . . .

At this point, as if from high up in the air, comes a Voice—monotonous, echoing, but clear:

VOICE. An ill-famed village, as there are still many, alas, in this wild island.

COTRONE [*hurriedly reassuring the* COUNT *and* COUNTESS *who hardly know where to look in their amazement*]. It's nothing. Just voices. Have no fear. Let me explain . . .

VOICE [*from the cypress*]. Where a man can be killed like a fly.

COUNTESS [*terrified*]. My God! Who's speaking?

COUNT. Where are these voices coming from?

COTRONE. Don't get upset, Countess; now don't get upset. They form in the air. I shall explain.

LA SGRICIA. They are those who have been murdered. Can you hear? Can you hear?

COTRONE, *smiling, makes a discreet sign to the* COUNTESS *as if to say, behind* LA SGRICIA's *back: 'Don't believe it, we're doing it for her.' But* LA SGRICIA *catches him at it and reacts angrily.*

LA SGRICIA. And why not? What about the little boy?

COTRONE [*anxiously, acting the part*]. The little boy, yes of course, the little boy . . . [*Then to* ILSE] They tell the story, Countess, of a carter who gave a lift one night to a small boy that he met on the high road somewhere round here.. Hearing two or three coppers jingling in the child's pocket, he killed him in his sleep and took the cash to buy some tobacco as soon as he reached the village. He tossed the little corpse behind a hedge, and, heigh-up! went singing on his way under the stars of heaven . . .

LA SGRICIA [*solemn and terrible*]. Under the eyes of God that were watching him! Eyes watching him so closely that you know what he did? When he reached the village at dawn, instead of going to his master, he stopped at the police station, and with the coins of that child still in his bloody hand, he reported his crime as if someone else were speaking through him. You see what God can do?

COTRONE. With a faith like that, you weren't afraid to set out at night.

LA SGRICIA. What night? I didn't have to leave at night. I wasn't supposed to leave till dawn. It was my neighbour's fault, the one I'd asked to lend me the donkey.

COTRONE. A farmer who'd asked her to marry him.

LA SGRICIA. That's got nothing to do with it. With his mind on getting the donkey ready for daybreak, he woke up in the middle of the night: there was moonlight and he mistook it for dawn. As soon as I saw the sky, I realized that it was moonlight not daylight. Well, old as I am, I crossed myself, climbed in the saddle, and set off. But when I was on the high road, at night, in open country, among those frightful shadows, in that silence where the dust muffles even the sound of the donkey's hooves . . . and that moon, and the long white road ahead . . . I pulled my shawl over my eyes, and, covered up like that . . . well, I don't rightly know how it was, what with the slow going and me feeling so weak . . . but the fact is that at a certain point I seemed to wake up and there I was between two long files of soldiers . . .

COTRONE [*as if drawing attention to the imminent miracle*]. Yes, now for it . . .

LA SGRICIA [*continuing*]. They marched on both sides of the road, those soldiers; and at their head, in front of me, in the middle of the way, on his majestic white horse, rode the Captain. I felt so much better when I saw them and I thanked God for seeing to it that on the very night of my journey those soldiers too should be on their way to Favara.* But why were they all so silent? Young lads of twenty, with an old woman on a donkey in the middle—and they weren't laughing; you couldn't even hear their footsteps; they didn't so much as raise the dust . . . Why? How? I found out at daybreak when we came in sight of the village. The Captain halted on his big white horse and waited for me to catch up with him. 'Sgricia,' he said, 'I am the Angel Hundred-and-One and these who have escorted you thus far are souls from Purgatory. As soon as you arrive, set yourself right with God, for before midday you will die.' And he vanished with his holy band.

COTRONE [*quickly*]. But now for the best part! When her sister saw her turn up like that, all pale and staring . . .

LA SGRICIA. 'What's the matter with you?', she screams. And me: 'Call me a confessor.'
'Are you feeling ill?'
'I'll die before midday.'

[*She spreads her arms out wide*] And in fact . . . [*She stoops to look the* COUNTESS *in the eyes and asks*] Do you by any chance think you're still alive? [*She wags a finger in her face to signal 'no'*]

VOICE [*from behind the cypress*]. Don't you believe it.

With an approving smile, the little old lady gestures to the COUNTESS *as if to say: 'You hear what he says?'; then, still smiling and satisfied, she goes back into the house.*

ILSE [*first turning towards the cypress, then looking at* COTRONE]. Does she think she's dead?

COTRONE. In another world, Countess, along with all of us.

ILSE [*very disturbed*]. What world? And these voices?

COTRONE. Accept them. Don't try to explain them. I could . . .

COUNT. But are they some kind of trick?

COTRONE [*to the* COUNT]. If they help her to enter into another truth, far from the one you know, so transient and unstable . . . [*To the* COUNTESS] stay there, stay in that distance and try to look with the eyes of this old woman who has seen the Angel. Give up all reasoning. Our life is made of this. Lacking everything, but with all the time in the world for ourselves: a wealth beyond counting, a ferment of dreams. The things around us speak and make sense only in those arbitrary forms that we chance to give them in our despair. Our own kind of despair, mind you. We are rather calm and lazy; as we sit around, we think up—what shall I say?—mythological enormities: quite natural ones too, given the sort of life we lead. One cannot live off nothing, and so our life is one long celestial binge. We breathe the air of fable. Angels come down among us as a matter of course; and everything that is born within us is a wonder to ourselves. We hear voices, laughter; we see enchantments shaped and rising in every shadowy corner, created by the colours left jumbled in our eyes, dazzled by this island's excessive sun. The unreplying dark is not for us. The shapes are not invented by us: they are the desires of our own eyes. [*He listens*] Now. I hear her coming. [*He shouts*] Magdalen! [*Then, pointing*] There, on the bridge.

MARY MAGDALEN * *appears on the bridge in the reddish light shed by the lamp in her hand. She is young, with tawny hair and golden skin. She wears a red peasant dress and looks like a flame.*

ILSE. God above, who is it?

COTRONE. The Red Lady. Don't be afraid, Countess, she's flesh and blood. Come here, come, Magdalen. [*And while* MAGDALEN *approaches, he adds*] A poor idiot-girl who can hear but not speak. She's all alone, with nobody left to turn to and she wanders through the countryside. Men have their way with her and she never understands what has happened to her all too often; she gives birth in the fields. Here she is. She's always like this, her lips and eyes smiling with the pleasure that she takes and gives. Almost every night she comes to shelter with us at the villa. Go on in, Magdalen.

Still with that smile, sweet on her lips but veiled with suffering in her eyes, MAGDALEN *nods her head several times and goes into the house.*

ILSE. Who owns this villa?

COTRONE. Us and nobody. The Spirits.

COUNT. What Spirits?

COTRONE. Yes. The villa is said to be haunted by Spirits. That's why the previous owners abandoned it in terror and even left the island, a long time ago.

ILSE. But you don't believe in Spirits . . .

COTRONE. Of course I do. We create them.

ILSE. Ah, you create them . . .

COTRONE. Forgive me, Countess. I never expected *you* to talk to me like that. It's impossible that you shouldn't believe in them, just as we do. You actors take phantoms and give them your bodies so that they can live—and they do live! We do the opposite: we take our bodies and turn them into phantoms: and we too make them live. Phantoms . . . no need to go looking for them: it's enough to just draw them out of ourselves. You called yourself a shadow of what you once were.

ILSE. Well, just look at me . . .

COTRONE. So there! The woman you once were. All you need to do is draw her out. Don't you think she's still living inside you? And what of the spirit of the young man who killed himself for you, isn't he still living? He's inside you as well.

ILSE. Inside me?

COTRONE. And I could make him appear. Look, he's in there. [*Pointing to the villa*]

ILSE [*getting up*]. No!

COTRONE. Here he is!

SPIZZI *appears on the threshold of the villa, dressed up as a young poet, like the one who killed himself for the* COUNTESS. *He has used clothes from the curious wardrobe that the villa reserves for apparitions—a black cloak thrown over his shoulders, the kind that used to go with formal evening dress; a white silk scarf round his neck; a top hat on his head. His hands hold the two corners of his cloak which billows out elegantly in front, allowing him to conceal an electric torch that he is also holding and that lights up his face from below with a ghostly effect. As soon as she sees him, the* COUNTESS *lets out a scream and falls back on the bench, hiding her face.*

SPIZZI [*running to her*]. No, Ilse . . . Oh my God . . . I meant it as a joke.

COUNT. You, Spizzi! Ilse, it's Spizzi . . .

COTRONE. Drawn out of himself to appear as a phantom.

COUNT [*angry*]. What have you got to say now?

COTRONE. The truth.

SPIZZI. I was only joking.

COTRONE. And I have always invented truths, my dear sir. And people have always thought I was telling lies. One never tells the truth as well as when one invents it. Here's the proof! [*He points to* SPIZZI] Only joking? It was an act of obedience. We don't choose our masks by chance. And here are more proofs, more proofs . . .

Back on stage, emerging from the villa, come DIAMANTE, BATTAGLIA, LUMACHI, *and* CROMO, *and in that order* COTRONE *will present them. They are dressed up in costumes from the wardrobe and lit by the various colours of the torches they hold hidden from view. All the others follow them.*

COTRONE [*taking* DIAMANTE *by the hand*]. You, of course, dressed as a countess . . . [*To the* COUNT] Did you, by any chance, have some function at court?

COUNT [*puzzled*]. No. Why?

COTRONE [*showing* DIAMANTE's *costume*]. Because this is very clearly the dress of a Lady-in-Waiting. [*Turning to* BATTAGLIA] And you, like a tortoise in its shell, found yourself perfectly at home as a bigoted old hag. [*Now he presents* LUMACHI *who has put on a donkey-skin with a cardboard head*] And you were thinking of the donkey you need so badly. [*Then, as he goes to shake hands with* CROMO] And you've made yourself into a Pasha. Congratulations. You obviously have a kind heart.

COUNT. But what *is* this? A carnival parade?

CROMO. Back in there [*referring to the villa*] there's a whole storeroom of ghost stuff.

LUMACHI. You should just see those costumes. You won't find more in any theatrical stores.

COTRONE. And each one of you went and took the mask that suited him best.

SPIZZI. Not me. I did it . . .

COUNT [*annoyed*]. For a joke? [*Pointing to* SPIZZI's *costume*] Is that get-up your idea of a joke?

ILSE. He was only obeying someone . . .

COUNT. Who is . . . ?

ILSE [*indicating* COTRONE]. Him. He's the one who plays the Magician. Didn't you hear?

COTRONE. No, Countess . . .

ILSE. You keep quiet. I know! Don't you invent the truth?

COTRONE. In all my life I've never done anything else. Without wanting to, Countess. All those truths that we consciously reject. I draw them out from the secret crannies of the senses or, in some cases, the most fearsome, from the dark caves of instinct. In my home town I invented so many that I had to run away, pursued by scandals. Here and now I try to dissolve such truths into evanescent phantoms. Passing shadows. With these friends of mine I contrive to blur and dissolve even external reality into a glowing mist, by pouring my soul, like flakes of coloured cloud, into the dreaming night.

CROMO. Like fireworks?

COTRONE. But without all the noise. Silent enchantments. Foolish folk get scared and stay away, so we are left here as masters. Masters of nothing and everything.

CROMO. And what do you live on?

COTRONE. Like this. On nothing and everything.

DOCCIA. You can't have everything, except when you've got nothing left.

CROMO [*to the* COUNT]. Hear that? That's us all right. So then, we must have everything.

COTRONE. Well, no; because you still *want* to have something. When you really don't want anything more, then yes.

MARA-MARA. You can sleep without a bed . . .

CROMO. Badly . . .

MARA-MARA. But still you sleep!

DOCCIA. Who can stop you sleeping when God, who wants you healthy, sends you sleep and tiredness like a benediction? Then you can sleep, even without a bed.

COTRONE. And you need hunger too, eh, Quaquèo? So that a crust of bread can give you the pleasure of eating in a way that all the rarest foods can never do when you're full or have no appetite.

Smiling and nodding his agreement, QUAQUÈO *rubs his stomach with his hand as children do when they want to show how much they enjoy what they are eating.*

DOCCIA. Only when you no longer have a home does all the world become yours. You walk and walk, and then let go, sink down into the grass beneath the silent skies; and you are everything and you are nothing . . . nothing and everything.

COTRONE. That's how beggars speak—refined people, Countess, with very special tastes—who have managed to reduce themselves to the exquisitely privileged condition of beggary. There are no mediocre beggars. The mediocre are all sensible and thrifty. Here we have Doccia as our banker. He spent thirty years putting aside that little extra cash which men dole out for the luxury of giving alms when asked; and he came here to devote it to the freedom of dreaming. He pays for everything.

DOCCIA. Yes, but if you don't go easy . . .

COTRONE. He acts the miser to make it last longer.

THE OTHER SCALOGNATI [*laughing*]. It's true, it's true.

COTRONE. Perhaps I too could have been a great man, Countess. I resigned. Resigned from everything—status, honour, dignity, virtue, all those things that, by God's grace, the animals in their blessed innocence know nothing of. Freed from all those hindrances, the soul is left vast as the air, full of sunshine and clouds, open to every lightning flash, abandoned to every wind, the superfluous and mysterious stuff of wonders that lifts and scatters us in fabled horizons. We look back at the earth, what sadness! Perhaps there is someone down there who imagines that he is living our life, but it isn't true. Not one of us is in the body that others see, but in the soul that speaks from who knows where; no one can know: semblance amid semblances, with this silly name of Cotrone . . . and Doccia for him, and Quaquèo for him. A body is death: darkness and stone. Pity the poor man who sees himself in his body and his name. We create phantoms. Phantoms of whatever comes to mind. Some are obligatory. For example, the Scotswoman with her umbrella [*points out* MARA-MARA] or the Dwarf and his blue cape. [QUAQUÈO's *gesture shows that this is his particular attribute*] Specialities of the villa. The others are all the fruit of our fantasy.

With the divine prerogative of children who take their games seriously, we pour the wonder that is within us into the things we play with, and let ourselves be enchanted by them. It is no longer a game, but a marvellous reality, a reality we live in, cut off from everything, even to the point of madness. So, ladies and gentlemen, let me say to you what they used to say to pilgrims: unfasten your sandals and put down your staff. You have reached your goal. For years I have been waiting for folk like you to give life to other phantoms that I have in mind. But we shall also put on your *Fable of the Changeling Son* as a wonder in itself without asking anything from anybody.

ILSE. Here?

COTRONE. Just for ourselves.

CROMO. He's inviting us to stay here for ever, don't you see?

COTRONE. Of course. What do you keep looking for in the world of men? Can't you see where it has got you?

QUAQUÈO AND MILORDINO. Yes, stay with us, stay here with us.

DOCCIA. Hold on, there are eight of them!

LUMACHI. I'm for it.

BATTAGLIA. It's a nice place.

ILSE. Which means that I shall have to go on by myself—at least to give readings of the *Fable* since I can't stage it.

SPIZZI. No, Ilse. Those who want can stay. I shall always follow you.

DIAMANTE. So shall I. [*To the* COUNT] You can always rely on me.

COTRONE. I understand that the Countess cannot renounce her mission.

ILSE. Never. To the very end.

COTRONE. So not even you want the work to live for itself—as it could only do here.

ILSE. It lives in me, but that's not enough. It must live in the world of men.

COTRONE. Poor play! Just as the poet had no love from you, so his play will have no glory from men. Enough. Now it's late and we had better get some rest. Since the Countess declines my offer, I have another idea: I shall propose it to you tomorrow at dawn.

COUNT. What idea?

COTRONE. Tomorrow at dawn, dear Count. The day is dazzlement, the night is for dreams, and only the twilight hours are made for men. Dawn for the future, sunset for the past. [*Showing the way into the villa with a sweep of his arm*] Until tomorrow!

Curtain

III

The storeroom for the apparitions, a large room in the middle of the villa with four doors, two on each side, indicating entry from two parallel corridors. The backdrop, flat and empty, can become transparent when required so that, as in a dream, one sees first a dawn sky with scudding white clouds, then the tender green of a gentle slope at the foot of the mountain, with trees around an oval pond; and finally (during the second dress rehearsal of The Fable of the Changeling Son*) a lovely seascape with harbour and lighthouse. The room seems to be filled with the oddest collection of household objects, furniture that is not real furniture but big dusty broken toys; yet everything in fact has been made ready so that the scenery of* The Fable of the Changeling Son *can be set up in the twinkling of an eye. There are also a number of musical instruments: a piano, a trombone, a drum, and five colossal skittles with human faces painted on their heads. Set awkwardly on the chairs are several puppets: three sailors, two little whores, a long-haired old man in a frock coat, and a sour-faced woman from the army stores.*

As the curtain rises the stage appears flooded with an unnatural light that seems to come from nowhere. In this light the puppets on the chairs look disturbingly human, even though the immobility of their masks reveals them as puppets. Through the first door on the left, running away from something, comes ILSE, *followed by the* COUNT *who seeks to restrain her.*

ILSE. No, I say, I want to go outside. [*Stopping all of a sudden, surprised and almost frightened*] Where are we?

COUNT [*also stopping*]. Hmm! Maybe it's what they call the apparition store.

ILSE. And this light, where does it come from?

COUNT [*pointing to the* PUPPETS]. Look at these. Are they puppets?

ILSE. They seem real . . .

COUNT. You're right, as if they were pretending not to see us. But look, you'd say they were made specially for us, to fill the gaps in the Company. Look, the 'Old Piano Man' and the 'Woman who Runs the Café', and the 'Three Little Sailors'* that we never manage to find.

ILSE. *He* must have set them up.

COUNT. Him? What does he know about it?

ILSE. I gave him the *Changeling Son* to read.

COUNT. Ah, that explains it. But what can we do with puppets? They can't speak. I still don't understand where we've ended up. And in this uncertainty I'd like to feel that you at least—[*Tender and timid, he moves to touch her*]

ILSE [*with a sudden exasperated start*]. God above, how do we get out of here?

COUNT. Do you really want to go outside?

ILSE. Yes, yes. Out, out!

COUNT. Out where?

ILSE. I don't know. Outside. In the open.

COUNT. At night? It's the middle of the night. Everybody's asleep. You don't want to be out in the cold at this hour?

ILSE. I have a horror of that bed.

COUNT. Yes, it is horrible, I agree. So high.

ILSE. With that moth-eaten purple coverlet.

COUNT. But after all it's still a bed.

ILSE. You go and sleep in it: I can't.

COUNT. And you?

ILSE. There's that bench outside, in front of the door.

COUNT. But you'll be even more afraid alone, outside. Up there at least you'll be with me.

ILSE. You're precisely the one I'm afraid of, dear, only you. Can't you understand?

COUNT [*taken aback*]. Afraid of me? Why?

ILSE. Because I know you. And I see you. You follow me around like a beggar.

COUNT. Shouldn't I be by your side?

ILSE. Not like that. Not looking at me like that. I feel somehow all sticky: yes, yes, sticky from your timid suppliant softness. It's in your eyes, your hands.

COUNT [*mortified*]. Because I love you.

ILSE. Thanks very much! You have a special gift of thinking of it in the wrong places or when I feel practically dead. All I can do is clear off. Or start screaming like a madwoman. You know something: yours is a horrible kind of usury.

COUNT. Usury?

ILSE. Yes, usury. Aren't you trying to get back out of me everything that you've lost?

COUNT. Ilse! How can you think such a thing?

ILSE. Go on. Now you'll force me to ask your pardon.

COUNT. Me? What can you mean? I've lost nothing. I don't feel that I've lost anything, as long as I have you. Is that what you call usury?

ILSE. Horrible. Unbearable. You're always trying to look into my eyes. I can't stand it.

COUNT. I feel that you're miles away. I want to call you back . . .

ILSE. Always for the same thing.

COUNT [*hurt*]. No. To what you once were for me.

ILSE. Ah, once! When? Tell me, in what other life? But can you really look at me and see the woman I used to be?

COUNT. Aren't you still and always my Ilse?

ILSE. I don't even recognize my own voice any more. I speak, and for some reason my voice, and the voices of others, and all the sounds around me—well, it's as if they fell on an air that's gone deaf to them; so that all the words are cruel to me. For heaven's sake, spare me those words!

COUNT [*after a pause*]. So it's true?

ILSE. What's true?

COUNT. That I'm alone. You no longer love me.

ILSE. What? I don't love you? What a thing to say, you silly man! When you know I can't imagine being without you. What I'm saying, dear, is that you mustn't *expect* it: because you know, good God, you know that for me it's only possible when you're not even thinking about it. You need to feel it, dear, without *thinking* about it. Come on, be reasonable.

COUNT. Well, I know I'm never supposed to think of myself.

ILSE. You always say you want the good of others.

COUNT. And my own too from time to time. If I could ever have imagined . . .

ILSE. I can't even think of anything that I regret any more.

COUNT. What I mean is that your feelings for me . . .

ILSE. They're the same, the same as always.

COUNT. No, it's not true. Before . . .

ILSE. Are you quite sure about before? Sure that my feelings would have lasted unchanged under those conditions? This way at least they last as best they can. But don't you see the way we are? It's a wonder we don't feel the certainty of our own bodies evaporating at the touch of our hands.

COUNT. That's just why.

ILSE. Why what?

COUNT. Why at least I want to feel you near me.

ILSE. Aren't I here with you now?

COUNT. Maybe it's a passing mood, but I feel totally lost. I have no idea where we are or where we're going.

ILSE. There's no going back now.

COUNT. And I see no way forward.

ILSE. This man here says that he invents the truth . . .

COUNT. Oh yes, he invents it, easy for him . . .

ILSE. The truth of dreams, he says, more true than we are ourselves.

COUNT. Him and his dreams!

ILSE. And really, look, no dream could be more absurd than this truth—that we're here tonight and that this is true. If you think about it, if we let ourselves get caught up, we'll go mad.

COUNT. I'm afraid we let ourselves get caught up a good while ago. We just kept on going and now we've arrived. I'm thinking of when we came down the steps of our old palace for the last time with all the servants there to say farewell. I was carrying poor little Riri. You never think about her; I always do. With that silky white coat.

ILSE. Once we start thinking about everything we've lost!

COUNT. All those candelabra lighting up the marble staircase! As we came down, we were so happy and confident that what we found outside, the cold, the rain, the dense dark mist . . .

ILSE [*after a pause*]. And yet, believe me, all told we've lost very little, even if it was a lot in material terms. If that wealth served to buy us this poverty, we shouldn't feel cast down.

COUNT. And you're saying this to me, Ilse? It's what I've always told you: you shouldn't feel cast down.

ILSE. Yes, yes; now let's go; you're a good man; let's go back upstairs. Maybe now I shall manage to get some rest.

They go out through the same door by which they entered. As soon as they have left, the PUPPETS *lean forward, place their hands on their knees and break into mocking laughter.*

PUPPETS. —How complicated, good Lord, how they complicate things!
—And then they end up by doing
—Just what they would have done quite naturally
—Without all those complications.

All by itself the trombone comments ironically with three grumbling notes; the drum, shaking like a sieve, beats its agreement without drumsticks, while the five skittles spring upright, showing their impudent heads. Then the PUPPETS *throw themselves back in their chairs with another mocking laugh—a 'hee-hee' this time, if the first was 'ho-ho'. All of a sudden they stop and resume their original positions just as the upstage right door opens and an exultant* SGRICIA *enters to announce:*

LA SGRICIA. The Angel Hundred-and-One! The Angel Hundred-and-One! He's come with all his cohort to take me. Here he comes. Here he comes. Down on your knees, everybody. On your knees!

At her command, the PUPPETS *automatically kneel while the large backdrop lights up and becomes transparent. Two columns of the souls in Purgatory file past in the form of winged angels and in their midst on a majestic white horse rides the* ANGEL HUNDRED-AND-ONE. *A chorus of soft treble voices accompanies the procession.*

Bearing the gentle arms of peace
When night bids strife and tumult cease,
With gifts of faith and love,
To those who struggle in the fray

And all poor souls who go astray
Help comes from God above.

When the procession is about to end, LA SGRICIA *gets up to follow it and goes out of the second door on the left which remains open after her exit. Behind the last pair of souls, as they gradually move out of sight, the backdrop becomes opaque again. The music lasts a little longer, slowly fading away. One by one the* PUPPETS *stand up and then fall back motionless on their chairs. A few moments later* CROMO *backs into the room through the door that has been left open. His appearance keeps changing in a dreamlike way: at first we see his face, then the mask of the 'Customer', and the nose of the 'Prime Minister' from* The Fable of the Changeling Son. *Although his backward steps would suggest that he is retreating in fear, he seems to be seeking in vain the source of some faint sound; he is quite certain that he has heard it and it seemed to come from the well at the end of the corridor. At the same time, through the first door on the right* DIAMANTE *enters dressed as the witch 'Vanna Scoma'* but with her mask pushed up on her forehead. She sees* CROMO *and calls out to him.*

DIAMANTE. Cromo! [*And as soon as* CROMO *turns round*] What's that face you're making?

CROMO. Me? Making a face? What about you? You're dressed up like Vanna Scoma and you've forgotten to lower your mask over your face.

DIAMANTE. Don't make me laugh. Me, as Vanna Scoma? Now you, you're dressed as the 'Customer' and you're wearing the nose of the 'Prime Minister'. I'm still dressed as a Lady-in-Waiting and I'm getting undressed. But you know something? I'm afraid I've swallowed a pin.

CROMO. Swallowed it? Is it serious?

DIAMANTE [*showing her throat*]. I can feel it here.

CROMO. But look here, do you really think you're still dressed as a Lady-in-Waiting?

DIAMANTE. I was getting undressed, I tell you; and just as I was getting undressed . . .

CROMO. Getting undressed? Come off it! Look what you're wearing. You're got up like Vanna Scoma. [*As she bends her head to look at her clothes, he flicks the mask down over her face*] And there's the mask.

DIAMANTE [*putting her hand to her throat*]. Oh God, now I can't speak.

CROMO. Is it because of the pin? Are you quite sure you swallowed it?

DIAMANTE. It's here! Here!

CROMO. Were you holding it between your teeth as you got undressed?

DIAMANTE. No. I think I just swallowed it right now. And there may even have been two.

CROMO. Pins?

DIAMANTE. Pins! Pins! Though the other one, I'm not so sure . . . perhaps I dreamt it. Or was it before the dream? But the fact is I feel it here.

CROMO. Now I get it: you must have dreamt about it because you feel a pricking in your throat. I bet your tonsils are inflamed, with little infected white spots.

DIAMANTE. Maybe. The damp, the stress.

CROMO. You must have fever too.

DIAMANTE. Perhaps.

CROMO [*in the same terse pitying tone*]. Drop dead!

DIAMANTE [*turning on him*]. Drop dead yourself!

CROMO. It's all that's left for us, my dear, with the kind of life we're leading.

DIAMANTE. Pins in my dress, yes, there was one, all rusty; but I remember pulling it out and throwing it away; I didn't put it between my teeth. Besides, if I'm no longer dressed as a Lady-in-Waiting . . .

BATTAGLIA *comes rushing in through the first left door like a man possessed.*

BATTAGLIA. Oh God, I've seen it! I've seen it!

DIAMANTE. Seen what?

BATTAGLIA. In the wall back there. Something horrible!

CROMO. Ah, if you say you've *seen* it, it must be true. Well, me too, me too, I've *heard* something.

DIAMANTE. What? Don't scare me. I'm running a fever.

CROMO. Down at the end of the corridor, just where the well is. Music, but what music!

DIAMANTE. Music?

CROMO [*taking them both by the hand*]. Here, come on.

DIAMANTE AND BATTAGLIA [*simultaneously drawing back*]. No, you're crazy. What music?

CROMO. So beautiful! Come with me. Music . . . what are you afraid of? [*They tiptoe towards the back of the stage*] But we need to find exactly the right place. It must be here. I heard it, there's no doubt about that. As if from the other world. It comes from the bottom of that well down there, can you see? [*Pointing out through the second left door*]

DIAMANTE. But what music?

CROMO. A concert in Paradise. Here, wait. It was like this. I moved away and I stopped hearing it; I came too near and I stopped hearing it. Then, suddenly, getting just the right spot . . . Here you are! Don't move! Can you hear it? Can you hear?

And indeed, muted but distinct, comes the sound of sweet soft music. The three stand in a line, leaning forward to listen, ecstatic and fearful.

DIAMANTE. God above, it's true.

BATTAGLIA. Couldn't it be Sgricia playing the organ?

CROMO. Not a chance. It's nothing earthly. And if we move one step, like this, we stop hearing it.

In fact, as soon as they move, the music stops.

DIAMANTE. No, once again! Let's hear it again!

They go back to where they were before and again they hear the music.

CROMO. Here it is again.

They stand listening for a while. Then CROMO *steps forward with the other two and the music stops.*

BATTAGLIA. I feel quite shattered by fear.

CROMO. In this villa you really do see and hear things.

BATTAGLIA. I tell you I saw it. The wall back there. It opened up.

DIAMANTE. Opened up?

BATTAGLIA. Yes, and you could see the sky through it.

DIAMANTE. Wasn't it the window?

BATTAGLIA. No, the window was on this side and closed. There was no window in the wall facing me. And it opened up, oh, with a moonlight like nothing you've ever seen, shining on a long stone bench so clearly that you could have counted the blades of grass in the tufts that grew around it. Then that idiot girl in the red dress came by, the one who smiles and never speaks, and sat down on the bench. And she was followed by some simpering dwarf.

CROMO. Quaquèo?

BATTAGLIA. Not Quaquèo. This one wore a dove-grey cloak which reached down to his feet and swung like a bell; and on top of it his tiny head and a face that looked stained with grape juice. He handed the woman a sparkling jewel-box and then jumped over the bench as if to run off. But, in fact, he was hiding behind the bench and poking his malicious head out every now and then to see if she would give in to temptation. But she didn't budge, just sat there with her head bent, smiling and staring at the jewel-box in her hands. I could even see her teeth between her lips as they half-opened in a smile.

CROMO. Sure you weren't dreaming?

BATTAGLIA. Of course I wasn't. I saw it, saw it the way I see you two here and now.

DIAMANTE. Oh Lord, Cromo. That pin then, I'm afraid I really did swallow it.

CROMO [*struck by a sudden idea*]. Wait, wait here: I have an idea: I'm going to my room and I'll be back right away. [*Exits through the same door by which he entered*]

DIAMANTE [*puzzled, to* BATTAGLIA]. Why's he going to his room?

BATTAGLIA. I don't know . . . I'm all of a tremble . . . don't leave me . . . Oh, don't you think those puppets have moved?

DIAMANTE. Did you see them move?

BATTAGLIA. One of them. I thought one moved.

DIAMANTE. No. They're just lying where they were put.

CROMO *re-enters, as excited as a schoolboy on holiday.*

CROMO. There. Just as I thought. I guessed as much. It's not us who are actually here, it's not us.

BATTAGLIA. What do you mean, it's not us?

CROMO. Cheer up! It's nothing to worry about. Just keep quiet. Go and look in your bedrooms and see for yourselves. You'll be convinced.

DIAMANTE. Of what? That we're not us?

BATTAGLIA. What did you see in your room?

DIAMANTE. And who are we then?

CROMO. Go and see. It's a laugh. Go on.

As soon as the two have gone out through the doors they came in by, the PUPPETS *straighten up, stretching themelves and exclaiming:*

PUPPETS. —At last!
            —Thank goodness, you've finally got the message.
            —It took long enough.
            —Couldn't have stood it much longer.

CROMO [*amazed at first to see them getting up, but then grasping the logic of the situation*]. Oh, you too? Well yes, sure; it's only right. You too. Why not?

ONE OF THE PUPPETS. Shall we stretch our legs a bit? How about it?

Two of them take him by the hand and form a circle with the others. As CROMO *and the* PUPPETS *dance in a ring, the musical instruments automatically strike up again in a discordant accompaniment. Meanwhile* BATTAGLIA *and* DIAMANTE *return looking thunderstruck.* BATTAGLIA *seems unaware that he is now dressed as one of the little whores with a rag of a hat on his head.*

DIAMANTE. I must be going mad. So this [*touching her body*] is not my body? And yet I'm touching it.

BATTAGLIA. So you saw yourself back there as well?

DIAMANTE [*pointing to the* PUPPETS]. And all these, standing up. Oh my God, where are we? I'm going to screee . . .

CROMO [*putting a hand over her mouth*]. Be quiet. There's no need to scream. I found my body too, back there deep in a splendid sleep. We awoke outside, do you see what I mean?

DIAMANTE. Outside? Outside what?

CROMO. Outside ourselves. We're dreaming. Can't you see? We're ourselves, but in a dream, outside our bodies which are sleeping back there.

DIAMANTE. And you're sure that our bodies are breathing and not dead?

CROMO. Dead, she says! My body's lying there snoring, happy as a pig, belly-up, chest rising and falling like a bellows.

BATTAGLIA [*hurt, sadly*]. Mine had its mouth wide open, yet I've always slept like a little angel.

ONE OF THE PUPPETS [*sneering*]. Like a little angel! How lovely!

ANOTHER PUPPET. Dribbling saliva down one side.

BATTAGLIA [*with a scared gesture towards the* PUPPETS]. And these?

CROMO. They're part of the dream too, you see. And look at yourself; you've become a little whore. Now here's a nice sailor-boy for you. Go on, give him a hug. [*He shoves him into the arms of one of the sailor-suited puppets*] Let's dance. Dance happily in the dream!

More music from the instruments. They dance but with the strange jerky movements of puppets who do not bend easily. Through the first door to the left comes SPIZZI *who elbows his way through the dancing couples. He is holding a rope.*

SPIZZI. Make way! Make way! Let me get through.

CROMO. Oh, Spizzi! You too. What's that in your hand? Where are you going?

SPIZZI. Let me go. I can't take it any more. I'm off to finish it.

CROMO. Finish it how? With this rope? [*He lifts* SPIZZI'*s arm and at the sight of the rope everyone bursts out laughing.* CROMO *shouts*] You fool, you're dreaming it. You're hanging yourself in a dream.

SPIZZI [*breaking loose and running off through the second door on the right*]. Yes, right; now you'll see if it's a dream or not.

CROMO. Poor lad. All for love of the Countess.

Greatly alarmed and distressed, LUMACHI *and* SACERDOTE *come bursting in through the first doors on right and left.*

LUMACHI. Oh my God, Spizzi's going to hang himself!

SACERDOTE. He's hanging himself. Spizzi's hanging himself.

CROMO. No, no, he isn't. You're dreaming it too.

BATTAGLIA. Spizzi's asleep in his bed.

DIAMANTE. And so are you. Go and have a look.

LUMACHI. Sleeping, you say? There he is. He's really gone and hanged himself. Look!

The backdrop becomes transparent again and SPIZZI *is seen hanging from a tree. There is a general scream of horror as everyone runs upstage. Suddenly the scene is plunged in darkness and, as the actors vanish like images in a dream, the stage resounds with mocking laughter from the* PUPPETS *returning to their chairs. The lights go up again and, apart from the* PUPPETS *in the same immobile postures as before, the stage is empty. A few moments pass before the* COUNTESS, COTRONE, *and the* COUNT *enter through the first door on the right.*

ILSE. I saw him. I saw him, I tell you. Hanging from a tree here behind the villa.

COTRONE. But there are no trees behind the villa.

ILSE. Of course there are. Round a pond.

COTRONE. There's no pond, Countess. You can go and see.

ILSE [*to her husband*]. How is that possible? You saw it as well.

COUNT. Yes I did.

COTRONE. Don't let it worry you, Countess. It's the villa itself. Every night it takes on this life of music and of dreams. And all unknown to the dreamer, the dreams come to life outside us, incoherent, just as when we dream them. Only poets can give coherence to dreams. Here is Signor Spizzi, you see him? In flesh and blood; and he must have started all this off by dreaming that he'd hanged himself.

SPIZZI *has, in fact, entered gloomily through the first left door. He reacts to* COTRONE'S *words with a sudden start, surprised and indignant.*

SPIZZI. How do you know?

COTRONE. But we all know, my dear fellow.

SPIZZI [*to the* COUNTESS]. You too?

ILSE. Yes, I dreamed it as well.

COUNT. And me.

SPIZZI. All of you? How can that be?

COTRONE. It's quite clear that you can have no secrets from anybody, not even when you're dreaming. I was just explaining to the Countess that this too is a special privilege of our villa. Always, when the moon rises, everything on earth begins to turn into the stuff of dreams, as if life had withdrawn leaving only a melancholy shade in the memory. Then dreams come forth and sometimes a passionate soul will decide to put a rope round his neck and hang himself on some imaginary tree. My dear young friend, we all speak and, having done so, almost always realize that we have spoken in vain. And so we retreat disenchanted into ourselves, like a dog to its kennel at night after barking at a shadow.

SPIZZI.   No, it's the curse of those words that I've been repeating for two years with all the feeling that their author put into them.

ILSE.   But those words are addressed to a mother.

SPIZZI.   Thanks. I know that. But the man who wrote those words wrote them for you, and he certainly wasn't thinking of you as a mother!

COTRONE.   My dear friends, since we're talking about the blame that he attaches to the words of his part, I have something to say: dawn is near and yesterday I promised that I would tell you the idea that struck me about where you could go to put on your *Fable of the Changeling Son* . . . if you really don't want to stay here with us. You should know that today there's going to be a huge marriage feast to celebrate the union between the two families known as the Mountain Giants.

COUNT [*worried because he is on the small side, raising an arm*].   Giants?

COTRONE.   Not really giants, dear Count. They're called that way because they are tall burly folk who live up on the mountain nearby. I suggest that you go and present yourselves to them. We'll go with you because you need to know how to handle them. The task that they've taken in hand up there, the constant physical effort, the sheer courage needed in their struggle with the risks and dangers of a colossal project——excavating, laying foundations, diverting streams into mountain reservoirs, building factories and roads, clearing new farmland—all this has not just given them massive muscles; it's also made them naturally thick-headed and slightly brutish. But the fact that they're puffed up with success gives one a handle on them: their vanity. Lay it on with a trowel and they soon soften up. You can leave that part to me while you think about your own business. It'll be no trouble for me to take you up the mountain to the wedding of Uma di Dornio and Lopardo d'Arcifa. And we'll ask for a hefty fee, because the more we ask for the more seriously they'll take what's on offer. But now there's another problem: how will you manage to perform the *Fable*?

SPIZZI. Don't the giants have a theatre up there?

COTRONE. The theatre's not the issue. Anywhere will do to set up a theatre. I'm thinking of the play you want to perform. Along with my friends, I've been up all night, until a short while ago, reading your *Fable of the Changeling Son*. And I'll say this, Count: you're pushing it a bit when you say that you've got everything you need and that you'll leave nothing out. There are only eight of you, and you need a whole crowd.

COUNT. Yes, we don't have people for the walk-on parts.

COTRONE. Walk-on parts? Come off it! They all speak.

COUNT. But we're enough for the main characters.

COTRONE. The problem's not with the main characters. What matters above all is the magic—I mean that's what creates the fascination of the tale.

ILSE. That's true.

COTRONE. And what can you create it with? You've got nothing. A choral work like this . . . Now I can see, Count, how you managed to spend your whole inheritance on it. As I was reading through it, I felt absolutely transported. It's just made to be given life right here, Countess, among us, believers in the reality of phantoms more than in that of bodies.

COUNT [*pointing to the* PUPPETS *on the chairs*]. We saw the puppets already prepared . . .

COTRONE. Already? Ah yes. They were quick about it. I didn't know.

COUNT [*amazed*]. You didn't know? Wasn't it you who got them ready?

COTRONE. Not me. But it's simple. All the time I was reading up there, they were getting themselves ready down here, on their own.

ILSE. On their own? How?

COTRONE. I did tell you, my good friends, that the villa is inhabited
by spirits. And I wasn't joking. Here we're never surprised at anything. Forgive me if I say that human pride is truly idiotic. There
are other beings living a natural life on this earth, dear Count,
beings that we humans simply cannot perceive under normal conditions. But this is only because of our own defects, our five very
limited senses. Well, every so often, when conditions are not
normal, these beings reveal themselves to us and scare us out of
our wits. Hardly surprising, since we never even guessed they
existed! Non-human denizens of the earth, my friends, spirits of
nature, of all kinds, living among us, unseen, in the rocks, the
woods, the air, the water, the fire. The ancients knew it well, and
the simple folk have always known it. And here we too know it
well, for we compete with the spirits, and often we win, forcing
them to give our magic wonders a meaning that they neither know
nor care about. If you still see life as restricted to the limits of the
natural and the possible, then I warn you, Countess, that you will
never understand anything here. We are beyond those limits,
thank God. It's enough for us to imagine things and straightaway
those images come to life of their own accord. If something is truly
alive in us, then by virtue of that same life it will emerge spontan-
eously. Birth is freely given to whatever must be born. At most, we
use what means we have to ease those births. These puppets, for
example. If the spirit of the characters they represent is embodied
in them, then you will see them move and speak. And the real
miracle will never be the representation, believe me, but always the
imagination of the poet where those characters were born alive, so
alive that you can see them even when they are not there in the
flesh. To translate them into a fictional reality on the stage is what
theatres are usually for. It's your function.

SPIZZI. So now you're putting us on the same level as those puppets
of yours.

COTRONE. No, not on the same level, I'm afraid; a little bit below
that, my friend.

SPIZZI. Even below?

COTRONE. If the spirit of the characters can be embodied in the
puppets so well that they can move and speak, then after all . . .

SPIZZI. I'd be very curious to see this miracle.

COTRONE. Ah, you'd be 'curious', would you? Well, you know, 'curiosity' won't help you to see these miracles. You need to believe in them, my friend, the way children do. Your poet has imagined a Mother who believes that witches put a changeling in the cradle in place of her baby son: yes, those wind-riding witches of the night that humble folk call 'the Women'. Educated people laugh at the idea, we know, and maybe you do too; but let me tell you that 'the Women' really do exist, my good friends. Many a time, on stormy winter nights, we've heard them round here, shrieking at the top of their voices as they flee past on the wind. Listen, if we want to, we can even conjure them up.

> At night they crawl into the houses
> Creeping down the chimneys like
> Smoke, black smoke.
> What can a poor mother know?
> Tired out, her day's work done,
> She sleeps at last, while in the dark
> Those bending figures lean and stretch
> Their scraggy fingers . . .

ILSE [*amazed*]. You even know the verses by heart already?

COTRONE. Even? But we can put on the whole *Fable* for you right now, Countess, from beginning to end, just to try out all those necessary things that you don't have and we do. For one moment, Countess, for one moment try to live out your part as the Mother, and I'll show you, just to give you an example. When was your son exchanged?

ILSE. When? You mean in the *Fable*?

COTRONE. Of course, where else?

ILSE.

> Lying asleep one night,
> I hear a plaintive cry, I wake,
> Grope in the darkness, in my bed,
> And by my side:
> Not there.
> Where could that crying come from?
> My little child, so tightly wrapped
> In swaddling bands, could not have stirred—

COTRONE. Why are you stopping? Go on. Ask the question. Ask it. Just as it is in the script: 'Is not that true? Is not that true?'

He has hardly finished the question before the stage, darkened for a second, is flooded as if at some magic touch by a new unearthly light, and the COUNTESS *finds herself flanked by two women, the* PEASANT NEIGHBOURS *of the first scene of* The Fable of the Changeling Son. *They immediately answer her:*

FIRST NEIGHBOUR. It's true. It's true.

SECOND NEIGHBOUR. A baby, six months old, how could he?

ILSE [*looks at them, listens to them and is seized by a fear which is shared by* SPIZZI *and the* COUNT *who recoil*]. Oh God, can it be them?

COUNT. How is this possible?

COTRONE [*shouting at the* COUNTESS]. Carry on, carry on! What's so surprising? You drew them here yourself. Don't break the spell and don't ask for explanations. Say: 'When I picked him up . . .'

ILSE [*obeying in a daze*].

> When I picked him up
> Where he'd been thrown—
> There—under the bed—

From some unknown source above comes a powerful derisive cry:

VOICE. He fell! He fell!

The COUNTESS *looks up in terror, as do the others.*

COTRONE [*quickly*]. Don't lose your place. It's in the script. Carry on!

ILSE [*surrendering to the spell*].

> Ah yes, I know.
> That's what they say: he fell.

FIRST NEIGHBOUR.

> He fell, they say
> Who did not see
> The way he was found
> Under the bed.

ILSE.

> Say it then, say it,

How he was found,
You who came running
As soon as I shouted:
How was he found?

FIRST NEIGHBOUR.

The wrong way round.

SECOND NEIGHBOUR.

Feet pointing to the bedhead.

FIRST NEIGHBOUR.

The swaddling bands in place
Stretched tightly round
The baby's little legs.

SECOND NEIGHBOUR.

Tied with a ribbon . . .

FIRST NEIGHBOUR.

All in order.

SECOND NEIGHBOUR.

So someone must have taken him,
Taken him from his mother's side,
And put him there under the bed
Out of sheer spite.

FIRST NEIGHBOUR.

If only it were simply spite!

ILSE.

When I picked him up . . .

FIRST NEIGHBOUR.

Such tears!

From offstage and all around come gales of incredulous laughter. The TWO
NEIGHBOURS *turn and shout as if to ward them off:*

THE TWO NEIGHBOURS.

> It was a different child,
> It wasn't him.
> We swear it!

For a moment darkness returns, still echoing with the laughter which ceases abruptly when the stage is once again lit as it was at the beginning of the act. Through the various doors, half-asleep as if just woken by the laughter, come CROMO, DIAMANTE, BATTAGLIA, LUMACHI, SACERDOTE *to find the* COUNT, *the* COUNTESS, *and* SPIZZI *stunned and perplexed by the mysterious source of the laughter and the sudden disappearance of the* TWO NEIGHBOURS *during that moment of darkness. They enter all speaking at once.*

CROMO. What's this? What's going on? Is this a rehearsal?

DIAMANTE. I can't manage it; I've got a sore throat.

LUMACHI. Ah, Spizzi, dear fellow! Thank God for that!

BATTAGLIA AND SACERDOTE. What's all this? What's all this?

COTRONE. You have been performing, Countess, with two living images, figures born directly from your poet's imagination.

ILSE. Where have they gone?

COTRONE. Vanished.

CROMO. Who are you talking about?

BATTAGLIA. What happened?

COUNT. The Two Neighbours appeared to us, from the first scene of the *Fable*.

DIAMANTE. 'Appeared'? How do you mean, 'appeared'?

COUNT. Here, here, all of a sudden, and started performing with her. [*Indicating the* COUNTESS]

CROMO. We heard the laughter.

LUMACHI. And how! Who was laughing so loud all over the place?

SPIZZI. A bag of tricks! All a set-up! Let's not be dazzled like a bunch of dummies. After all, we're in the same business.

COTRONE. Ah no, my dear fellow, if you put it like that, then you're not in the same business. There's something that's more important to you. If you really were in the same business, you'd be the first to let yourself be dazzled, because that's the one sure sign that you belong. I've told you already to learn from children who first invent a game and then believe it and live it as true.

SPIZZI. But we're not children.

COTRONE. If we were children once, we can always be children. And, in fact, you too were amazed when those two figures appeared.

CROMO. Yes, but how? How did they appear?

COTRONE. Right on cue. And right on cue they said what they had to say: isn't that enough? All the rest, just how they appeared and whether they are real or not, that doesn't matter. I just wanted to give you a sample, Countess, to prove that only here can your *Fable* come to life. But if you insist on taking it out amid the world of men, so be it! Away from here, however, I shall have only my companions to offer in your service. I place them and myself at your disposal.

At this point, fortissimo from offstage comes the thunderous noise of the Mountain Giants riding down into the village to celebrate the wedding of Uma di Dornio to Lopardo d'Arcifa with wild music and shouting. The walls of the villa tremble at the sound. QUAQUÈO, DOCCIA, MARA-MARA, LA SGRICIA, MILORDINO, MAGDALEN *burst onto the stage in a state of high excitement.*

QUAQUÈO. Here come the giants! Here come the giants!

MILORDINO. They're coming down from the mountain.

MARA-MARA. All on horseback. Dressed up to the nines.

QUAQUÈO. Do you hear that? Do you hear? They're like the Lords of the Earth.

MILORDINO. They're on their way to church for the wedding.

DIAMANTE. Come on, let's go and see.

COTRONE [*with a powerful commanding voice that halts all those who were about to run off with* DIAMANTE]. No. Nobody move! Nobody show his face outside—not if we want to go up there and offer a performance. Let's stay here and see about the rehearsal.

COUNT [*drawing the* COUNTESS *aside*]. Aren't you afraid, Ilse? Don't you hear them?

SPIZZI [*joining them, terrified*]. The walls are shaking.

CROMO [*following suit*]. It's like the wild ride of some savage horde.

DIAMANTE. I'm frightened! So frightened!

*They all stand listening, tense with fear, while the music and the uproar
die away in the distance.*

Curtain

IV

Here is the action of the third act (or fourth 'moment') of The Mountain Giants, *as well as I can reconstruct it from what my father told me and with the meaning it was intended to have.*

This is as much as I know and, though I have unfortunately done it less than justice, I trust I have made no arbitrary changes. But I cannot know what, at the end, might have emerged from the imagination of my father which, throughout the penultimate night of his life, was busy with those phantoms—so much so that in the morning he told me that he had suffered the terrible strain of composing the whole of the third act in his head and that now, with all obstacles overcome, he hoped to get a little rest. He was also glad to think that, as soon as he was well, it would take him only a few days to set down everything that he had conceived during those hours of the night. I cannot know, and nobody can ever know, whether, in that last act of mental composition, he may not have found another shape for the dramatic material, different developments for the action, or higher meanings for the Myth. All I learned from him that morning was that he had found a saracen olive.* 'In the middle of the stage', he said with a smile, 'there is a large saracen olive; and this solves all my problems.' And since I didn't understand, he added: 'To hitch up the curtain . . .'. Then I realized that he had been worrying about this practical question, perhaps for days on end. He was delighted to have found the answer.

The third act is set on the mountain, in an open space before a dwelling of the 'Giants'. It opens with the arrival of the actors, tired from the journey, pulling their cart and accompanied by some of the Scalognati; the whole group is led by Cotrone.

The arrival of these strange and unexpected visitors arouses the curiosity of the inhabitants—not the 'Giants' who never appear on the stage, but their servants and the crews of workmen employed on their massive projects. These are all seated at a great banquet upstage, where the long tables seem to extend over a vast space out of sight of the audience. Some of the nearer banqueters get up to enquire about the newcomers whom they regard with a blend of astonishment and attraction as if they were beings dropped from some other planet.

Cotrone finds an overseer with an air of authority and explains the intentions of his companions: they are actors and have everything ready to offer this distinguished public an artistic spectacle of the very highest order in the hope of adding lustre to the wedding festivities which are already under way.

From this first scene, with the orgiastic songs and shouting of its Gargantuan banquet and its dancing fuelled by noisy fountains of wine, it is clear what kind of entertainment the 'Giants' provide for their people and how those people enjoy it. So the actors lose heart when they realize that these folk have no notion whatsoever of what a theatrical performance involves, and things become even worse when someone who has heard of the theatre comes forward to persuade all the others what great fun it is; for it is soon all too obvious that he is thinking of the Punch and Judy shows with their thumping and spanking, of the slapstick of clowns, or the exhibitions of nightclub dancers and chanteuses. But, while Cotrone goes off with the Overseer to propose the performance to the 'Giants', the actors take comfort in the hope, which they try to argue into a certainty, that the masters before whom they are to perform cannot possibly be as uncouth as their servants and workers; and even if it may be doubted whether they will grasp the full beauty of *The Fable of the Changeling Son*, they will at least listen politely. In the meantime they have trouble warding off the coarse chattering curiosity of the rabble around them as they wait impatiently for Cotrone to return with an answer.

But Cotrone returns to report that, though the 'Giants' accept the offer of a performance and are willing to pay handsomely, they unfortunately have no time to spend on such things, so many and so great are the tasks to which they must attend, even at this festive time. So let the performance be for the people who benefit from being offered the means of spiritual elevation every now and then. And the people greet this gift of a new amusement with a frenetic enthusiasm.

The actors are divided in their response. Some, led by Cromo, say they feel they are being fed to the lions, there is nothing to be done before such abysmal ignorance, better give up the whole project. Others, like the Countess, emboldened by the very spectacle of beastliness that disheartens and appals the others, declare that it is precisely before such ignorance that the power of art should be put to the test; and they have no doubt that the beauty of the *Fable* will conquer those virgin souls; and there is the ecstatic Spizzi, already girding himself for this extraordinary performance as for an enterprise worthy of some noble knight of old, persuading the hesitant to join him by shaming them with his example. The Count meanwhile would at least like to shield the Countess from the surrounding vulgarity that disgusts and embitters him.

Cotrone sees and tries to point out the unbridgeable gap that separates these two worlds that have been brought so strangely into contact: on the one hand, the world of the actors for whom the voice of the poet is not only the highest expression of life, but indeed the only certain reality in which and through which life is possible; on the other hand, that of the populace who, led by the 'Giants', are intent on vast projects to possess the powers and riches of the earth; in this huge unceasing common effort they find their norm, and in every conquest over matter they fulfil a purpose of their lives and take pride in an achievement that is both shared and deeply individual. But Ilse is so happy and so eager for the test that Cotrone has to admit that anything is possible and that she may even triumph, intense as she is. 'Quick, quick,' she says, 'where do we perform?' 'Right here where people are already gathered for the banquet. All we need to do is fix up a curtain to hide the actors while they make up and put on their costumes.'

In the middle of the stage there is an old saracen olive, so they hang the curtain on a cord stretched across from the tree to the wall of the house.

While the actors are getting ready, nervous and constantly disturbed by people peeping in and calling others to come and jeer, Cotrone decides it would be a good idea to tell this uninformed audience something about the play. He goes out through the curtain to speak to them, but is immediately greeted by an outburst of jibes, catcalls, shouts, and rude laughter. The Magician returns cast down; they have not let him say a word.

'Don't let such a little thing get you down, we're used to it,' says Cromo the character actor in dry consolation; 'you'll soon see how it turns out.'

The actors explain to Cotrone that he was shouted down because he has no experience with an audience: but now one of them will go out instead—Cromo, who is already dressed and has his Prime

Minister's nose on, will improvise an introductory explanation; he will know how to get their attention by starting off with a couple of jokes. And indeed a noisy chorus of approving laughter, applause, and cheers of encouragement soon testifies to his success.

The reception given to Cromo does something to raise the spirits of the actors so that Ilse, Spizzi, and Diamante, the most eager and ardent of the troupe, can dismiss the fears of Cotrone who now realizes that it will end up badly and makes one last despairing effort to dissuade them. He sadly reminds them of the happiness they are giving up, he recalls the enchanted night they spent at the villa when all the phantom spirits of poetry came to life in them so easily—and could still continue to live if only they would return and remain there for ever.

Meanwhile the hilarity aroused by Cromo is so great that he too fails in his attempt to put the audience in the right mood for the poetic spectacle that is being offered. Cromo returns wet through and dripping with water because some spectators have turned a hosepipe on him to add to the fun. On the other side of the curtain bedlam has broken loose: they are shouting for the actors to come out and for the play to begin. What can be done? Ilse, who is alone on the stage at the start of the *Fable*, moves away from her husband and Cotrone and steps beyond the curtain, as if to a supreme sacrifice, resolved to fight with all her strength to impose the word of the poet.

At this point, the basic conflict, now about to explode into dramatic action, has already been set out. Inevitably the fanatics of art, convinced that they alone are the true guardians of the spirit, faced by the incomprehension and derision of the Giants' servants, will be led to despise and insult them as people devoid of all spirituality; the other side, fanatics of a very different ideal of life, cannot believe the words of such puppets as the actors seem in their eyes—not because they are dressed up, but because the spectators sense that these poor devils, so fixed and earnest in their tone and gesture, have, for some reason, placed themselves definitively outside life. Puppets: and as puppets expected to provide amusement. After the initial amazement, the great groans of boredom and the crude questions ('Who's she supposed to be?', 'What's she on about?'), the audience tell the Countess to drop her inspired declamation of incompehensible words and give them a nice little song and dance. Frustrated by Ilse's persistence, they begin to turn violent. Behind the curtain the drama of

Ilse's struggle with her public is reflected in the agitation of the other actors and the anxious reactions of Cotrone and the Count. Ever more threatening, the gathering storm suddenly bursts onto the makeshift stage when the Countess hurls insults at the spectators and calls them a bunch of brutes. Spizzi and Diamante rush to help her; the Count faints. Cromo shouts that they should all get started on a dance and goes onto the stage himself in an attempt to divert the public's unbridled anger away from Ilse. The pandemonium outside can be seen in the shadowy images cast on the curtain, gigantic gestures, huge bodies locked in combat, cyclopean arms and fists raised to strike. But now it is too late. Suddenly there is a great silence. The actors re-enter carrying the body of Ilse, snapped like a broken puppet. A brief last agony and Ilse dies. Spizzi and Diamante, who had rushed into the fray to defend her, have been torn in pieces: no trace of their bodies can be found.

The Count comes to himself and cries out over his wife's body that men have destroyed poetry in the world. But Cotrone understands that nobody is to blame for what has happened. No, it is not that poetry has been rejected, but only this: the poor fanatical servants of life, in whom the spirit does not speak today but may yet speak someday, have in their innocence broken, like rebellious puppets, the fanatical servants of art who are incapable of speaking to men because they have withdrawn from life—yet not so far withdrawn as to be content with their own dreams but still seeking to impose them on people who have other things to do than believe in them.

And when, deeply mortified, the Overseer arrives to offer the apologies of the Giants, together with fitting financial compensation, Cotrone persuades the grieving Count to accept. Almost angrily the Count announces that, yes, he will accept; and he will use this blood-money to erect a noble and eternal monument to his wife. But one senses that although he weeps and protests a noble fidelity to the dead spirit of Poetry, he feels suddenly relieved, as if freed from a nightmare; and the same is true of Cromo and the other actors.

They depart as they came, carrying the body of Ilse on the cart.

Stefano Pirandello

APPENDIX I

MANY years ago (but it seems like yesterday) a nimble little handmaid entered the service of my art, and although she is no longer young she is still perfectly good at her job.

Her name is Fantasy.

She is a bit of a joker and somewhat malicious and, though she likes to dress in black, it cannot be denied that she is often downright bizzare; nor can it be thought that she always does everything in earnest and in the same way. She sticks a hand in her pocket and pulls out a cap and bells, shoves it on her head, red as a cockscomb, and dashes off. Here today, there tomorrow. And she amuses herself by bringing home the most discontented folk in the world for me to draw stories, novels, and plays out of them—men, women, and children, all involved in strange inextricable situations, their plans have been frustrated and their hopes dashed, and often, indeed, it is truly painful to deal with them.

Well now, several years ago, this handmaid Fantasy had the unfortunate inspiration or ill-omened whim to bring home a whole family. I have no idea where or how she fished them out, but she was convinced that they would provide me with material for a splendid novel.

This was the group I found before me: a man of about fifty, wearing a black jacket and light-coloured trousers, with a frowning air and eyes that spoke of mortification and defiance; a poor woman in widow's weeds holding a four-year-old girl by the hand and with a boy of little more than ten at her side; a bold seductive-looking girl, also wearing black but with an equivocal and brazen ostentation, trembling all over with a keenly-relished biting disdain for the mortified older man and for a youth of about twenty who was standing aloof and self-absorbed as if he despised them all. In short, the six characters who are seen coming onto the stage at the beginning of the play. And first one and then the other, but often one overpowering the other, they embarked on the story of their misfortunes, shouting at me as each argued his or her own case and thrusting their disorderly passions in my face, much as they do in the play to the unfortunate Director.

What author can ever say how or why a given character is born in his fantasy? The mystery of artistic creation is the same mystery as birth itself. A woman in love may desire to become a mother, but the desire alone, however intense, will not suffice. One fine day she will find herself a mother without any precise awareness of when it began. In the same way an artist absorbs so many germs of life and can never say how and why at a given moment one of those vital germs finds its way into his fantasy to become a living creature on a plane of life superior to mutable everyday existence.

I can only say that, without having consciously looked for them, I found them there before me, so alive that they could be touched, so alive that I could even hear them breathe, those six characters who are now seen on the stage. And all present there, each with his or her secret torment, bound together by the birth and development of their intertwined affairs, they were waiting for me to grant them access to the world of art, constructing from their persons, their passions, their adventures, a drama or at least a story.

Born alive, they wished to live.

Now it should be said that I have never been satisfied with portraying the figure of a man or a woman, however special or characteristic, for the mere pleasure of portrayal; or with narrating a particular episode, happy or sad, for the mere pleasure of narration; or with describing a landscape for the mere pleasure of description.

There are certain writers (and not a few) who do take such pleasure and, once satisfied, seek nothing more. These are writers more accurately defined as being of a historical nature.

But there are others who, beyond such pleasure, feel a more profound spiritual need, so that they cannot accept figures, episodes, or landscapes that are not imbued, so to say, with a distinct sense of life from which they acquire a universal significance. These are writers more accurately defined as philosophical.

I have the misfortune to belong with the latter.

I detest symbolic art in which the representation loses all spontaneous movement to become a mechanism, an allegory—a futile and misconceived effort because the very fact of giving an allegorical meaning to a representation shows that we are dealing with a fable which of itself has neither literal truth nor the truth of fantasy, being made only for the demonstration of some moral truth. Except occasionally when it serves an elevated irony (as with Ariosto), such allegorical symbolism cannot appease the spiritual need of which I speak. Allegorical symbolism starts from an idea, indeed, it *is* an idea which evolves or seeks to evolve into an image. What I speak of, on the contrary, seeks in the image, which must remain living and free throughout its expression, a meaning that gives it value.

Now, however hard I tried, I could not find that meaning in those six characters. And so I judged that it was not worth bringing them to life

I thought to myself: 'I have already afflicted my readers with hundreds and hundreds of stories: why should I afflict them yet again with the misfortunes of these six poor devils?'

And thus I sent them packing. Or rather I did everything I could to send them packing.

But not for nothing does one give life to a character.

Creatures of my spirit, those six were already living a life that was their own and no longer mine, a life that I no longer had the power to deny them.

So much so that, when I persisted in my determination to drive them from my mind, they continued to live on their own account, almost completely detached from any narrative support, like characters from a novel, escaped by some miracle from the pages of the book that contained them. They chose certain moments of the day to reappear before me in the solitude of my study, sometimes one by one and sometimes in pairs, coming to tempt me, to suggest this or that scene for representation or description, arguing the particular effects that could be achieved, the singular interest that could be awakened by a given unusual situation, and so on.

For a moment I would let myself be won over; and every time this concession, this slight slackening of resistance, was enough to give them a longer lease of life, an increasingly concrete presence, and therefore a greater power of persuasion over me. Thus it gradually became more difficult for me to go back and free myself from them, and easier for them to come back and tempt me. At a certain point they had become a real obsession: but then, all of a sudden, the solution flashed upon me.

'Now why,' I said to myself, 'why don't I represent this extraordinary situation of an author who refuses to give life to some of his characters, and the situation of those characters who, born in his fantasy and already infused with life, cannot resign themselves to exclusion from the world of art? They have already detached themselves from me, have their own life, have acquired voice and movement; on their own, therefore, in this struggle for life that they have had to wage against me, they have already become dramatic characters, characters who can move and speak on their own; they already see themselves as such; they have learned to defend themselves from me; they will also know how to defend themselves from others. Well then, let them go where dramatic characters usually go to have life—on a stage. And then let us see how it turns out.'

That is what I did. And naturally what happened was what had to happen: a blend of the tragic and the comic, of the fantastic and the realistic, in a totally new and highly complex humorous situation: a drama which, simply through the characters who carry it and suffer it within, breathing, speaking, and self-moving, seeks at all costs the way to its own realization; and the comedy of the vain attempt at an improvised stage performance. First, the surprise of those poor actors of a theatre company rehearsing a play by day on a bare stage without flats or scenery; surprise and incredulity at the appearance before them of those six characters who announce themselves as such and in search of an author; then, immediately afterwards, provoked by the sudden faint of the black-veiled Mother, their instinctive interest in the drama which they glimpse in her and in the other members of that strange family, an obscure ambiguous drama suddenly invading an empty stage unready to receive it. And the gradual growth of this interest as they see the outburst of the conflicting passions of the Father, Stepdaughter and Son, and of that poor Mother—passions that, as I have said, seek to overpower each other with a tragic, lacerating fury.

And there we are: now that they have taken the stage, that universal significance, first sought in vain in those six characters, is found by the characters in themselves amid the agitation of the desperate struggle that each of them wages against the others and that all of them wage against the Director and the actors who fail to understand them.

Without wishing it, without knowing it, in the strife of their troubled souls, each one of them defends himself against the accusations of the others by expressing, as his own living passion and torment, the same pangs that I myself have suffered over so many years: the illusion of mutual understanding, irremediably based on the empty abstraction of words; the multiple personality of every individual according to all the possibilities of being to be found within each one of us; and finally the inherent tragic conflict between life which is ever-moving, ever-changing, and form which fixes it, immutable.

Two especially of those six characters, the Father and the Stepdaughter, speak of that atrocious inescapable fixity of their form, in which both of them see their essence expressed for ever and immutably—that essence which for the one means punishment and for the other vengeance. And they defend it against the artificial affectations and involuntary mutability of the actors; they try to impose it on the conventional Director who seeks to modify it and adapt it to the so-called requirements of the theatre.

On the face of it, not all the six characters have been developed to the same level, but this is not because some are figures of first and others of second rank, in the sense of leading parts and supporting roles (which would be a matter of the elementary perspective essential to all theatrical or narrative structure); nor is it that they have not all been fully formed for the purpose they serve. All six are at the same point of artistic realization, and all six are on the same level of reality, which is the play's level of fantasy. Except that the Father, the Stepdaughter, and also the Son are realized as mind, the Mother as nature, and as 'presences' the Young Boy who observes and performs a single gesture and the Little Girl who is wholly inert. This fact gives rise to a new kind of perspective among them. I had had the unconscious impression that some of them needed to be more fully realized (from an artistic standpoint) and others less, while yet others would be barely sketched in as elements of an episode to be narrated or represented.

The most living characters, the most fully realized, are the Father and the Stepdaughter who naturally come to the fore, lead the way, and drag along with them the almost dead weight of the others—the Son who comes reluctantly and the Mother, a resigned victim between the two children who have practically no substance beyond their appearance and who need to be led by the hand.

And yes, indeed! Indeed, each of them needed to appear in exactly that stage of creation which they had reached in the mind of the author at the moment when he wanted to send them packing.

If I think back on my intuition of that necessity, on my unconscious discovery that the solution lay in a new perspective, and on the way I managed to create it—all these things seem miraculous. The fact is that the play was truly conceived in one of those spontaneous illuminations of the fantasy where, by some marvel, all the elements of the mind respond to each other and work together in divine accord. No human brain, working in cool consciousness, however hard it struggled, would ever have succeeded in grasping and satisfying all the requirements of the play's form. So the explanations that I shall give to clarify the significance of the play should not be understood as intentions that I conceived in advance of its creation and which I now set out to defend, but only as discoveries that I myself have made in tranquil retrospect.

I wanted to present six characters who seek an author. Their drama fails to be represented precisely because the author they seek is lacking; what gets represented instead is the comedy of their vain attempt, with all that it contains of tragedy in that these characters have been rejected.

But can one represent and reject a character at the same time? Obviously, if one represents him, he must first be accepted into one's fantasy and then expressed. And in fact I did accept and realize these six characters: but I accepted and realized them as rejected and in search of another author.

Now I should explain what it is of these characters that I have rejected. Not themselves, obviously, but their drama which, no doubt, concerns them first and foremost, but did not concern me in the least, for reasons I have already suggested.

And for a character, what is his drama?

In order to exist, every creation of fantasy, every creature of art, must have his drama, that is, a drama which allows him to be a character and by virtue of which he is a character. This drama is the reason for the character's being, the vital function that he needs in order to exist.

In these six, then, I accepted the being while refusing the reason for being; I took the organism and entrusted to it, instead of its own proper function, another more complex function into which its own function entered only as a basic fact. A terrible and desperate situation this, especially for the two characters, Father and Stepdaughter, who more than the others, insist on coming to life and are aware of themselves as characters, meaning that they are absolutely in need of a drama, their own drama which is the only one they can imagine and which they now see denied them. It is an 'impossible' situation from which they feel they must escape at whatever cost, a question of life and death. It is true that I have given them another reason for being, another function, which is precisely that 'impossible' situation, the drama of being in search of an author, of being rejected. But that it should be a reason for being, that for them who already had a life of their own it should have become their true function, necessary and sufficient for their existence, this they cannot even suspect. If someone were to tell them so, they would not believe him, for it is impossible to believe that the sole reason for our existence lies wholly in a torment which appears to us unjust and inexplicable.

I cannot fathom, therefore, what could justify the charge made against me that the character of the Father was not what it should have been in that it overstepped its capacity and position as a character and sometimes encroached on and usurped the functions of the author. I understand those who cannot understand me and I can see that the accusation comes from the fact that this character expresses as his own a mental torment that is recognizably mine. Which is perfectly normal and has absolutely no significance. Quite apart from the fact that the mental torment suffered and lived by the character of the Father derives from causes and reasons that have nothing to do with my own experience (something that of itself shows that the criticism has no substance), I want to make it clear that one thing is my own inherent mental torment, a torment which—so long as it has an organic place there—I can legitimately reflect in a character; another thing entirely is the activity of my mind in the realization of this work—the activity, that is, that succeeds in creating the drama of these six characters in search of an author. If the Father were to participate in this activity, if he were to collaborate in creating the drama of being without an author, then and only then would there be some justification in saying that on occasions he becomes the author himself and therefore not what he should be. But the Father suffers and does not create his existence as 'a character in search of an author'. He suffers it as an inexplicable fatality and as a situation which he rebels against with all his strength and seeks to remedy. He is indeed, therefore, 'a character in search of an author' and nothing more, even if he does express as his own the mental torment that is mine. If he participated in the activity of the author then that fatality would be perfectly explicable insofar as he would see himself accepted, even if only as a rejected character—accepted nonetheless into the creative matrix of the poet, he would no longer need to suffer the despair of being unable to find anyone to affirm and construct his life as a character. I mean that he would accept with a good grace the reason for being that the author gives him and would renounce his own without regrets, casting off the Director and the actors to whom instead he has turned as his only recourse.

There is, however, one character, the Mother, who cares nothing about being alive (if we consider being alive as an end in itself). It never even dawns on her that she is not alive; nor has it ever occurred to her to wonder how and why and in what manner she lives. In short, she is unaware of being a character, insofar as she is never, even for a moment, detached from her role. She does not know she has a role.

This makes her perfectly organic. In fact, her role as Mother does not in itself, in its naturalness, involve any mental activity; and she does not live as a mind; she lives in a continuity of feeling that is never broken and therefore she cannot acquire awareness of her life—which is to say of her existence as a character. And yet, despite all this, she also, in her own way and for her own ends, seeks an author. At a certain point she seems happy to have been brought before the Director. Perhaps because she too hopes he can give her life? No: because she hopes that the Director will make her act out a scene with the Son into which she would put so much of her own life. But it is a scene that does not exist, that has never and could never take place. That is how unaware she is of being a character, unaware of the life she can have, all fixed and determined, moment by moment, in every gesture and every word.

She appears on stage with the other characters, but without understanding what they are making her do. Obviously she imagines that the rage for life which possesses her husband and daughter and which is the cause of her own presence on the stage is only one of the usual incomprehensible eccentricities of that tormented tormenting man, and also—horrible, most horrible— another equivocal act of rebellion by that poor erring girl. She is completely passive. The events of her life, and the meaning they have assumed in her eyes, her own temperament—these are all things that are spoken by the others and which she contradicts on only one occasion, which is when the maternal instinct rebels within her and rises up to make it clear that she never chose to abandon her husband or her son. Because her son was taken from her and her husband himself forced her to leave him. But she is rectifying matters of fact: she knows and explains nothing.

In short, she is nature—a nature fixed in the figure of a mother.

This character gave me a new kind of satisfaction which should not be passed over in silence. My critics usually define all my creatures, without exception, as 'unhuman'—this being apparently their peculiar and incorrigible nature. But with the Mother the vast majority have been kind enough to note 'with genuine pleasure' that at last my fantasy has produced 'a very human figure'. I explain this praise as follows: this poor Mother of mine is totally bound to her natural behaviour as Mother, denied all free mental activity, little more than a lump of flesh, fully alive in her functions of procreating and breastfeeding, nursing and loving her young; she has, therefore, absolutely no need to use her brain and she realizes in herself the true and perfect 'human type'. This must be the case, because nothing in a human organism seems more superfluous than the mind.

But even with that praise, the critics were trying to get shut of the Mother without bothering to grasp the nucleus of poetic values that the character signifies in the play. A very human figure, yes, because mindless, unaware of what she is, or not concerned to explain it to herself. But not knowing that she is a character does not prevent her from being one. That is her drama in my play. And it is when the Director urges her to think that the whole story has happened already and therefore cannot be the cause of new lamenting that this drama bursts forth most strongly as she cries: 'No, it's happening now, it happens all the time. My agony's not feigned, sir. I'm alive and present, always, in every moment of my torment which is itself renewed, alive and ever-present.' This she *feels*, in an unconscious way that makes it inexplicable: but she feels it so terribly that it never even strikes her that it might be something to explain to herself or to others. She feels it and that is all. She feels it as pain, and this pain immediately cries out. Thus she reflects that fixity of life in a form that also, in a different way, torments the Father and the Stepdaughter. In them, mind: in her, nature. The mind rebels or, as best it can, seeks to profit from the situation: nature, if it is not aroused by sensory stimuli, weeps at it.

Conflict between form and the movement of life is the inherent and inexorable condition not only of the mental but also of the physical order. The life that, in order to exist, has become fixed in our corporeal form, gradually kills that form. Nature thus fixed weeps for the continuous irreparable ageing of our bodies. In the same way, the tears of the Mother are passive and perpetual. Revealed in three faces, given significance in three distinct and simultaneous dramas, that inherent conflict finds in this play its most complete expression. Moreover, in her cry to the Director, the Mother declares the particular significance of artistic form, a form which does not confine or destroy its own life, and which life does not consume. If the Father and the Stepdaughter were to keep starting their scene a hundred thousand times over, always, at the given point, at the moment when it must serve to express the life of the work of art, that cry would resound—unchanged and unchangeable in its form, but not as a mechanical repetition, not as a return determined by external necessities, but rather, each time, alive and as new, suddenly born thus for ever, embalmed alive in its incorruptible form.

Thus, always, on opening the book, we shall find a Francesca alive and confessing to Dante her sweet sin; and if we return to that passage a hundred thousand times, then a hundred thousand times Francesca will say those words again, never repeating them mechanically, but saying them each time for the first time with such intense and sudden passion that every time Dante will swoon. Everything that lives, by the very fact that it lives, has form and therefore must die; except for the work of art, the one thing that lives for ever, insofar as it is form.

The birth of a creature of human fantasy, a birth that is a step over the threshold between nothingness and eternity, can sometimes happen suddenly, brought about by some necessity. An imagined drama needs a character who does or says a certain necessary thing; thus such a character is born and is exactly what he or she had to be. This is how, amid the six characters, Madame Pace is born and why she seems a miracle, indeed a trick, on that realistically presented stage. But it is not a trick. The birth is real; the new character is alive not because she was alive already, but because she now has an opportune birth befitting her nature as a character who might be called 'obligatory'. What has occurred, therefore, is a fracture, a sudden change in the scenic level of reality, because a character can be born in this way only in the poet's fantasy, and certainly not on the boards of a stage. All of a sudden, without anyone noticing, I have changed the scene, gathering it back into my fantasy but without removing it from the eyes of the spectators—I mean that, instead of the stage, I have shown them my own mind in the act of creation under the appearance of that very stage. When what is visually observed suddenly and uncontrollably shifts from one level of reality to another the effect is that of a miracle performed by a saint who makes his own statue move, which in that moment is surely no longer wood or stone. But the miracle is not arbitrary. The stage, partly because it accepts the reality of the six characters, does not exist of itself as a fixed and immutable fact—just as nothing in this play exists as given and preconceived: everything is in the making, everything moves, everything is an unforeseen experiment. Thus there may be organic shifts even in the reality-level of the place in which this unformed life changes and changes yet again in its quest for form. When I first thought of having Madame Pace born there and then on that stage, I felt that I could do it, and I did it. I certainly would not have done so if I had realized that this birth, instantly, silently and unobtrusively, was unhingeing and reshaping the reality-level of the scene; I would have been paralysed by its apparent lack of logic. And I would have inflicted a fatal injury on the beauty of my work. I was saved from this by the fervour of my mind, because, despite the deceptive logic of appearances, that birth from fantasy is sustained by a genuine necessity in mysterious and organic relation to the whole life of the work.

When someone tells me now that this play does not have all the significance it could have because its expression is disorderly and chaotic and because it errs on the side of romanticism, I can only smile.

I can understand why such an observation has been made: because of the apparently tumultuous and unfailingly disorderly way my work presents the drama in which the six characters are involved; there is no logical development, no proper sequence of events. Very true. Even if I had gone out of my way to do so, I could not have found a more disorderly, a more bizarre, a more arbitrary and complicated—in short, a more romantic—way of presenting 'the drama in which the six characters are involved'. Very true. But I have simply not presented that drama; I have presented another—and I am not going to keep repeating what it is—in which, among other fine things to suit all tastes, there is actually a discreet satire of romantic procedures. It lies in those characters of mine, all so heated by their strife for primacy in the roles that each of them plays in a given drama, while I present them as characters in another play which they neither know nor suspect, so that all that passionate agitation, so typical of romantic procedures, is 'humorously' situated, based on the void. And the drama of the characters, not organized as it would have been if accepted by my fantasy, but presented like this, as a drama rejected, could only exist in my work as a 'situation', with some small development, and could only emerge in hints, stormy and disordered, in violent foreshortenings, in a chaotic manner, constantly interrupted, sidetracked, contradicted; by one of its characters denied, and by two others not even lived.

There is, in fact, one character, the Son, who denies the drama that makes him a character and who derives all his prominence and significance from being a character not of the play in the making—for he hardly figures as such—but of my representation of it. He is, in short, the only one who lives solely as a 'character in search of an author'; the more so in that the author he seeks is not a playwright. And this too could not have been otherwise. Just as the character's attitude is organic to my conception of the work, so it is logical that, given the situation, it should generate greater confusion and disorder, and yet another element of romantic conflict.

But this organic and natural chaos is precisely what I had to represent; and to represent a chaos in no way implies representation in a chaotic and hence romantic manner. And that my representation, far from being confused, is very clear, simple, and orderly is proved by the clarity with which audiences all over the world have grasped the plot, the characters, the fantastic, realistic, dramatic, and comic levels of the work; and also by the way the unusual kinds of significance that it encloses have emerged for those with a more penetrating vision.

Great is the confusion of tongues among men if such criticisms can be expressed in words. No less great than this confusion is the perfection of the intrinsic order, the law which, obeyed in every point, makes my work classical and typical and which forbids any words at its tragic conclusion. When, indeed, everyone has understood that life cannot be created by artifice and that the drama of the six characters cannot be presented without the author to give it significance, the Director remains conventionally eager to know just how things turned out. At his urging, the Son then recounts the conclusion, the facts of the case in their concrete succession, without any meaning and therefore with no need of a human voice. That conclusion, stark and senseless, is triggered by the detonation of a mechanical weapon on stage, and it shatters and dissolves the sterile experiment of the characters and the actors, made apparently without any assistance from the poet.

Meanwhile, unknown to them, as if he had been watching from afar throughout, the poet has been intent on making with and of that experiment his own creative work.

APPENDIX II
THE HISTORICAL HENRY IV

IN the first act of *Henry IV* Pirandello is careful to remind his audience of what they need to know about the 'tragic emperor' whose identity has been assumed by the unnamed protagonist of the play. A cultivated Italian public could, in any case, be counted on to at least know about the meeting between Henry IV and Pope Gregory VII at Canossa. There is, however, no formal recapitulation of the emperor's career and no chronological order in the way the protagonist's imagination shifts rapidly from one event to another. The setting may be an imitation of the throne room at Goslar, but, as the supposed privy counsellors inform us, this does not prevent the protagonist from imagining himself to be at Worms or the Harzburg, in Saxony, Lombardy, or on the Rhine. English readers, therefore, may be grateful for a brief summary of the relevant history.

Henry IV, third emperor of the Salian dynasty, was born in 1050, became King of the Germans on the death of his father Henry III in 1056, and was crowned Holy Roman Emperor in 1084. For the first six years of his reign, his mother Agnes of Poitou acted as Regent, advised by Bishop Heinrich of Augsburg who was rumoured to be her lover. In 1062 a group of German nobles kidnapped the young king at Kaiserswerth and took him to Cologne where their leader, Archbishop Anno, assumed the reins of government while Agnes retired to a convent. Restive under the stern control of Anno, Henry confided increasingly in his second guardian Bishop Adalbert of Bremen who, in 1065, succeeded in taking over from Anno as the dominant force in the Crown Council. When Adalbert in his turn was forced from power at the diet of Tribur in 1066, Henry became effectively his own master.

Henry's reign was marked by constant struggle on two fronts: on the one hand there was the hostility of Swabians, Thuringians, and, above all, Saxons, who opposed his attempts to affirm and extend imperial power in Germany; on the other, there was his own resistance to papal authority in what is known as the Investiture Controversy. There is, however, no need for us to trace the complex interaction between these two contests: in *Henry IV* it is clearly the strife with the papacy that takes centre stage.

The first clash came in 1068 when Henry's attempt to repudiate Bertha of Susa, the wife who had been chosen for him and whom he had married two years earlier, was blocked by the papal legate Peter Damian. Tensions between Empire and Church increased when the austere reformist monk

Hildebrand was elected as Pope Gregory VII in 1073. Not only was Gregory elected without the customary consultation with the emperor, but he soon began to make unprecedented claims for papal authority. At the Roman Synod of 1075 the appointment (investiture) of bishops by lay authorities was declared sinful and in the document *Dictatus Papae* of the same year Gregory asserted his right as Pope to depose emperors and to release subjects from their obedience to unworthy rulers. Henry, meanwhile, had continued to appoint bishops to dioceses in northern Italy, including the important archdiocese of Milan. Confrontation could not be avoided and in 1076 Henry summoned a synod at Worms where Gregory, 'no longer Pope, but a false monk', was formally deposed. Gregory, in his turn, declared the emperor deposed, released all his subjects from obedience, and excommunicated both Henry and all the bishops who had supported him. Henry had, in fact, overestimated his authority and, in August 1076, at the Diet of Tribur, an assembly of German princes, egged on by the ever-hostile Saxons, called on the emperor to repent and seek absolution before attending a meeting with the Pope scheduled for early in the following year. Apparently unrepentant, Henry crossed the Alps, counting on the hostility of northern Italian nobles and clergy towards Gregory who, on his way north to Augsburg, was forced to take refuge in the Apennine castle of Canossa, a possession of his powerful ally, Countess Matilda of Tuscany.

It was now, in January 1077, that Henry performed the dramatic action that has been associated with his name ever since. Instead of profiting immediately from what seemed to be an advantageous situation, he presented himself as a penitent at the castle gates, standing in the snow for three days, until Gregory finally agreed to absolve him. The depth of this humiliation is reflected in traditional iconography of the scene which usually shows him barefoot, clad in sackcloth, and presumably fasting. On the face of it, this was a huge victory for the papacy, but subsequent events soon proved Henry's abject acknowledgement of papal authority to be no more than a temporizing stratagem. He could now return to Germany to announce that he had fulfilled the conditions imposed on him by the German princes while his Lombard allies still prevented the Pope from travelling to Augsburg. The struggle continued. Arguing that at Canossa he had pardoned Henry as a sinner but not reinstated him as king, Gregory renewed the sentence of excommunication. Henry called a synod of bishops at Brixen (1080) and deposed the Pope yet again. In 1084 his troops entered Rome and he was crowned emperor by his chosen antipope Clement III. Gregory died at Salerno in 1085, defiant to the last: 'I have loved righteousness and hated iniquity: therefore I die in exile.'

Henry's later efforts, whether in resisting the papacy or strengthening the empire, were not crowned with any lasting success. Matilda of Tuscany remained a formidable enemy, the Saxons were not reconciled or overcome, and both of his sons turned against him. The peace proclaimed at a diet in Mainz (1103) proved short-lived. Imprisoned and forced to abdicate in 1105, he escaped to win one last victory over his son (Henry V) before dying in 1106.

As John C. Barnes has demonstrated,[1] Pirandello's interest in Henry IV dated back to his years of study in Bonn (1889–91) and to his reading of Karl Geib's *Die Sagen und Geschichten des Rheinlandes* ('The Sagas and Histories of the Rhineland', 1836). Geib's romanticized version of events was supplemented before the writing of *Henry IV* with serious works of history such as Hans Prutz's *Staatengeschichte des Abendlandes in Mittelalter* ('History of the Medieval States in the West', 1884) which Pirandello read in an Italian translation that is quoted verbatim at the end of Act Two. Pirandello may also have been aware that the figure of Henry IV already belonged to German theatrical tradition. Landolph remarks that 'the story of Henry IV would be matter enough for several tragedies, not just one' (*HIV*, pp. 66–7) and, indeed, between 1768 and 1910, it had provided dramatic material for Johann Jakob Bodmer, Julius Graf von Soden, Hans Köster, Friedrich Rückert, Ferdinand von Saar, Wilhelm Ressel, Carl Biedermann, Ernst von Wildenbruch, and Paul Ernst. In the second half of the nineteenth century, when Bismarck's attitude towards the Catholic Church was summed up in his famous 'We shall not go to Canossa', German historiography and literature tended to elevate Henry IV into a hero of national resistance against papal aggression. Though the Italian play is in no sense political, this aspect of the 'tragic emperor', together with his concern for the welfare of the common people, must have appealed to Pirandello's Garibaldian anticlerical instincts.

[1] John C. Barnes, 'Why Henry? Pirandello's Choice of Historical Identity for the Protagonist *Enrico IV*', *Pirandello Studies*, 26 (2006), 6–21.

EXPLANATORY NOTES

SIX CHARACTERS IN SEARCH OF AN AUTHOR

3 *The Rules of the Game*: one of Pirandello's most successful plays before *Six Characters*, first performance Rome, 6 December 1918.

4 *Can't see . . . please*: opening line of the play in the first edition (1921) which does not contain the exchange between the Stage Manager and the Technician, the dancing of the Actors, or the late arrival of the Leading Lady. The definitive 1925 edition shows how much Pirandello had learned from Pitoëff's 1923 Paris production, especially as regards the need to reinforce the presence of the Actors in relation to the dominant Six Characters.

6 *Yes, sir . . . the puppet of yourself*: a sly piece of self-parody.

11 *Sancho Panza . . . Don Abbondio*: the down-to-earth servant in Cervantes's *Don Quixote* and the pusillanimous parish priest in Alessandro Manzoni's novel, *The Betrothed*.

12 *Chu Chin Chow*: hugely successful musical with music by Edward Norton, opened in London in 1916 and ran for a record-breaking five years. Dave Stamper's song was a spin-off composed for the Ziegfeld Follies in 1917. The French version sung by the Stepdaughter may be translated as: 'What clever folk the Chinese are! | From Peking to Shanghai | They've put up placards everywhere: | "Beware of Chu Chin Chow!"'

16 *Robes et Manteaux*: dresses and coats. The use of French suggests a tawdry pretentiousness just as *Madame* hints at Mme Pace's real profession.

23 *each one of us . . . we do*: the passage anticipates both the title and the theme of Pirandello's novel *One, No One, One Hundred Thousand* (1926).

27 *Commedia dell'Arte*: a form of popular theatre that flourished in Italy from the mid-sixteenth to the early eighteenth century; the actors were trained to improvise on the basis of a rudimentary scenario involving a relatively invariable set of instantly recognizable comic types (the rich elderly cuckold, the lovers, the wily servant, the braggart soldier, etc).

34 *shaped by the stage itself*: for the sudden apparition of Madame Pace see *PSC*, p. 194.

36 *'viejo señor' . . . 'amusarse con migo'*: old gentleman . . . amuse himself with me (Spanish).

43 *impossible on the stage*: these fears are well founded: in 1922, even without the threatened nudity, the play was banned in England by the Lord Chamberlain and was only given a private performance by the Stage Society thanks to the advocacy of Bernard Shaw.

45 *alive and ever-present*: see *PSC*, p. 194, for a comparison with Francesca da Rimini in Dante, *Inferno*, v.

59 *waste a whole day*: this is where the play ends, brusquely and somewhat flatly, in the 1921 version. The 1925 version leaves the Characters in possession of a stage that they will continue to haunt in search of the dramatic realization that they have been denied.

HENRY IV

63 *Goslar . . . the Harzburg . . . Worms*: all places connected with Henry IV: Goslar, his birthplace, site of the imperial palace in Lower Saxony; the Harzburg, a castle built to protect Goslar, destroyed during the Saxon rebellion in 1074; Worms, where Henry called a synod to depose Pope Gregory VII (see Appendix II).

64 *the French one*: Henry IV, King of France (r. 1589–1610).

65 *1071, we're at Canossa . . .*: this should be 1077; probably a slip of the pen, unless Pirandello wants to undermine our trust in Landolph as a historian.

66 *Berthold of the folk tale*: in the Italian folk tale Bertoldo is the apparently simple-minded rustic whose practical peasant wisdom earns him an unlikely appointment as royal counsellor.

76 *Charles of Anjou*: King of Sicily, son of Louis VIII of France; driven out in 1282 by the revolt known as the Sicilian Vespers.

   Bonn: German university where Kaiser Wilhelm II had studied as crown prince; also where Pirandello obtained his doctorate in 1891.

83 *Adelaide, the mother*: Adelaide of Susa, mother of Henry IV's wife Bertha. Lady Matilda is tactful enough not to resume her old role as Matilda, Countess of Tuscany.

84 *Hugh of Cluny*: St Hugh (1024–1109), Benedictine monk, reforming Abbot of Cluny, adviser of Henry IV's mother Agnes of Poitou, but also supporter of Pope Gregory VII.

87 *Peter Damian*: St Peter Damian (1007–72), austere reformer and ally of Pope Gregory VII, prevented Henry IV's repudiation of his wife Bertha (see Appendix II).

   Bishop of Mainz: Siegfried, archbishop of Mainz from 1060 to 1084, at first supported Henry IV against Pope Gregory VII but later changed sides.

   Tribur: the Diet of Tribur in 1076 (see Appendix II).

88 *Six years old*: presumably referring to the Kaiserwerth episode (1062) when Henry IV was, in fact, 12 years old (see Appendix II).

   she's dead: Henry associates the death of his sister with that of Henry IV's mother Agnes of Poitou which occurred at the end of the same year (1077) that saw the Emperor's spectacular penitence at Canossa.

90 *Brixen*: the Synod of Brixen (1080) where bishops and nobles favourable to Henry IV once again pronounced the destitution of Pope Gregory VII.

91 *Robert Guiscard*: Norman conqueror of southern Italy, eventually came to the help of Gregory VII and drove Henry IV's forces from Rome (1084).

This is a solemn . . . that he is: Pirandello felt that this passage, set here within square brackets, slowed down the action and should be omitted in performance.

101 *Quantité négligeable*: an insignificant quantity (French), Belcredi's false self-deprecation.

114 *humble monk*: possibly an allusion to the anonymous author of the *Vita Heinrici IV Imperatoris* (*The Life of Emperor Henry IV*), written shortly after the emperor's death.

The peace . . . the latter: transcribed from the Italian translation of Hans Prutz, *History of the Medieval States in the West from Charlemagne to Maximilian* (*Staatengeschichte des Abendlandes im Mittelalter von Karl dem Grossen bis auf Maximilian*, 1884).

THE MOUNTAIN GIANTS

126 *Villa 'La Scalogna' (the Scalognati)*: literally 'Villa Misfortune' and 'the Unfortunate', but in this case a better translation might be 'Misfit House' and the 'Misfits'.

132 *the Countess*: Pirandello certainly remembered Countess Olga De Dieterichs Ferrari who staged plays in her own Roman house and whose touring company, founded in 1926, proved a financial disaster.

134 *If you would stay . . . cruel fate*: these lines and all subsequent passages in verse are taken from *The Fable of the Changeling Son* (see Introduction, p. xxiii).

135 *the Women*: malevolent witchlike figures in *The Fable of the Changeling Son*.

146 *cinema*: Pirandello's initial reaction to the cinema was the blend of scepticism and fascination that can be seen in his novel *Shoot* (1916). Even as late as 1929, in a *Corriere della Sera* article, he argued that the introduction of the talking film would result in a pale imitation of the theatre (*SP*, pp. 1030–6). He did, however, collaborate with the film industry and many of his works reached the screen, including *The Late Mattia Pascal* and, with Greta Garbo and Erich von Stroheim, *As You Desire Me* (1932).

149 *the Angel Hundred-and-One*: taken from his 1910 short story, *The Starling and the Angel Hundred-and-One* (*NA* ii. 502–12).

152 *Favara*: small town near Agrigento; the 'indeterminate' setting is, after all, Sicily.

153 *Mary Magdalen*: character already described by Pirandello in a 1929 piece for *Corriere della Sera* (*SP*, p. 1248).

160 *Old Piano Man . . . Sailors*: characters from *The Fable of the Changeling Son*.

165 *'Vanna Scoma'*: a sorceress in *The Fable of the Changeling Son*.

181 *saracen olive*: indicating an olive tree of great age; the saracen olive had strong personal associations for Pirandello who may have seen it as a symbol of endurance under harsh conditions or of his own rootedness in the soil of Sicily.

The Oxford World's Classics Website

www.worldsclassics.co.uk

- Browse the full range of Oxford World's Classics online

- Sign up for our monthly e-alert to receive information on new titles

- Read extracts from the Introductions

- Listen to our editors and translators talk about the world's greatest literature with our Oxford World's Classics audio guides

- Join the conversation, follow us on Twitter at OWC_Oxford

- Teachers and lecturers can order inspection copies quickly and simply via our website

www.worldsclassics.co.uk